Seven Sisters Collection
Volume 2
By
M.L. Bullock

The Stars that Fell
By M.L. Bullock

This book is dedicated to Lula Mae, a true Southern lady—strong, gentle and always believing the best in all those you love.

Though my soul may set in darkness, it will rise in perfect light;
I have loved the stars too fondly to be fearful of the night.

—Sarah Williams, 1868

Prologue

Mobile, Alabama, 1851

Hoyt Page never wanted to become a physician, but his family's good name required him to take up a respectable occupation. Since he loathed the prospect of a lifetime of military service or the pretense of local politics, medicine appeared his only option. To his and his family's surprise, he excelled at his craft.

Generally, Hoyt did not care to engage people in conversation unless the topic touched on a subject he held an interest in, like astronomy or pedigree horses. Too many times, he stood awkwardly through sessions of idle chitchat only to excuse himself before he made the unforgivable mistake of yawning. However, people in pain—that was quite another story. Those he could speak with all day, listening to their list of symptoms, offering comfort and wisdom. Hoyt found he had a mile-wide streak of compassion for the sick and infirm. He himself was a healthy man and had been a healthy child, but his concern for the sick was real and nothing he intentionally cultivated. Hoyt was committed to his work and did not mind the midnight calls, the long rides and the bone-aching weariness. Even those terrifying moments when he left a home feeling powerless to heal—yes, even in those moments, he knew he was walking in his unique purpose.

Just like tonight. He left Seven Sisters with his stiff black hat in his hands, his bag feeling unusually heavy. Every step he took away from the mansion brought him both relief and extreme regret. Jeremiah Cottonwood was an evil, reprehensible man, probably the angriest man Hoyt had ever known. Even Hoyt's father's temperament could not compare to Cottonwood's. The man married Christine Beaumont, the most beautiful woman in the state, but had that satisfied the arrogant bastard? Had her wealth and quiet beauty calmed his rambunctious spirit? No, of course not. Jeremiah Cottonwood had used her with hopes of getting a son—the son he needed to maintain control of his wife's extraordinary wealth. Hoyt's own cynicism surprised him. He shuddered and stoked the fire, which had died hours ago in his absence.

How many times had Hoyt visited the sheriff to voice his concerns over the treatment of Christine and her daughter Calpurnia? At least four now, but nothing had changed. What could he do? With a grimace, he recalled the conversation he'd just had with the sheriff of Mobile.

"Come now, Dr. Page. You should leave the gossip to the ladies. It's not seemly for a man in your position to engage in this kind of speculation," Sheriff Rice had said as his deputy and oldest son had snickered and leaned back on his dirty boot heels. Hoyt had cast a glance at the deputy over his shoulder but continued undaunted, determined to help Christine. "Do you have any proof that Mr. Cottonwood has abused either of them?" the sheriff had asked.

"What kind of proof do you need, sir? I know starvation when I see it. The girl is nothing but skin and bones, and her skin is sallow—both obvious signs of starvation. Her mother can't even speak—she's catatonic, unable to do anything by herself. Something is going on in that house."

"Did they complain to you, doctor?"

"No," Hoyt had said with a surge of desperation, "but I want it on record as the family's physician that I made a formal complaint. I cannot sit idly by while the man starves his daughter to death. God only knows what Christine—Mrs. Cottonwood—has had to endure. Have you ever known me to gossip about a patient or any family that I have cared for? Won't you at least investigate what I am reporting?"

"Surely you understand how sensitive this type of matter is, Dr. Page." Rice had stroked his greasy black beard like it was his favorite cat. His dark eyes were steady and fierce; they seemed to bore into Hoyt's soul. Hoyt had been unnerved that he couldn't read him.

"I am not asking you to arrest anyone. Just investigate. Please, sheriff. I would consider this a personal favor." Hoyt understood what that meant. The next time another fool deputy shot his toe or another one of Rice's relatives developed syphilis, Hoyt would offer his care for free—until Rice said otherwise. *No matter. It is worth it if it helps Christine!*

Sheriff Rice's wooden chair had squeaked as he'd sprung to his feet and offered Hoyt his hand. Hoyt had shook it tentatively and thanked him. "If it will ease your mind, Dr. Page, I will do it. If I see any cause to intervene, I will. You have my word."

With a nod, Hoyt had left the office, hoping to make it home before the rain began to fall. That was earlier that evening—it was now near midnight. It was a fortunate thing that the sheriff had been in his office. He had felt hopeful at first, but it hadn't lasted.

Knowing the sheriff's character, it was doubtful that Christine, Calpurnia and now the new baby would receive any help at all. He sat at his writing desk, wondering to whom he should write—who would help him? There was a judge, Judge Klein, who used to serve as a circuit judge. But what influence would he have here now? He sighed again and reached for the small cedar box hidden in the secret drawer of his desk. Not even his sister knew of his personal treasure trove.

Dearest Dr. Page,

Against the desires of my own heart, I have consented to marry Jeremiah Cottonwood. As this pleases my parents, it also pleases me. Had my father not suffered so extreme a shame at the hands of my sister, Olivia, I may have better resisted his pleas. Olivia has brought a cloud upon our name, and I dare not speak her name in public, not in the presence of a living soul.

Even Louis agrees that my marriage to Mr. Cottonwood is the wisest course of action for our family, although he continues to respect and admire your noble character. Truthfully, he does not express much care for my intended but assures me that he will remain by my side to guide me in my new role as the lady of Seven Sisters.

My friend (I call you this because you are still my dear friend despite this troubling news), you cannot imagine how unhappy I am at the possibility that I will no longer receive your Kind and Enjoyable Favor.

Please forgive me,

C.B.

He had not written back. In fact, it had been a full year before he saw her again. It had been at the Ferguson-Mays Christmas Ball at the Idlewood Mansion. He closed his eyes and remembered that night. The Greek revival home had been full of Mobile's elite....

***

Fragrant greenery decorated the balustrades and mantelpieces, and white and red candles flickered everywhere. The dark wooden panels of the parlor gleamed, and even the servants wore fine cuffs and tails.

Snow fell for the first time in a decade, and the gentlefolk spent a great deal of time gathered at the massive windows, watching the sparkling snow and dancing flakes in the comfort and warmth of the mansion. Two young cocker spaniels leaped up on the back of one of the couches and began barking excitedly. The partiers laughed at the entertainment, and this was the scene to which he entered. With the recent surge of influenza and other illnesses, it was a welcome picture of joy that he rarely witnessed. He handed his hat and coat to a servant and politely nodded to those who greeted him.

Immediately, his eyes fell upon Christine. Her dark blond hair no longer hung prettily down her back in carefully combed tendrils; instead she wore it in an elegant swirl at the back of her head, as a respectable married woman would. Delicate pearls dangled from her pretty ears, and she wore an expensive dark red dress. Some women could not wear such a shade without looking pale, but Christine's beautiful shoulders and bright skin made her look like a crimson angel. Hoyt drew himself up straight, suddenly proud of his height—he was well over six feet and easily one of the tallest men in the room. Although he was thirty, he maintained a trim physique and a healthy metabolism. Some women found him attractive, he gathered, but he considered his brown hair and hazel eyes rather plain.

Hoyt stared—he could not help himself. That he had thus far managed to avoid socializing with Christine had been nothing short of sheer luck. Now that he stood so close, he felt his heart melt. Yes, she had chosen Jeremiah Cottonwood over him, but how could he blame her? She, the obedient daughter of the Beaumonts, could do nothing but obey her father's wishes. Strangely enough, that made Hoyt love her more. Her sense of duty was as fierce as his own. All this time, he had asked himself if he had really loved her, and now he knew the answer. Indeed he had, and he loved her still.

Hoyt silently prayed that Christine would look in his direction, but she was engrossed in a conversation with one of the Maples twins. The hostess of the ball, Margaret Ferguson, suddenly stepped into his line of sight. "I am so happy to see you, Dr. Page. It has been far too long since you stepped foot in Idlewood. How long must it be? Two years? And how is your sister? Still not well? I miss my friend."

Returning Mrs. Ferguson's smile, Hoyt offered Claudette's formal apologies. "Alas, Mrs. Ferguson, she hasn't the strength right now for a night of dancing. But I feel sure another few weeks will have her right as rain. She asks that you excuse her just this once, and she promises she will return to your side in time for the church auction in January."

Her smile deepened, and she gave him a courteous nod. "Of course I excuse her, poor thing. This year's flu has wreaked havoc here too. Almost all my servants have succumbed to it, and now our boy is sick...."

"I pray it leaves your household soon, ma'am." Suddenly, he could hear the swell of violins and the sliding of the wooden panels that transformed the front parlors into a spacious ballroom.

Mrs. Ferguson leaned toward him and whispered, "Would it be vile of me to ask you to check on my Charles before you leave? My husband does not trust physicians, I am afraid; however, I would value your opinion. I cannot imagine what I would do if..." She sniffled as she confessed her greatest fear to him.

"I will be happy to examine the boy, but I am afraid I left my bag in my coach."

Her nervous smile reappeared. "I will ask Daniel to bring the bag up to you. Would it be possible for you to visit Charles now? That way my husband will not suspect anything. I do not think he knows yet that you are here."

"Of course, as you wish."

"His room is up the stairs, to the right. I will go find Daniel now."

"Leave him in my hands. All will be well."

"Thank you so much, Dr. Page."

Although with all his heart Hoyt wanted to greet Christine, he went up the stairs just as Mrs. Ferguson asked. He walked with his hands clasped behind his back, and his stiff collar felt hot and uncomfortable on his skin. He pushed open one door and found a young black woman busily folding linen. "Excuse me," he whispered as he closed the door behind him and continued to the second door. There was a low lamp lit on a desk in the second room, and Hoyt could discern the shadows of furniture, toys and books. *This must be the nursery.* A light glimmered on the other side of the room, and he could hear a child coughing.

He walked quietly through the nursery to the child's room and noticed a draft. He made a mental note to mention that to Mrs. Ferguson. The boy rolled over in his bed and looked up at him.

"Hello, young sir. You must be Charles. Your mother asked me to come see you. I am a doctor. Would you mind if I took a look at your eyes, nose and ears?"

The child said nothing, but his dark eyes had a shadowy, sickly look. Hoyt's heart went out to the poor little fellow. As he sat on the bed, a young man came into the room with his bag. Absently, Hoyt thanked him and opened the bag, looking for his liniment. He felt the child's head—he had a fever, and a high one. Fevers were child killers. He moved the lamp closer to the child's face and examined his eyes. The pupils were dilated slightly, and his throat felt swollen. "Oh, yes. That hurts, doesn't it?"

The frail boy nodded, and Hoyt continued his examination, peering into the youth's red ears and inspecting his runny nose. Fortunately, the mucus was clear with no obvious signs of infection. Either the boy's case was early in the going or this was not the flu. A sharp knock on the door grabbed the pair's attention. Hoyt stood quickly, wondering what he would say if Lane Ferguson came barging in wondering why Hoyt was examining his son. The door opened and Christine entered, her soft red dress filling the small room with happy color. Hoyt's heart leaped in his chest.

"Who are you?" the boy whispered, his voice sounding scratchy and hoarse.

"Why, I am Christine. I am Dr. Page's nurse."

"You don't look like a nurse, ma'am. You're too pretty to be a nurse."

"How charming you are, sir," she answered with a smile. "How is the patient, doctor?" Her dainty hand grasped the post of the twin bed as she smiled down at him.

Hoyt's mouth was as wide as the child's astonished eyes. He could tell that the young boy was quite infatuated with Christine, but who could blame him? His heart beat fast in his chest, and he felt a smile stretch across his lips. "Our patient will recover as long as he gets plenty of rest and drinks all the soup his mother brings him. Can you do that?"

"Yes, I can do that."

Hoyt stuffed his tools back in his bag, tousled the lad's hair and walked toward the door. What should he do? What should he say now?

"Goodbye, nurse. I hope you come see me again."

"I shall, I promise, young man. Good night." She walked out of the drafty room and Hoyt followed her, his bag in hand. They walked into the nursery, where several tiny lights bounced and shimmered; she must have lit the candles before she entered the bedroom. Swells of music rose from the lower floor, and candlelight sparkled from the greenery-decked mantelpiece. Christine took Hoyt's hand and led him to a tufted couch at the corner of the room.

Hoyt's hands were freezing, and panic gripped him. *Should I take her hand or refrain? Should I...what should I do?* He stared at her, not daring to touch her or ask why she had come upstairs. Just as he summoned the courage to touch her cheek and speak his mind, Christine turned her attention to the window. She made a comment about the snow—how beautiful it was, how quickly it would be gone—but Hoyt barely listened. The small talk made him impatient, and he rose to join her. Standing behind her, he quietly examined her hair, her elegant neck, the milk-white skin of her bosom. None of these had he ever had permission to touch or appreciate. How he'd fantasized about her hair falling through his fingers, her upturned face tilting toward his. Christine spun around, the silk of her dress rustling as she did.

Here was the moment he had been waiting for! He grasped her thin arms, pulling her close to him. He wanted to rail at her, yell at her for leaving him, but he couldn't. Her sweet lips beckoned him and he kissed her, softly, chastely at first, then more ardently.

"What if your husband..." Hoyt couldn't help himself. The unwanted words came tumbling forth.

"No! Do not mention his name! Don't spoil this, Hoyt! Let this moment be for you and me!" The two embraced, uncaring that anyone could enter the room and find them. In a ragged whisper she said, "All I need is this moment. That's all I need. Then I can go on."

There was a message in her confession—a desperation that made Hoyt both protective and angry. He felt it with every inch of his being.

Before he could seek the source of her anxiety, she whispered, "Come to me at four o'clock tomorrow, Hoyt. If you don't come, I don't know how I will make it. I need your strength. You have always been my friend and...even more. Promise me you will come."

"Where shall I meet you?"

"Come to Seven Sisters. Ann-Sheila will lead you to me."

"What of Cottonwood? Won't he be suspicious to see me calling upon you?"

"He leaves in the morning. Tell Stokes you've come to check up on Ann. She's been ill recently. He won't suspect anything."

"I will come, Christine."

"I had better go now, before someone misses me. Until tomorrow." She squeezed his hand and smiled at him.

Hoyt's heart banged happily in his chest as he watched her leave the room. He tried to gather himself, wandering around the room and pretending to be interested in the impressive selection of children's fairy stories on the shelf next to the couch. As patiently as he could, he forced himself to wait. No one must know their intentions. Mobile society was unforgiving when it came to infidelity, but was this truly infidelity? Weren't they meant for one another? Besides, Hoyt knew the secrets of just about all these old families—including his own. After what seemed like a lifetime, he walked out of the room and discreetly passed his bag to Daniel, who took it to his carriage.

Hoyt danced a mere four times, drank two hot whiskeys and discreetly excused himself far earlier than his sister would have liked. The entire night, he did not speak to Christine—it wasn't seemly to dance with a married woman unless she was a cousin or a sister-in-law. He could not bear to think he might bring her scandal or heartache.

Jeremiah Cottonwood greeted him during the course of the evening, preening like a peacock and showing everyone the gold chain and watch his eminent father-in-law had given him. After a few drinks, he began to share bawdy jokes. He was careful not to speak ill of his rich wife, but Hoyt was sure he was tempted to do so. As far as Cottonwood believed, he was the luckiest man in the room—twice as wealthy as anyone there and four times as wealthy as his hosts. But that did not humble the man at all. Hoyt considered it a pleasure to leave his company.

He spent a restless night in his modest two-story brick home, tossing and turning, wishing sleep would come and make the time go faster. The next day, he went out for a haircut and a shave, purchased a new shirt and came back home and watched the grandfather clock move ever so slowly. At three, he saddled up his horse and rode toward Seven Sisters. With any luck, Cottonwood would not be home and Hoyt could spend time with the woman he loved.

Ann-Sheila, Christine's constant companion, greeted him at the door. That was highly unusual, as Stokes was such a fixture there. Hoyt was so surprised that he inquired about Stokes' health, but Ann-Sheila assured him he was well and only away on business for Mr. Cottonwood. He knew her; she had been always present during his attempts to court his beloved. With a perfect smile and natural grace, she welcomed him into the plantation. It was a marvelous place with dark plum settees and plush carpets, the likes of which he had never seen. The only problem—it belonged to Cottonwood. Ann-Sheila led Hoyt to the ladies' parlor and began to give him a list of her false symptoms. Eventually the two were alone and the young woman leaned forward and whispered into his ear. "She's waiting for you in the Rose Garden. Out the side entrance just there."

Unable to wait any longer, Hoyt handed her his hat, bag and riding crop. He scrambled out the French doors, his steps hastening him to his deepest desire. The hedges surrounding the garden grew thick but were well-manicured by obviously talented gardeners. Hoyt had never been in this garden, but his beloved left clues for him along the way. A glove here, a book there, and finally he found her.

She sat under a wisteria-wrapped oak, her pale, perfect hands resting peacefully in her lap. When she spotted him, she rose and ran toward him, her eyes never wavering. "I wasn't sure you would come."

"How could you wonder?"

Her arms went around his neck, and they kissed like they were always meant to—with complete and utter abandon.

Finally, when he couldn't stand the tension anymore he asked her, "Where can we go?" Taking him by the hand, Christine led him out of the maze to a sandy, narrow path. He could hear water rushing nearby, perhaps the Mobile River. Hoyt never questioned her; he followed obediently until they were alone in a small white cottage. How hurried they had been, that first time together! That stolen hour had been too brief but so passionate. They didn't talk about Jeremiah; in fact, Hoyt rarely thought about him except for on the few unhappy occasions he had to face him.

The following year, Hoyt had the pleasure of helping Christine bring their child into the world. It was an experience he had never expected, and it moved him deeply. He never doubted that the child was his—Christine confided in him that Cottonwood rarely sought her bed, and when he did his drunkenness made it impossible for him to perform his duty; however, she always left him so that he believed he had done the deed.

* * *

Hoyt took a swig of his brandy—it had been a gift from his sister. How close they used to be. How could he tell her about his secret life? Like their mother, Claudette would die of shame if she knew about his love for Christine. He poured another drink and thought about how wretched his situation had become. That night, he had held another baby; looking down at her sweet face filled him with joy, but even that had not roused Christine. His beloved was unresponsive, even when he whispered to her. Hoyt never claimed the child—that would bring Christine to ruin. But what should he do? He must take action! Surely he must! Regardless of the cost to his reputation or that of his family. But for now, he would wait a little bit longer. There was always hope that Christine would arise from her bed, her mind refreshed. Then what would she say to him?

Hoyt loved Christine as if she were his own wife, as she rightfully should have been. Now, they had delivered another one of their children into this world, only Christine could not see the baby, or Hoyt or anyone she had loved. Ann-Sheila, Christine's faithful friend, had been killed years ago, and since then, his sweetheart had been a broken person. Now here was his child, *their* child, yet he could not claim her. This was a sacrifice he must make—for his beloved and their children.

After Calpurnia was born, he and Christine experienced loss after loss, their children dying after a few days at most. Now tonight, another baby, likely their last, was born. Christine was now catatonic from some unknown, unspoken suffering, obviously at the hands of Cottonwood. If he could get his hands on that bastard just one time, he would show him how it felt. How often he fantasized about killing the man—how easy that would be! Cottonwood was a known drunk, yet he had powerful friends, including the sheriff and a few notable politicians.

With a surge of anger, he sent his glass crashing across the room, the warm liquid streaming down the carefully painted gray wall. Finally he cried, collapsing on his couch, the complete powerlessness overwhelming him at last. It was there where he slept until an urgent rap at the door woke him. He'd been dreaming—something vile, something horrible.

He woke in complete darkness, the fire almost gone and the room as cold as death. He squinted at the grandfather clock, but he couldn't make out the time without his glasses. The knocking continued, and he could hear something else...the sound of a baby crying.

Exhausted but curious, he walked to the front door. It was raining—he could hear fat droplets splashing against the windowpanes in the parlor. Lightning cracked across the sky. Hoyt opened the door and blinked against a nearby burst of bright light. His natural instinct was to insist that the young woman at the door come inside out of the rain, but he could not do so yet. It was illegal to give aid and comfort to a runaway slave, and he couldn't be sure she was here on behalf of her owner. She slid back her cloak so he could see her anguished face. Hoyt could tell that she had been crying, perhaps as much as the baby had.

"What are you doing out here with the baby? With Mrs. Cottonwood's baby? Have you lost your mind?" Then the thought suddenly came to him. *What if she was here because of Christine—what if his love had died?* "Has something happened to Mrs. Cottonwood or Miss Calpurnia?"

"No, sir. I mean, I don't know of anything. I'm here because of the baby."

"What? Why would you bring the baby out in a thunderstorm, Hannah? That's your name, correct?"

"Yes, sir, that's my name." Another pop of lightning lit up the narrow lane. Hannah gasped, and the baby began to cry in earnest. "But I had to come, lightning or no! The master said this baby is dead. You have to take it!" She handed the writhing bundle to him.

Puzzled, Hoyt stared at her. "What? She's alive! I hear her crying! Take her home."

Hannah screamed in agony, "No! No, Dr. Hoyt! Please don't send the baby back. Please listen! Hooney told me to come—the master says this baby is dead."

Still stymied, Hoyt pressed on. "Come inside, Hannah, and warm yourself by the fire. Let's figure out exactly what you are saying."

"No, I can't go in there. Hooney said I was to come right back because Miss Calpurnia would need me. The master told us, 'The baby is dead.' He don't want no dead baby! We was to get rid of it."

Awareness rose like a black sun in Hoyt's mind. Would Cottonwood murder a baby? A baby he believed was his child? Hoyt snatched the bundle away from her in desperation. The baby's cries were now more pitiful and heartbreaking. Crying loudly herself, Hannah ran from Hoyt, no doubt back to Seven Sisters.

Hoyt stood in the doorway as the enveloping darkness swallowed Hannah's tiny figure. She was gone from sight in seconds. He brought his daughter indoors and found a warm blanket to wrap her in. As she cried, Hoyt stoked the fire, his mind working to figure out what he should do next. What did this mean for Christine? If it weren't for the baby, he would have driven the carriage back to Seven Sisters right away—thunderstorm be damned!

Leaving the unhappy baby crying on the settee, Hoyt ran to his neighbor's door and banged on it until she answered. He managed to acquire a pint of milk without giving too many details about why. Mixing a little sugar in the milk so the child would sleep better, he fed his hungry daughter until she fell asleep, satisfied at last. He arranged her on his bed, wrapping her tenderly in the soft blanket. He left her only long enough to raise a warm fire in the bedroom fireplace.

For the first and last time, he slept peacefully beside his child, knowing in his heart that tomorrow he must let her go. He had to protect Christine. Let the world believe the child was dead—he knew that she wasn't. She was beautiful, perfect and alive! As he lay in the dark, smelling her hair and allowing her tiny fingers to wrap around his finger, he cried. At least he had this moment—it was more than he deserved. He prayed for Christine and asked God to forgive him for all their trespasses.

He knew what he had to do. He could not keep his daughter, but he had to take her somewhere safe. No foundling hospital. He remembered the young couple on the other side of the county, the Iversons, who owned a small store. They had lost a baby two weeks ago. Surely, they would welcome a child of their own now. But for now, he held his baby close. Staring at her in the dim light, he could see Christine's perfect bow lips, his own eyes and his beloved's tapered, elegant fingers. He lingered in the moment, knowing it would disappear with the rising of the sun. His life had been unconventional, not at all the way he had envisioned, but it was his. Soon he fell asleep, dreaming of nothing and no one.

Sometime during the night, he felt a draft blow through the room.

He smelled roses, the sweet, large blooms of wild roses that grow only on vines. Those had been Christine's favorite. He must have been dreaming—what a pleasant dream! Hoyt whispered her name and felt her cool hand upon his brow and then his cheek. He attempted to rouse himself, but the brandy and the weariness of the day made it impossible to move even his arms. She was near him, somehow, watching over him and their daughter. She kissed his forehead and Hoyt opened his eyes to smile at her. He felt peace and then surprise when he saw that she wasn't there at all. She had been there—he could still smell the roses—but now Christine had gone.

Yes, now she was gone.

Chapter 1

I hadn't had a dream in six months, but I couldn't worry about that right now. Seventy-five of Mobile's most elite and notable women had gathered at the Bragg-Mitchell Mansion to hear me speak about my work at Seven Sisters. I was sure some had come to hear about the crystal chandeliers, the antique ceiling medallions and the expansive Moonlight Garden, but most probably wanted to know how I had "landed" Ashland Stuart. A few others likely wondered if the rumors they had heard about ghosts and such were true. To this crowd of local nobility, I was a nobody, at least in the genealogical sort of way. Even though most Mobilians, the average Jane and Joe, didn't give a hoot about these kinds of things, they really mattered to the old families. For Ashland's sake, I wanted them to accept me on some level.

I had arrived thirty minutes early, and a throng of excited women greeted me at the massive front doors of the mansion. Most were polite, but there were a few unfriendly faces in the crowd. Fortunately, the unspoken rules of polite society did not allow the more curious of my greeters to simply jump in and ask me pointed questions, although it was plain that many of them wanted to.

"You are so lovely! No wonder *our* Ashland was so taken with you," one woman said. She introduced herself, but I instantly forgot her name. I was not too good at remembering the names of the living.

"She certainly is, Margaret! How Sheila cried when she heard Ashland had run off and gotten married!" I wanted desperately to roll my eyes at the idea of Ashland and me "running off" together like naughty teenagers, but I slapped a smile on my face instead. *How do I respond to that?* For the moment, I didn't have to. The ladies remarked on my hair, my pink sheath dress and my fitted green jacket with the three-quarter sleeves.

Is that a Bobbie Brooks dress?
Who does your nails?
Love those shoes! Are they Italian?

I nodded through more introductions and politely smiled as each shared some detail about Ashland with me. Naturally, or so it seemed to the women gathering around me, the conversation steered around to my family name. One lady emerged as the unofficial leader of the group. She was an older woman, my height, with a slim figure and a suspiciously wrinkle-free forehead. She wore pale pink lipstick and expertly applied brown eyeliner that flattered her brown eyes. I couldn't remember her name.

"You from New Orleans, darling? I knew some Jardines from New Orleans once. The family had a delicatessen and muffaletta shop down on Toulouse Street, but it got washed away when the storm came through." The five women surrounding her paused their mini-conversations and observations to listen to my answer. It was unnerving to say the least. *What am I doing here? I almost failed public speaking in college!*

Like a white-haired angel, Bette came to my rescue. "That was Hurricane Katrina," she offered politely. My friend tried to run interference for me, bless her. After all, she had insisted months ago that I come speak about the old house, and I couldn't really refuse her. Bette and I had been through a lot together—we both survived Mia.

"Yes, that's the storm I'm speaking of, Bette." My interrogator continued undeterred, "So you say you're from New Orleans, Miss Jardine—I mean Mrs. Stuart?" She sipped from a white china teacup with a gold band around the rim and an elegantly scripted "B."

"No, I didn't say that. I may have family there, but my mother is from the East Coast."

"Your mother? What about your father? Isn't he a Jardine? Or is that your mother's name?" The older redhead with the perfect afternoon chignon raised her eyebrow as if she had discovered something shocking. I knew my mistake immediately. I wasn't supposed to admit that I didn't know my father or have his last name. *I knew I would screw this up.*

Bette's delighted squeal broke the silence. "Oh look, there is Detra Ann! I am sorry to steal Carrie Jo from you, Mrs. Betbeze, but I have to deliver our speaker to Miss Dowd. No doubt y'all will speak again." Without waiting for a dismissal, Bette gently steered me by the elbow toward a busy Detra Ann, who was greeting a few stragglers. Bette whispered to me as we walked across the perfectly polished wooden floor. "Don't you let that old bat bother you. I have seen her drunk as a foreign sailor and doing the bump at the Mystics Mardi Gras ball, and I swunny! If you shook her family tree, there's no telling what would fall out! Did you know she has an albino sister that nobody sees?"

"Thank you for stepping in."

"No problem. She's as mean as a snake! A snake in designer clothing! The only claim to fame that family has is Yolande Betbeze. She was Miss America in 1951 and, by all accounts, quite a beautiful young woman. Holliday Betbeze needs to get over herself—1951 was a long time ago. Though there's quite a story about Yolande."

Bette always made me smile. I had no idea what "doing the bump" meant, but I laughed thinking about Holliday Betbeze drunk at a ball. "It's okay. It's not like I can hide who I am. You'll have to tell me all about Yolande Betbeze sometime."

"Actually, I was hoping to talk to you later." We stopped about ten feet shy of Detra Ann, who still had not spotted me. "A lot has happened since you've been gone." She dropped her voice and looked around the room before continuing. "I think I found something you should see."

"Really? I'm intrigued." I wanted to know what she was talking about, but it was clear that she was not going to divulge the information with so many ears perked up around us.

As Bette squeezed my hand, her clunky costume ring dug into my skin, but I didn't complain. "You have a special gift, Carrie Jo, and you're not afraid to use it. I admire you for that. It must be hard to dream about someone else's life all the time.

Anyway, I won't get into what I wanted to talk about now, but maybe you could come by later this week?"

I nodded, but I felt like such a fake. What would Bette think when I told her the truth? *I don't dream anymore.* What could I say to her? *Sorry, I burned up all my "magic" beating the ghosts of Seven Sisters.*

My dreaming dry spell had me questioning everything. What did it mean? Was it natural? Had I really short-circuited my "power" trying to defeat Isla? I had no idea and knew no one who could mentor me. Funny how you don't appreciate something until you don't have it anymore. I spent so many years trying to pretend that I was normal, and now I would give anything to see Calpurnia and Muncie again.

"Carrie Jo! It's so nice to see you. It has been too long! You look lovely and so tanned—looks like married life has treated you well." Detra Ann had colored her hair during my absence, and the change only made her look more attractive. I could never go blonde—I'd had a bad experience with Sun-In when I was in middle school, and I was sure bleaching my hair would only be worse. The leggy blonde had an angular, beautiful face, and she hugged me as if we were old friends.

At one time her mother had hoped that she and Ashland would hit it off, but fortunately for me, it didn't happen. Detra Ann had fallen hard for Terrence Dale, a talented contractor who worked with us at Seven Sisters. Well, until the supernatural activities weirded him out to the point that he quit. Who could blame him? I sure didn't. I liked TD. We had hit it off from day one. I liked Detra Ann too, but as friendly as she was at this moment, she was changeable. I think Detra Ann primarily did what she wanted to do. As far as marketing went, she was a whiz—but as a future BFF? Probably not. Besides, I had trust issues. My longtime bestie had turned out to be a crazed killer. Apparently, I wasn't too good at judging someone's character.

"I'd say so! Good to see you too. How are things going at the house?" I did not regret our decision to give the house to the City of Mobile, but I did miss it. I longed for the coolness of the Blue Room. I missed the fragrance of the magnolia petals in the Moonlight Garden—I even missed the squeaky stairs and doors. I remembered the first time I walked up the staircase, the cool, smooth wood felt familiar under my fingers. How that first view from the top floor of the grounds below astounded me! It had been love at first sight. Then to discover that I had a heritage there, in a roundabout sort of way, well, that was just incredible.

I did miss it. Even after all the sadness, murder and mystery, I missed Seven Sisters.

"Quite well. We've been packed since the doors opened—people love it, Carrie Jo. You and your team did a remarkable job—you really captured the spirit of the house."

I must have turned a few shades of red because she quickly added, "You know what I mean. We are a month away from Halloween, and we're finally having our first ball." She smiled politely, but Detra Ann was well aware that this subject had been a source of contention between the two of us. When we first met, hosting a ball at Seven Sisters seemed somewhat sacrilegious to me. After all, the ghosts of the past were lingering, unwilling to let go of their lives and their agendas. But that was then—perhaps they'd put all their old bones to rest now. I wanted to believe that, but I knew it wasn't true. Something was undone. Something wasn't right. I could feel the supernatural approaching again, like a lone drum beating in the distance. And just as before, it filled me with anxiety.

Masking my thoughts as well as I could, I smiled at the beautiful, blue-eyed blonde.

"You know it wouldn't be right to have our first ball without you and Ashland in attendance. Would you consider coming?"

"I'll talk to Ashland. He's been so busy with the Dauphin Street project I barely see him. I guess the honeymoon is over now." It was intended as a joke, but it sounded harsh and unhappy.

Bette chimed in, "Now, don't you get discouraged. It takes some adjustment being married. I think you'll find he will come around. He'll balance things out soon. Ashland has a strong work ethic."

Detra Ann chuckled. "He's all work, that's for sure. Please let me know if you can come to the ball. I'll save two tickets for you, just in case. Bette has promised to come—and bring a date."

"Wow, Bette. I'm gone for three months and you find Mr. Right." She chuckled but didn't offer any more information about her mystery date. I wondered if it was her "Steve McQueen" she'd been so crazy about before. "I will do that, Detra Ann. I know that Seven Sisters is in good hands if you're there." I meant it. Like Ashland, Detra Ann loved Mobile and the house. I had no worries that those hallowed grounds would be mistreated.

My heart hurt—I wanted to go home.

"We're offering nightly tours all October, did you hear? Rachel is the best guide—you'd be so proud of her." I smiled thinking of Rachel Kowalski be-bopping from room to room, explaining to the tourists how we acquired the mantelpieces and where the Augusta Evans book collection came from. I wondered what else she might tell them. *'Here's where Hollis Matthews was murdered by an insane historian…and over here, we found the body of Louis Beaumont."*

"I am sure I would be. Rachel is very passionate about local history. I am glad she stayed on with you. How is your mother? Recovering okay?"

Detra Ann frowned and gave an exasperated sigh. "Driving her friends and her nurse crazy. You would hardly know she had surgery; she is on her phone and laptop all the time, still working on behalf of the Historical Society. No way she will be out four more weeks. My guess is she will be back in two, tops. I can't say I'll be sad. That means I can move back to my place even sooner."

I had heard rumors that she and TD had been "playing house" as Bette called it. I was not judging her, but I was curious to hear how he was doing. "I am sure TD will be glad to have you back home."

Her beautiful smile disappeared, and she glanced at Bette reproachfully. "I, uh, TD hasn't been well. He took a trip up to Montgomery, but I think he's home now." She glanced at her watch and promptly changed the subject, "Oh, we better get started." Detra Ann walked away and left me standing by the open French doors.

"Bette? Is TD okay? I get the feeling I said something wrong. What just happened?"

"He left her high and dry." She froze and pressed her lips together thoughtfully. "All men get a little crazy now and then, but that I didn't figure. From all accounts, he's not doing too well. I hear he's had some sort of breakdown."

"Breakdown? What kind of breakdown? Like a mental breakdown? Oh no, this is all my fault."

"No, no, no. Don't take that on yourself. We better head to our seats. My table is right at the back if you need anything." She half hugged me, and I obediently walked toward my seat at the front. I wanted to fuss over my hair and clothing but refrained. My heart sank at the thought that TD was hurting. I remembered seeing his face in the garden the night we fought Isla. He'd dug the hole like a furious dog, trying to locate the box. We'd found it, but at what cost?

I sat in the chair, staring at my empty teacup and saucer. Trays of sweets and sandwiches decorated my table, but I didn't sample any. *Focus on the moment, CJ. You can find out more about TD later.*

I scanned the room as Detra Ann called the meeting to order. Thankfully, most of the tables and guests were behind me so I didn't have to stare at all the faces. Instead, I took in the details of the mansion. This shindig was in one of the front rooms. This particular room had lovely high ceilings, cheerful yellow walls and tons of white molding, decorative columns and a shiny white mantelpiece. A carved marble mantelpiece—in the Federal style, I guessed. The event planner had opted for an intimate setting; there were at least a dozen round tables covered with white linen tablecloths and matching wooden chairs. If I hadn't been so heartsick about TD, I would have cherished every minute of this experience. The Bragg-Mitchell Mansion wasn't as fine as Seven Sisters, but it was one of the loveliest antebellum homes I'd seen in Mobile.

"Now, please make welcome this month's speaker, Carrie Jo Stuart." People began to clap, and I clumsily rose from my chair. Why had I worn heels? Had I learned nothing from history? I was a historian, for Pete's sake.

Carrie Jo Stuart. I still wasn't used to hearing my new name, and I could not help but smile at the friendly applause. I thanked Detra Ann and stood behind the podium, clumsily arranging my notes. My throat felt dry as I stared out at the anxious audience. More than anything, I wanted to jump into the details about our most prized acquisitions. The amazing sculpture in the men's parlor—the delicately carved cherub faces on the mahogany mantelpiece that TD placed in Christine's room. But I didn't.

I decided I would start things a little differently.

Might as well give them something to talk about.

Chapter 2

"Ashland! Are you up there?" I scampered up the stairs to the second floor of our two-story Victorian searching for my husband. According to Ashland, purchasing one of the old homes on Anthony Street was nothing less than miraculous. People loved these homes, and I can't say that I blamed them. From the smooth white exterior to the black cast-iron details, it was a lovely place. Naturally we had worked our magic on the inside, replacing the horrible windows with double-paned Victorian reproductions. This house—Our Little Home, we called it—was indeed little, but it had some historical importance. It was once home to an inventor and author, Mills Broughton. Still, it just didn't feel like home yet.

What did I think? That I would spend my days swanning down the staircase of Seven Sisters, greeting callers in the Blue Room?

"In here!" Ashland called from one of the guest rooms. The soft blue carpet runner felt luxurious underfoot. I pushed on the half-open door and found him rummaging through the closet. "How did it go?" he asked without looking up from his task.

"I nailed it—no tripping or stuttering."

He gave me a disbelieving look.

"Okay, I did get tongue-tied once or twice. Honestly, I am fine." He grinned at me and, as always, I felt my heart do somersaults. He continued to rifle through my carefully stacked closet. I paused to add, "I may have shocked them just a little." I suppose I needn't have told them about my life in Savannah, my brief stint in foster care and how much Mobile felt like home.

"What do you mean? I am sure you were great." His distracted attitude hurt me a little.

"I mean, I told them that I didn't come from an old Southern family. I was just Carrie Jo, historian and researcher."

"Nobody cares about that, CJ. Just you. If you give people a chance, they might surprise you." His voice sounded tired, and I could tell he was in one of his quiet, sulky moods. I wasn't the kind of person to push someone into talking, as I hated that myself, but there were many times in our short history when I wished I knew what he was thinking.

He finally pulled a suitcase from the closet, which triggered a landslide of boxes and bins down on top of him. Laughing, I helped him pick up the books that tumbled out of a blue plastic tub. "We've really got to think about getting a bigger place. Or at least put some things in storage."

"Or you could get rid of some of this stuff. I think most of these are full of your old books and papers."

"I don't have all that much, and I need those for my research. Remember I am supposed to be consulting on the Tillman House. These are important for that project. What about you? I had no idea that you were such a pack rat. You have boxes of baseball cards taking up half the closet." I didn't mean to complain—and I wouldn't have if he hadn't said something first.

"Me? At least I confine my items to the closet. The whole dining room table has become your research center." He frowned, tossing the suitcase on the down coverlet of the queen-sized bed.

Wow, that stung just a tad. His junk didn't really bother me, but I sensed he was angry about something—something about me. "Okay...well, I will do my best to finish my office and keep things off the kitchen table. Um, I'm going to change my clothes—maybe get a shower."

"No need to rush," he said with a sigh, his hands on his hips. "I have to go to New Orleans for a couple of days. I should be back on Sunday."

My shoulders stiffened and my chin jutted out. No way on God's green earth was I going to ask him where he was going. Now I didn't really care! "Two days should be enough time for me to get my office in order. Have fun on your trip."

"It's not that kind of trip—it's mostly for work. I've got to see some people. You can tag along if you like."

"No thanks. Tagging along isn't my style, and I have an office to organize." I strolled out of the room, my hands curled into angry fists intended to keep me from crying.

"Wait. I'm sorry, Carrie Jo. Come back." He shoved a tennis racket and a box of miscellaneous items back into the closet and closed the door. "I didn't mean that crack about your stuff."

I nodded and said, "Okay," leaving the room before he saw the tears in my eyes. It wasn't just this incident—it was where we were now. Like two unhappy strangers forced to live away from home. I walked away, closing the bedroom door behind me, just to let him know that I wanted to be alone for a little while. I knew whatever had ticked him off was not my office.

Everything had been fine during our months in Haiti and the Bahamas, and even afterward when we spent some time on the Happy Go Lucky, Ashland's boat. But those three months were gone, and real life piled in on us. I couldn't help but think maybe we just weren't meant to be together. Perhaps we had rushed into things; the supernatural drama of Seven Sisters forced us to move too fast, too soon. I wondered if that could be true—I suspected he did too. We were from two different worlds. His was respectable, full of tradition, and he was from a family of wealth and means. The world I stepped out of had none of those things. Everything I'd ever had, I had to work hard for, harder than my peers did.

Despite my momentary anger, divorce wasn't a consideration—not for me. I loved Ashland, and I would do my best to make it work, but no way did I plan to be a pushover. *Tag along? What was he thinking?*

Let him go to New Orleans—I could use the time to myself anyway. I stepped into my closet and looked for something to wear. I reached for a pair of old jeans and a soft grey V-neck t-shirt, then went to turn on the shower. As I chewed my fingernail nervously, I heard my phone whistle in my purse. I walked to the dresser and dug it out. It was a text from Ashland.

I'm a jerk.

Walking back into the bathroom, I turned on the shower and stared at the phone. I tapped in my response. *What do you want me to say? That you're not?*

That would be nice.

Sorry. I'm all out of nice.

I threw the phone on the bed, stripped off my clothing and stepped into the warm water. It felt good to be mean for a moment. I typically wasn't very good at mean, but I found married life made me better at it. Not that Ashland wasn't wonderful, thoughtful and completely patient, but living with someone was a new thing for me. I barely had roommates in college because I so treasured my privacy.

When he didn't text me back after a minute or two, guilt washed over me. Maybe this was a good time to test out that old adage that making up was much more fun than breaking up. I wondered how he felt about taking an afternoon shower with me. Before I could call out to him and ask him to join me, I heard the front door slam closed. *Oh well, there goes that idea.*

I rubbed my body down with a thick, soft towel and shimmied into my panties and blue jeans. I pulled on the t-shirt and tucked it into my jeans. I wrapped my waist with a luxurious black leather belt and opted for some black sandals. I pulled my damp hair on top of my head so I could focus on putting on makeup without fighting my wayward wet curls. I laughed when I saw myself in the mirror. I looked, as they sometimes say in Mobile, like a "hot mess." Nothing like Calpurnia and her carefully coiled braids. How times had changed!

"I miss you Calpurnia. Muncie—Janjak, I miss you so much! I hope you're happy where you are," I said to the air around me. I didn't expect to hear anything, and I didn't, but I sensed they were with me still. That both comforted and troubled me. Why weren't they at rest now? For the second time that day, I felt that nagging feeling, like I'd left the water running or the oven on. Something missing, something forgotten—something disturbing.

Putting down the mascara wand for a moment, I closed my eyes. *What is wrong?* I listened to my heart, hoping it would give me a clue, but I heard nothing but the birds chirping outside my spacious bathroom window.

Talking to the air around me I said, "You know, if you're unhappy, all you have to do is tell me. But please—no scary stuff." My phone rang loudly beside me, and I jumped up and out of my vanity chair. "Oh my gosh! You guys have a sense of humor, don't you?" I stared at the phone and picked it up. When I read the screen, my jaw nearly hit the floor. The call was from Terrence Dale!

"Hi, this is Carrie Jo."

"Can you hear me?"

"Yes, I can hear you. How are you, TD?"

"Fine. I need to talk to you—face to face. Can I come by and see you? Or maybe you could come to my place tomorrow? Around four? I should be home by then."

"Sure, I can do that. I'll come to you. Are you still over off Clairborne Street?" I smiled into the phone. I was happy to hear from him.

"Yes, on the corner. I think you've been here once before to pick up something."

"That's right. I'll be there. Would you like me to bring Ashland too?" Reuniting the friends would be a dream come true.

"If it's okay, I'd like it to be the two of us." He didn't offer much explanation, but I chalked it up to male pride. Southern male pride at that. Whatever he wanted to talk about, he didn't want Ashland to know about it.

"I'll see you at four tomorrow."

"Sounds great. Thanks for taking my call."

"Happy to hear from you."

TD hung up the phone, and I walked to the big window that overlooked the backyard. The garden was in a sorry state. The gardenia was overgrown and wilting in the heat, and riotous weeds overran the walkway stones. I couldn't help but think about the Moonlight Garden and how proud TD had been when he finished that project. It had been a thing of beauty—until the three of us tore it up digging for lost treasure.

I held the phone in my hand and pulled up Ashland's name from my contact list but then changed my mind. Why should I tell him about the phone call? He wasn't in an all-fired hurry to tell me who he would see this weekend. Besides, this was just two friends meeting to talk. What was the harm in that?

I felt guilty, even though I had done nothing wrong. Did I really want to start keeping secrets from the man I loved? I walked down the stairs, shocked to see that the front door stood wide open. Crunchy fall leaves had blown in and were strewn down the hall. Piles of them were heaped on the hallway floor as if someone had raked them into a tidy piles. I didn't remember it being so breezy out.

"Ashland?" I stepped out on the porch, past the cheery pumpkins and potted mums. It was only two o'clock, but it was getting cloudy and dark. I could smell the rain on the wind. Looking up and down the sidewalk, I didn't see a soul. Ashland's truck was gone. I walked back inside and called again. Nobody answered. I locked the door and pulled on the knob. I'd have to deal with these leaves but right now, I just wanted to think. I pushed on the door again—now it was closed tight, without even a draft of air around it. I flipped on a light and leaned my back against the door. I coached myself, "Alright, don't be a baby. He probably didn't close the door properly. There's no one here."

Just to be sure I wasn't lying to myself, I walked through the house. Like a teenage girl, I opened every closet just to make sure I was alone. When I had satisfied my overactive imagination, I turned on the radio to a local jazz station. It was too early for wine, but I did help myself to a glass of the peach iced tea Doreen had made us earlier. I had never had a housekeeper before, and the idea had made me uncomfortable at first. But Ashland assured me that he paid Doreen and the rest of his staff well.

Hmm…maybe Doreen had popped in while I was in the shower. Yeah, that was probably it. Anyway, no harm, no foul.

I pretended I didn't hear the faint sound of giggling.

Chapter 3

By six o'clock, I had made a significant dent in the chaos. The built-in bookcases in my office, gifts from Ashland, were full of my research books and a decent collection of leather-bound classics. I arranged them by color first, then changed my mind and lined them up by author. When I was finally satisfied with my library, I turned my attention to the various papers, pictures and other materials I had collected over the years. Ashland had also surprised me with a custom-made desk, deep enough to allow me to spread out my papers but not so long that it hindered access to the French doors leading to the private backyard garden that would one day spring to life. I did love this room; it reminded me of a study in an old 1940s movie, like *Rebecca*, down to the small fireplace on the outside wall. I imagined spending long days here, happily buried in forgotten manuscripts. I wanted to continue working simply because I loved it. That was one reason why I volunteered to help Roz Tillman organize her family's estate. What else would I do with my time if I wasn't working?

One day, Ashland and I would raise a family—I believed that—but now wasn't the time.

Sipping my iced tea, I walked to the window and pulled back the white linen curtain. The sun was sliding down the sky. It would have been the perfect sunset to watch on the Happy Go Lucky. I had meant to catch the sunset earlier, but time had gotten away from me. The jazz station played something by Etta James, which made me miss Ashland all the more. I had stopped checking my phone half an hour ago. He would probably be in New Orleans by now. Maybe I should have tagged along after all.

I opened the door and breathed in the fresh air. The gas lamp kicked on, its amber light casting a few fall shadows in the baleful garden. The all-too-brief rainstorm earlier had blown through, taking with it all the warmth of the day. I closed my eyes and enjoyed the coolness. I toyed with the idea of abandoning my office project and maybe grabbing a bite to eat somewhere—I'd made so much progress already—but then my neighbor stepped out on his porch. I couldn't see him, but I could hear his very private phone conversation. Closing the door as discreetly as I could, I stepped back inside. I turned the lock and nearly jumped out of my skin for the second time.

Someone walked past my door quickly and without saying a word to me.

"Doreen? Is that you?" Setting the glass down on the corner of the desk, I walked into the hallway. "Doreen?" I froze—the front door was standing wide open once again. More leaves were in the hallway, as if someone had deliberately brought in baskets of shriveled leaves and scattered them on the hardwood floor. My half hour of work sweeping them all out earlier had been for naught. I turned off the radio and called again, "Doreen? Ashland?" Chills ran down my spine. *I know I saw someone!* I walked to the front door and closed it again. *And I know I locked this door!*

I didn't bother calling again. Something was happening, but the ghosts of the past were silent, at least the ones I knew personally. The urge to flee was overwhelming. I ran back to the dining room and grabbed my keys and purse off the sideboard. Just as I turned to walk out, I noticed a fat, worn envelope resting on top of a stack of unopened envelopes. As frightened as I felt, it caught my attention. I didn't remember ever seeing it, and I had been working in this room and the adjoining one all afternoon. It was addressed to me with no return address, but that didn't matter. I recognized the tight, controlled handwriting.

This was from Mia! Had she been here? Had she escaped from the facility?

I stared at the return postmark. It had arrived a month ago—no wonder I hadn't seen it. Ashland and I had been gone for months. Why would Doreen set this here and not where she put the rest of the mail? That familiar, unsettled feeling began to creep over me. No, I didn't want to be here anymore. Not right now. Taking the envelope with me, I left my Victorian home behind. I pulled onto Government Street and headed to Bette's house. Anywhere would be better than here, and I could use some comfort and advice. As I closed the door behind me, I heard a stifled giggle. It was her—Isla was here! In my house!

Stopping at the red light just past my house, I reminded myself to breathe. My knuckles were white—I had a death grip on the steering wheel. This was no time to freak out. Surely I was wrong. We had defeated Isla, right? Breaking my rule about using my phone while driving, I dug in my purse. I had to talk to Ashland, now! Trying to beat the light change, I tapped on the screen and called my husband. "Hi, this is Ashland…" Voicemail. Rats! How would that message sound? *"Honey, please come home. I think the ghost is back."* I tossed the phone back in my purse.

Focus on the road, girl! It was a pleasant drive for a Friday night. Not a ton of cars out on the normally busy street, and many of the old houses along Government were decorated for fall. The sight of porches full of pumpkins and the trees draped with goofy sheets meant to look like ghosts helped calm my nerves. Still a bit panicked, I pulled into Bette's driveway. From the road I could see that she wasn't home, and my heart sank in my chest. Her light blue convertible, a gift from Ashland and me, was gone and the house lights except the side porch light were off. I pulled into the driveway just to have a place to think for a minute. I checked my phone again but Ashland hadn't bothered to call me back. *What was going on with him?*

Glancing up at my old apartment, I wished I could barge in and make myself at home. That's where my life here in Mobile had begun, in Bette's over-the-garage apartment. I missed that place. Bienville, Bette's orange tabby, was nowhere to be found. I spied Iberville, his less than friendly brother, staring at me from the gardenias that grew beneath Bette's kitchen window. Now what? My appetite had disappeared, but I didn't want to go back to the house right now. I tore open the package on the seat next to me. All that was inside was a scrap of paper and a worn leather-bound book. With some trepidation, I unfolded the note. Yes, this was from Mia.

Nothing I can say will ever make up for what I have done. However, after reading this, maybe you will understand. – M

Refolding the note, I examined the unusual book cover. The leather cover was embossed with the image of a peacock showing his feathers. Flipping on the map light, I studied it closer: *The Stars that Fell* by E. Halderon. I didn't see anything that jumped out at me as I leafed through the pages, just faded letters on delicate paper. I closed the book and slid it back in the envelope. Now wasn't the time to read an old book from a former friend. Lightning cracked across the sky in the distance. I had to go somewhere—I couldn't just hang out in Bette's driveway all night.

Seven Sisters! Detra Ann mentioned that they were having nightly tours during October. I put the car in reverse and made the quick trip to the plantation. It had been three months since I had stepped foot on the property, and the thought of returning thrilled me. Maybe my former intern and fellow historian Rachel Kowalski would be there. I turned down the long drive that led to the house. Someone had trimmed back the hedges, and I could see the top floor of Seven Sisters shining brightly all the way down the driveway.

It was barely dark, but there were half a dozen cars in the driveway, presumably to take the Halloween tour. I was thankful there were no inflatable cartoon witches on the lawn or plastic bats hanging from the live oaks. Detra Ann and her crew had lined the pathway to the house with hurricane glasses that held white flameless candles. It was lovely and simple, evoking a certain understated magic.

I parked the car, stuffed Mia's envelope in my purse and followed the sidewalk to the massive front steps. I paused at the bottom, remembering the first moment I stood here, the night I met Ashland. He had emerged from the overgrown brush like a phantom, but his easy smile had won my heart.

Standing near the front door was a perky young woman, an Azalea Trail Maid, according to her massive purple antebellum dress. The gown moved as she waved to me and walked to the porch edge. She handed me a tour brochure. "Hi! The next tour starts in 30 minutes, but you can step into the foyer and enjoy some refreshments."

"No, thank you. I am not here for the tour. Is Rachel around? Rachel Kowalski?"

"Um, I'm not sure. I don't really work here, but the lady in charge, Miss Dowd, is inside. Maybe she can help you."

"Alright, thank you." I smiled at the teenager and walked through the open door. How different it was now than the first moment I saw it! No more lumpy carpet and musty rooms. The walls were meticulously painted, and hardwood floors shone brilliantly throughout the house. Someone had placed a round table in the foyer, covered with more brochures and information about local historical landmarks. I didn't like that, but the house wasn't mine anymore. Not that it ever really was. It had belonged to Ashland's family, but now it was just another historical property owned by the City of Mobile. Nobody greeted me in the lobby, so I made myself at home. I walked first to the ladies' parlor, where everything was exactly where I left it. As I looked around the room, scenes from my dreams played out in my head. Over by the fireplace was where Calpurnia had first laid eyes on David Garrett. It was such a sad room, really. The side door was closed, but I could hear voices in the Rose Garden.

"I'm sorry, ma'am, but the tour is in the Moonlight Garden now. Just out the back door. Oh, Carrie Jo! I didn't know you were here." It was Detra Ann, surprised but polite.

Suddenly, I didn't know what to say. "I was just in the neighborhood. I mean, I thought I could..."

"No need to explain. Come on into the Blue Room. We can chat in there unless you prefer to sit in here."

"No, the Blue Room is fine." I followed behind her, anxious to see what my old office looked like now. The walls were still painted a cool blue. Calpurnia's painting hung over the fireplace, as it should. All of our desks and equipment had been removed, replaced with period furniture. There was a modern piece, a small love seat, by one of the tall windows. Detra Ann and I sat, and I fumbled for what to say. I needn't have worried; she was still the take-charge kind of gal. *Like I used to be before all this. What happened to me?*

"What can I help you with, Carrie Jo?"

"I, uh, I just wanted to come by and see the place. It feels like forever since I walked these halls."

Detra Ann sat with perfect posture on the couch beside me. I felt an awkward smile stretch across my face. She gave me a sweet smile of her own in return. "I understand that. This place must feel like home. You are always welcome to stop by, Carrie Jo. You know, you're kind of a legend around here. Chip and Rachel just adore you."

"That's sweet to say. Those two were hard workers, and I am glad that at least Rachel is still here. I guess Chip got the job at the Mobile Museum?"

"No, he didn't. To his credit, there was some stiff competition. He has been lurking around here, mostly to see Rachel, I think. He spends a lot of time working with his professor in the northern part of the county. Some project trying to find the old fort, Fort Louis de La Louisiane."

"That's interesting. Wow, if they found the actual location—that would be such an important find." She nodded and then we sat quietly again, the sound of the clock ticking on the fireplace filling the emptiness between us. Seven Sisters still had the comforting smell of wet paint and fresh wood. Maybe we had done something good after all, Ashland and I.

Detra Ann's blue eyes scrutinized me. "I know why you're really here, Carrie Jo."

I caught my breath. "You do?" *You know that I'm hearing and seeing things again? That I'm not dreaming and that my husband barely talks to me anymore?*

"Yes, you're here about TD. Aren't you?"

I didn't know what to say. *I came here because I think Isla Beaumont is in my house.* "I won't deny that I am curious. What's actually going on, Detra Ann? Bette mentioned he had some sort of breakdown?"

She leaned back against the love seat, her posture collapsing under the obvious weight of their relationship. She slipped off her heels and sighed. "You could call it that. All I know is that things were going along fine, and then the incident in the Moonlight Garden happened. Everything went downhill after that. He tried to get over it—I tried to help him—but it didn't happen. He had nightmares, bad nightmares. He'd wake up screaming."

I hadn't known that. How would I have? "Did you ever get him to go to church? You mentioned giving that a try."

She nodded. "He went, but I guess he never found the answers he was looking for. Honestly, I don't know how to help him. I am crazy about him—as you well know—but I am not going to date a man who refuses to work and mopes around all day. Have you seen him lately?"

Now was the time for some honesty. I couldn't keep it from her. "He called me earlier. Says he wants to talk. I am supposed to meet him tomorrow afternoon."

"Carrie Jo, I know you have a big heart, and I care about TD too. But he's not the same guy you remember. He is angry all the time. The littlest things set him off. I mean, I do not think he would harm you, but then again, he is not the laid-back, sweet person we used to know. He is moody and…" Her pretty freckled nose crinkled. "He drinks a lot. One of my brothers is an alcoholic. I know the signs, and I refuse to enable TD."

"I owe this to him. I feel responsible for what happened. If it were not for me, for my dreaming, we would have never been in that garden digging around. I am the reason he is drinking. I have to make it right."

Detra Ann reached across the love seat and took my hand. "You can't help who you are, any more than I can or anyone else can. You did not make TD drink. He fell apart on his own." I nodded, but I was not convinced. "Look at all the good that has happened, Carrie Jo. Now we know what happened here. Calpurnia can rest now. All of them, they can rest because we all know the truth. That's no small thing."

"No, it's not," I agreed. *But they're not all resting!*

Chapter 4

"Detra Ann, I have a huge favor to ask you. You do not have to say yes, but I need to ask it anyway."

"Okay, what is it?" She looked at me intently, waiting for me to spill the beans. Would she think I was crazy? Until this conversation, I would never have believed that Detra Ann cared about how I felt, not one bit.

"First, I promise you, I will help TD. Whatever has passed between you two, I know you belong together, just like Ashland and I do. I can't explain it, but I know." She gave a tiny smile. "Fight for what you have—what you want, Detra Ann. Pray for it. Be patient…he's going to come back around. Whatever is bothering him, we'll uncover it, but I need you to help me."

"What do you mean? I don't understand."

How to explain when I wasn't sure myself? "TD had a part in what we uncovered. He helped us—he's probably experiencing the same kind of resistance we have."

Her big blue eyes widened. "You mean like spiritual resistance?"

"That would be my guess. Now you see why I have to help him—I know Ashland would want that too. Honestly, ever since that night, nothing has been the same. Not for me, not for Ashland. Obviously not for TD."

Detra Ann's eyes betrayed her feelings. She was telling the truth: she didn't understand, and she was definitely afraid.

"You have to keep fighting. There's nothing anyone, dead or alive, can do to keep you apart—not if you were meant to be together!"

At that moment, a glass figurine from a nearby side table, one of the less expensive ones in the arrangement, flew off the mantelpiece and shattered on the floor at our feet. Both of us jumped up, careful to avoid the glass.

Detra Ann clutched my hands, and we just stood there and waited for more strange activity, but nothing happened. Detra Ann breathed a sigh of relief. "What just happened?"

"I'm not really sure, but someone or something did not like our conversation. That means we're going the right way! That's where I need your help."

"Anything. What is it?" Still looking around the room nervously, Detra Ann slipped her heels back on.

"I want to spend the night here, in Calpurnia's room—no, wait. In Christine's room. I won't harm anything, and I can't really explain it, but I feel compelled to stay. You see, I know I missed something. A piece of the puzzle is missing. When I find it, all will be well."

"You want to dream, don't you? I don't know. What would Ashland say about this, Carrie Jo? He loves you so much. If you were hurt, or if something happened to you, he would never forgive me."

"Nothing is going to happen. I am going to sleep with the lights on, but I need to try and dream here. I can't help but feel that I left something undone. I missed something. We missed something. I have to find out what and make it right. Worst of all, Isla is still wandering around. Although I haven't seen her yet, not fully, I know it's her. I need her to be gone! Please, let me stay just this one time."

Detra Ann smiled. "Okay, on one condition—no, two conditions. First, I stay with you, and second, you come to the Halloween Ball here. Agreed?"

"That's not necessary. I can stay alone. I swear I'm not afraid to be alone."

"I am sure you aren't, but you won't be. That's the deal, take it or leave it." She wasn't budging, and strangely enough, I was glad. I hated the idea of taking part in a ball. I was the worst dancer on the planet! But if it meant I could stay at Seven Sisters, I would just have to put on my dancing shoes and a smile.

"Fine, agreed, but we can't sleep together." Her look of surprise spoke volumes. I chuckled. "No! I mean in the same bed. You see, when I dream, there is a chance I can transfer and see your dreams too. I don't want to know what you are thinking when you are dreaming. That's an invasion of your privacy. You can stay in the other room or set up a cot in Christine's room. But are you sure you want to do this?"

"Yes! I want to see a real dream catcher in action! This is all new to me!"

"Well, I'll go call Ashland. I hate to go back to the house tonight. It's getting late."

"No worries, I'll call my housekeeper. She can bring us both some clothes and toothbrushes and toothpaste, whatever we need." We made a little list, including some food, and waited until the guests left. At about 10 p.m., we walked up the stairs to go to bed. My call with Ashland didn't happen. I did get a hold of him once, but the music in the background was so loud that I couldn't hear him. Angry, I hung up and put my phone on mute. I didn't want to hear it if he called me back. I had to focus now. I had to rein in my emotions and focus on Christine.

Maybe that's what I'd missed! What happened to her? To her baby? That had to be it!

I opened the door to Christine's room. I loved this room— it never got a ton of sunshine during the day, but it was bright and had a serene view, even in Christine's day. After I changed into the pinstriped capri pajamas that Detra Ann brought me and we chitchatted a while, we lay down to sleep. I took the bed, which wasn't the original but was in the right spot in the room. We'd brought in a rollaway bed for Detra Ann. She moved it to the corner of the room and made it up neatly with pink sheets.

She piled her blond hair on top of her head in a ponytail and looked at me expectantly. She didn't look a bit tired. "I'm nervous as heck. What do I do?"

I smiled at her. "You don't have to do a thing. I might read a little before I go to sleep. Sometimes it helps me relax."

"Listen, do you really think this will help TD? You weren't just putting me on?"

"I would never joke about this kind of thing, but it's just a hunch. You see, we all had a connection. Ashland was connected to Calpurnia, I was connected to Muncie, but TD…I'm not sure about."

"I see."

"I sound like a crazy person, but all I can tell you is what I think and feel. There are no books I can read that teach me about all this stuff. You know, growing up, I never considered myself a spiritual person. But I guess I am. Weird how that works."

"No, I get it. I've never seen anything. Except that fan stopping on the porch and the figurine crashing earlier. And both of those things happened with you around."

I hadn't thought about that before. She had a point.

"Another thing. If everyone involved is connected, who was Mia connected to?"

"That's what we need to figure out—and what happened to Christine. That's important, that much I know."

We chatted some more until Detra Ann began to yawn. "If you don't mind, I'm going to plug in my headphones and listen to some music. It's kind of my nighttime routine. I love sleeping to music. It drives TD crazy, but it helps me sleep."

"Sure, go ahead. Is this light going to bother you?"

"Not at all. I don't have a problem sleeping with the lights on. In fact, it might help because I admit I'm a little freaked out. Not because of you—because of what happened earlier."

"I get that. Me too, but I don't feel any sort of presence right now. Thanks, by the way. I appreciate you allowing me to do this."

She was quiet for a minute. "I have never known anyone like you, Carrie Jo. Before I met you, I thought that supernatural stuff was nothing but hokum—just shills trying to make money on whoever would believe them. But you're not like that. You're just a real person. Have you always dreamed about ghosts?"

I had never thought of it like that, and I admitted it to her. "I always just thought of it as dreaming. When I was a kid, I thought everyone did it, but I learned the hard way that I was wrong. Completely."

"What did your parents think? Are they supportive about your...powers?"

"I would hardly call it a power," I said with a laugh, "but I can see why someone would think that. Until I came to Seven Sisters I considered it more of an impediment. It used to drive my mother crazy. I don't think she knew what to do with me. She never quite got it. She thought I could turn it off, like I was having these dreams on purpose. It upset her to think I could see people's dreams."

"So she wasn't a dreamer? A dream catcher?"

"If she was, she never told me."

"What about your dad? Did he dream?"

"I don't know. I never met him."

"Oh, I'm sorry."

"It's okay. You can't miss what you've never known, right?"

"I guess that's true. Well, Ashland sure loves you." She stretched out on the rollaway and smiled. "I've known him all my life and have never seen him fall in love before—ever. Don't get me wrong, there have been plenty of girls interested in him, but he's always been kind of standoffish. Never committing to anyone. I am so glad he has you."

I was curious to hear about my husband from someone who knew him better than I did. "Bette told me that your mother used to hope the two of you would get together."

She chuckled. "My mother is a control freak. Ashland and I kind of got one another—we left each other alone. He was always talking about what he'd like to do for Mobile, how he wanted to restore his family's name. I was always talking about leaving this city. Little did I know I would end up loving it too." She chewed her lip and added, "Everyone in Ashland's world wanted something from him. Hollis wasn't the only one who wanted his money. I felt sorry for him—he got used a lot. Our senior year, we used to skip school together and go to the beach, but I swear nothing ever happened. We didn't like each other that way."

I smiled. "I'm glad he had a friend."

"What else did Bette tell you about me?"

"Nothing bad. Well, except that you were cross-eyed. Imagine my surprise when I met you and you were just drop-dead gorgeous."

"Ha! Don't I wish!" She laughed aloud. "I had a lazy eye for like one summer, but the eye doctor corrected it with a patch. What an amazing summer that was—me wearing a patch for three months, all the guys running the other way. It did do one thing, though. It made me more sympathetic toward people with physical challenges."

"Yes, I guess it would."

She yawned and smiled. "I guess I'm going to try and sleep. If you need me, I'm right here. Kick that fan up a notch, will you?"

"Sure." I slid out of bed and turned up the oscillating fan. It was comfortable to me, but then again this old house didn't have central air and heating. Before I got back into bed, I dug the envelope out of my purse.

Detra Ann had her back to me; she was playing on her phone listening to music. I examined the envelope again and sighed. Why was I doing this? Could I trust anything that Mia might tell me? What did I care about her reasons for trying to kill me—and William? She did kill Hollis Matthews and God knows who else.

Nothing else to see, just my name and new address and a crumpled envelope. I pulled out the book inside and held it under the yellow lamp light. It was apparently the first in a collection of biographies of actors and actresses. The words *THE STARS THAT FELL* were embossed with gold, or they had been. I could see a just fleck or two of gold now. I ran my fingers over the peacock and opened the cover.

Published in 1921 by the Nelson-Howell Publishing Company. Well, so what? What did this have to do with Mia? Another delusion?

I leaned back against the pillows and closed my eyes for a minute. Mia was crazy—there was no doubt about that—but she had been right about so many things. When it came to research and hunches, she was the best. I felt a twinge of sadness. Mia had been the first to discover that the Beaumont treasure was real and the first to have an idea of where it might be. She was right about the fact that the statues were a map, a map that was echoed with the markers in the Cottonwood cemetery. She knew, even before I did, that Calpurnia had never found the treasure.

I held the book to my chest and took a deep breath. I guess it was time to know what else Mia knew. I hoped I wouldn't regret this.

I probably would.

Chapter 5

I could tell the book was old by the font and the page layout. And I recognized that "old book" scent, probably one of my favorite smells in the world. The book began with a note from the author and some commentary about his subjects, which included a woman named Delilah Iverson.

Dear Reader,

I am not merely an author but a collector of unusual lives. THE STARS THAT FELL is a representation of my life's work. Many of you, no doubt, will recognize some of the more famous names like Delilah Iverson, Nate Daniels and Edwin McCarthy.

I must confess that it took some convincing on my part to compel my first subject, the talented Miss Iverson, to agree to speak to us concerning personal matters. In the end, she graciously yielded to my pleas and allowed me that privilege. As I have such great respect for the lady and consider her a dear friend, her story begins THE STARS THAT FELL.

Your Faithful Scribe,

Ernesto Halderon

I flipped to the first chapter and read the first few sentences. Nothing unusual yet. I sighed and hunkered down in my bed, reading by the dim light. A light pattering of rain began tapping against the window. The house was quiet except for the occasional squeak of wood, which one would expect in a house as old as this.

Dear Ernesto,

What should I say? So, you wish to hear my story? I am willing to tell it, but I insist on doing the telling. Perhaps if you knew how crowded my mind would become with the faces of those who are gone, those I have loved and lost, you would forget this idea, have mercy and find a more worthy muse for your book. Yet I can see by the anxious look on your face that you will not allow me to depart without first having told all.

For myself, I cannot imagine that any intelligent person would care to read about my life, for I have not found it so unusual or interesting. Surprising? Yes! But it was my life, and I have enjoyed every sun-filled and rainy day included within it. Even when the storms came and the war rolled over the South like the devil drove it, I wanted to live! I guess you could say that I have a strong will to live. As I am now seventy, this I certainly have proven.

Where shall I start? Should I tell you all my secrets? Whom I have loved and whom I have hated? Should I tell you about the stolen kisses, the promises we made and the inevitable betrayals? Should I tell you about the time I missed my happiness by mere minutes? Oh, but those were the times when I felt the most alive, alive in my pain! If it's a tale you want, then a tale you shall get.

Hmm... I liked her already.

***

My life began quite happily, dear Ernesto. I was not born with a silver spoon in my mouth—quite the contrary! At an early age, I learned the value of hard work, and it is not a lesson I regret having learned. Yet we had fine things when it was possible. Hard work has paid me well, as you can see by my many achievements here. But things were different then.

My parents, Jacob and Katharine Iverson, owned a sundries shop in downtown Mobile, Alabama. My father was also a master carpenter, and his fine Norwegian workmanship was always in high demand. Our shop was right on Conception Street, across from the Irish church that rang bells for matins and whenever a good Catholic child was born in the parish that surrounded it. Near our shop was the dress and hat shop where I later went to work. Our home was above the sundries shop. It was nothing large, but I had my own room, which was quite a treat for the time.

My brother and I spent many happy days there until right before the war. My parents loved America, but my father had no desire to take sides in a war that would divide the great country he so passionately loved. My parents weren't quite Southerners yet, although they loved living in Mobile. My mother always said that Norway was the most beautiful place on Earth but Alabama was certainly the warmest. She liked that. She told me on many occasions that the cold hurt her bones.

My brother had other ideas. Neither he nor I remembered Norway, although he was born there. I was four years younger than Adam, and we were very close, as close as a brother and sister could be. I was born an American, born at home in Mobile. Although he had been born in Norway, Adam was a Southerner through and through. I still remember him young and happy. He had the blondest hair; it always fell in his eyes. Mother would say, "Delilah, cut your brother's hair. He looks like a sheepdog." We would take the chair out behind the shop, and I would cut his hair as best I could. He was kind to me, even when I cut gaps into his hair or made him look like a beggar boy. He would say, "Yes, this is what I wanted, thank you, Delilah." I would smile, and he would give me a coin, just like I had been a true barber. He always had a way of making me feel special.

When other young men his age began to sign up to serve in the Confederate Army, he felt it his duty to do the same. Mind you, we were not slave owners; my parents abhorred slavery, but they equally abhorred the heavy taxation by the Northern states—it was a concern for all local businessmen and indeed businessmen everywhere I would imagine. For many men, that alone was enough reason to go to war. They were fighting for their wealth and happiness. There were plenty of raw materials in the South but no way to manufacture anything. All those factories were up North. Mobile was the Cotton Queen, but she had nary a one cotton processing company.

What arguments my father and Adam would have on this subject! That was a difficult time for all of us. I was only fifteen when the talks of war turned serious; Adam was nineteen and a young man—ready to prove himself as such. My Uncle Lars wrote us inviting us to travel to Canada until the war was over. That idea didn't sit well with my brother; he knew that the local families would call our father and him a yellow coward.

"It's always better to fight," Adam would say to Poppa. Then Poppa would speak Norwegian, and Adam would join him. I couldn't understand a word they were saying. I always regretted that. Eventually, it would become clear that Adam had lost the argument. At the request of Uncle Lars, we prepared to head north to Canada to ride out the war. I didn't want to leave my hometown, but I also didn't want to see the city destroyed. It surely would be—and to some degree it was! Adam was angry, of course. As a grown man, he could make his own decision. I knew he wanted to leave us. I couldn't let him go!

I had followed Adam that afternoon. I watched him walk into the military station and talk to the sergeant. He had not yet signed up, but I knew he was intending to do so. That evening, when Poppa put the violin away and Mother finished the dinner dishes, I ran upstairs and went into

Adam's room. He was in bed, wearing his nightgown, his hands behind his head. He stared out the far window, looking at the moon.

"What is it, Lila?"

I sulked toward him and crawled in the bed with him. "You cannot leave me, Adam. You would send me all the way to a land where I know no one. All the way to Canada."

"Hush now. You want me to be a kid forever. It's only for a little while, and then I will be home with my jacket full of metals and ribbons."

"That's not what will happen, and you know it." *I held him tight as if it could really be the last time I saw him. He held me too.*

"I don't know anything of the sort." *He rubbed my hair playfully.* "Wouldn't you feel proud to have a brother who served in the war? Wouldn't you want me to show them that I am not a coward?"

"Yes, you could show them, but then I would lose you. That's not fair, Adam. You would do this just to show off?" *I sat up, my dark curls falling around my face.*

Adam took my hand and kissed it. "You'd better go to bed, Lila. Tomorrow's going to be a big day."

I walked slowly to the wooden door, my lower lip quivering. "Please don't do this, Adam. Will you make me a promise?"

He rolled back over to face me. "What is it?"

"If it is raining in the morning, you will stay with us. If it's sunny, you will go. Isn't that fair?"

"Really? That's the deal you want me to make?" *He smiled sadly and covered back up. I was an excellent deal maker—just ask anyone who came to the shop.* "That's too easy. You know it's going to rain tomorrow."

"Okay then, let's say that if you see a rainbow in the morning sometime before 8 a.m., you will stay." *Even as I said the words, I could see Adam actually seeing the rainbow and then looking at the clock. My mother called it intuition; I mostly kept my knowings and seeings to myself, but that day was special.*

Adam laughed at the idea. "Not giving yourself much of a chance to win, Lila. You do like these silly tests, don't you? Okay, I agree. If I see a rainbow tomorrow before 8 a.m., I will stay with you and our parents. We will go to Canada. If not, I go to join the Army. That is a deal. Now go to bed."

"Thank you, Adam!" I slipped out of his room feeling as if I had won the argument. Somehow I knew that God was on my side. Adam would see a rainbow, and he would be okay. Best of all, we would be together. Little did I know he would hate me for it later.

Chapter 6

Closing the book quietly, I placed it on the nightstand. I didn't want to sleep with it. She wasn't the girl I wanted to see right now. Her story was beginning to intrigue me, especially in light of the fact that THE STARS THAT FELL was on Mia's required reading list.

The truth was I wanted to see Christine, to dream about her. Strangely enough, I felt complete peace. I knew I was doing the right thing. I felt no fear that I would see snakes or be chased by horrible monsters. I simply whispered "Christine Beaumont Cottonwood..." quietly until I slipped into my dream.

The air around me moved fast at first, and then suddenly it stopped. I was in Miss Christine's room, standing at the end of the bed. I was standing behind the doctor who was sweating so hard he asked me to wipe his brow with my apron. I did as I was told. My name was Hannah, and I was new to Seven Sisters. I came from some place called Philadelphia, a long way from here. My former mistress, a woman who ran a house of ill repute in the Blue District, lost me in a card game to one of her rich lovers. It had been a joke to her, sending me away from the only family I had ever known. How she laughed and drank and laughed some more that night. Fortunately, my new master was a nice man who taught piano. He moved to Mobile, but he died quite suddenly from pains in his chest.

I come upstairs to bring him his morning cornbread and milk mush, and the old man was cold dead. I didn't know what to do, so I sat down, ate the mush and then walked down to the sheriff's office to tell him the news. Soon, I was sold to another family, and some folks say I was very lucky to get to work at Seven Sisters. It was a grand place with many rooms and plenty of food to eat. But it was full of sadness. Everyone here was sad. At least at Madame LaMont's everyone was happy, but that was probably because they were always drunk. Here, in this big fine house, it was like they was all under some sort of magical spell, the kind that slowly crept in and couldn't be removed no matter how many prayers you say.

The baby's head began to show, but Miss Christine never made a sound. She tried to sit up a few times but refused to speak. She just stared up at the ceiling. Her mouth was slack, and Hooney had to wipe it often. "Miss Christine, please try. Push that baby out, Miss Christine. You'll feel so much better if you do." Hooney pleaded with her kindly, but the woman was gone. She was like the living dead. It broke my heart.

"Hannah, come up here for a minute and let me come help the doctor. You stand right here and wipe her mouth when she needs it. And talk to her kindly. Help her remember who she is and what she is doing. We need her to push that baby out, or the doctor here might have to cut her open."

Hooney's voice was dead serious, and I didn't want that to happen to Miss Christine. She had been a nice lady. She'd given me a new cotton dress and apron when I got here. She'd even made sure that I found a pair of secondhand shoes that fit me well.

"Miss Christine, please wake up." Hannah patted my face with her hand and suddenly....

I wasn't Hannah anymore. How weird was this? My gift was changing, and I didn't understand it at all.

Now I was Christine.

I feel warm, like I have too many clothes on. Oh, to be alone and naked with Hoyt! I would take a thousand beatings for him. How I love that man! When will I see him again? Look! There's our daughter! There's Calpurnia, over there in the corner. Why does she look so sad? Don't cry, Callie. I have something for you. I know you will find it.

I wrote you a note, dearest. "Find your True Self, and you will Find a Treasure." I hope you understand. You are our treasured daughter, our daughter. I wish I could tell you...

Oh...why does my stomach hurt so badly? I scream and scream and scream, but nobody hears me. Whose dark face is that leaning over me? I want Ann-Sheila! Where is my friend? No, she's gone. Like Louis.

Louis! Louie! Come back to me!

Look, there's baby Calpurnia trying to walk in her new shoes. How proud I am! My daughter! How she would hate me if she knew my secret! Oh, the pain is excruciating! Why can't someone see that I am in pain?

My Mother used to say that pain was proof that you were alive. That pain was essential for living. Once we stopped hurting, we stopped living. I want you now, Mother! How you would disapprove of Hoyt and me, but he is a good man! I married the man Father wanted me to marry, and see what it has brought me? Nothing but sadness and ruin. Mother, Mother, please don't go. Take me with you.

I try to sit up and follow her, but she leaves the room, a swirl of blue silk behind her.

I see another face now...Isla! NO! NO! *Get her away from me! So much like Olivia but so evil! She is my tormentor. The things she told me! I feel the darkness surrounding me!*

The lies! Oh the lies she tells me, Louis! My beautiful brother! It cannot be true!

Hoyt! Hoyt! I hear your voice. Help me, please, my love! My own darling! Help me. Please watch over our children. They need you—I need you. Maybe the day will come when you and I can be together truly. How I long for that day. No more sneaking to the cottage, hoping and praying that no one catches us! I would do it all again, all for love, all for my family!

What lovely roses! Who so kindly brought me roses? May I smell them? Bring them closer.

Again, the dark-faced girl is leaning over me. I barely see her smile as she shows me a baby. Is that Calpurnia? I feel a surge of wetness between my legs, but the pain has gone. What has happened? The room has darkened! It is too dark, and I hear voices that I cannot understand.

No, the voices have stopped. All is quiet. All is quiet. A little rest now...

What is that sound? It is the sound of thunder—it is Jeremiah! Make him leave, Hoyt! You do not know how he beats me. How he hurts me. If only you could hear me. Where am I?

I am coming, Calpurnia. My child is crying. Mother is coming now!

Hannah wiped at Christine's face again.

Wait...Christine saw me! I saw her look at me! She saw me!

Who are you? her mind asked. Her face did not move.

I am a friend, Christine. I am here to help you.

Are you an angel? Are you here to take me to heaven?

My heart melted in my chest. How could this be happening? She couldn't really see me, could she?

Before I could answer her, I was Hannah again.

"Get that baby out of my sight!"

I winced at the master's anger. He would never hit me with his leather strap, but he had beaten many others at Seven Sisters. He leaned over the bed and yelled at Miss Christine, who could not hear him. I muffled a cry as I watched him.

"You were supposed to get me a son, wife! Not another daughter! A son! You have failed me for the last time! Everyone out!"

The doctor stood to face him, his face wet with sweat or tears or both. "No, sir, I shall not leave my patient, even if you beat me with an inch of my life. Your wife has wounds that will kill her if we leave them like this. I will not allow you to harm her!"

"Damn you too, Page! You nosy bastard! Always here sniffing around, sniffing at the skirts in this house. You do what you have to do, then you get out of here. Or I will call the sheriff to come and drag you out. You forget your place, sir."

"On the contrary, I forget nothing." Dr. Page stood up and tossed a bloody cloth to the ground, his hands clenched in angry fists.

With a grunt of disapproval, the master left us alone, at least for a little while. The doctor finished his ministrations but lingered at Miss Christine's bedside. He held her hand and spoke to her quietly, but the missus never looked his way. I thought maybe I saw a hint of a smile on her face, and then nothing but emptiness. Hooney stood on the other side of the bed, sniffing and wiping tears from her face. She whispered prayers, the kind of prayers the missus often said, and made the sign of the cross.

The doctor gave Hooney instructions on how often to give the medicine he was leaving. "I shall be back in the morning to see her. These drops will only help with the pain, nothing else. She needs to be in a hospital. I'll see what I can do to make that happen. In the meantime, you keep him away from her."

"I don't know who can stop him if he means to get to her. All we can do is pray."

"Well, don't defy him, but at least send for me. Surely you can do that. I will not stand by while he kills his wife. The lady needs to rest if she's ever to come out of her sickness."

Hooney promised and put the sleeping baby in my arms. I peered down at her face: she was peaceful, unaware that her Daddy was evil and that her Momma had lost her mind. I wondered what kind of life she would have.

A few hours later, the doctor was long gone and the master was deep into a bottle of corn whiskey. He came staggering back up the stairs, yelling for his wife. Instead, he found me in the nursery with his baby daughter. "That baby is dead," he growled, wavering on his feet.

"What? No, sir. She's not dead—she's sleeping like an angel. She is a beautiful little girl." I smiled, but my insides were frightened and my alarm was screaming at me to run.

"I don't think you heard me right, girl. That baby is dead. You hear me? Dead! Now get rid of it. I don't want no dead baby around here stinking up the place."

I stared at him, blinking wildly. What should I do?

Mr. Cottonwood cast an evil grin. "Want me to show you it's dead?" He reeled toward me but I stepped back, avoiding his snatch easily. The baby began to stir and fuss.

"No! Please! I understand, sir! This baby is dead. I will get rid of it right now." I ran out of the room before he could change his mind. The master shouted something at me, but I moved too quickly to hear but a few words. "Oh Lord, Jesus, Mary and Joseph! Help me!" I whispered as I practically flew down the stairs and out the front door.

"That baby is dead, you hear me!"

I cried as I ran, and Hooney ran after me. "Wait, Hannah! Where you going?" I paused, but only for a moment. I wept as I told her what happened.

"Did you hear him, Hooney? He says this baby is dead. I think he is going to kill her."

"Nothing you can do but take that baby away. The master says that baby is dead, it's dead. Take her somewhere where he can't harm her. I know where you should go—to the doctor! Quick, go now! Follow the road until it forks, then go left like you're going to town. It's the yellow house with the green windows! Go, Hannah!"

The master yelled again, and his voice sounded closer and closer. Oh Lord, he's like the devil chasing me! What will he do to us if he finds us, baby child?

The rain began to fall, but I did not let that slow me. I kept my eyes slitted against the raindrops as I flew down the red clay road. I had to get the baby to a safe place. I had to, for Miss Christine! Imagine someone wanting to kill an innocent baby!

Not tonight. Not if I had anything to say about it!

Chapter 7

"CJ—Carrie Jo! Wake up! Carrie Jo! Now!" Detra Ann's concerned face hovered over me as she roughly shook my shoulders. "Hey, are you with me, girl?"

"What? Is everything okay? Was I talking in my sleep?"

"Try screaming! You almost gave me a heart attack," she said with a nervous laugh. "I thought the boogeyman was chasing you and…" her voice dropped to a whisper, "I thought I heard something downstairs."

Her cool hands grabbed mine, and I could see in the dim light that her eyes were wide and fearful.

"I'm sure it's nothing. Just me scaring up some nightmares. I apologize, Detra Ann. Let's try to get some sleep. I'll keep quiet now, I promise."

She nodded but didn't move. She was convinced she'd heard something. I glanced at my watch; it was 4:30. We remained quiet, holding hands, waiting for any sound. I felt the hair on my arm prickle up in alarm and anticipation. Yep, something or someone was with us at Seven Sisters.

After a minute, I asked in a whisper, "What did it sound like?"

"Kind of like…" Before Detra Ann could answer, I heard a loud thump coming from the bottom floor. "Like that!" The willowy blonde froze, unsure what to do.

"I heard it too this time." The thump was a footstep. Someone was walking—no, stomping—up the wooden staircase. *Stomp, shuffle, stomp, shuffle…*

"What do we do?"

I slung the covers off and ran to the door as quietly as I could. Yes, I had set the lock, but I was not leaving anything to chance. "Hand me that wooden chair!" Detra Ann did as I asked, and I slid the chair under the doorknob hoping that would protect us.

Stomp, shuffle, stomp.

"Is that Ashland? Is this some kind of joke?"

"What? No!" I whispered furiously. "He doesn't even know we're here—nobody does!" The stomping continued, and the sound was very close to us now.

"Oh my God! It's at the top of the stairs now! What do we do?" Detra Ann was nearly in tears.

I grabbed my phone off the nightstand and dragged her by the hand to the far corner of the room, nearest the window. It was too late to call anyone—the intruder was here with us. The fear mounted as the stomps sounded louder and more threatening. Suddenly, the sound stopped, and I squeezed Detra Ann's hand as fiercely as she squeezed mine. I watched in terror as the doorknob began to turn ever so slowly. I heard Detra Ann gasp. The doorknob turned easily now, more quickly. I was just about ready to call out, to scare away whoever stood outside the door, when I heard a voice growl, "Christine!" I knew that voice—it was Jeremiah Cottonwood! There would be no reasoning with him—not in this life or any other.

"Oh, hell!" I began to pat the wall frantically. I shoved the phone in the pocket of my pajama pants and searched in the near dark.

"What are you doing?" Detra Ann exclaimed, nearly frightened out of her mind.

"Looking for a door! There has to be a way out of here!"

"There is! Move that picture!"

I lifted the heavy-framed picture off the wall and set it on the floor. The ridge was discernible now, but only barely.

"Christine!" the voice insisted, angry that he could be denied access. The doorknob continued to rattle until the door opened a tiny bit. I heard the wooden chair crack and creak. The phantom paused his assault, and it seemed I could hear him breathing. *But that can't be true! He can't breathe! He's been dead for over a hundred and fifty years!*

"Here!" Detra Ann pushed on the corner of the hidden door, and the latch gave way. A small door, just big enough for one person at a time to fit through opened, and she scurried through. I climbed in behind her, closing the door furiously just in time to hear Christine's bedroom door, the chair or both splinter behind us.

"Run, Detra Ann!" I yelled at her.

I heard her sob, "I can't see!"

I stepped in front of her. "It's okay. I have my phone. Follow me." We began to move quickly. The dust under my feet felt sticky and thick. I held her hand and turned on the flashlight app on my phone so we could work through the stuffy labyrinth. Finally, we came to a short set of stairs. We almost fell down them, but we managed to control our fear long enough to get downstairs without killing ourselves.

Above us, we could hear the stomping grow louder. Thank God, the malevolent ghost of Jeremiah wasn't in here with us. Detra Ann sobbed again, and I tried to comfort her. "It's okay, I promise. We'll be out of here soon."

"If we leave our hiding spot, won't we still be in the house with that thing?"

"Just stay close." At some point during our frantic escape, I hit my mouth. My lip felt swollen, and I could taste blood. Still, I was alive—we were alive! The air smelled stale, but I forced myself to breathe as normally as I could. We walked past another hidden door; I could see an unearthly light shining from behind it. I thought about pushing it open, but a fleeting shadow passed across the light. Nope! Not this one! I couldn't tell where we were—probably somewhere behind the dining hall wall. In the distance, I could hear what sounded like a piano crash and the furious stomping became louder, so loud that it sounded like a freight train. Forget controlling my breathing—it was so hard that my chest hurt; sweat dripped down my face and neck. I dragged Detra Ann behind me and ran on into the dusty darkness. She stumbled as I came to a stop. I flashed my light against the wall. It had to be here somewhere! It had to be! Suddenly, the door popped open without any help from us. We froze on the spot, neither of us breathing or moving. Nothing came. I pushed it open.

We couldn't stay trapped in the wall all night. At any moment Jeremiah Cottonwood could decide to appear, and who or what could stop him? "When we get out, run to the right to the back door. You ready?"

"I don't know, but let's do this." Even in the shadows, I could see the determined look on her face. "Don't you dare let me go!"

"You either!"

I pushed the door open wider. It struck a small side table, slinging picture frames and porcelain pieces to the ground. We were out of the wall and didn't waste time dawdling in the dining room.

"Christine," the disembodied voice growled at us from somewhere near. We couldn't see him, but it was as if he were everywhere at once. Suddenly, the stomping above us stopped but there was another sound coming from the window. A windstorm blew outside, and the branches of the live oaks were slapping at the windows viciously as if they would whip us too. For some reason, it entranced me.

"Don't stop!" Detra Ann yelled at me. It was her turn to drag me now. She ran toward the open door; her ponytail had come undone, and her blond hair flew behind her. I held onto her hand for dear life.

"Christine! You are mine!" I heard the voice yell— Jeremiah's anger was palpable. I slid on the freshly waxed wooden floor of the hallway that led to the back door. I ungracefully sailed against the wall and crashed to the ground, and my knee crunched as I landed. Detra Ann struggled to help me up, and I yelped in pain.

"Run, Detra Ann! Go!"

"I'm not leaving you, so get your ass up—now!" Her adrenaline surging, she practically jerked me up off the ground, snatched my arm and slung it over her shoulder. The green potted palms begin to move under the influence of the unearthly wind. The brochures and flyers that had been so neatly arranged on the welcome table were now scattered about the room. I heard a distinct giggle—a familiar giggle. Then whispered words sent chills deep into my soul: "You'll be worm food now, I suppose!" *Isla! They were both here!*

The massive double doors that led to the back garden seemed so far away, but we awkwardly ran together. I ignored the pain, determined not to hinder Detra Ann from escaping Seven Sisters.

"Oh God—oh God—oh God!" she whispered like a chant. We could feel the supernatural presence surging, swelling behind us like a cloud of evil that threatened to overwhelm us and steal our warm bodies from the land of the living. If we turned to look, I was sure we would see something awful, something we would never forget. There wasn't a chance that I was going to look behind me. I closed my eyes and ran for the door on my damaged knee.

"Keep moving!" I shouted to myself and to Detra Ann, and then my phone began to ring in my pocket. Only it wasn't my ring tone that played—it was the tune from Christine's music box! No way was I going to stop to look and see who called me.

It was my turn to panic. "Oh God!" Somehow, we made it to the back door. I hung on Detra Ann's shoulder as she flipped the dead bolt. This time I did look—I saw Isla hovering against a wall, floating above us, grinning as she watched us fight for our lives. I did not see Jeremiah Cottonwood, but a solid black cloud was moving toward us from the stairway. He was coming! My phone rang nonstop in my pocket; Christine's song played at an unearthly decibel. Suddenly, Detra Ann swung open the door and everything stopped. Isla and the black cloud disappeared. The stomping, the laughter, the wind—it all stopped.

"Come on, CJ! No looking back. Let's go!"

I don't know how we managed it, but we made it to the first cast-iron bench in the Moonlight Garden. It was pitch-black out. The skies were clear, with no storms at all, but the stars had begun to fade. The sun would make its appearance soon. I leaned on Detra Ann's shoulder, trying to catch my breath.

"We're okay. We're alright," she panted, her voice filled with relief. She hugged me and began to cry.

I patted her back to comfort her and finally whispered, "Yes, we are." *Please let this be the end of it!* I reached in my pocket and pulled out my phone.

The message on my screen read: *You Have 2 Missed Calls!* Curious to see what it would say, I tapped on the screen. *Unknown Caller at 5:00 AM.*

We sat staring at the open door, but nothing ever emerged. I didn't know what Detra Ann was thinking, but I was ready for this dream catching experience to be over. My knee was screaming, and my blood was still pumping furiously from our unexpected run through the house.

"Is it always like that?"

"No, it's not, I promise. Or I would lose my mind."

"I'm not sure I haven't lost mine. I don't know how you live with this. Now I see why TD is having such a hard time dealing with his experience."

"It's a rare thing, but it is disturbing when it happens. Something happened tonight, something triggered Jeremiah Cottonwood's anger. He didn't like us in his wife's room."

"Maybe he's worried that you might find another treasure?" I could tell she was doing her best to reason away the spirit's attack.

"Maybe he was—but I don't think so. He wasn't after the treasure; he wanted Christine, remember? He kept calling her. I don't know what just happened. I need time to think."

"So do I! I'm ready to go, but my keys are upstairs. You need to go to the hospital."

"Not me. I'm fine. What about you?" My knee was throbbing, but I didn't want to go anywhere until I was sure we were safe.

"Well, there appears to be only one thing to do."

"Detra Ann—you can't go back in there!"

"No worries, girl. I don't plan on it! The police will be here soon. We tripped the silent alarm when we walked outside without entering the code in the keypad."

"Oh, thank God. Then maybe we can go home. I have had enough fun for one night." I put my arms around her and hugged her. She'd said she wanted to hang out with a dream catcher. Well, be careful what you wish for. Sometimes the dream sticks around and follows you home! I hoped Jeremiah would stay within the confines of Seven Sisters and not show up at my new place as I suspected Isla had been doing.

There had to be something I could do—then I remembered something Henri Devecheaux once told me. "Spirits don't come unless they are welcomed, and they only stay when they have a claim to something. You want to keep a spirit away? Don't welcome it, and don't give it a claim on anything you own."

That might be easier said than done, though. I was beginning to think Isla had her sights set on Ashland.

And alive or dead—she never played by the rules.

Chapter 8

Thankfully, it wasn't Detective Simmons who responded to the alarm. It must have been too early in the day for her. No doubt if she had heard the call, she would have been here, ready to lick her pencil and give me unbelieving stares. We'd certainly given her enough to think about. That reminded me—I needed to call her about Mia. I felt sure that the woman who tried to kill me shouldn't know my new address, and she sure as heck didn't need to be writing me.

During our ten-minute wait, Detra Ann and I concocted a story to explain why the house was in such a state and why we didn't want to go inside. We'd say a squirrel found its way in the house and we ran out. That might also explain why it looked like a tornado had blown through the downstairs foyer. The officer, an older gentleman, didn't doubt us—he seemed happy to "rescue" two pretty young women from a dangerous rodent. He did a search of the house and declared that whatever animal it was must have made a break for it because the house was all clear.

"That's great, but I'm not staying. If you wouldn't mind, we'll just grab our things and leave."

Officer Thornton looked tired after his sweep. "I can't understand why you were here to begin with. This isn't a residence, is it?"

"We were working late getting some things ready for the Halloween Tour and figured we'd just spend the night. Then that rowdy squirrel came in and liked to have scared us to death." Detra Ann was doing a marvelous job playing her role as the helpless blonde who needed a big strong man to rescue her. I found it funny to say the least.

"Oh, I see. Ended up scaring yourselves silly, did you?"

I could tell by the way Detra Ann's back stiffened that she didn't care for his tone. I smiled and said, "Well, you know how it is in these big old houses. Give us just a minute." We walked up the stairs and gathered our stuff.

"What a jerk!"

"Let's just get out of here. I guess we should change first. I can't drive through Mobile in my pajamas. People think I'm nuts anyway."

"Only Holliday Betbeze," Detra Ann said with a giggle as she pulled on her jeans. "That was quite a speech you gave at the Historical Society. I can't believe you told those women your mother was mentally ill."

"They would have heard about it eventually. I figured why put off the inevitable? I believe in taking charge of my life in every way possible." We didn't bother making the beds or cleaning up the foyer. The clock said 5:30—still too early to be up. I wanted nothing more than to go home and climb into bed with Ashland, but he wasn't there. I didn't want to be alone again, not right now.

As if she'd read my mind, Detra Ann asked, "Want to grab some breakfast? I don't think I'm ready to go home right now."

"Me either. That sounds wonderful." We thanked Officer Thornton, and Detra Ann locked up Seven Sisters again. I wondered what her employees would think when they saw the mess we'd made.

Still a bit jumpy, I rode in my car alone—I refused to leave it on the property. I turned the radio to a boring talk radio station. Just something to keep my mind busy, make me feel normal again. With a sigh, I followed Detra Ann, wondering what we would talk about over breakfast. I didn't know where she was going, and I didn't really care—I just wanted to get away from Seven Sisters. I kept hoping to see the fat orange sun climb above the Mobile Bay. I wanted this night to be officially over! Instead, steel gray clouds shielded the sun, so I was left listening to WPMX for comfort. Mike and Dave were no less boring than usual. I needed boring at the moment.

I turned up the volume, listening to Mike extol the virtues of the new roundabout that the city had installed on Old Government Street. He was making some good points when the radio began to distort. I hit the tune button, but to no avail. "Well, rats." Watching the road with one eye, I tapped on the radio buttons in search of another channel. I felt tired and still a bit freaked out. I switched from the FM radio to the satellite radio, and still nothing. *What? How is that possible? Something should be working.*

Stupidly, I turned up the volume as if that would help.

Help me...

Help me...I can't see...

The voice was faint, almost indiscernible. I turned up the volume again but heard nothing.

"Hello? Is someone there?"

You...help me... You saw me...

Suddenly and with perfect clarity, I knew who was talking to me. It was Christine! We had connected in the dream—somehow, she had seen me. Now here she was being spooky in my radio. Out of sheer fright, I turned off the radio. The light changed and Detra Ann was making a right turn into By the Bay Bed and Breakfast. I pulled into the spot beside her and put the car in park.

What had I done? Why had I gone back to Seven Sisters? Ashland warned me to stay away, but I didn't heed his advice. Now my radio was talking to me and angry ghosts chased me out of the home I'd loved. I laid my tired head on the steering wheel, but I didn't cry. I was too tired to cry.

Detra Ann opened the car door, squatted down beside me and patted my back. A few moments later, she said, "Let's go have some coffee. Hardly anybody comes here, and I know the owner. We can sit on the back porch and look at the water. We don't have to talk if you don't want to. Sound good?"

"Sure." Coffee sounded really good right now. I grabbed my bag and followed her to the back porch dining area. There was an old man sitting at a faraway table reading his Mobile Press Register and drinking coffee. He politely raised his cup to us and then went back to his paper.

A middle-aged woman wearing a Smuckers jam apron walked out on the porch with a pot of coffee and two cups. "Good morning, Detra Ann. Y'all having coffee this morning? You're up awful early."

"Good morning, Gloria. Yes, ma'am, and a basket of biscuits too, please."

"Sure thing. You want those with fig or peach preserves?"

"How about both?"

Our friendly server smiled as if she'd just been told she won the lottery. "Wonderful! I'll be right back." She laid a small laminated menu on our table along with the coffee and cups. Detra Ann poured two steaming cups of black coffee and placed one in front of me.

We sipped for a minute, and the silence was wonderful. Gloria came back with the promised hot biscuits, and I helped myself to one. They smelled buttery and delicious—how could I resist? This was normal, this was what I needed, to drink coffee with a friend. She was a friend, wasn't she? I placed an order for scrambled eggs and bacon, and Detra Ann asked for grits and eggs.

"I heard a voice on the radio," I confessed.

"What? Like a talk show?" Her tired eyes were apprehensive. She had to be thinking I was nuts.

"No, not like a talk show. Something happened in my dream tonight, something that has never happened before. Christine saw me. I think, no, I *know* she knew I was there! She asked me who I was—she thought I was an angel come to take her to heaven!"

"What? That's impossible, CJ."

"No more impossible than dreaming about the past and going back in time! No more impossible than a dead man chasing us out of his house!"

"Don't get mad. This is all new to me. What happened? I mean, how does it normally work? Is it like a vision?"

"I transferred tonight—I saw from different viewpoints. That means instead of being just one person, I was two. There was a girl there, Hannah—she was a young slave. At times, I was looking through her eyes, and at other times I was Christine Cottonwood. It seemed that when they touched, I switched viewpoints, like I was watching a movie. That's never happened before. I wonder what it means."

"I'm dying to know, what did you see?"

"I saw Christine giving birth to a baby, and she didn't even know she was there. Her mind was so fragmented, so fragile. Isla really did a number on her, and so did Jeremiah. I think he'd been abusing his wife to the point that when she heard Louis was dead, she checked out. But that's only a guess right now."

"Checked out how?"

With shaking hands I put another biscuit on a china plate and buttered it. Ooh...I felt dizzy. I realized it had been way too long since I'd eaten.

What a pretty pattern! Blue butterflies dancing around the rim, such a happy dish. I loved butterflies. I had forgotten how much...

"Carrie Jo?"

"What?"

She laughed nervously. "Checked out how?"

"Oh, when I was her, she went from one thing to the next, with no logical train of thought. One minute she was seeing Calpurnia dancing in the corner of the room, and the next she was walking through a garden with her brother. She couldn't have been older than twelve. Next she was... oh my gosh!" I took a sip of my coffee, hardly believing what I was remembering. My brain felt tired—no, sticky, as if there were some type of residue left over from my dream catching. I felt off—weird.

"Christine was *avoir une liaison* with her doctor, and it wasn't just a one-time thing. She was in love with him—she thought of him as her *vrai mari*. Christine loved him more than anyone, except her daughter."

Detra Ann laughed again. "I didn't know you spoke French. You are a girl of hidden talents, Carrie Jo." She smeared peach preserves on a biscuit and popped a piece in her mouth.

I stared at her like she'd slapped me. "I don't speak French. I never have."

"Surely you must. You just spoke it perfectly. Maybe you took a high school or college course?"

"I didn't take French ever. I took Spanish and Latin." We stared at one another.

What a pretty lady. Such vibrant blue eyes, trustworthy eyes. Louis says the eyes are the windows of the soul. Such a poet he is!

What was happening to me? I clutched my napkin like it was a life preserver and I was drowning.

"Well, you must have heard Christine speaking French and the words stuck in your brain. That makes sense—well, as much sense as any of this does. Hey, are you okay?"

"I...uh...yeah. I'm fine."

"So Christine and her doctor? That's kind of scandalous, especially for those days. Tell me what you know."

Hoyt! Where are you, Hoyt?

Oh my God! I am going nuts! I should have listened to Ashland. I should never have gone back to Seven Sisters. What was I thinking? ...Hoyt?

I practically leapt out of my chair. "Detra Ann, thank you for breakfast, but I think I better go home. I'm tired and my mind is racing..."

"Aw, but we're just getting to the good part."

I reached for my bag. She was chewing on her biscuit, and I could see our food approaching. I couldn't stay—I couldn't have a meltdown here in the middle of this nice bed and breakfast.

"I'm sorry. I'll call you later." I stumbled trying to get off the porch but I kept on walking. *I have to go home...take me home!*

Detra Ann followed me to the car. She was talking to me, but my ears weren't listening. I felt tired, ready to go to sleep. *Yes, maybe a nap would calm my nerves. Calpurnia...come lie down with Mother.*

"Carrie Jo? Let me come with you. You don't look well."

"Je vais bien," I lied with a smile, feigning happiness, "really I am."

"But you just..."

"Please, let me get some rest and I will call you later. I promise." I closed the door and pulled out of the gravel parking lot. As I turned on to the side road, I glanced at myself in the mirror. Yes, I was still Carrie Jo Jardine Stuart, but there was something else going on behind those green eyes. I couldn't see her, but I knew she was there.

Now it all made sense. Why Jeremiah chased us through the house! Why he tried so desperately to stop us from leaving! She had made her escape through me! She had been with us the whole time, and her husband knew it.

Somehow, Christine Beaumont Cottonwood had returned, but why? And for how long? How would this end?

This time, I really had gone too far.

Chapter 9

Carrie Jo drove away, kicking up rocks from the back tires of her tan Cadillac. She sped out of the parking lot without even a courtesy wave. *Ashland is going to kill me!* I walked back to the porch and made excuses to Gloria about why my friend took off so suddenly. "She's not been feeling well. This looks delicious!" I smiled and Gloria walked away, happy that at least I was staying to enjoy her home-cooked breakfast.

I took my phone out of my purse and stared at it as I poured myself another cup of coffee. What was I going to say to him?

Sorry. I had a sleepover at Seven Sisters with your wife, and now she's gone a little nuts.

No. That wasn't true. She believed what she told me about her dream catching. That much I was sure of. CJ had her secret power, but I had one too. Well, a couple actually. I was a human lie detector. Whenever someone lied to me, big or small, bells went off. Carrie Jo didn't have an inch of dishonesty in her—not until she told me everything was okay. In general, she had a unique honesty about her, but now my "bells" were ringing like crazy. She wasn't okay, and that was partially my fault.

Ashland had asked me to befriend his wife and help her get to know our circle of friends. But with everything going south with TD, and with the added responsibility of my sick mother, I just hadn't gotten around to it. I'd had every intention of hosting a party for the new couple or something, but then I got started on the Halloween Ball. At least Carrie Jo had promised to attend. That would be the perfect time to present her to everyone…if we got that far. I wasn't sure she'd ever want to step into Seven Sisters again—me either for that matter. I didn't know what happened with her dreams, except the little she told me. But what happened afterwards, that was completely real.

In just about an hour, I would call Rachel Kowalski and give her a heads up on the mess we had left behind. I planned to use the invading squirrel defense, the same as we had with the cop. Hopefully she wouldn't ask too many questions.

It was early, but I called Ashland. He needed to know what happened. I figured I might as well fess up and get it over with.

"Hey, did I wake you?"

"Of course not. What's up?"

"It's Carrie Jo."

"What is it? Is she okay?" I could hear the desperation in his voice, which made me feel even guiltier. What kind of friend was I? So far, he'd proven to be a better friend to me than I had been to him. I would never forget what he did for me—how he stayed by my side after Fred Price assaulted me. He was there every step of the way, and I could never repay him. I had five brothers, but Ashland had proven to be a better brother than any of them. It was too bad we didn't have romantic feelings for one another. According to my mother, we should have skipped the love part.

"Love can come after marriage, Detra Ann," she'd said. "Compatibility is much more important to a happy marriage."

I had replied, "Not for me. One day, I'll fall madly in love and that will be it." I knew the truth—she wasn't actually concerned about my happiness. The only thing she truly cared about was where our family ranked on the city's "Most Wealthy" list. My marriage to Ashland Stuart would have permanently secured for her the top spot, right over the head of Holliday Betbeze. *Sorry, Mom. I'm not going to use my friend to help you get a better parking spot and boost your ego—or your bank account.*

"Yes, she is fine—at least I think she is. She came to the house last night, Ash, to Seven Sisters."

"What? Why?"

"I think she wanted to talk about TD, but then I made a mistake. Don't be mad, but I let her stay there last night."

"Are you crazy? That's the last thing she needs!"

"For the record, you never told me to lock her out! Besides, I was with her. As much as I love you, I'm not your wife's keeper!" The old man across the porch gave me an irritated glare and then turned the page of his newspaper, pretending that he wasn't listening.

He sighed heavily into the phone. "What makes you think she's not okay? What happened? She had a dream?"

In a whisper I told him, "Yes, but the real strangeness didn't happen until after she woke up. I think she brought something back with her. We got chased out of the house this morning—whatever it was nearly tore the place up. We got out okay, but it was the weirdest thing I have ever experienced. This ghost—this entity, it was after us, Ashland. After her, I think. I thought she was handling it all well. I mean, I'm the one that should be freaking out—I had no idea this would happen. But then it just went wrong. I took her to breakfast, and that's when she went all strange."

"Strange how?"

I gestured wildly with my hands, as if he could see me. "All daydreamy and confused. And another thing...does she know French?"

"No, I don't think so. We were just in Haiti, and she never spoke it there."

"She's speaking French."

"What?"

"I can't be sure, but I think she's kind of losing it, you know, mentally. Did you know that her mother is mentally ill? She told the entire Historical Society, Ash."

"I know all about Carrie Jo, and she's no crazier than you or I. Where is she now, Detra Ann?"

"I took her to breakfast at Gloria's place, but she went home before our food arrived. She should be there now. You should call her."

"I've been trying! Now I know why she hasn't been answering. I need you to go there and stay with her until I get home. Please don't leave her alone. If you can't go, then I can call Bette. I'm on the way, and I can be there in an hour and a half—two at the most."

I poked at my eggs with my fork and leaned back in the wicker chair. "Fine. I'll go, but I'd like to go home and change first. And when you get home, we've got to talk about that house. How am I supposed to go back there now?"

"Don't wait, please. I need you to go now."

"What am I supposed to say to her? 'Please let me in—your husband sent me over to spy on you?'"

"No, but you can tell her that I heard she wasn't feeling good and that I asked you to come over. It's the truth—she hasn't been taking my calls, and I *am* worried about her. We've not been…well, we have had some problems lately."

My heart sank a little. Carrie Jo had hinted at this. I wanted Ashland to be happy—I knew he cared for Carrie Jo a great deal—probably more than anyone else I'd seen him with. For goodness' sake, he married her.

"Okay, I'll do it. Be safe. I'll see you there."

I hung up and finished off my breakfast. I sent Rachel a super long text about the "squirrel" and explained that I would be coming in late. She sent back an "Okay" and that was that. I was sure she'd light up my phone after she saw what had taken place inside. Then what would I say?

Yeah, sorry about the mess the stark-raving ghost left us. Try not to upset him, and don't mention the name Christine.

Gloria picked up my plates, and I gathered my belongings. I paid the bill and drove to Carrie Jo's house. Unfortunately, I was behind a street cleaning truck that refused to get out of the way. I knew he saw me waving at him, but he still didn't budge.

"This is just great," I complained to the truck. My phone rang and started singing "Thank God I'm a Country Boy." I knew it was TD. I couldn't dig the phone out of my purse fast enough. We hadn't spoken in weeks, and our last conversation wasn't anything nice. I'd given him an ultimatum and he gave me his answer—I came home to find all his things gone. I'd cried all night but hadn't called him. He had not called me either.

"Hey!" I said as casually as I could while juggling the phone and the steering wheel. *Keep your game face on, girl, and don't get wimpy!*

"Hey, beautiful." I loved his warm voice, and I especially loved it when he called me that. He had a delicious Southern accent that made him sound uber-sexy. His accent was distinct and fine in a way that set him apart from the other guys around here. He could talk excitedly about projects and buildings, but when it came to him and me—he was slow and on purpose. I'd loved that.

"Good to hear from you, TD. How have you been?" *Be cool, be aloof!*

"Things are good and getting better—especially now that I am talking to you. I have so much to say to you, beautiful. I was hoping we might have coffee this morning—if you'd be willing to see me. I know I have been wrong about so much—I would like to apologize and talk about our future—if you think we might have one."

Uh-oh, something doesn't feel right. Probably just some apprehension left over from last night. So why is my "lie detector" going off like crazy?

"I would like that, but I have to visit a sick friend this morning. I am going to go check on her now. I'll be available in a few hours. Is that okay?"

"Yes, we could meet later this morning, if you have some time for me."

"Are you sure you are okay, TD?"

He chuckled. It sounded insincere, kind of forced. "Never better! Just can't wait to see your gorgeous face." *He was lying to me—but about what?*

"Alright... so where should we meet?"

"Why don't you come to my place? I would like to talk somewhere private, talk things over, see what I can do to make it up to you. I know I've been a jerk."

Nope. This is a bad idea.

"I think I would like to take things a bit slower. Can we meet at Starbucks, the one on Airport?"

"Alright. I'll be there. See you at ten?"

"Okay, I'll see you then."

"Detra Ann?"

"Yes?"

"Thanks for agreeing to see me."

"See you later, TD." I hung up the phone, caught a break in the traffic and whizzed around the truck. If I weren't such a lady, I would have given that guy a piece of my mind—or at least an ugly gesture. When I got to Carrie Jo's house, her shiny new car was in the driveway. I pulled the BMW up behind it and wondered what I would say to her. *Why am I here? If something creepy is going on, I'm out of here. I can't take another creepy thing! I don't even believe in ghosts!*

I dropped my keys in my purse and slung it over my shoulder. I hoped this wouldn't take too long. All I had to do was check on her and ask her to call Ashland.

"Oh no," I said to myself when I walked up the sidewalk. The front door stood wide open, and dead magnolia leaves from the front yard had blown into the house. This didn't look right—not one little bit. I stood on the pavement wondering what to do next. Visions of my own attack five years ago flashed in my head. I practically ran to the open door. "Carrie Jo?" There wasn't a sound in return except the sound of rustling leaves. I hadn't noticed the breeze until now—it picked up a swirl of dry leaves and tossed them around the foyer. She wasn't answering, and I couldn't leave here until I knew she was okay. I just couldn't.

I stepped into the foyer, a layer of leaves crunching under my feet. I continued to call her name, when I heard a sound from upstairs and froze in my tracks. Oh my God! What if someone else was here—an attacker like Fred Price? I dug in my purse for my tiny pearl-handled gun. I wasn't taking any chances. This could be a dangerous area at times—I mean, I loved Mobile, but we had our share of violent criminals. I walked through the entire lower hallway and checked all the rooms as if I were a rookie police officer.

"Carrie Jo?" I said again, this time in a whisper. I heard another sound—definitely coming from upstairs. She could be hurt up there; I had no choice but to climb those stairs. I left my bag on the lower steps and began to work my way up. *Thank God I'm not wearing my usual high heels today.* Between the leaves and the wooden steps whoever was up there, if anyone at all, would know I was coming long before I got there.

I called her name again. This time I plainly heard a door close. The sound wasn't too far away either. I gritted my teeth and kept moving up. I was just three steps from the top now. *Not too late to change your mind. Go outside and call the police.* I stopped and lowered my gun. Maybe that was what I should do. What was I thinking? How was I qualified to do this? Just because I had once been a victim didn't mean I was now an expert. Before I could sneak back down, the door closest to me opened and out walked Carrie Jo in a terry robe with a towel wrapped around her head. She jumped back in surprise, and suddenly I felt a cruel punch in my gut. My gun flew out of my hand. I could hear the sound of the shot.

I screamed as the sensation of falling overwhelmed me. My arms reached out for something, anything, to help me stop my fall, but I couldn't grasp a hold of the rail. I heard a loud pop, then a thud, and everything went dark.

Chapter 10

"Detra Ann!" I screamed in horror as I scrambled down the stairs after the fallen blonde. Blood poured out of her side, and the smell of gunpowder filled the air. I hadn't touched her but she'd fallen somehow. "Detra Ann!" I screamed and ran to her side. I squatted next to her in the blood and felt for a pulse. She was alive—at least for now.

Doreen walked inside and stifled a yell behind her hands. "Oh my God! Oh my God!"

"Doreen! Call 911, now! Please!"

She dropped her grocery bags on the floor and ran for the phone. "Yes, we have an emergency." She handed me the phone and ran to get towels for Detra Ann, who was still unconscious.

"Yes! I need help. My friend fell down the stairs. She was carrying a gun, and I think she's been shot. Please come! She's bleeding pretty bad. Please help us."

"Okay, ma'am. They are on the way. It won't be but a minute. Is she breathing? Can you see?"

"Yes, but it's shallow."

"Okay, now you say she's been shot?"

"Yes, oh my God! Please hurry!"

"Where has she been shot?"

"In the side, around her waist. I think she lost control of the gun as she fell. I don't know! Oh my God! She's my friend, but she's not supposed to be here. I came out of the bathroom and she was here."

"It's okay. Don't worry about that right now. Let's see if we can stop the bleeding. Do you have some towels?" asked the friendly dispatcher.

"Yes, I do now."

"Fold a towel and press it to the area where's she been shot. That should slow down any blood loss."

"Make them hurry! She's bleeding through the towel. Please, Detra Ann. Don't you dare die!"

I could hear the ambulance tearing down Government Street. Doreen scrambled to her feet and opened the door and then ran to the laundry room.

"Detra Ann, stay with me! Can you hear me?"

Her dark eyelashes fluttered, but she never opened her eyes completely. I saw her body sag just as the EMTs came barging in the front door.

"What happened?"

"I don't know. I think she tripped and fell—her gun went off. I didn't even know she had a gun! She's been shot." I got out of the way as the two young men squatted down beside her.

"What's her name?"

"Detra Ann. Please, is she going to be alright?"

"We'll do our best to help her."

I watched as they assessed her quickly and prepared her for transport. They braced her neck and expertly moved her body to the gurney.

"Here, ma'am. I got you some clothes." Doreen handed me a tote bag with a shirt, jeans, underwear and sandals.

"Thank you. Please call Mr. Stuart for me. Tell him to come to the hospital."

"I will!"

I followed the men to the ambulance and didn't wait for an invitation to join them. I climbed inside and sat out of the way on the only available metal bench. While working furiously to stop the bleeding they asked me questions about allergies and blood type. I didn't know what to tell them—I didn't know any of these things. The sight of Detra Ann near death, her normally tanned face pale and lifeless, sent shockwaves through my psyche. What had she been doing in my house? How did she get in, and why did she have a gun? I couldn't answer any of those questions but whatever the answer, I prayed that she would live. The rest of the ride was a blur. When we arrived at the hospital, I ran after the gurney. The EMTs paused in the ER hallway only long enough to call for a doctor. "She's bleeding out! Code Six!" They whirred past me through a set of self-locking doors. I wanted to chase them into the operating room, but a sympathetic nurse blocked my way.

"I'll meet you at the registration area in a couple of minutes. In the meantime, you can change. There are some scrubs in here," she said kindly, pointing to a nearby closet.

"Thanks, but I have clothes. Is there a bathroom I can use?"

"Right through there." She hurried away, following after Detra Ann and the team that had assembled around her. I couldn't stop shaking. I stumbled into the bathroom and changed my clothes quickly. Fortunately for me, Doreen had enough foresight to include my cell phone. What a relief!

With shaking fingers, I called Ashland. Strangely enough, he was already on the line. He'd been trying to call me. I let out a sob. "Baby? Are you there?"

"Yes, Carrie Jo. Are you okay? Doreen called me. What have they told you about Detra Ann?"

"I'm fine. I'm at the hospital, Springhill. They haven't said much yet. They just took her back. Are you on the way?" I was in full-blown crying mode now.

"I .am—I'll be there in about an hour. Do you have someone with you? Maybe Bette?"

"No, I'll be fine." I scurried out of the bathroom and went in search of the nurse at the registration desk. "I have to go. The nurse wants to talk with me. I don't know what to tell her."

"I'll call Cynthia and tell her to get down there. She can answer their questions. Just take a deep breath, and I'll be there soon."

"Ashland?"

"Yes?"

"Hurry, please."

"I will. I'll talk to you soon."

He hung up, and I stood at the registration desk waiting for the nurse. When she didn't return I called Terrence Dale. He didn't answer, so I left him a message. "Hey, this is Carrie Jo. I'm calling because Detra Ann is at Springhill. She's had an accident, and I think it might be a good idea for you to be here. I'm in the emergency waiting room. Bye." Fifteen minutes later, I took a seat in the waiting room, hoping that the nurse would come back eventually.

The first person to arrive was TD. Detra Ann was right, he did look different. He was thinner now, and his silky brown hair brushed his shoulders. Not an unattractive look, just different. Even his clothing style had evolved. Now the young contractor wore torn blue jeans and a vintage T-shirt with the emblem of an old rock band on the chest. No more khakis and polo shirts, I supposed. "TD!" I said, throwing my arms around his neck. He tentatively hugged me and awkwardly stepped back.

"What's happened?"

"I'm not sure, really. I came out of the shower, and she was there on the stairs with a gun. I don't know if I startled her or what, but she fell and the gun went off. Now she's shot! In the side! I'm waiting and waiting, but nobody will tell me anything."

"She tried to shoot you?"

"No! I don't think so—I don't know what she was doing, but she is hurt really bad. I witnessed the whole thing, but it all happened so fast. I can't tell you much about what happened."

He hugged me again and helped me find a seat. He said, "Wait here. I'll go see what I can find out."

I watched him chat with the receptionist. She nodded and smiled at him, and he waved at me. "Thank you," he said to her when she pressed the button to let us back. "She's in surgery, but they're allowing us to sit in the surgery waiting room. The doctor will come speak to us when he's finished."

"Oh God! Ashland is on his way in from New Orleans. He said he would call her mother. I haven't heard anything else." We shuffled through the bleach-scented halls of Springhill Memorial until we came to the surgery waiting room.

"Yeah, she knows—she called me too. She was in Foley— she'll be here in about 45 minutes." He plopped down beside me. "The woman hates me. I can't say that I blame her. Detra Ann was way too good for me. Damn—that's her calling me now. Excuse me." He stepped just outside the door and took the call.

With a growing numbness, I sat in the smaller, colder waiting room. There were only a couple of people there. I stared absently at the muted television and waited for TD to return. He came back looking somber—it had been a long time since I'd seen him smile.

"I was supposed to meet her this morning. She said her friend was sick—she was going to check on her and then meet me afterwards. I can't believe this." His head was in his hands, his shoulders slumped. "I've been such a jackass," his voice broke in a sob.

I must have been the sick friend she was referring to. Still, that didn't explain why Detra Ann was in my house with a loaded gun. I knew I had locked that front door, but the hallway was full of leaves again. *I wonder if...I can't figure this out right now!*

"I'm listening." I put a hand on his back as he cried. This was what he needed—he needed to talk. "It's okay—Detra Ann is strong. She'll survive this."

After a few minutes, he stopped crying, and a kind nurse stopped by with a bottle of water and some tissues. "Anything yet?" he asked. "The patient is Detra Ann Dowd."

"No sir. She's still in surgery, but the doctor will come right out when he's finished. If y'all need anything, I'm right outside."

"Thank you."

"TD, I know this is none of my business, and you can tell me to shut up if you like, but what happened? With you and Detra Ann? She's just crazy about you."

"She didn't tell you?" I could see the shame in his brown eyes.

"Well, I heard a little, but I'd like to hear it from you."

"I really don't want to talk about it."

"We don't have to. I'm sorry I asked."

Leaning back in the plastic chair, he sighed. "No, I said I wasn't going to do that anymore. I'm facing my demons. I promised Detra Ann that I had changed. I can't drink away what I saw—what I know I saw." He rubbed his eyes and looked at me. "For a long time I hated you and Ashland—you know, for that night. It was like from that night forward everything went wrong, and I do mean everything. I couldn't focus—tools came up missing—I even got robbed. I lost jobs—I think I lost my mind for a while—a long while."

"I'm truly sorry, TD. I never meant for any of that to happen. I guess I—we didn't count the costs before we went looking for Calpurnia and the treasure. I really am sorry."

"I believe you. I meant to tell Detra Ann something today, but I guess it's not her I'm meant to tell. It's you."

I turned sideways in the chair, my arm on the back, my hand under my chin. "What is it?"

"When I was in high school, my sophomore year, I was in a car accident on I-65. I'd been dating this girl—Ashley Dubose was her name. Sweet girl. We hadn't been dating long, but I was crazy about her. You know, like you are in the tenth grade. One Friday night, we drove downtown to the Saenger Theater to see *Gone with the Wind*, her favorite film. She lived in Theodore, so after the film I took the interstate to get her home faster. Her dad was strict about her curfew, but I didn't mind. I liked her a lot. Everything was great. She was chattering on about Scarlett O'Hara—I was half listening when she kissed my cheek to thank me for taking her. I half-turned to kiss her and took my eyes off the road for only a second. That split second changed everything."

"What happened?"

"A truck sideswiped us and we went spinning. Ashley died. I walked away from the accident with just a scratch on my arm."

"I'm sorry. That must have been so difficult to process."

"It was, but it only got worse. For the next six months, I saw Ashley everywhere I went. Not like a face in a crowd or someone that looked like her. It was her, bleeding, with her empty eyes that stared through me—just like she looked in the car, you know, afterwards. I felt like a crazy person. Imagine sitting in economics class and your dead girlfriend is standing in the corner of the room. Only no one else can see her—just you. Just staring and bleeding. It happened every day for months."

"That sounds horrible. How did you cope?"

"My parents tried every way they could to help me. They're nice people. Medication, grief counseling, therapy—nothing worked. Finally, one afternoon my grandmother picked me up. It had been a rough weekend—it had gotten so bad I didn't want to leave the house. Not even for school. Anyway, Granny Kaye came over one day—she knew all about what I'd been going through. She didn't tell me where we were going or anything. We pulled into the parking lot of Valhalla Cemetery, and she grabbed my hands and started praying for me. When she was done, she handed me a note card and a pen. She told me to write Ashley a note. I thought that was a crazy idea, but she was adamant. I wrote five words: *I'm sorry. I loved you.* We took the card and some flowers to Ashley's grave." He took a deep breath and continued, "She told me to read it out loud, and I did. I cried the whole time, but I read it. I left the card and the flowers on the grave, and I didn't see Ashley ever again after that. Granny and I never talked about it for the rest of her life, but I will always be grateful for what she did."

"Wow, that is incredible. It must have been so terrifying to see her over and over again like that. I'm glad you had some resolution, though."

"I did until that night in the Moonlight Garden."

"Oh my gosh! You mean she came back?"

"No, it was the other one that I saw, the one that was reaching out for Ashland. Isla, I think her name was."

I shivered and nodded. "You saw her? Where?"

"Everywhere. And worse. Sometimes…"

"What? What is it?"

"Sometimes I'd wake up and she'd be on top of me. I'd scream, and she would disappear. I think I scared Detra Ann to death. She thought I was having nightmares, but they weren't like nightmares. CJ—they were real. She visited me, and I didn't want her to. She was really there, just like Ashley. Only I could smell her, feel her…even taste her. And when I fought her, she would change and I would be kissing a dead thing. I wanted to die. My soul was dying. Anyway, that's when I started drinking. I thought if I was drunk I wouldn't see her. It worked for a little while."

"I am so sorry. I had no idea that you were going through that." Impulsively, I put my arms around his neck and hugged him.

"The problem is I am still going through it, and I don't know what to do."

"Why didn't you tell us? We're your friends, TD. We care about you. Ashland and I would never let you fight her by yourself."

"What does she want? I don't have Granny Kaye in my corner this time, unless you believe in heaven and such. I know she did. She was a praying woman, and I've never been much for faith and prayer. Detra Ann tried to help me, just like Granny Kaye, but she couldn't. She didn't know what to do, and she has no idea about Ashley…" His voice dropped to a whisper. "Or that Isla is lurking around. I can't blame her for dumping me. I am a mess! I don't blame her, and I don't blame you, Carrie Jo."

"Now I know, and together we can fight her. We will figure out why this is happening! Believe it or not, I think I've seen her too." I admitted to TD something I hadn't been ready to tell my own husband. *What am I doing?* "I think she's been at my house."

His brown eyes widened in surprise. "What do you mean?"

"Well, I found this package in my house. It's Mia's handwriting. It was in my house for a month, and there is no way that Ashland or I would have missed it. Isla made sure I found it. I guess it was her. Something did, anyway." I chewed on my lip remembering the shadow that sailed past my door. "I opened the envelope, and inside was a small book—a collection of biographies, but the main story was about an actress named Delilah Iverson."

"I've never heard of her."

"Me either. I haven't finished reading it yet, so I'm not sure how it fits in. That's the kind of thing Isla would do. Death hasn't slowed her down. But besides that unexpected package, I keep seeing someone move out of the corner of my eye. If I am alone in my house, she sails past my door and I hear her giggle. It's bone-chilling." I shivered with the memory.

"I know that feeling," he said. "Yes, it is."

"She's been leaving my front door open and scattering leaves everywhere too. I don't know what to do about her. When Ashland comes home, I guess we'll all be having a 'come to Jesus meeting' because *she* is affecting us all. And there's more…"

Before I could tell him what I knew about Hoyt and Christine, we were interrupted.

"Isn't this cozy? So happy that you two found my daughter's surgery so unimportant that you can't behave respectably."

"What?" TD and I stared at Cynthia Dowd in surprise. She didn't elaborate on her accusations.

Ignoring TD, she addressed me coldly, "How are you, Mrs. Stuart? How is your mother? I hear she's ill."

The gossip from the Historical Society luncheon had traveled quickly. Well, what of it? I had nothing to hide, and I wasn't going to be cowed by my friend's overbearing mother. Before I could open my mouth to speak, the ginger-haired Detective Simmons joined us. She was dressed in a poorly fitting pantsuit with a gaudy pin at the lapel and wore no makeup except some feeble attempts at mascara and an overabundance of lipstick. She was a sharp contrast to the well-dressed Cynthia with her perfect bob cut, Mary Kay makeup and a trim yellow suit. If the difference in statuses bothered the detective, she didn't show it. As usual she pulled out a notebook and a small pencil.

"Just the person I was looking for—Mrs. Stuart. May I talk to you for a minute?"

"Can't it wait, Detective? I am in the middle of a conversation here."

"Suit yourself. We can either talk here or talk down on Government Street in the squad room." She wasn't messing about today. It was her way or the highway apparently.

"Fine, if you'll excuse me, Mrs. Dowd, TD." Only TD acknowledged me.

I followed her down the hall and saw that she was intending to walk out of the hospital. "Where are we going?"

"To my office. Like I said, we need to talk."

"You gave me a choice—I chose to talk to you here. I have no intention of leaving Detra Ann right now. She had an accident, in case you didn't know." I didn't mean to sound snappy, but the abrasive detective had caught me at the wrong moment.

She turned around and stared at me, her pencil in her hand. "In your house! You think I don't know what happens on my beat? I know everything. Would you care to tell me how she got shot in your house?"

"I don't know exactly, or why she was even there. As far as I knew, she had stayed behind to finish her breakfast at By the Bay Bed and Breakfast. I hadn't invited her over."

"So she just broke in and shot herself?" Simmons said with a smirk.

"No, not exactly. After I got home, I went upstairs to take a shower. I needed to relax. When I walked out of the bathroom, Detra Ann was walking up my stairs with her gun drawn. She lost her balance, fell backward and down the steps. As she fell, the gun went off. That was it. That's all I know."

"That seems a bit farfetched, don't you think?"

"I can't help that, Detective. It's the truth."

"You say this woman is your friend?"

"Yes, she is. We've been—we've been working on a project together. I like her, and I am sure the feeling is mutual. She isn't dangerous!"

"You have a hard time keeping friends from killing you, don't you?"

"What?" I stared at her incredulously. I knew what she meant. Mia had tried to kill me, so why not Detra Ann? But I knew Detra Ann would never harm me. Even if we weren't besties, she loved Ashland—I was sure of that.

"It's the truth. People you hang around have a nasty way of getting killed, Miss Jardine—I mean, Mrs. Stuart. Now I want you to come downtown to take a test."

"What kind of test?"

"The kind that tests your hands for gunshot residue. That way, we'll know what happened. It would be a good way to clear your name, ma'am." She raised an eyebrow and scrutinized me.

"What's going on here?" I looked over to see Ashland beside me. I could smell his expensive cologne and felt his warm hand rest gently on my shoulder. "My wife isn't taking any kind of test unless our lawyer says so. Here's her card. Now if you'll excuse us, we have a friend who needs us."

I wanted to kiss him for being there, for coming to my rescue, but I had no reason to run. I knew I was innocent—if I could quickly prove it, why wouldn't I? "Wait, Ashland. I don't mind taking that test. I never fired that gun. I never touched it. If it will clear me, I will do it."

"That's not necessary, CJ. You don't have to do it."

"No, I want to. If it helps the detective, I don't mind. May I come down after I see Detra Ann? She's in surgery right now. I don't know how long that will be."

She nodded begrudgingly. "Sure, that will be fine." She scribbled something on a piece of notebook paper and handed the note to me. "Present this to the officer at the front desk when you get there. They'll get you to the place you need to be. Just walk in and take the test. They wipe your hands with a special cloth, and you wait for the results. They'll know if you fired a gun. If you fired that gun or handled it after it was fired, you will have residue on your hands. If that's the case, you will be arrested."

"Hey…" Ashland started to protest. "She's cooperating, detective."

"No, it's okay. I haven't done anything. I didn't touch that gun! Not before—not afterwards—and sure as heck not during! I will come down soon, Detective. Thank you."

"Fine. Since the patient is in surgery, I can't interview her, but I will send the team to check her hands too. Y'all have a good evening now."

We shook our heads as she left. "What is she thinking?" Ashland asked. "That you would try to kill Detra Ann? What kind of theory is she working? If she had bothered to ask, she would know that I sent Detra Ann to the house. She'd called me and told me you were upset."

"Really? But why did she have her gun out?"

"I don't know. She must have thought something was going on inside—she must have thought you were in danger."

I thought about the door standing wide open. How many times had that happened in the past twenty-four hours? And Ashland didn't even know about it. I decided right then and there that I was going to come clean with him as soon as we were alone. He needed to know that I hadn't been dreaming, until last night, that I'd been seeing Isla and that TD had seen her too. This wasn't over—it seemed the house wasn't through with us yet. But for now, I had to push it aside.

"I don't know, but I am so glad you are here. TD is here, and so is Detra Ann's mother."

"Detra Ann told me what you two did. That you stayed at Seven Sisters. Is that why you weren't answering my calls and why you kept hanging up on me?"

"I only hung up once, and that was because I couldn't hear you. I didn't know you called me."

"How is that possible? I called you like six times, Carrie Jo."

"I don't know what to say except I never got a call from you."

We walked back in silence toward the surgery waiting room. More and more I believed that something was trying to keep us apart—trying to destroy us all. *Oh my God! I am crazy like my mother!*

"When did Mrs. Dowd get here?"

"Just a few minutes ago. I gather she thinks I am involved in the shooting. She made some snide comment about my mother. I guess she heard about my speech at the society lunch."

"I've been meaning to talk to you. You know, your family history is your own business. Why did you open yourself up for ridicule like that?"

"I don't know. Because they are a bunch of busy bees that love to gossip? I figured they would find out the truth anyway, so why not be straight about it. Holliday Betbeze led the pack on that. I'm sorry if I embarrassed you."

"Stop that, Carrie Jo. It's like you don't even know me. I never said you embarrassed me. You've seen how warped and twisted my family is—haven't you?"

"Ashland, I wasn't raised in your kind of world." We stopped in the hallway outside the waiting room. "Where I come from, you tell it like it is. There's no sense in prettying things up. My mother is mentally ill. End of discussion. They kept poking me about her, and I told them. That's it."

He sighed and went in the waiting room. I followed behind him and tried to hide my frustration. *We really are in trouble, aren't we?* Well, at least he came. He was here with me. Or maybe he just came to see Detra Ann. No matter, he was here. And that meant the world to me.

The pieces were beginning to fall into place. Isla was on the move, and she wanted something from TD. I wondered what the trickster had in mind. And I wondered if, once and for all, I could actually defeat her.

Chapter 11

When we left the hospital a few hours later, Detra Ann was sleeping peacefully. The surgeon said she had been very lucky. The bullet had missed her major organs, and there were no fragments left behind. However, she had to be watched the next twenty-four hours. She had lost a lot of blood and had a history of bad reactions to anesthesia.

Mrs. Dowd had appeared genuinely happy that Ashland had come to see her. She'd tolerated TD and me, which was fine with both of us. Ashland tried to include us, but Cynthia had made up her mind to hate us, at least for the moment. After a while, none of us spoke. We sat waiting and staring at Detra Ann, who slept through the whole uncomfortable exchange.

We said our goodbyes, and TD promised to call when she woke up. Ashland still didn't want me to take the gunshot residue test, but I had to. I was innocent! I wanted to prove them all wrong. The faster I was cleared, the more quickly Simmons would start looking at other scenarios. A dull worry began to creep up within me…what if Isla was responsible? I knew she had been there—the open door and the scattered leaves attested to that. Who would ever believe it? The only person who could tell us what really happened was Detra Ann, and she wasn't awake yet.

We drove in silence down Government Street to the Mobile Police Department Headquarters. The only sound was the radio playing softly.

Wait, I know that voice. It was William Bettencourt singing "The Heart of Love." I couldn't help but smile. He deserved the break. I was happy for him. I hummed along to the tune.

"Seriously, CJ?"

"I'm happy that he got his big break."

"Thanks to you. He almost got you killed. I'm not convinced he was so squeaky clean. If he hadn't gotten his name in the papers…"

"That's completely unfair. He saved my life, Ashland." Neither of us moved out of our seats. "I love you, Ashland Stuart. Not William or anyone else."

"I love you too. You ready?" Ashland appeared nervous, unsure. I hoped that his doubts weren't about me. Surely he didn't believe that I actually shot Detra Ann.

"Yes, I want to get this over with and go home. It's been one heck of a day."

"You know I can call our attorney and have her down here in no time."

"I don't need an attorney, Ash. I haven't done anything wrong."

"That doesn't always matter. We have been on the local authorities' radar recently, what with Hollis' murder and Louis Beaumont's body in the backyard. They aren't exactly in our fan club."

I knew it was true, but we were innocent of wrongdoing. We parked, put some change in the meter and walked in, hand and hand. I explained to the on-duty officer why I was there and showed her the written order from Simmons. She led us to the lab and there we sat, taking in the stark ambiance until the lab tech and a uniformed officer appeared. I couldn't help but notice that the police officer had his cuffs handy. True to her word, Simmons wasn't taking any chances. If she could arrest me, she would—she'd promised me that. Now it was my turn to look at Ashland nervously. I gave the tech my name, and then they proceeded with the test. Unsealing the small damp cloth from the package, she rubbed my hands vigorously, both tops and bottoms.

"I'll be right back," she told the officer. He let her pass and stood by the door, his arms folded across his chest. We didn't make any small talk with him or even with each other. It was a nerve-wracking experience to say the least.

"She's clean. Not even a trace." She wrote something on a piece of paper and handed it to me. "Detective Simmons will be in touch with you soon. Keep this for your records."

"That's it? I can go?"

"The detective may have more questions later, but we're all done with you today, Mrs. Stuart."

"Okay."

"If you all would follow me, I'll lead you out." I had had no idea that the entry doors had been locked behind us. Suddenly, the whole thing seemed surreal. Actually, the past forty-eight hours had been surreal. We walked back to the car and got in. I leaned back in the seat and let out a sigh of relief. Lightning cracked over the bay, and the sky darkened ominously above us.

"Take me home, Ashland." I felt so tired. The anxiety from this morning, the strangeness, was creeping back into my mind. "I'm ready to go home."

"Home where? Our new home or Seven Sisters?" I didn't know if he was joking or what, but I wasn't in the mood.

"*Notre petite maison*. I just want to be with you." I sighed and closed my eyes.

"What did you say?"

"I said I want to go to Our Little Home. Not Seven Sisters."

"No, you said '*notre petite maison*'. But you don't speak French. What's that about?"

I felt the blood drain from my face. *What was going on?* I smiled awkwardly. "Maybe I heard that somewhere."

He frowned and eyed me suspiciously. "Let's go, then. I'll cook us something, and we can talk."

I nodded my head against his shoulder. "I would like that." *I have so much to tell you.* When we arrived home, thankfully the front door was neatly closed and there were no leaves on the porch and sidewalk. Doreen's car was gone, but she had left the house neat and tidy. Lightning cracked again, and this time the rain began to fall, heavy, soaking drops. I tossed my purse on the foyer table under the gilded mirror and stared at the stairs. Doreen had dutifully cleaned up the blood, and you'd never know what had happened earlier. I was glad for that and happy that Simmons hadn't taken the liberty of wrapping yellow tape across our front door. Wouldn't the neighbors have loved that?

Ashland wrapped his strong arms around me, and we kissed like we hadn't kissed since our honeymoon. He led me gently by the hand to the bottom of the stairs, but my feet wouldn't let me go up. I couldn't go up there, not right now, but I wanted him as much as he wanted me.

"No, I have a better idea." We had a barely used guest room on the other side of the kitchen. I smiled and pulled him in that direction. Ashland's sexy grin told me he liked the idea, and he followed me into the room. It felt cool and fresh—and presumably free of lurking ghosts and unhappy entities. I liked this room. We fell on the soft down comforter together and spent the next half hour lost in one another's arms. How wonderful to be with the man I loved! We needed this. I needed him! I loved him with every fiber of my being.

"I love you, Ashland Gregory Stuart." He showered my neck with kisses, and I laughed as his lips whispered across my skin.

Hoyt! Hoyt, I love you! Christine's pleading voice whispered in my head. I smothered the urge to spring up from the bed. Instead, I closed my eyes and forced myself to focus on the moment—this moment, in this lifetime. I was alive and here with my husband.

What do I do about you, Christine? What am I supposed to do? Ashland stroked my cheek with his finger and I whispered, "Hold me tight, Ashland."

"I love you, my wife. Are you hungry yet?"

"Starving! Are you sure you want to cook, though? You've had a long day already."

"I like cooking for you. And believe it or not, I couldn't find a decent meal in New Orleans."

"I do find that hard to believe!" I said with a laugh. "Okay, well, at least let me chop up some vegetables or toss a salad or something."

"That's a deal." We kissed and got dressed, and then I padded off to the restroom to work up a decent-looking ponytail. I took a ponytail holder out of the bathroom closet and checked my hair in the mirror. I didn't mind a sloppy ponytail, but my curls could look crazy if I didn't have a care for the finished product. Unhappy with the ponytail I'd made, I took it down and tried again.

Can you hear me? I know you can hear me. Please help me!

This couldn't be happening! *Go away!*

Suddenly the mirror began to reflect a smoky image. I looked behind me, but there was nothing. I stumbled back against the wicker hamper and stared at the mirror. I didn't speak, I couldn't! All I could do was gape at the outline of a woman's face struggling to appear in the smoke.

"Christine?" I gasped at the apparition.

"Hey, did you hear me?" Ashland barged into the bathroom, and I turned my attention from the mirror for a second. Even the voice had quieted in Ashland's presence. "What is it, Carrie Jo? You look like you've seen a…" His smile disappeared, and he pushed the door all the way open.

"I think I have."

"What? Here?"

I reached for his hand, and he pulled me out of the bathroom. "Okay, let's forget dinner. We'll order out—we have to talk."

"I agree. And I need a drink. How about you?"

"Yes, please." I followed him into the living room and flopped on the suede blue leather couch. I couldn't stop shaking. I wasn't necessarily afraid of Christine, but encountering ghosts or whatever that was always set my nerves on edge. It wasn't a natural thing. Not at all.

Help me.

Unleashing my wild hair from the ponytail holder, I accepted the small snifter of brandy that Ashland handed me and moved the pillow so he could sit beside me. "I don't know where to begin."

"When did all this start? Have you been dreaming about the house again?"

"That's the thing. I haven't been dreaming. In fact, until yesterday, I haven't had a dream in about three months. But I've been so happy with our new life and all, I haven't thought

much about it. Then I started to experience this feeling, like
something was…what's the word I'm looking for?"

"Undone?"

"Exactly. Undone. Like a wrong note played in a song you
know or a whisper that you can't quite make out."

"I've felt the same thing. I thought it was just me."

I squeezed his hand, and we sipped our drinks. "Do you
think we missed something?"

"Maybe. I'm not the expert, though."

"I'm sure not either," I said wryly.

"What else? Tell me what else has happened?"

"That feeling I described, it got stronger as the weeks went
by. Then when you left for New Orleans, I felt like a jerk. I
went downstairs to catch you before you left and found the
door wide open. Not only that, but there were piles of leaves all
over the place, like the door had been left open for days. That
happened a few times. Including this morning, when Detra
Ann got shot. And that's not all."

"Yes?"

"She's here…Isla. I've heard her giggling."

"Are you sure?"

"Well, I can't say a hundred percent, but I am pretty sure.
The day you left I was working in the office when she went
sailing by my door. She's back, and that can only mean one
thing—we missed something."

He swirled the amber drink in his glass and downed it.
"Damn," he muttered, setting the glass on the coffee table. "I
wonder what it could be."

It was my turn to down my drink. "More, please." Ashland
took our glasses and refilled them. A branch began to tap on
the window; the storm outside had kicked up the evening
breeze and the rain continued to fall.

"After that, I decided to get out of the house as quickly as I
could. I drove to Bette's house, but she wasn't home. All I
could think was to go to Seven Sisters. Detra Ann told me at
the luncheon about the night tours, so I thought I might see

Rachel and kill some time until I felt brave enough to come back here."

"You should have called me. I would have come right home, or you could have driven to New Orleans."

"Really? Because when you left I wasn't getting that vibe from you at all. It felt like you wanted to be alone, so I left you alone. For the record, I did call. You were at a party."

He laughed. "I wasn't at a party, CJ. I was at a supper club, Henri's club in New Orleans. I didn't tell you because I didn't want you to worry. I guess I was just trying to protect you."

"You saw Henri?" I couldn't help but smile. Even though he'd been caught up in Mia's web, at least at the beginning, he'd proven to be a worthy friend to Ashland and me. He'd left Mobile after the incident in the Moonlight Garden. I didn't blame him. Not one bit.

"I did. I haven't been completely honest with you. I've been back to the house too."

"What? Why?"

"That same feeling that something was off. Detra Ann called me a few weeks ago and reminded me that I left a few crates there. I should have told you, and I'm sorry I didn't. I admit I was happy to get the call—that was my excuse to go back. Especially after all the fuss I made about deeding the house to the city. I loaded up the crates and then took a walk around the property."

"And?"

"And nothing—not at first. There were tons of visitors there, walking through the house and the gardens. It was so crowded." I could tell he was pleased about that. I was too. "Re-enactors were scattered around the property, talking to guests and pointing out some of the architectural details and the 'acceptable' history. It was exactly as we hoped. The people love it, CJ."

I smiled, happy that he was happy. Restoring Seven Sisters had been a real dream of his. "You knew they would."

"I hoped. You helped make that happen." He sipped his brandy again and continued, "I walked through the gardens toward the back of the property, where it meets the Mobile River. The grounds team that TD hired did a remarkable job of cleaning it up and bringing it back to life. I decided to walk down to the riverbank. It was a good hike, but I wanted the time to think. I felt like I was being watched, but I kept walking. I wasn't sure where I was going, but then I saw a woman peeking out from behind a tree. She wore a full-skirted gray dress with black lace trim. I thought for a minute she might be one of the re-enactors from the house, but as I got closer, I knew she wasn't."

"What did she look like?"

"Attractive, but not beautiful like Calpurnia. Sweet. She had a sweet, round face. She was about your height, maybe an inch shorter, and looked to be in her early thirties."

"Okay. What else?"

"Thinking she needed help, I shouted to her, 'Are you okay?' She stepped on to the path and faced me—she was about fifty feet away." Ashland took another sip of his drink. Anxiety crept over me—what happened next? I didn't rush him, but it took great restraint. "She raised her hand above her eyes, like you do when you're trying to block the sun. But the weird thing was, the sun was behind her. She called out, 'Hoyt! Is that you?'"

The hair on my arms began to crackle. I froze—my eyes widened at hearing someone else speak that name. "Oh, no," I whispered.

"I said, 'No, ma'am. I'm Ashland. May I help you?' Without a word, she ducked back into the woods and ran from me. I called after her, asking her if she needed help, but she didn't answer. I could hear the leaves crunching under her shoes and the swishing of her skirts, but when I made it to the point in the path where she had stood, she'd disappeared. But there was no pathway. And she couldn't have run through that section of woods, too much underbrush. No way she would have made it with those skirts. I ducked through, trying to look for any trace of her, maybe a footprint or a bit of cloth, but I didn't find anything."

Peering into the brown liquid in the glass, I asked, "Didn't you recognize her, Ashland?"

"I don't think so. It wasn't Calpurnia. I know her face. And it certainly wasn't Isla."

"No, it was neither one of them. You saw Christine, Calpurnia's mother, and she's looking for the man she loves—she's looking for Hoyt Page."

"Hoyt? Who's Hoyt?"

"He's the man she should have married. I believe he is Calpurnia's father."

"What? Who is he?"

Taking my drink with me, I walked to the back door and pushed open the curtain. The rain still streamed down, and the gutters were full of water; they poured off the side of the house. Somewhere, a cat begged to come inside. I touched the crystal glass to my lip. The scent of brandy comforted me.

Hoyt! Where are you?

For the next hour, I told Ashland everything. About the dream. About connecting with Christine. About running from Jeremiah. He didn't question me or interrupt me. It felt good to tell it, to tell it all.

"That's it. We have to find this other daughter, the one that's missing. Christine needs to know she's okay. Right? Is that what this is about?"

"I don't know. I would think so. At least, it's a place to start."

"But where do we start? Have you seen this girl?"

"I haven't…but I think Mia has. She sent me this book, that's the book I found the day you left for New Orleans. In the note, Mia says that once I read it, I will understand why she did what she did. I don't know if that's true or not, but I think there could be something significant in there."

"Well, we don't have any other clues to go on. Sounds like you, Mrs. Researcher, will be doing some research." Suddenly, Ashland laughed. It was a strange sound after everything we'd talked about. "You know, if this historian thing doesn't work out for you, you could open a detective business. Mysteries seem to follow you, Carrie Jo."

I raised my eyebrows and shook my head. "No thanks. I prefer dusty old books to voices in my head and bad dreams. Thank you, by the way, for believing me."

"Of course. If you're crazy, I'm crazy too. I've seen a few things myself, remember. I hope I never see Isla again."

"That's another thing. TD has seen her and is scared to death."

"Why would she show herself to him?"

"Why not? When she was alive, she was quite lovely. And if she thought she could use him for her own means, then…"

"That doesn't sound right. We found the treasure—why is she hanging around? Where are Calpurnia and Muncie?"

"I'm sure they are resting, Ash. Their part in this craziness is over, at least I think it is, but Christine's isn't yet. As long as there are secrets, Isla will have some measure of power."

"Great. That's just great."

"I think you're in the clear. You stood up to her. But we have to help TD. She's terrorizing him, Ashland, and he doesn't know what to do. Instead of doing this by ourselves, we have friends who will help us. We just need to come up with a plan."

"Then it's a good thing I went to see Henri."

"Why do you say that?"

"Because he's willing to help. Because he knows more than we do about all this stuff. And because, like you, I trust him."

"I think you should call him and ask him to come back to Mobile." Despite all the supernatural storytelling, I felt warm and comfortable now. Maybe it was the brandy or just being with Ashland. The rain had begun to slack now, and we cuddled up together on the couch. Neither of us was ready to break the mood.

"I will do that. You ready to go to bed?"

We'd forgotten all about eating, and I was too drowsy to think about it now. "Can't we sleep here tonight?"

His arm was behind his head, and I was lying on his chest. Sometime during our chat, I'd grabbed the chenille throw off the back of the couch and covered us with it.

"Sounds perfect," he said, kissing the top of my head. Smiling, I snuggled up to him and listened to the sound of his heart beating. I loved him so much. I couldn't believe how lucky I had been to find him. I wished Christine had had a happy ending. How many times did she lie on Hoyt's chest and listen to his heart beat?

Christine, I'm sorry for what happened to you.

I fell asleep and stepped into a dream, but it wasn't mine.

Chapter 12

"*Calpurnia, dearest. Come show Mother what you found. Oh, look at this, Hoyt.*"

The little girl danced in a circle, swirling her skirts about her. The tiny ladybug on her finger refused to fly.

Screwing up her face, she stared at it. "*She won't fly, Mother. Why won't she fly?*"

"*Maybe she needs a rest, dearest. Proper ladybugs rest in between flights.*"

"*Is that true, Dr. Page?*" With an untrusting look, the four-year-old tilted her pretty head and questioned her mother's friend.

"*Yes, that is quite true.*"

Christine plucked at the petals of the white daisy she held. How childish to play games like "*He Loves Me, He Loves Me Not.*" Even her soul knew that Hoyt Henry Page loved her beyond reasoning—as much as she loved him. What a picture the three of them made! Quite like a happy family enjoying a summer day by the water. But that was only a picture— an ever-fading dream buried in her heart.

Calpurnia spun around again, trying in earnest to force the bug to fly.

"*Your sister came calling yesterday, Hoyt.*"

"*Claudette? I suppose she came to bring Calpurnia a birthday gift?*"

"*No. In fact, she did not mention her at all.*"

Hoyt rose from his reclining position. He dusted the elbow of his sleeve and looked at her. He didn't dare hold her hand or touch her in public, but he had the sudden urge to do so. Christine knew this, and it assured her of his love.

"*What then was her business?*"

Christine tossed the now-bare flower aside and smiled at him. "*She requested a meeting with Mr. Cottonwood. When I pressed her, she implied that it was business, but I know better.*"

"*I see. What did Claudette say that would lead you to that conclusion?*"

Christine raised her hand to her eyes to shield them from the sun. "*Calpurnia! Come back this way. Stay away from the water!*"

Frustrated, Hoyt scolded her, "*Christine, you're being evasive.*"

"*My daughter is perilously close to the river, Hoyt. Calpurnia!*"

Hoyt stung at the phrase "my daughter." It was just the two of them. Couldn't Christine even then say "Our daughter?"

He brushed off her concern and tried not to appear hurt. "She will come to no harm. See? She's just spinning about. Now tell me what troubles you about my sister's visit?"

"It was a pretense, Hoyt. She has no real business with Jeremiah, none at all. She came to tell him. About us. I am sure of it."

He laughed. "She knows nothing. I have told her nothing. She has seen nothing." He tossed his hat on the blanket beside him and secretively reached for her pale hand. Such a lovely hand. Well-sculpted like a Grecian statue. "For the record, Claudette has a keen business sense. She handles all my finances."

Christine pulled her hand away in frustration. "Always willing to defend her. She knows, and she will make sure that my husband hears her out. Why has she never married? Perhaps if she were married, she would be less prone to interfere with matters that do not concern her."

"That is just her way, Christine. I promise you that I will speak to her this evening and see what is on her mind. Do not worry so."

Her heart felt instantly lighter but before she could thank him, a loud splash into the nearby water grabbed her attention. "Calpurnia!" she screamed in terror. "Ma fille!" Hoyt raced past her and in a few seconds had leaped into the water after the child. Christine stood on the riverbank, her chest heaving, anguished tears in her eyes.

Immediately she began to plead, "God, punish me but not my child! Please, not my child!" She began to pray to the Virgin as Hoyt swam to Callie, whose sweet face was immersed in the troubled waters of the river.

"Calpurnia! Calpurnia!" Finally Hoyt reached her and turned her upright. The child did not move but floated like a dead leaf on the water. "Calpurnia!" Hoyt struggled against the current but finally reached the muddy shore. Exhausted, he lifted the child out of the water and collapsed on the bank. Christine ran to them, crying and pleading with God to save her daughter.

She peeled long strands of wet hair off the child's face and gasped. Calpurnia's lips were blue, her skin cold and clammy. "She is dead. Oh mon ame! Come back to me, my child!"

Hoyt shook off the weariness and lifted the child up to his shoulder. He patted her back, attempting to force the water from her lungs. He wept as he smacked her tiny back until finally, he heard her wheeze.

"Hoyt!" Christine's face appeared unbelieving for a second, then a smile flashed across it. "She's moving! She is alive! Grace a Dieu!"

"Let's get the child home. She needs some attention. Get the carriage, Christine."

"Yes, of course." She ran back to the lane and appeared in a few minutes with Hoyt's open carriage. Calpurnia had not roused, but she was breathing. She was alive—and that was all that mattered to Christine. They did not talk as they raced back to Seven Sisters. Christine held her water-logged child to her chest and kissed her head repeatedly. "You will be alright, cherie. See? We are almost home, dearest." The child could not open her eyes, but her tiny chest rose and fell. Christine watched each breath with worry. They raced down the red clay lane that led to Seven Sisters. In seconds, tall, gangly Stokes ran out to meet them. Christine handed him the child and said, "Take her to her room."

"Yes, ma'am. Mr. Cottonwood is looking for you in his study." He did not look Christine in the eye but took the damp bundle she presented him.

"I will see him. Take her upstairs to her room and give Dr. Page whatever he needs. I'll come as soon as I can." She searched his face for a clue about her husband's request, but there were none forthcoming. Stokes had been and always would be the master's most dependable slave, faithful above all others.

"Yes, ma'am."

Now that the immediate emergency had been handled, Christine could breathe again. Hoyt would see to it that their daughter would recover. She knew it. Her gown was wet and muddy, and she imagined that her hair was messy, but there was nothing she could do about that now. Jeremiah insisted that she appear like a lady at all times, but surely such an emergency as this warranted a measure of latitude. She went in the house, down the hallway to Jeremiah's study. Nobody came to greet her or attend to her, a sure sign that something was amiss. Jeremiah stood at the window, an unlit cigar in his mouth. He wore no coat; Christine spotted his blue jacket resting on the arm of his chair. Immediately she began to worry. He wouldn't harm her with Hoyt in the house—surely not with

Hoyt there. How different he looked from the man she had first met. He had been so accommodating, so eager to please her during their courtship. Christine had never had any illusions that he loved her, or she him, but she would have never dreamed that she would be so unhappy—and he so cruel.

"You wanted to see me, Jeremiah?"

He did not look at her at first, and when he did, he showed no surprise at her appearance. He barely looked in her direction. She might as well have been one of the slaves.

"I would ask you to sit, but your gown would stain my chair, I am afraid." He set the cigar in the massive crystal ashtray that rested on the edge of his desk. "You cannot know how unhappy I am, Christine. I have had a letter from your father today."

"Mon pere?"

"Yes, and please refrain from speaking French. It will do you no good. I am immune to your feminine wiles."

"Wiles?" Christine felt her pulse race. She reminded herself to remain calm. "What do you mean? I have no wiles."

Jeremiah leered at her. He strode to his desk and picked up the letter. "He says, and I quote, 'Make my good daughter aware of my correspondence, and please relay to her my fondness and pride in her situation.'"

She did not know how to respond, still unsure what crime he imagined she had committed. Her inner voice urged her again to remain calm. "I shall go write to him immediately and thank him for his kind words. Thank you for sharing them with me." She turned to leave, holding her breath for luck as she did. In just four steps he was behind her.

Grasping her arm savagely, he pulled her to him. His breath smelled stale, a sickening combination of whiskey and salted pork. "Do not walk away from me, wife! Never walk away from me. Do you understand?"

Her silver earbobs jingled as she nodded. She didn't pull away, for that would only enrage him further. She had to keep quiet until she could discern the source of his rage. Christine prayed that Claudette Page had not been successful in her desire to educate him, to fill his ears with the one thing that could destroy Christine completely. He would kill her—that much she was sure of.

"Why is he coming here? Why, Christine?"

"*Who? Dr. Page? Calpurnia fell into the river, and he happened to be passing by and gave assistance. If it weren't for Dr. Page, our daughter would be…*" *The words began to pour out of her mouth. She detested lying. She never mastered "mensonge discrete," discreet lying as some called it. But for Hoyt, for Calpurnia, she would lie to the holy angels themselves.*

"*Don't play coy with me! I am speaking of your brother!*" *He shoved the letter at her and commanded her to read it. Fearful of what he might do next, she hastily began to read. 'Esteemed Son-In-Law…'*"

"*Damnation! Skip down to the last paragraph. Read it! Convince me that you did not call him here!*"

"*In the interest of our mutual benefit and kind relationship, please receive my son Louis with all courtesy when he arrives at the end of this month. I have entrusted him to carry out my business and have requested his assistance in procuring the adjoining lands to the south of Seven Sisters. He has also requested a review of the most recent financial records, and I trust you will accommodate him in this matter.*'"

"*Louis is coming here? I swear, mon mari—I mean, my husband—I did not know! I have not written him or my father since this spring. He has not come at my request.*"

He stomped toward Christine and snatched the letter from her, reading it silently to himself. Fighting every instinct in her soul, mind and body, she stood rigidly, almost defiantly. In this she was innocent!

"*You think I believe you? I know you swoon and pant after Louis Beaumont. He is the only man you have ever truly loved, isn't he, Christine.*" *He stomped back to his desk and sat in the heavy wooden chair.*

"*He is my brother, Jeremiah! How dare you suggest such a thing?!*"

"*Don't play the frightened damsel with me, wife.*"

She could bear the insults. It was nothing in comparison to the truth, was it? "I swear to you, Jeremiah, on everything I treasure, I did not write to Louis. Whatever he and my father have planned, I know nothing."

"*So you say. How can I trust you?*" *He poured himself another glass of whiskey, tossed it back and closed his eyes. Christine breathed a quiet sigh of relief. He didn't know! He knew nothing about Hoyt! Not yet. Bravely, she continued to stand before him. Eventually he looked up, his eyes bleary and red. "Go, and for God's sake, do something with yourself. No more gardening today, Christine.*"

With a curt nod, she left the room, closing the doors behind her. As quickly as she could, she ran up the stairs to her daughter and Hoyt. Her heart skipped a beat when she heard her daughter crying loudly.

Just a little longer together, Hoyt! We have just a little longer!

I'm coming, Calpurnia! Mother is coming!

Chapter 13

"Momma?" My eyes felt heavy, and my entire body hurt like I'd been hit by a Mack truck, especially my left side. Confusion and pain collided, and I caught my breath.

"Detra Ann! You're awake! Nurse! She's..." The words sounded muffled and I strained to hear but fell asleep again. Suddenly a beam of light hit my left eye, and I felt my eyes flutter open.

"Momma? Where am I?"

I began to see clearly now. Sunlight peeked through cheap plastic blinds, and the walls were a horrid mauve with grey plastic trim. Medical machines were beeping around me. My mother hovered over me, her pearls dangling from her neck and ears; she was wearing her yellow suit, the one with the tiny yellow flowers at the lapel. She always wanted to look like she'd stepped out of the Sears and Roebuck catalog, she said. How sad that they don't send out those catalogs anymore. Still, my mother could be kind, if a bit overprotective.

"Are you awake again? Detra Ann?"

"Yes, I'm awake."

"You are at the hospital," she said slowly and loudly like I was hearing-impaired.

I tried to sit up, but a sharp, stabbing pain tore through my side.

"Don't move, alright? The doctor is on...his...way."

"I'm not deaf, Momma. Please, can you get me a glass of water?"

"I don't think you're supposed to drink anything yet. Not this soon after surgery."

"Surgery? Please get me some water."

"Detra Ann? You're awake." TD hovered over me now. I ignored Mother's pursed lips and the eye roll that seemed to accompany all her conversations or interactions with him. He kissed my hand—he was as handsome as ever. His hair was slightly longer and messier than I last remembered...I kind of liked it. I touched it as he leaned forward. No matter how lost he was, TD always smelled like sawdust and sunshine.

"Hey, baby. Does this mean we're back together?" Oh Lord! I was never this needy—what was I saying?

"I'm here, Detra Ann, and your mother is too."

I whispered through dry lips, "I need something to drink."

"Be right back."

As he disappeared from my view, I struggled to get my bearings. The pain in my side was excruciating—I had nothing to compare it to. I'd never had children or any major surgery, except for that time I broke my finger on the playground. That had been Ashland's fault, but I never told anyone. He hadn't meant to smash my finger with that teeter-totter. Oh, and I'd had my wisdom teeth removed too. How sick I had been that night. Something about the pain medicine made me sick. Oh my God! The pain was unbearable.

"Listen, dear, the doctor has you on a drip—see the tube? The button is right here. When you start hurting, press the button. You will recover, but it is going to hurt for a while. Don't be a hero, Detra Ann."

"I won't," I said glumly, immediately pressing the button.

"What happened? Why were you in that woman's house?"

"Somebody pushed me, I think." I remembered climbing up the stairs, calling for Carrie Jo… "Carrie Jo…is she okay? Did they hurt her too?"

TD returned with a cup, and I prayed it was water. I could see the IV bag pumping fluids into my body, but I was so thirsty.

"The nurse says you can't drink any water but you can have ice chips, if that makes any sense. Here you go, baby."

I took the cup in my hands as Momma slowly eased my bed up a few inches. "That's good. It hurts too bad to move up any higher. Thanks for the ice." The pain medicine was working again—I felt no pain at all now. I scooped up a few ice chips in my mouth and crunched them. They were the best things I had ever put in my mouth. "Somebody hit me in the stomach and I fell down the stairs. I couldn't see who it was, but it wasn't

Carrie Jo. She was in the hallway. Wait, I do remember someone being on the stair with me. What was her name? Why can't I think?" My brain felt like it was wrapped in damp cotton.

"It's the pain medicine," my mother whispered to TD.

"Wait, she's not supposed to be there. She lives at Seven Sisters, right? I wonder why she was at Carrie Jo's house."

"Who, baby?" My mother patted my forehead with a damp cloth.

"Isla. Yeah, that's it."

TD's face turned deathly pale. He said, "What did you say, babe? Isla?"

"Yes, she pushed me down the stairs at CJ's house. Oh, TD! It was the scariest thing I ever saw. She was right in front of me—she just popped up out of nowhere. I found the front door open, and I got worried for Carrie Jo. She'd had a bad night at the house, we both did. Jeremiah Cottonwood tried to get us, but we ran and ran…"

"What are you talking about?" My mother's face reflected her shock. "Is she talking about *the* Jeremiah Cottonwood? Is that who you mean? He is dead, Detra Ann, and has been dead for over a hundred years."

"Cynthia, I think it's the meds talking. Don't take anything she says seriously," TD lied to my mother. He knew that what was happening at Seven Sisters was real—very real.

"How can you say that, TD? I saw her. I know I did." I summoned up her face from my fragmented memory. She had appeared just inches in front of my face. I wasn't sure how I knew her name or how she knew mine, but she did.

Go home, Detra Ann! Her face twisted into a snarl, the voice in my head full of inhuman viciousness. I remembered that she'd startled me and then struck me hard in the gut. "I'm so tired."

"Rest now. I'll be here when you wake up," TD whispered in my ear. "I love you."

"I love you too," I said, at least in my mind.

Then I wasn't in the hospital room anymore.

I found myself standing in the ballroom of Seven Sisters. Shadowy couples dressed in black swirled about me, dancing to a macabre waltz played by an invisible orchestra. The massive chandelier above me shone with amber light that cast living shadows on the walls of the room. The black-clad dancers did not seem to notice me, but I could feel the silk rubbing against my skin as they moved around and around. With escalating alarm, I pushed my way through the couples; their indiscernible faces did not acknowledge me, but somehow I knew they were aware of my presence—and I was an unwanted guest. I didn't belong here. My side hurt and my skin grew cold, the thin hospital gown providing me little comfort. I stumbled forward, terror rising inside me. What if I could not get out?

"Please," I shouted, "please let me out!" I reached out to touch the shoulder of a man who swung by me in a perfect circle. He robotically turned his face to me, but none of his features were clear except his hate-filled eyes.

"Where is your invitation?" he demanded as he and his partner swooped around me.

Sobbing now, I pushed on. My side burned, and I imagined that I felt blood dripping from the wound. Time had no meaning here in this ballroom of specters, but I knew I had walked much further than was necessary to reach that door. Again silk slapped my face and bodies pushed against me as I shoved my way to the exit.

"Let me go! Let me out!"

My cries went unheard over the noise of the scratchy violins. Finally, in the briefest of moments, the couples in front of me moved and I could plainly see the door. I was almost there! Again they shoved against me. Weeping and reaching, I said, "You have no right to keep me here!"

Then the chandelier dimmed as I made a final push to escape the spinning crowd. I extended my shaking hand toward the door with every ounce of energy I had. Somehow I knew this was my last push, my last try. If I wasn't successful now, if I couldn't break free, I would be here forever. I felt the tears welling up in my eyes.

Then she appeared—Isla! Hovering between me and the door. With a kittenish smile and fierce eyes, she floated closer. I had nowhere to go. The dancers whirled behind me in their evil circles—the only way out was before me.

"No, Christine. You can't leave yet. You haven't been properly received, and he's waiting for you. He's been waiting, and now the wait is over. Take my hand, Christine, and it will all be over." She reached her hand out to me, only a few feet away. I stared at it. It was a lifeless, pale thing, so small and childlike. So young, so perfect.

So dead.

I opened my mouth to protest, but all that came out was a scream.

Chapter 14

I woke up to the smells of breakfast and the sound of Ashland calling my name. I stretched like a lazy cat and followed my nose to the kitchen. My husband had taken a shower, set the bar for breakfast and had everything ready for me before I got up. "Morning," he said, "How did you sleep?"

"Great. How is your shoulder? I hope I didn't drool on you."

He laughed. "No but you do talk in your sleep."

Sitting at the bar, I slid my plate his way to accept a few spoonfuls of scrambled eggs. "Did I at least say anything interesting?"

"I'll never tell," he teased.

I sipped the hot coffee and wolfed down my bacon and eggs. It felt like forever since I'd eaten. I had managed to grab some chips from the vending machine at the hospital but had never opened them. "Boy, that was delicious. Anything else in there?"

"Check the fridge. I think there is some fruit salad if you want that."

"Yuck, I'll pass. I better get a shower before we head to Springhill. I assume we're going first thing?"

"I'd like to. I'll tidy up here."

Hopping out of the chair, I kissed his cheek and took my coffee cup with me. "Give me ten minutes."

"You got it."

During my walk up the stairs, I focused on not spilling my coffee, not on the spot where Detra Ann fell or on the tiny hole in the wall from the bullet. I hoped she was going to be all right. As quickly as I could, I rummaged for some casual yet presentable clothing and then headed to the shower. I didn't look in any mirrors or even glance around the room. If there was something here, I didn't want to know. Drinking down the last swigs of my coffee, I took my shower and got dressed in record time. No sense in dawdling and giving Isla a chance to reappear. I stopped for a moment. Nope, nothing. Hmm… things were oddly quiet this morning.

Ashland rapped on the door. "Almost done," I called.

"We have to go. Something's happened to Detra Ann!"

"What?" I flung the door open as I buttoned up my pants. "What happened?"

"I don't know. TD said something about a seizure—now she's in a coma. I don't know. Are you ready?"

"Yes, let me grab my shoes and purse."

"I'll be in the car."

"Okay, be there in a sec!" I towel-dried my hair and grabbed a hair clip. *Not fooling with my hair today.* Two minutes later I ran after him, grabbing my purse off the foyer table as I practically ran out the door. Locking it behind me, I yelled up the stairwell, "You're not going to win, Isla!" I don't know why I did it, but it felt good. I was angry, angrier than I had been in a long time. I didn't hear a sound, not even a giggle.

As Ashland navigated the busy streets, I sent TD a few texts to let him know we were close, but he didn't answer. "Must be with Detra Ann," I told Ashland. "God, I hope she's okay."

"Me too. She's like a sister to me, you know. She is the nearest thing to family that I have. Besides you, of course." His voice shook as he turned into the parking lot.

I didn't know what to say. I rubbed his shoulder as we whizzed down Springhill Avenue. A few minutes later, we pulled into an open spot. It was a good thing we'd gotten here early, as the parking lot was nearly full. A few minutes later we were stepping off the elevator onto the fifth floor of the hospital. When the doors opened Ashland and I both froze—the place was full of women from the Historical Society. A nurse approached our group and asked us to relocate to the waiting room. We complied, but some of the society did not go without some mild protests.

"Ashland! Carrie Jo!" People hugged me like they'd known me all my life. "So sad what's happened! How in the world did she get shot? Now she's in a coma!"

My plan was to let Ashland field these questions. I'd stay in the background until I could see Detra Ann. But Holliday Betbeze had other plans. She found an empty seat beside me and attempted to probe me for more information.

"Were you robbed? Is that what happened? Did Detra Ann protect you from a thief? You know, that is a very dangerous part of town. My own cousin was robbed down there just two streets over."

"I didn't know that," I said, attempting to deflect her questioning.

"Tell me the truth, why on earth did you and Ashland ever give up that big old house? I would have stayed there until they drug me out by my shoelaces."

"You know you don't own a pair of shoelaces, Holliday," another woman chimed in. For a few minutes, they forgot about me and chatted about the tragedy and the "Seven Sisters" curse. After a while, Cynthia came out of her daughter's room and soon became the group's new center of gravity. Ashland hugged her and said something in her ear. She nodded and smiled weakly before patting him gently on the shoulder. After a few seconds, he walked out of the room, leaving me behind without a word. I gave Cynthia a polite smile and tried to follow after him as quickly as I could. It didn't happen.

"Wait, Carrie Jo." Cynthia stepped in front of me. The crowd stopped their chattering, waiting to see what happened next. In a quiet voice she said, "I want to apologize to you. I said some very rude things yesterday, and I regret them. Detra Ann told me that it wasn't your fault—and she told me what she thinks happened. And that lady detective called me to say you aren't a suspect. I was wrong. I jumped to the wrong conclusion, and I am truly sorry for that." Cynthia didn't wait for my response. She scooped me up in her thin arms and hugged me.

I squeezed her shoulders and whispered, "Don't worry about me. We're here if you need us."

She wiped at her eyes with a crumpled tissue. "Is there anything you can tell me? Anything at all? My daughter mentioned that someone else was there. Isla, I think her name was. Is she a friend of yours?"

How should I answer this? "The only person I saw was Detra Ann. I swear to you, I didn't see anyone else."

She touched my arm and nodded. "It must have been the pain medication. She's never been able to tolerate it." She walked away slowly, and I went down the hall in the direction Ashland had gone. I pushed the door open to Detra Ann's room. TD sat in the chair next to her, his long hair tucked behind his ears, his eyes bloodshot and tired-looking. Ashland stood on the other side of the bed staring down at her. Detra Ann's blond hair was spread around her like a golden halo. Her face was serene; she reminded me of Sleeping Beauty. Even though she was the picture of peace, the air around her was not.

Bette popped in the room, and she practically ran into me. "How have you been, Bette? I came by to see you, but you weren't there. Are you okay?"

With tears in her eyes, Bette nodded. I could see that she was a big old mix of emotions right now, but I had no idea why. I had not gotten the idea that she and Detra Ann were all that close. Maybe they were after all. People deal with situations like this differently.

For about the sixth time today I received an unexpected hug. But this wasn't just an "I'm here for you" hug. Bette was heartbroken. "Bette, please. You're scaring me. What has happened? Is it your son? Your boyfriend?"

She looked from me to Ashland, her heart on her sleeve. Her perfect white curls bounced as she shook her head. "Now isn't the right time to share my news. As soon as Detra Ann is better, I will tell you everything. Right now, I just wanted to see you. And I know this may sound strange, Carrie Jo, but I wanted you to know that I love you. And you too, Ashland. I love you both. No matter what happens. Now I have to go help Cynthia. I'm going to make sure she eats, even if it is in the lousy hospital cafeteria. We'll talk soon." With that, she walked out. Ashland's eyes met mine—he looked as confused as I did. What was going on with Bette?

"Ashland, we have to do something." TD sounded desperate. "What can we do? I've been here with Detra Ann, praying for her. Can you believe that? Me, praying? I won't quit, but there has to be something else. I have to do something."

I nodded and said, "I agree. Of all the people in the world, this shouldn't be happening to Detra Ann. She didn't do anything to deserve this. I think we all know that this wasn't an accident. Isla did this, and I can't understand why. I thought her power was broken, but I guess she never left."

"I can't stand sitting back and waiting. I hate playing defense." TD's deep voice shook with a mixture of anger and grief. I could tell he was considering having a drink—or five. I touched his shoulder to remind him that he wasn't alone.

Ashland shook his head. "No, we won't sit back and wait for the other shoe to drop. I'm making the call. Henri needs to be here, and whatever he tells us, we're going to do, right? Everyone agree?"

"I don't know what else we can do," I said.

"If it helps Detra Ann, of course. I'm in." He reached out, took her hand and kissed it.

"I'll go make the call." With a resolute look, Ashland left the room. That was my Ashland, always ready to rescue someone. I sighed, hoping that he was right—that Henri knew more than we did.

I sat next to TD and quietly prayed for Detra Ann. Soon, the room felt and even looked lighter. The bells on her machine rang less and her heart rate was calm.

I knew it. We weren't alone. And maybe this time, we'd get it right.

Chapter 15

An hour later, it was quiet, which was a relief. The ladies had left, deciding to each cook a dish for Cynthia Dowd. It was like a wake lunch, only Detra Ann wasn't dead. It was morbid, if you asked me, but I guessed they did things differently down here in Mobile. Just one of the social quirks that made this place so unique.

I settled on a corner couch in one of the many waiting rooms in Springhill Memorial. I had a water bottle, a bag of dried pineapple from the vending machine and the book that Mia had sent me. Ashland and TD were counting on me to get to the bottom of the problem—find out why Mia and Isla felt they still had a claim on Seven Sisters. When I knew what it was, we could come up with a plan. We needed a plan, big time! I'd deliberately left the ICU floor, at Ashland's urging, in favor of the fourth-floor waiting room. There were more people here but they didn't know me or try to chat with me. I needed quiet to read, but I didn't want to go home. Not without Ashland, and he understandably wasn't leaving until Detra Ann was better.

He'd gone home and grabbed me some snacks, a toothbrush, a pillow and my favorite chenille blanket. I hated the idea of dreaming here in the hospital, but I thought I'd gotten better at controlling who I dreamed about. I'd gotten quite good at calling out names and entering the right dreams. But I was the first to admit that I had a lot to learn about dream catching.

I hunkered down on the couch, which was remarkably comfortable given the circumstances. Kicking off my shoes, I examined the book again. It felt old, small and certainly not magical. It was a plain brown leather book, but hopefully there were some words inside that were going to set us all free. Especially Detra Ann.

I skimmed through the part I'd already read. I flipped through the section about Delilah's time in Canada. Surely, whatever I needed to know about her had to do with her time in Mobile, after the war. No sense in wondering. It was time to find out.

For five years Canada was home even though it didn't feel like it. I missed Mobile, but we were surrounded by people who loved us. The Iverson clan was a hearty lot with plenty of children to keep me entertained during those long, tedious winter months locked inside away from the cold Canadian wilderness. During our stay, I had picked up a bit of our mother tongue and developed a propensity for storytelling, which according to my mother was a family tradition. I got quite good at telling stories and even began to write my own stories and plays.

Uncle Lars and his wife Aida treated me well, but their daughters were far from friendly and liked to refer to me as the "dark bird." I assumed they were referring to my dark hair and eyes, which were so markedly different from their own blond hair and blue eyes. Still, the small children liked me, and many of my male cousins treated me affectionately.

In fact, some of my cousins were so friendly that Adam came to me one afternoon and instructed me to behave less warmly with them. I admit that at the time, I was quite naïve about such things and didn't know why he was making such a fuss. It wasn't until one of my cousins proposed to me that I understood Adam warning. Marriage to a beloved cousin was an honorable thing to my family, and indeed to many people at that time, even though such an idea seems repugnant in today's world. I had no mind to marry anyone at that time, even though I am sure my parents would have found such a match pleasing and acceptable. A year after our escape from Mobile, my mother died rather quickly. Right until the end she worked in the Iversons' store alongside her sister-in-law until the morning we found her dead in her bed. Poor gentle Mother—she had been the sun in our sky, the warm embrace that held us all together.

Adam and I grieved like orphans even though our father was still very much alive. After our relocation, he spent much of his time on the trade routes with his brothers and didn't know about Mother's demise for several months. I had set pen to paper many times, but where would I send a letter? What would I say? After the trading season ended, he returned home to discover her long gone and buried. We found him there at her grave one afternoon, unable to speak or move his left arm and leg. Eating became impossible, and soon he shrank into a husk of the strapping man we knew.

He followed Mother into heaven just a month after his return home. And then we were orphans in the truest since of the word.

One would think that such a tragedy, the loss of parents, would drive two siblings closer, but it did not. Adam became sullen, often angry at the mere sight of me. In turn, I did my best to avoid him, spending as much time as I could with my aunt and her many grandchildren. His moods were unpredictable—at times he would leave me bouquets of purple flowers on the sideboard. Other times, he would pore over his newspapers, reading news of the war, and would slam the door in my face if I approached his room. Soon he took to leaving me alone for days on end. I went to him once, begging him to speak to me, but he refused—until one spring evening. He'd been drinking from the brown jug that Father had kept in his desk drawer. I thought that odd because Adam never drank and showed little regard for those who did.

I had retreated to my room, shed my day dress and brushed my hair before braiding it to make ready for bed. It had been a long day. Adam had sold our parents' cabin on the outskirts of town, and we had moved into the rooms above the store as a way to save money. Adam had steady work, with many orders for new tables and chairs coming in all the time, but we had no need for a home with three bedrooms.

"Delilah!" I heard him call me. I didn't go right away, for I dreaded the idea of squabbling with the brother I loved so much. "Delilah, please come see me." Unable to resist his gentler tone, I walked into the other room, waiting to hear what he had to say. I sat in a chair near the hearth. It was chilly in my nightdress, and spring had yet to yield warmer temperatures. Adam's blond hair shone bright in the candlelight, his cheeks were pink from working outdoors.

"I think we should go home."

"We cannot go back. You sold our home, remember?"

"No." He shoved a cork in the jug and set it back in its place in Father's desk drawer. "I mean home to Mobile."

"What? This is our home now, Adam. We have no one to go back for. How can you suggest that we leave our parents?"

"Our parents are dead, Delilah. We have property in Alabama, did you know that? We retain ownership of the carpentry shop and the store— even though they are empty. I had an inquiry from a woman, a Miss Page, *who wants to buy them, but I can't part with them. We could do it—we could make something for ourselves."*

"What are you saying, Adam? Is the war over?"

"Yes, and Mobile is rebuilding. We should be there to help. I know you miss it! You often talk about it, the warm creeks, the hummingbirds, the blackberries."

"We aren't children anymore, Adam. We have a life here. How can we leave Uncle Lars and Aunt Aida now? After all they have done for us?"

"We have worked and earned what we have. Father left us very wealthy, Lila." He moved his chair closer to me. "Please, come with me."

"You sound as if you've made up your mind already. After weeks of not talking to me, of treating me like a stranger, you have the nerve to ask me to leave with you? What will you do, leave me in the wilderness somewhere?" Tears stung my eyes. How could I leave my parents behind? How could he ask me this? I would never be able to pull the weeds from their graves or visit them whenever I needed to talk.

"I love you, Delilah. With all my heart I love you." His blue eyes were full of pain, and I suddenly felt sorry for him. I squeezed his hand and kissed his cheek. How could I stay mad at my own brother? He was all the family I had now.

"I love you too, Adam. Tell me, what has been the matter? Why have you been so distant? Is it because of the war? You blame me, don't you?"

"It's not that. I can't talk about it. Please don't ask me to explain—I will one day, I promise."

That would have to do for now. Adam was an Iverson, stubborn through and through. Pressing him would only lead to more bickering. "If I agree to this, how soon would we leave?"

He smiled his beautiful smile as if he'd already won the argument. "It would take us a few weeks to settle our affairs here and to find passage south, and I would have to find a solicitor for our legal needs. Probably by the end of May, I would think."

"I haven't said yes yet. Let me sleep on it so that I may keep at least a shred of dignity." He hugged me, holding me close to him. I welcomed his embrace; it had been too long since we had been kind to one another. Suddenly, Adam kissed me tenderly on the neck and then released me. He walked out the door, and I watched him leave. He had never kissed me

before, much less in such a personal way, and I hardly knew what to think of it. I still remember that night. How I tossed and turned, how I dwelt upon that kiss.

The next morning, I rose early to prepare his breakfast. I tried not to see the eager look on his face, but I could see he wasn't going to allow me to avoid giving my answer. "Although I am loath to leave our family, I am willing to return to Mobile if you like, at least to settle our affairs there. I want you to promise me that if I choose to return, you will not stop me."

"Why should you return here? Has anyone asked for your hand?"

"No, of course not."

He smiled again and said, "Agreed. I shall tell Uncle Lars this morning after breakfast."

"Adam, if I had said no, would you have left anyway?" What prompted me to ask such a question, I do not know, but I did want to know his answer.

He poured a cup of dark coffee and stared at me. "Does it matter now? To Mobile and to our future!" He raised his cup to me and drank from it cheerfully. He chattered about details that did not concern me. Soon he left to see our uncle. Usually I would dress and go downstairs to help in the store. Sometimes my aunt needed help moving things, and I had a knack for selling. None of her daughters came to the shop except Elsa, the oldest. Her swollen belly kept her from helping now—her new baby would arrive very soon. That morning, I dawdled amongst our things, mentally making a list of what I would keep, what I would give to my aunt and what I truly didn't need.

Walking over to the rolltop desk, I rolled back the lid. My father had built the desk when he was a boy, and it still rolled smoothly. This I would take with me. I sat down on the cushioned chair and stared at the neatly stacked letters. Taking one in my hand, I ran my finger over the script, missing him more than I had in months. I didn't cry, but my heart broke to read his letters even though they were all business transactions. I read them all, and when I was through, I opened other drawers and found other stacks of letters. Again, many of these were business-related, but finally I found one that was not.

It was a worn envelope addressed to me. I had never seen it, nor had anyone ever read it to me.

Dear Delilah,

I call you this because I hear that is what your family calls you. My name is Dr. Hoyt Page. I am a physician living in Mobile, Alabama, and I am writing to inform you that you are my daughter. Forgive me for my bluntness, but as I am ill and not likely to live through the night, I feel a sense of urgency to reach out to my only living child.

As I have stated, I am your father. Your mother was Christine Beaumont Cottonwood..."

I couldn't believe what I was reading! Delilah was the baby! I immediately sent Ashland a text.

Big news in book! I'm going to keep reading, but I will come up and see you in about an hour. You still there??

A few seconds later he responded: *Yes, Detra Ann is stable now but still unconscious. I will be here.*

I scanned the waiting room. I could hardly believe this bombshell I was reading. Nobody paid me a bit of attention, which was great. I tucked in my headphones, tapped on an instrumental song on my phone and continued to read. I couldn't stop now!

Your mother was Christine Beaumont Cottonwood, and she died the night you were born. There is no way, my dear, to pretty up the facts. Christine was a married woman, married to a horrible man, Jeremiah Cottonwood, whom I recently killed. It was quite easy to do, as I have hated him for such a long time. I set upon him as he was riding drunk on his way home again to Seven Sisters. I stepped out of the shadows and shot him dead. Now he had paid for his crimes against your dear mother. The man was a monster and deserved his fate. I have avenged your mother's death, and soon I will join her. Please do not think too meanly of me to have done this deed—how could I allow him to go on living? In the case of your mother, justice moved too slowly for us all.

What else should I say to you except that I am sorry, truly sorry, for the misfortune that fate seems to have dealt you? You are the daughter of a Beaumont. That may not seem like much at the moment, but it is a special thing. You are also my daughter, the child of a prosperous doctor, and I have left everything I own to you. Won't my sister be surprised to learn about you! Your aunt, Claudette, is not a woman to be crossed, so be kind to her. Perhaps you can give her one of the houses I have bequeathed to you.

I wish we had had a different life, Christine and I, but it wasn't to be. We had our moment in the sun, and you are our proof that our love was real. You had a sister, Calpurnia, but she has been missing for nearly seventeen years. I cannot prove this, but I feel sure that Mr. Cottonwood killed her after your own dear mother died, knowing that Christine would have left your sister the heir to her fortune. I hope that somehow you will forgive me, forgive us, for not being the kind of people who could care for someone as special and lovely as you.

I imagine you often. I wonder if you like singing and playing music as Christine did, or maybe you prefer drawing, reading and writing as did your sister. I wish you were here so I could steal a look at you, as I did so many times when you were a child.

Please know that if I had believed the Iversons to be unsuitable people to serve as parents for my daughter, I would have taken you from them without a word or thought. But even I, a man who has never had a wife and family to call his own, could see that you were happy. I saw you many times, working in the shop and sometimes in attendance at church. I had hoped one day that you would return to Mobile to see me or that perhaps, once the war was over, I might go to see you, but such a visit is impossible now.

I love you more than I love my last breath. I love you more than I love even my own sister. I pray that you have a happy life. Think of me not as a vulgar man but as a fallible one who loved your mother and my children the best way I knew how.

Yours truly,
Your father,
Dr. Henry Hoyt Page

Can you imagine, Ernesto, what I felt as I read that letter? Knowing the truth forever changed me! I imagine some might feel betrayed to know that her parents were not her blood kin. Some women might feel angry at being pushed to the side so that her parents could continue their illicit affair undisturbed. Others might begrudge the inevitable title of "bastard," but I felt no shame about it.

No! I was free, Ernesto! Free like the Great Wind that blew through Shakespeare's plays. Free like a young colt that's discovered there is life outside the prison of the corral! Everything made sense now! I clutched the letter to my heart and spun about the room. I did not know this man who claimed to be my father; indeed, I did not even know if his words were true. I did know that now, more than anything else, I wanted to go to Mobile. I had to go and see what my true father had left me. I wanted to know about him and my mother. I would always love my Iverson family, but I was old enough now to know the truth about who I was! I truly was the "dark bird!" A bird of another flock!

But what about Adam? What did this mean for him? Was it my property he was thinking of claiming for himself? I tucked the letter in my dress pocket and continued to search. In the hidden compartment under the desk I found three more letters. One was from the Miss Page that Adam had spoken about. With shaking fingers I opened the letter and read it feverishly.

...wish to purchase the sundries store on Royal Street. Please let me know...

Thank God! How would I feel knowing that my own brother would be willing to steal from me, his sister? Wait! I was not his sister. We were raised as such, but there was not an ounce of Iverson blood in my body. And Adam, well, he was a Norwegian through and through. Suddenly, I heard him bounding up the stairs. He must have received a happy answer from our—his—uncle. He came into the room with a smile on his face, but it quickly faded as he saw the letter in my hand and the state of the desk.

"Adam," I whispered, unsure of what I wanted to say. He didn't ask any questions; he tossed his hat on the table and closed the door behind him. I walked toward him, Miss Page's letter in my hands. All of a sudden I knew the truth, the mind-blowing truth: I loved him. I loved him like a woman loves a man. By the kiss he had given me earlier, I knew he felt the same way. He knew the truth and had probably known for some time but had kept it from me.

I didn't know what I should say, so I said nothing at first. Then, with a trembling voice I said, "I know who I am now. I know that I am not your sister."

He nodded, looking relieved, his fair complexion an embarrassed pink. At last, the weight of the truth lifted off of him, but he didn't move. I knew that he would never care that some might call me bastard. He didn't care what anyone thought, and neither did I. For the first time, I kissed him. *Chastely at first and then passionately. It sounds strange, doesn't it, Ernesto? That I could so freely kiss a man whom I had previously considered my brother. It sounds strange and unholy to me even now, but I think we always knew.*

We did not kiss again after that, not for many weeks. We spent our time packing and preparing for our trip. I asked him one quiet evening while we sat in the nearly empty house how long he had known the truth. He confessed that he had always known, that he remembered the day I came to live with his family, a frail child who cried constantly. But it wasn't until recently that he realized he loved me. He had promised our mother that he would never tell me, but my discovery of the letter had freed him from that constraint.

Adam advised me to refrain from telling the Iversons about our relationship, for they would not approve. In the Old World, adopted children are considered blood kin. So we kept our secret and left with their blessing. I genuinely felt heartsick about leaving my aunt and her grandchildren.

I won't bore you, Ernesto, with the details of our trip. The days were long and tedious with too much riding and not enough walking. Adam treated me well, making sure that I was as comfortable as possible in whatever carriage, train or wagon we found ourselves in. However, he was still changeable. At times, he introduced me as his sister, at other times as his fiancée, although he had not actually proposed. It did not escape my notice that these "sister" introductions were typically made in the presence of other young women, women that Adam might have had an eye for.

Truth be told, I spent half the journey to the Gulf Coast not speaking to him. For two months we traveled and never did he kiss me again.

We arrived in Mobile on a Tuesday. The dirt streets in front of our shops were muddy, but from the wagon we could see that somehow the businesses had made it through the war without any missing walls or fallen roofs. "See! That's a sign!" Adam said excitedly. We looked for lodgings for the next few nights, as our plan was to live again in the apartment above our sundries store. We would have to paint, make small repairs and then set about the task of becoming reacquainted with the community. A daunting task if ever there was one! I shall never forget how hopeful Adam was—how sure he was that everything would be okay.

For my part, I was as nervous as a cat in a room full of rocking chairs! Besides the change in scenery, I faced the prospect of navigating the social community knowing the truth about my own parentage. I had to find my own solicitor, present my letter and proceed with claiming my inheritance. I didn't know Claudette Page, but what woman would want to hear the news that her brother had had a child out of wedlock—two, if you included my missing sister—who would be the heir to the fortune she thought she had inherited? As Adam tended to his legal affairs, I tended to mine. I found a lawyer named Mr. Peyton on Royal Street, not too far from our shop. With some surprise, he listened to my story and read the letter.

"How amazing! To think, I knew the man and never knew that he…well, I never knew he had a daughter."

"Two daughters. He has two daughters, Mr. Peyton."

"Well, technically, just one living heir. Calpurnia Cottonwood was declared dead years ago. Her inheritance from her mother was claimed by her father, or the man we believed was her father. How incredible!" He twisted his waxed mustache tips and stared with wide eyes. "I suppose you have something that would corroborate your story. A will, perhaps, or some other documentation."

The question surprised me. I had not expected that I would need to prove my identity. I confessed as much to the attorney.

"Let me speak frankly to you, my dear. This is quite a thing to present to a judge. He may not believe that this letter is from Dr. Page or that it is a true document. I am almost certain that before we proceed, we need something else. At least something that we can use to authenticate the handwriting."

"What? Who would make up such a thing? I would never…"

"I believe you. I am on your side, and I want you to have what belongs to you, but…well…have you met Claudette Page? Dr. Page's sister?"

"No, I haven't."

"There is no way that lady is going to lie down for this. Not for one minute! I have never met such an independent-minded woman, and she is most disagreeable. To top it all off, you'll be accusing her brother of a great lapse in virtue, a topic that is particularly important to the lady. She is one of our city's strongest advocates for 'greater Christian morality,' as she calls it. I heard a rumor—it can't be true, though—that even the local pastors *consult her before they preach their sermons. Apparently, they were becoming too liberal here for her liking."*

"She must be very influential to hold such sway over the community." I fiddled with my gloves, unsure what to do next. How could the man who claimed to be my father do this to me?

"Still, if Hoyt—I mean, Dr. Page—took the trouble to send you this letter, then chances are he made some record of it somewhere. I'll check with the courthouse to see if there is anything useful there. My friend Mr. Schumacher is the director of our bank. I can inquire with him about any accounts or safety deposit boxes. If we cannot produce supporting documents, we will have no choice but to meet with Miss Page personally. I am sure she would want to avoid a scandal, so that should work in our favor."

"I don't wish to cause a scandal, and I'm not here to take anything that's not mine, Mr. Peyton. I confess I am just as surprised about all this as anyone else is." I paused and then asked the question I was dying to ask. *"What do you know about my mother and sister?"*

"Until today, I would have sworn that Christine Beaumont was a saint. Never had a bad word to say about anyone, and she lived with the devil himself! I don't blame her too harshly for wanting to find some happiness in this world outside that cold fish of a husband. However, as your attorney, I advise you to keep that letter to yourself. No one, not even Miss Page, needs to read Hoyt's confession."

"I will keep it to myself." He rose to see me out, but I had one more question. *"What about Calpurnia? What can you tell me about her?"*

"I didn't know her personally, but I did attend her coming-out party. My son Gerald was quite taken with her, but unfortunately for him, she showed no interest. I do remember she was very shy, some might even say bookish, but still a lovely young woman. You look very much like her. Yes, if anyone saw you, they might look twice. That might help your case, Miss Iverson—I mean, Miss Page."

I rose to my feet smiling. I liked the sound of my true name. *"I will leave this to you then, Mr. Peyton. My brother and I are staying at the Iverson Sundries Store."*

"Oh yes! I'll be in touch soon."

I walked back to the store and set about cleaning the place. What would my parents think about all this? I tried not to think about it.

Maybe it was best that I gave it up—left the name behind and spent the rest of my days as an Iverson. It was certainly something I needed to think about. As I swept up the dust, thinking and stewing over the fact that Adam was gone yet again, a shadow darkened my doorway. A woman dressed in black from head to toe blocked the sunlight, her tall, lace-lined bonnet adding height to her already imposing figure. I raised a hand to my eyes and asked, "May I help you, madam? Our store isn't open yet, but if you'd like to place an order for something specific…"

She walked in and untied the bow under her chin. With an unimpressed expression, she looked around the store and then finally at me. "Delilah Iverson, I presume?"

"Yes. May I help you?" I smiled at the sunlit figure.

"I was just getting to know your brother at the carpentry shop. We haven't been properly introduced. My name is Claudette—Claudette Page." She didn't offer me a hand of friendship or even a smile. She held her bonnet to her as if she were afraid that the dust might soil her hat beyond repair. As she stepped out of the light, I could see her features more clearly now. She had pale skin, carefully curled black hair and full lips. I imagined at one time she had been an attractive woman but never one prone to smiling.

"Miss Page, nice to meet you. May I help you?"

"Are you or are you not Delilah Iverson?" So the swords were sharpening, were they? Miss Page did not know me if she thought I would be cowed by her unfriendly attitude. I knew who she was but not why she was here.

"That depends on who you ask, Miss Page."

"You have the look of your mother," she said as she stared around the room at the crates and boxes.

I didn't know what to say. Who was I to argue with such an observation? I had never laid eyes on my mother. I felt my chin rise and I clung to my broom handle, fighting the urge to hit her with it repeatedly. "The nature of your visit confuses me, Miss Page."

"Oh, I just wanted to have a look around."

"I see," I said.

"You know, I wrote to your brother while you were in Canada. I offered to buy this place so you wouldn't have to come all this way. I mean, the economy here isn't what it used to be. You might find it difficult to turn

a profit, Miss Iverson. Mobile already has a sundries shop. Do we really need two?"

"A little competition is good for the economy, at least that's what I've read. Do you have a different theory?"

"Yes, I have a theory. I think you're an opportunist, Miss Iverson. Your coward brother ran from the war, and now the two of you are back to exploit the hardworking people of Mobile. But I won't let you do that!"

"How dare you talk about my brother in such an offensive manner! My brother is no coward!"

"So you see how it is then." Her voice was like sharpened steel. "I care for my brother as you care for yours. Why sully Hoyt's name now that he's gone, now that he's dead. Let sleeping dogs lie, Miss Iverson, and I'll do the same for you."

"Are you threatening me, Miss Page?"

Another shadow appeared in the back door. It was Adam!

"Come now. Do I need to threaten such a sensible girl as yourself? Lay down your claim to my brother, and I will do the same for yours."

Adam walked into the shop from the stockroom, shock written all over his face. "What? What claim are you referring to, Miss Page?"

"Isn't it interesting that when the war came to our fair city, you were nowhere to be found?" Adam's face turned beet red, and he walked to the half-open door and held it open. "If Miss Iverson leaves her ridiculous claim at the courthouse door, I will keep my opinions to myself. No one has to know that you were a coward, Adam."

"How dare you!" My voice rose in anger. "Get out of my store! I will make no such promise! Who do you think you are that you can come here and threaten me—threaten us? Get out!" She stomped out, leaving us alone. I turned to Adam, but the damage was already done.

All his hopes were dashed now—his male Norwegian pride crushed like flowers under a bootheel. His worst fears were realized. The gossip had begun—Adam Iverson was a coward. Adam Iverson was yellow. I could hear his imagination at work already.

"Adam!" I called after him, but I didn't see him until late that evening. And so it was for two weeks until I heard again from my attorney...

I forced myself to close the small, worn book. I didn't have time to focus on another mystery like what happened to Delilah

Iverson. Detra Ann was fighting for her life, and the gravity of the situation became very real to me. I needed to help my friend.

Finally, I knew how I could do it.

Chapter 16

Cynthia Dowd walked out of the tiny hospital bathroom and gasped.

"Oh, I'm sorry. I didn't mean to startle you. How is she?"

With a worried expression, she glanced at her comatose daughter and whispered, "I think she's doing better. See, she's got color in her cheeks this evening. I think she knows we are here, don't you?"

I politely agreed with her and followed her back to Detra Ann's bedside. I sat in the noisy pleather seat and tried to be quiet. I needed Cynthia to leave—this would be dangerous, but I had to do it. Making contact with Detra Ann could only help. At least that's what I believed. Since Cynthia was whispering, I whispered to her, "Have you seen Ashland and TD?"

"Yes, they went to grab a bite to eat. Ashland told me he wanted to bring you something too. You must have just missed him. They went to Jumpers for takeout. They'll be back soon."

"What about you, Cynthia? Don't you need to eat something?"

"No, I can't eat. Not while she's like this."

I sighed. "Yes, I can see that." I sat quietly again, trying to work out how I could get her out of here. I needed to be alone with Detra Ann, and I needed enough time to fall asleep and make contact with her. I prayed that I wasn't making a terrible mistake by attempting this.

She leaned back in the seat beside me and said with a smile, "Wasn't it nice that the ladies came to see me this morning?"

"Yes, very nice indeed. Bette seems to truly care about you." Bette! As discreetly as I could I reached for my phone and texted her while Cynthia sat staring at her daughter.

Bette, this is Nancy Drew. I need your help. Can you come to the hospital? I need to get Cynthia out of the room.

My "Nancy Drew" reference was an observation that Detective Simmons had made about Bette and me during the Mia incident. She'd called us Angela Lansbury and Nancy Drew. It had tickled Bette tremendously.

On the way. What do you have in mind?
Can't share now but it's crucial. Please help.
Roger that.

Bette added a smiley face and I tapped one back. For the next fifteen minutes, I chitchatted with Cynthia as she talked about Detra Ann's last beauty pageant, how she'd shocked the committee by performing "Dixie" on her flute while leading her white poodle through an obstacle course. It was quite humorous to hear, and I was sure that Detra Ann would be mortified that her mother would tell such childhood secrets.

The door opened, but it wasn't Bette. Ashland and TD were back with food. "There you are," Ashland said. "What's up with not answering your phone?" I checked it and noticed his two messages.

"Oops, sorry. I don't know how I missed those," I whispered.

"Why are we whispering?" Ashland asked me, but it was Cynthia who answered.

"Because she's asleep. She'll wake up when she's ready. Now you boys go out in the hall and let her rest a while."

"Hey, everybody!" Bette missed the speech about whispering, but Cynthia didn't say a word to her. "How is our princess doing, Cynthia? Oh, look at her. I think I see color in those pretty cheeks. I'd say she's on the mend. Have the doctors come in recently?"

"They won't be in until morning."

"You know what? You don't look so hot, Cynthia. I mean, you look pale, darling." I loved the way Bette said "darling." It was the long drawn out version, "daw-lin." It just kind of lingered there.

"I don't care what I look like right now."

"I'm not talking about your gorgeous face, Cynth. You can't neglect your health right now. Not when Detra Ann is going to need you so much. When was the last time you had some fresh air?"

"I don't know. This morning, maybe?"

"I tell you what, let's go for a walk. Maybe visit the gift shop and find her some flowers. She'll like seeing those when she wakes up."

"No, Bette! I can't leave her. What happens if she wakes up and I'm not here?"

"You won't be gone long, and Carrie Jo is here. You can trust her to stay, right?"

"Oh, yes, ma'am. I'll stay. Ashland brought me some food, and I have a pillow and blanket. Take all the time you want."

"I won't be gone long, though," Cynthia said, stretching her back before she walked over to the mirror. She stared at herself disapprovingly. I felt bad for manipulating her, but I needed her to leave. Ashland watched the whole thing quietly and didn't interfere, but he knew something was up. I'd have to explain what I was doing. That would be tricky.

Bette kept her game face on as they left and didn't give a clue that I had called her. Now that was a true friend. I would have to thank her somehow later.

"What's up, beautiful? You're up to something. You might as well tell me now."

"Yes, I am up to something." I arranged the pillow and blanket in the chair next to Detra Ann. I reached over and held her hand lovingly. Through tear-filled eyes, I stared at her perfect pink manicured nails. She'd tried to help me, to save me from something in my house—probably Isla—and now she was trapped, trapped in another world. I had to go help her. Suddenly awareness crept across Ashland's face.

"No, Carrie Jo. This isn't a good idea! What happens if you make contact with her and then you're in a coma too?"

TD broke in, "Wait! Ashland's right. Detra Ann wouldn't want that."

"I have my friend's hand, that's all. I'm tired and am going to take a nap now. If I see her, I will talk to her, maybe get her to come back to us."

"You can do that?" TD sounded unsure but willing to give it a shot if it brought Detra Ann back to him.

"I've never done it before, TD, but I would like to try. With all my heart I will try. She loves you so much. I can't imagine that she'd want to be too far away from you."

"Ashland, I don't want to put her in danger, but if she can find her…"

"I know. Okay, Carrie Jo. I guess it's okay, not that you needed my permission. I know you. You would have done it anyway."

"I sure would have. Now turn out the light, please, and try to keep the nurses occupied for the next thirty minutes."

"Sure, but I am going to be right outside. If I hear something, I am coming in."

"Fair enough."

Ashland turned off the light and held onto the doorknob for a minute. I smiled at him to reassure him and then closed my eyes. Sleep didn't come immediately; there were too many distractions. To make matters worse, I could hear Henri's deep, booming voice in the hallway. He'd come! But I had to focus on Detra Ann.

Detra Ann, where are you? Why won't you come back to us?

I rubbed her hand gently, just like my mother would do for me when I was sick as a child, before she became sick herself. It had always comforted me; hopefully it would help me make a connection with Detra Ann.

All of a sudden, I stepped out of reality and into the dream world, and what I saw terrified me. I wasn't holding the hand of beautiful, tanned Detra Ann—I was holding the hand of Christine Beaumont!

I looked down at Christine, only I wasn't a character in a dream or some ghost from the past—I was me! Wrapped around her arms and legs were black snake-like cords that held her in place. "Help me! They won't let me go!" I stared, but only for a moment. A disturbing sound from the hallway, like a demonic train, shook the building and threatened to bust through the wall. I began to furiously untie the cords and free her from the hospital bed. At first, I didn't think I could release her, but suddenly the cords fell off. She sat up in the bed and put her arms around me.

"You can see me! You have to help me! He won't let me go! Where is Hoyt? Hurry!"

With frightened fingers I untied the last tie. "I will help you, Christine—but where is my friend, Detra Ann? I have to know!" The crashing train noise ceased, and suddenly the room became foggy so quickly that I could barely see Christine. But I didn't release her hand, and she clung to mine. She slid off the bed, her full skirts rustling as she did. The gray fog cleared and she stared at me, then recognition crossed her face. She squeezed my hand even tighter—I thought she would hug me again.

"I don't understand how you are here, my own dearest. How I have missed you! Please help me! Oh no! They're here, Calpurnia—run!" she sobbed. Her brow beaded with sweat, and her dark blond hair became wet with it.

I pulled on her hand. "I'm not Calpurnia. I'm Carrie Jo. What about Detra Ann? Where is she?"

"We have to go now, Isla is coming—my tormentor, the one who tied me here!" The door blew open, and the sound of a thousand angry invisible bees filled the room. It was the same sound I'd heard in the Moonlight Garden the night Ashland, TD and I defeated Isla—or thought we had.

"Christine! Where are you going? I've only just begun to play with you. So happy that Calpurnia could join us," Isla purred, her perfect blond ringlets bouncing against her cherubic cheeks.

"I'm not Calpurnia!" I shouted, but who was going to hear me over the furious noise? Christine tugged on my hand, and we ran pell-mell down the hallway to the back wall. I screamed, preparing for the pain of running into the wall, but nothing happened. Instead I opened my eyes to find myself and Christine standing in the ballroom of Seven Sisters.

A lone candelabrum provided light in the dreary blackness that surrounded us. Catching my breath—I thankfully still had breath—I noticed a figure walking toward us. It was Jeremiah

Cottonwood. He wore all black except for shiny silver coat buttons that glittered in the dimness. He looked as if he were going to a funeral, and then it occurred to me that this was how he must have been dressed for his own funeral. Hoyt Page had killed him over a hundred and fifty years ago.

"Christine, daughter...how nice of you to come to my party. More guests will be arriving soon. Come closer and embrace me." He stretched out his arms to us with a devilish smile, and I noticed that the tiny silver buttons weren't buttons at all but spiders that fell off his velvet suit and scrambled across the hardwood floor. I shuddered at the sight.

"Stay away from us, Jeremiah."

His evil smile vanished, his mouth opened and an unearthly scream rose—it penetrated my very bones. "I'm alive! I'm still alive," I kept telling myself. I hoped it was true. How could I be here?

Still, Christine squeezed my hand. "We have each other now, Calpurnia, and nothing will stop us from going to our peace. Nothing! Step aside, Jeremiah! Your curse has been broken."

He did not move but stared at us, his neck bent down, his head tilted up. The evil smile had returned, and his dark eyes shimmered strangely. He observed us like an animal would, an animal stalking its prey.

Fearlessly, Christine continued. She walked around him with sure steps, never letting go of my hand. "Remember the words you whispered in my ear the night you killed me? You cursed me. You said no one would ever love me again, not now and not for eternity." She stepped toward him bravely, ignoring his angry, purple face and the beastly, guttural sounds he made. "You are a liar! I am loved!"

"I loved you!"

She smiled at him. "Yes, I remember how you loved me, Jeremiah. I remember how you slid the rope around my neck. I remember how you tightened it and raised me from the ground until I swung higher and higher. Oh yes, I remember your love! You exacted your revenge and stole my life, and now you think you can keep me in death too? What justice is that? I will be free!"

"What do you know of love, Christine?" He hissed at her.

"You condemned me and then killed me, but what you didn't know was that you set me free. Free from you who cannot love!"

"Don't speak to me about love, harlot!"

"Call me what you will, but I have love. My daughter loves me! The power of our love breaks your curse, Jeremiah!"

"But I'm not..." I started to explain myself, but then the invisible bees began to circle me again. It was Isla, here to serve Jeremiah, to see to it that he exacted his revenge on us for all eternity. Briefly I wondered what debt she was paying by serving him in death, for I knew in life she cared nothing for him. He had been amusing to her and, like most men, a means to whatever end she imagined or schemed.

"What kind of fool do you take me for, Christine? This is not Calpurnia, your bastard daughter."

Suddenly, Jeremiah reached for Christine with a gnarled hand and snatched her viciously from my grip with such force that I fell backward. He slid his arm around her neck. The look of fear had returned to her face, and I could see her surprise. She'd failed. How could she have confused me for Calpurnia?

Whatever the reason, I had failed Christine. And I had failed Detra Ann.

"This can't be," she yelled. "Calpurnia?"

"You are mine, Christine! And now another has come to join our party! Bring in our guest, Isla." Isla stepped out of the outer darkness and with a wave of her hands made candlelight appear around the room—it looked just as it had the night of her coming-out party. Wax candles burned bright, an orchestra played in the corner of the room and black-clad dancers took their places on the floor. My skin felt cold and clammy, as if death were nearby. It was, wasn't it? She wore a purple dress with white ribbons at the sleeves, and her invisible hemline never touched the ground.

I couldn't be here! I couldn't be! How is this even possible?

"Hoyt!" I heard Christine scream with all her might. "Hoyt! Help me, my love!"

I swung my head to the door and wanted to run to him but couldn't get up. I suddenly felt heavy, as if my limbs were covered with concrete. I couldn't move or get up—only helplessly watch whatever was about to happen. *Oh my God! That's TD! Why can't she see it's Terrence Dale and not Hoyt Page?*

"I'm here, Christine." Then, TD wasn't TD anymore. He was taller, thinner with darker hair, and he wore a tailored brown suit. "I failed you before, but I will not fail you now, my love. Come to me. Let her go, Cottonwood. You have no claim on her."

She wrangled free from Jeremiah but only for a second. Grinning, Cottonwood slid his arm around her neck again and said savagely, "She's mine, Page. She always will be mine. You may have her heart, but I have a covenant that cannot be broken, the covenant of marriage. I am on the side of right."

Hoyt stormed toward Jeremiah, determined to rescue Christine, but he ran into the invisible force that Isla seemed to manipulate so easily with just her hands.

"Isla! Stop this! How can you let him use you like this?" I pleaded with her. I was desperate.

She giggled and pressed her hands together, a move that forced me almost flat to the hardwood floor.

"How can you set her free, Page? See, she is mine still."

"You are a murderer! You murdered Christine. You are an unjust man, and you have no right to keep her here! You would have killed our daughter too, if I had allowed it. I saved her, Christine. I saved Delilah!"

"Let me go, Jeremiah. Please I beg you." Christine struggled less now, and I could see that she was giving up. "Don't keep me here anymore. I can't bear it. I want to be with Hoyt and my children."

"Did you think that I didn't know about you and Hoyt, about your bastard children—the ones you tried to pass off as mine? What a fine game player you were, dear! Granted it took me years to discover that Calpurnia was his ill-begotten stock, but once I knew, everything changed. You stole that from me! I will never let you leave, not now—not ever!"

"Christine! Christine! Come to me now! Please! Before it's too late!" Hoyt cried out from his knees. Isla whirled around us, and this time she sailed by so close that I could smell honeysuckle and something else...death. I could feel her excitement as she waited to kill me.

"I can't, he won't let me go! It's no use, Hoyt," Christine cried pitifully. For a second, her face faded—I could plainly see Detra Ann! Jeremiah was holding Detra Ann!

"Fight, Detra Ann! Fight!" My friend struggled with renewed vigor, but it lasted only a few seconds.

Isla growled, but I continued to shout, "Fight! You are not Christine, you are Detra Ann Dowd. You are my friend, and I care about you! Now fight, damn it!"

Jeremiah seemed confused, but then Detra Ann's face disappeared and it was just Christine again, crying hopelessly.

"Let her go, Jeremiah! She's not Christine!" Finally, I could stand. I reached for Hoyt and helped him up too. A swell of terrible music rose in the ballroom, and the once-frozen dancers began to dance around us. The stale air moved like a brewing storm.

"You are a guest in my house now, my dear. Please join the dance," Jeremiah said, squeezing Detra Ann's neck, choking the life from her.

"NO! Detra Ann! TD, do something!" I screamed as a faceless man in a black suit whipped his arm around my waist and spun me about, lifting me a few feet from the ground. We danced in a circle, his invisible hand on my waist, pulling me tighter and tighter.

"Calpurnia, my darling," he whispered. I recognized that voice! David Garrett! He was here too, trapped with everyone else! It took everything I had not to scream my head off as I struggled between my fear of falling to the ground and my terror at being held by this faceless ghoul.

The doors opened again, and the dancers froze to see who else had arrived. It was Bette!

I gasped and then screamed at the top of my lungs, "Bette! Run! Leave before it's too late!" But she didn't appear to hear me. The ghost that held me swirled us back to the ground, and I violently pushed away from him. I made my way through the dancers—I had to get to Bette!

"Let her go!" she commanded Jeremiah. "Now!" Bette stepped toward Christine as he visibly released his hold on her. Then the oddest thing happened—Bette transformed before my very eyes. Her perfect puffs of white curls grew, and her hair darkened to a lustrous dark brown. She appeared tall and thin, like Hoyt. In a flash, her blue capris with the yellow daisies all over were replaced with a flowing pink and white gown and a lovely white hat with a soft ivory-colored feather. She walked toward the center of the room and stood between Hoyt and Jeremiah. The bees went silent, and I noticed that even Isla slid as far away from Bette as she could. Fear, which had been tangible and sovereign just moments ago, fled into the shadows like a wild animal along with Isla and her cohorts. Peace filled the room. I alone stood out from the darkness. Hoyt (or TD, I wasn't sure which) was only a few feet away from me. He watched with a rapt expression of pure love.

Bette wasn't Bette. She was young and beautiful—she was Delilah Iverson.

"Can it be?" Christine's hand flew to her chest, and she took a step away from Jeremiah. He did not reach for her again. I noticed that he too had retreated a little.

"Yes, Mother. I am Delilah, your daughter. I am here to take you home."

In one bold move, Christine covered the distance between them and embraced her tightly. After a moment, Delilah stepped away, touching her arm as she walked toward Jeremiah. His typical haughty expression had vanished, replaced with a look of abject despair and anger.

"My mother doesn't belong to you anymore. You were wrong—she is loved. I love her, just as my sister loves her. We are leaving here now, Jeremiah Cottonwood, and don't think to stop us."

He backed away as a light surrounded her. I couldn't explain it, but love shone through her like a big bright candle. No. Like a star.

Arm in arm, they walked toward the outside door. Another light, brighter and bigger than even Delilah, shone brilliantly. As the door swung open, that light filled the ballroom in a flash.

Hoyt stumbled after them, pleading, "You can't leave me again, Christine. I love you and always will. Don't leave me now."

Christine paused on the garden path and gave him a beautiful smile. She reached out her hand, and he ran to her.

"Wait! TD! You can't go!" I cried out, unsure what to think about what was happening. I watched their glowing figures walk through the Moonlight Garden, Delilah on the right, Hoyt on the left and Christine in the middle. I didn't dare take my eyes off of them, but I could "feel" the others around me disappearing into nothingness.

Instead of giggling, I heard Isla crying. Crying that her life and afterlife were now completely over. She would go down into the grave and be gone forever.

Worm food now, I suppose…

Jeremiah didn't whimper or wail, but simply slid into a small black hole that appeared in the floor. He didn't even make a sound as he slipped away down into the abyss. The hole closed, leaving only a small scorch mark on the floor.

I looked back up and saw the three lights, Delilah, Christine and Hoyt, fading away into the dark night. They were together at last. I wondered if they would simply go to sleep or if they would have time, their time—the time that was stolen from them. I didn't know. I hoped they found Calpurnia waiting wherever they were going.

I sat on the hardwood floor and cried my eyes out.

Epilogue

Ashland and Carrie Jo stepped out onto the dais and faced the excited crowd. It was springtime in Mobile, bright and cool—the perfect day for unveiling the new Bette Marshall Museum and the Terrence Dale House. The new museum housed the extension of the Seven Sisters art collection, while the Dale House was the rebuilt slave quarters, reconstructed according to TD's plans. It had been next on his list after restoring the Moonlight Garden. Ashland and TD had wanted to restore the plantation to be as historically accurate as they could make it, and this addition would do just that. Carrie Jo had commissioned a painting of Muncie that now hung in the foyer of the Marshall Museum. It was one of my favorite places to visit.

I wondered what our missing friends would think about the honors we bestowed upon them today. I wondered if TD remembered me—I liked to imagine that he did. I thought about him every day. At first, he was all I could think about. How could he have simply walked out of the hospital and disappeared? But slowly, the space between the crashing waves of grief grew, and eventually I found the strength to continue. But my future was forever changed by his absence.

Ashland made his speech, and the crowd applauded. I watched Carrie Jo as she stood smiling by his side. Funny how close we were now. She was like the sister I never had. I couldn't imagine life without her, and I would forever be in her debt for what she did.

"But none of this would be possible without the help of Detra Ann Dowd, the director of the Seven Sisters Living Museum. Please make her welcome." The crowd again applauded, and I solemnly took the podium. I closed my eyes for a second and let the sunlight beam down on me. We'd worked like dogs to make this happen in such a short time, but at least it was done. These weren't just important landmarks and museums. They were memorials to our friends.

It was the least we could do.

According to the papers, Bette Marshall had died of a sudden heart attack in her home. TD had simply disappeared. For a while, rumors circulated that he'd fallen off the wagon again, but when he didn't reappear, everyone changed their mind. I knew the truth. So did Ashland, Henri and Carrie Jo. That was all that mattered.

"Thank you, everyone, for your support throughout this process. Special thanks to the Historical Society for your tireless commitment to Seven Sisters…." I read my notes and tried to keep a smile in my voice. I thought I did okay. When my speech was finished, I took a seat on the dais. Carrie Jo reached for my hand and squeezed it. Suddenly, I missed TD so badly that I almost cried. I squeezed her hand back, and she didn't let go. I was glad for that.

When the ceremony ended, we stepped off the dais and I fell into Henri's big arms. He'd become a dear friend to me these past six months. I was glad that he had decided to move back to Mobile. Within a month, he'd purchased the Cotton City Treasures antiques store, and I'd spent a bit of time there helping him set up his displays. It was peaceful work, and he seemed to value my opinion. Despite what some of the wagging tongues might think, we weren't romantically involved. But I cared deeply for him.

We spent the next thirty minutes greeting visitors and answering questions. When it was over, I gave a sigh of relief. I was leaving Seven Sisters at the end of the month. My assistant, Rachel Kowalski, was taking over the directorship. I knew I was leaving the house in good hands. Of that, I had no worries. I'd given enough to the house. We all had.

It was time to leave the past behind…time to say goodbye to Seven Sisters. I took a walk through the Moonlight Garden. I touched the flowers and breathed in the scent of magnolias and roses. I picked a few petals off the ground and walked to the Atlas fountain.

"Goodbye, TD." I tossed the petals into the water and watched them spin wildly and then slowly sink to the bottom.

I turned my face to the sun once more and felt peace wash over me. I couldn't say for sure, but in that moment I believed he heard me.

For the last time, I walked out of the maze and back to the house. Henri, Ashland and Carrie Jo waited for me. We walked through the house and closed the door behind us.

We didn't look back.

The Stars We Walked Upon
By M.L. Bullock

This book is dedicated to all the fans of the *Seven Sisters* series. Thank you for walking through the Blue Room and strolling down the shady paths of the Moonlight Garden with me. May you have many dreams, and may they all come true.

O Stars and Dreams and Gentle Night;
O Night and Stars return!
And hide me from the hostile light
That does not warm, but burn
That drains the blood of suffering men;
Drinks tears, instead of dew:
Let me sleep through his blinding reign,
And only wake with you!
—Emily Bronte
Excerpt from "Stars"

Prologue

Mobile, AL, 1851

Sunlight splashed through the tall conservatory windows, and I leaned back in the comfortable parlor chair, a glass of brandy in my hand. I closed my eyes, allowing the music to carry me to places far and away. The sound of the piano lent to the illusion of sanity and comfort, two things perpetually absent from my world of escalating darkness. The notes were light and choppy and full of happiness. If I allowed myself to, I could imagine I was in the music room of some talented debutante hoping to impress me, the elegant Captain David Garrett.

How many times had this been the case? How many musical recitals had been performed for me?

Sipping my brandy, I scanned through the memories with pleasure. The first face I recalled was that of the delightful Katrina Phelps, the daughter of Christian and Mary Beth Phelps of Savannah, Georgia. A pretty thing with light brown eyes, a sharp, clever wit and a sultry voice, a voice too sultry for one so young. Still, as charming as her face and figure were, she had not yielded to my ardent desire despite my best efforts to persuade her. The Phelps family welcomed me into their particular society; that is until that wretched letter arrived. And then Katrina was lost to me.

Ah, but there was always a fly in the ointment. One sour spinster who could not or would not leave the past alone. Yes, the past was my constant companion. I shook the memory of Miss Phelps and her tearstained face away. How she cried over me! At the time, I believed that I loved her—imagine that!

Oh yes, then there was Miss Virginia Lewis. The mother was so keen to make my acquaintance that I barely knew whom to seduce—the mother or the daughter. However, after meeting the woman's husband, I decided that the latter would suffice. Unlike many of the maidens I dabbled with, I had not been able to control myself, so willing was she. I did partake of the young woman's delights and so perhaps deserved the disdain of Red Hills' society, but in the end, what did I care? Red Hills was no Savannah, nor Charleston nor even a Mobile. It was merely a farm community, and Miss Virginia Lewis nothing more than a glamorous wealthy farm girl with hefty arms, pink cheeks and skin that tasted like butter. My cheeks warmed at the thought of her, or perhaps it was the brandy. I smiled remembering our times together in the milk shed, the store cupboard, the floor of the carriage. But I had been a much younger man then, just hitting my prime.

The piano's notes climbed higher and the music became lighter. I yielded myself to the tune, pausing only to sip the decadent drink in my crystal glass. I felt as if the notes could almost carry me to heaven—it was probably as close to that holy place as I could ever hope to reach.

Especially after what happened to Miss Cottonwood. Dear, sweet, gentle Miss Cottonwood. Now she had been a true lady. *That had not been entirely my fault.* The girl must have been out of her mind to seek me aboard the Delta Queen—or been encouraged to do so by someone other than me. With slitted eyes I observed my nude piano player. Loose coils of long blond hair hung down her back and stuck to her skin. How she sweated when we made love! She was no pasty-faced farm girl happy to endure whatever pleased me. No, she was an active participant—curious, hungry and eager to please and be pleased. It occurred to me that I should love her. After all, we were bound together in a dark world of our own making; perhaps I did love her in my own perverse way.

Although I told myself that she was the bane of my existence I admired her ambition, her skilled depravities. How I loved her constant scheming—her spirited aspirations far exceeded mine. She was like that biblical hussy Jezebel, and she deserved to be thrown out of the tower. I was the doomed Ahab.

I knew all this, and yet I was her slave.

Suddenly the piano made a crashing noise as her hands slammed down on the keys. Quick as a flash she was off her tufted stool and standing before me. Her damp tresses covered her goblet-shaped breasts.

"What are you thinking? I demand you tell me!"

As subtly as I could, I glanced at her hands to make sure that they held no object that might injure me, for my love had a deadly temper. Seeing no scissors, knitting needles or any other type of blade, I smiled at her peacefully.

"I think of nothing but you, my love. What else should I think of?"

"You're a fool! Tell me you're not thinking of her!" Her hands went to the curve of her naked hips, and she stared at me with unbelieving eyes.

"Calm down, dearest. Sit in my lap. Let us talk of the future—not the past. You promised, remember?"

I could see the struggle in her eyes as she gave in to my request and smiled that catlike smile. Her arms snaked about my neck, and her frame was as light as a feather as she perched in my lap. With insincere calmness I stroked her hair as she plunged her hand in my open shirt and rubbed my chest lightly. "Now. Where shall we go next, darling?" I spoke carefully in soothing tones. "To Paris? Perhaps to Boston? Where shall I take you?" She kissed my neck with her childlike lips—lips that always tasted of lemonade. How she loved the drink! "Nectar of the gods," she called it as she added ridiculous amounts of gin into her glass.

"I want to see *all* of those places, my darling captain. All of them! But we must wait a little while."

I wondered what plan she had concocted in her feverish brain. Isla Beaumont rarely kept me in mind when she planned a scheme. Why should today be any different? She took my hand with her small one and kissed it. "Good news, my love. I am with child."

I was shocked into silence. I weighed her mood to determine how to proceed.

"Isn't that delightful?"

I responded with a confident smile. "If you are happy, I am happy. I must say I have never considered myself a family man. My, how you have changed me."

She giggled. "Oh no, darling. I am quite sure that I am carrying a Cottonwood. A long-awaited boy for Jeremiah Cottonwood. Won't he be delighted to hear the news that he will finally have a son!" She hopped out of my lap and spun about as if she were in the ballroom.

It was my turn to laugh. The whole thing seemed so outlandish I could not wrap my mind around it. "You and Cottonwood? Tell me, my clever love. How did you ever manage that? It was my understanding that the man had no appreciation for young beauties such as yourself, not of the female persuasion."

She curtsied graciously, lifting the edges of a pretend dress. "Never underestimate my skills. That would be a mistake. He was like clay in my hands." She giggled again and pretended to hide a nonexistent blush.

I raised my glass to her and said, "Well done."

She frowned. "You do not seem as pleased as I imagined you would be. Isn't this the cleverest thing? Just think. In a few months we will have what we wanted—Seven Sisters! Oh, and that is just the beginning! Imagine me with a fat little baby and all that money. Won't that be funny?"

"Not to doubt your amazing ability to make men do whatever you desire, but what makes you believe that Mr. Cottonwood will welcome this news? We all know that man is an evil-tempered drunk."

"I have it all planned out."

"I had no doubt of that."

"You must trust me, dear Captain. I will tell you more later, but now I need a distraction—a 'faveur discrète'. Let us go upstairs and celebrate!"

I swirled the rest of my brandy and tossed it down my throat. The warmth of it invigorated me. Now wasn't the time to consider the meaning of all this. I would do that when she slept—whenever she slept. Sometimes she would not sleep for days. I pulled her close to me and stared down into her cherub-like face. How could such a face hide such a mind?

"You are full of surprises, my sweet one."

"Happy surprises?" Her coy look stirred my loins.

"Are there any other kind?" I scooped her up in my arms. She kissed my neck as I stepped over the body of our hostess. I accidentally kicked her and foolishly offered an "Excuse me."

To that, she giggled again. "David," she whispered in my ear, "Lennie Ree can't hear you. She's dead."

By the time we made it upstairs, I was nearly naked and completely hers.

***

Hours later I slipped out of our stolen bed to go downstairs in search of food. I was thinking not only for myself but also for my beloved, who was always ravenous after a murder. Now that she was with child, I was sure she would be even hungrier. But I needed food myself too. This was no small house—surely there would be something hidden in a larder somewhere. Maybe even some lemonade for my Isla.

Being the lover of the demanding, demented cherub took a lot of energy, and I needed to build my strength. I walked down the stairs holding up my trousers with one hand and whistling. I paused at the bottom step to give a respectful nod to our dead hostess. Just as I stepped over her the front door opened—there was nowhere to hide. The housekeeper, a tall, thin woman dressed in all black, did not see me at first. She set her basket down on the entryway table and left her purse there while she removed her plain black hat. I could see by her demeanor she was not someone to be trifled with—a no-nonsense kind of woman.

I decided to take the bull by the horns. Some women preferred to be charmed into doing whatever it was I wanted them to do; others preferred the direct approach. I chose the second option and hoped for the right results. If she failed to amuse me, then of course we would simply have to kill her too.

"And who might you be?" I asked in a commanding voice.

The woman appeared calm, not shocked in the least by what she saw or by my question. She had not run out the door, which she very well could have. Out of respect, I buttoned my trousers and my open shirt.

"Docie Loxley is my name. I am the housekeeper."

"Well, Miss Loxley, it appears that my hostess has had an accident and died."

"That much I see, and it is a shame. I have not been paid in six months. Who's going to give me my wages now?" She walked toward the stiff body of Lennie Ree Meadows and touched her with the toe of her black boot as if she wanted to make sure she was dead. She needn't have bothered.

Isla said from behind me, "We should bury her. But somewhere where dogs won't find her. You don't want the dead to come back. They smell awful." She hopped on my back as if she were a child and I a child's party entertainer. I did not argue but gave her a piggyback ride up and down the stairs. Isla giggled with pleasure. At least she was clothed now, although her hair was mussed and she smelled of our lovemaking. She slid off my back and stepped gingerly over our hostess. She presented herself to the housekeeper, her hands on her hips. If the housekeeper knew that her life was in the young woman's hands, if she understood that Isla could and would kill her if it pleased her, she gave no sign. She sighed and said to her, "You needn't bother yourself with this mess. I will bury her after breakfast. She's not in any hurry. Are you hungry?"

Apparently deciding the housekeeper should live, Isla bobbed alongside, free spirit that she was, and followed her into the larder. I heard Isla ask her as if it were the most natural thing, "After you bury the old lady, would you mind helping me get my hair in order? It's a rat's nest."

I didn't hear the woman's reply but if she had given the wrong one, I would have heard Isla's angry scream. As they left, I stole a tablecloth from a nearby table and covered the deceased woman's body. "Again, my apologies, madam." Leaving her in Miss Loxley's hands, I walked away from the whole mess in search of more brandy.

Now there were three of us—three savages and all with black hearts.

Chapter 1—Carrie Jo

"Dang it!" I woke myself up again faced with a choice— either put my size-seven foot on Ashland's behind and kick him off our brand new canopy bed or get up and leave. After five nights of unintentional access into his less than faithful dreams I had had about enough. It was too late to get into a knock-down, drag-out fight, so I decided to take the high road. In an angry huff, I sat up like a snapped rubber band and threw back the covers. Naturally, he didn't flinch.

Of course not! Why should he stop dreaming about some curvaceous supermodel while I'm fuming right beside him?

I stared down at the perfectly peaceful face of my sleeping husband, and my heart was a ball of feelings—none of them good. I couldn't decide which I hated more: that I couldn't control my dream catching or that I couldn't stop thinking about what I saw. Maybe it was just that I wouldn't be able to sleep for the rest of the night—God, I was tired! Call me sensitive, but the images of wanton women twisting under my husband in the throes of passion were just a bit more than I could bear. The last thing I wanted to do was fall asleep again and "enjoy" the big finish.

He's lucky we have a housekeeper who likes to cook for him because I sure as hell won't be making him breakfast! Not this morning!

Still, in the back of my mind I knew how this would play out. He'd wake up as chipper as a beaver with a new log without a clue as to why I was so pissed. I sure couldn't come out and tell him. Nope. No way was I giving up the high ground now. I might have issues, but I wasn't the cheater. I'd slap a big ol' fake Carrie Jo smile on my face and pretend that everything was right as rain. Thankfully, he did not have women's intuition. For someone who had extrasensory gifts, Ashland Stuart was none too perceptive—at least not when it came to me.

Swearing under my breath, I got out of bed and walked to the large round window across the room. The moon glowed round and near-perfect above the city of Mobile. A few wisps of clouds passed in front of it, but they quickly skittered away as the breeze blew in and along with it the fog from the nearby bay. According to the weatherman, the temperatures were never this warm in January, but people didn't seem to mind. They liked wearing flip-flops and T-shirts even in the dead of winter. As my old friend Bette used to tell me, "If you don't like the weather in Mobile, just wait a few minutes, dah-ling. It will change!" She'd chuckle and shake her head in amusement, white curls bouncing with every shake. I wondered what advice she'd have for me now. She loved Ashland, that much I knew. I had known her less than a year and she was thirty years my senior, but she had truly become one of my best friends ever. I missed her every single day. She had been a second mom—a confidante, my protector. I loved her.

I leaned against the window with arms crossed and stared down at the quiet downtown streets below. From the top floor of our Victorian home, the view was peaceful, with the exception of the occasional siren from the nearby police station. My friend and assistant Rachel informed me that the quiet façade would quickly fade when Mardi Gras kicked off in a few weeks. Apparently it was such a parking and traffic nightmare that she'd already developed maps to help us navigate traffic and avoid the bead-hungry, moon-pie-seeking masses. We even changed our office hours to accommodate the local parade calendar. I looked over my shoulder at Ashland— he didn't stir. Typical.

Think about something else, Carrie Jo!

I tried to distract myself with thoughts of work. I still couldn't believe I had an office—a real business of my own. Word had gotten out about my role in the restoration of Seven Sisters and the additions to the facility. Those old plantation owners were beginning to see what a lucrative venture restoring these beautiful downtown homes truly was. Of course I could not take all the credit. It took a team, and many of those team members were no longer with us. Like it did so often recently, my mind traveled back to the first time I visited this charming yet dangerous city. Some people called Mobile the Azalea City;

others called it the Port City. In my own experience I believed a better name would be the Supernatural City. I had never been to New Orleans, but I was pretty sure that old city had nothing on this one.

I nervously spun the white gold wedding band on my finger and stared at the shiny ring in the moonlight. Tears flooded my eyes. We'd fought so hard to keep it all together, and now here I was staring out the window unable to sleep beside the man I loved. I did love him, and he loved me. I would just have to figure out a way to get my dream catching under control.

Suddenly I felt two hands on my shoulders. I gasped and nearly jumped out of my skin. I turned to find a laughing Ashland standing behind me with his hands raised in surrender. "Sorry! I thought you heard me. I didn't mean to startle you."

"What the hell?"

He laughed again. Normally I would find the sound cheerful, even sexy. Now I just wanted to slap him. He said in a softer voice, "You were deep in thought. I didn't mean to scare you like that."

"Well, you did. Let me catch my breath."

"I've got a better idea. Why don't you come back to bed? Maybe I can find a way to soothe your nerves?" He rubbed my shoulder, but I didn't encourage him.

I stammered for a moment, then stomped to the bed and grabbed my blanket, intending to find sleep elsewhere. "I can't sleep. You go to bed. No sense in both of us being tired." Playfully he grabbed the other end. He still had no clue how mad I really was. He had no idea that I knew about his breast-centric dreams. "Let go, Ashland!"

"What did I do? I said I was sorry. Now come to bed."

I glared at him. Unless I was willing to tell him the truth, I would have to do as he asked. "Fine! I just hope I can sleep. My eyes are going to look horrible in the morning, and I have to meet with Desmond Taylor. You know, you've had me up every night this week."

"What? Have I been snoring? I'm sorry, Carrie Jo. Maybe I should get some of those strips for my nose—the kind that keeps your airways open. You should have said something sooner." I flopped in the bed and turned my back to him, beating my pillow into submission. He tucked the blanket around me and kissed me on the cheek.

Darn him! How dare he be kind! I like being mad at him.

"I promise to pick some up tomorrow, and don't worry about Taylor. You're a genius. He would be lucky to have you work on his project. In the meantime, if my snoring gets really bad I can go sleep in the guest room. Should I?"

I sighed, guilt over my snooping washing over me. "That won't be necessary." As he put his arm around me and held me, I realized I was being a fool. A man's mind was his own territory—it belonged solely to him, and that included his dreams. How would I like it if Ashland saw a few of my dreams? I never planned to dream some of the crazy stuff I did, but it happened. I let him cuddle up to me, and I enjoyed his clean sandalwood scent and his strong arms. *Well, as long as he's only dreaming about it and not acting upon it, then we should be okay. Chances are he doesn't even remember them. Most people don't remember their dreams at all.* Still, I had to do something if I wanted to stay married. And indeed I did.

I glanced back at the clock on the bedside table. It was 4:45. Weird. What were the odds of that happening again? I had woken myself up early every day since Monday. Now it was Friday night—no, make that Saturday morning. As I pondered the puzzle, my eyes grew heavy and I soon fell back to sleep.

I chose to think about something else for a while. Like Delilah Iverson. I'd put her to the side too long. I had promised myself after my friends died (they did die, didn't they?) that I would dig in deeper. If for no other reason than to honor their lives. I hadn't kept my word, which wasn't like me at all.

Conjuring her image from my memory of our ballroom encounter, I whispered her name. It felt right to seek the ghosts of the past. Maybe that's what I needed to do if I wanted to stay out of Ashland's head. Since I could not turn my dream catching off, I needed to learn how to focus on using it productively.

It seemed like a good idea at the time.

Chapter 2—Delilah

Another hot summer day passed by without a single customer darkening the door of the Iverson Sundries Store. A small, greasy-faced child plastered his face on the front glass of the store before he was shooed away by his rotund mother, but that was the closest thing to a customer we had. A stray cat had made his way in the back door, which I'd absently left open, but I showed him the way out with the help of one of my new Shoemaker brooms. Around 4 o'clock, after sweeping the floors for the third time, counting spools of thread and repeatedly climbing the ladder to check the top shelf of my stock, I gave up. Miss Page had been true to her word. Nobody wanted to have anything to do with me or my business. For weeks I had managed to ignore the hisses and unfriendly faces, but now it was all too much. Mobilians had clearly cast their vote for the respectable Claudette Page. Friendless, hopeless and feeling defeated, I decided to call it a day. It was sad to say, but even the newly arriving northerners avoided my store. It was a hard pill to swallow.

In contrast, Adam's woodworking business continued to increase—there was never a lack of activity at his shop. It took hard work to get it moving; I had to give him credit for that. In the beginning nobody had wanted to give him a chance either, but he'd been persistent. And it didn't hurt that he had a handsome face and friendly demeanor. Funny how nobody wanted to have anything to do with me, but my "brother" was perfectly acceptable. But then again, he wasn't an illegitimate bastard, a social usurper. What would my parents say about all this? What would I say to them?

I strolled down the wooden sidewalk, making a right turn toward Adam's shop—I was happy to make the turn off Dauphin Street away from the snooty shoppers who crowded every store but mine.

With a tinge of bitterness, I recalled this morning's conversation with the only other Iverson in this town. "It seems to me that Mobile has far too many aspiring female woodworkers. For God's sake, Adam, don't encourage them."

"What am I supposed to do, Delilah? Close the shop door and forbid anyone to walk inside without your permission? You cannot tell me you're worried about a few silly girls. You know only you have my heart."

We rarely spoke openly about how we felt about one another, and I was beginning to think that he was doing so now only to prevent further argument. Any other time he did not want to talk about our future together, or love, or feelings— except after the lamp blew out. I welcomed the guilt that came with the memory of our first time together. It had been awkward but wonderful until the sunlight streamed into the room and I woke up alone. He barely spoke to me in the days that followed, but he could not keep up the isolation since we lived in the same apartment above the store.

Well, I only had myself to blame. I loved a man who most of the county considered my brother. For the hundredth time I asked myself, "What was I trying to prove?" It's not like I needed money—both Dr. Page and my parents had been generous in their bequests to me—but I enjoyed working in the shop. It was the only life I knew, and now Claudette Page had seemingly put an end to all that. Mounting pressure from the unofficial leader of the local moral society had taken its toll.

The afternoon heat rolled up from the sidewalk like an unseen blanket. I suddenly missed the coolness of Canada; even my unfriendly cousins were not as cruel as Mobile society. Unwilling to witness their collective disdain any longer, I kept my eyes on the path in front of me until I crashed into another pedestrian. My victim was a young woman, slightly taller than me but wearing more fashionable attire than mine—a moss-green dress that flattered her wide gray eyes. Despite her otherwise polished appearance, she had a bundle of tight curly red hair that appeared barely controlled by a diamond-shaped green hat. Before I could mumble an apology and continue on my way, she said, "Miss Iverson? Adam Iverson's sister?"

"I am Delilah. May I help you?"

"Your brother tells me you are an excellent dressmaker. I happen to be in need of an excellent dressmaker." She rocked back on her heels delightedly, as if she were doing me the greatest favor imaginable by offering me a job. The young lady appeared oblivious to the stir our collision had caused. When I did not respond immediately she added, "Oh, my manners. My name is Maundy Weaver. I own the dress shop two streets over." She stuck her lace-gloved hand out to me, and I shook it.

"I had no idea my brother made a habit of visiting dress shops. Thank you, but I don't need a job." I tried to get by her, but she touched my arm.

"If I could have just a minute of your time. Would you join me for a glass of something cool?"

She quietly added, "My shop is just a minute away."

I was curious now, so I nodded and followed behind this mysterious Maundy Weaver. Her shop was indeed just two minutes away. I was surprised I had never seen it, but then again I had not spent much time exploring the area. I wondered how well my "brother" knew the woman and why she believed I needed a job. With a polite smile, she opened the side door and we stepped into a small parlor. She waved me to a seat at a polished two-person table. I recognized the work—Adam had built this. As Miss Weaver poured us a glass of something that looked like iced tea, I looked about me. Through an adjoining door I could see into her store. She had customers, busy dressmakers and an endless sea of colorful fabrics neatly arranged along the walls. In her parlor there was no evidence of her dressmaking business. However, I could see that she was fond of pink roses for her china, and many decorations displayed that painted theme.

"I am glad I caught you. When it gets this hot out, many shops close early. I suppose you find this climate a bit oppressive after Canada." She placed the glass in front of me, and I could not resist taking a sip. The drink was not tea at all but something much more delicious. She laughed at my reaction. "Sarsaparilla. I like the flavor, don't you?"

"Yes, I do. I see quite a bit of Adam's handiwork here in your parlor. I didn't know you were a customer, but I think there's some mistake. I'm not looking for a job. As you know, I have my own store. Iverson Sundries on Dauphin Street."

"Miss Iverson, if I may be direct?" I nodded slowly. "I know all about your story and would like to help."

"Really? How much of my story do you think you know?" I set the glass down and stood. How dare Adam talk to this woman about our private matters!

"Please, sit. I am a woman who appreciates the direct approach. I did not mean to offend you; it's just that I too have crossed swords with Claudette. I know what a vicious adversary she can be, but you can beat her."

"So you think closing my store and coming to work for you as a dressmaker will beat her? I'm afraid I don't follow your logic." I sat back down, suddenly feeling tired.

"Of course you don't. You have no idea who I am or what I can do, Miss Iverson—or do you prefer Miss Page?"

"Delilah will do fine."

"I have just learned that your attorney, Mr. Peyton, has every intention of advising you to withdraw your case."

I could not hide my shock. "He can't do that!"

She laughed dryly. "Oh yes, he can. He's her cousin—and yours since you are a Page too. And as such, you can take him to court. You may not get much, but it will be on record and that might come in handy later. He should've shared with you his connection with her at your first meeting. It's what legal folks call a 'conflict of interest.'" I sank back in the chair. Could this day get any worse? Miss Weaver seemed to pick up on my thoughts. "Are you ready to quit?" She removed her hat pin and her hat and tossed it on the table beside her. She didn't attempt to tame her wild red hair as she leaned toward me with one arm on the table, waiting for my answer.

"I don't quit so easily. Why does my situation interest you so much, Ms. Weaver?"

With a smile she answered me, "Maundy, please. Why shouldn't it? You're a woman. I'm a woman. I believe we women should stick together. This world is an unfriendly place for us, hence my offer. I am not merely offering you a job; I offer you a way to get even. You need something—and you need it very badly. I can help you get it."

Her tone of voice made the fine hairs on the back of my neck stand up. "And what is it you think I need?" The thought that I should never cross this woman flashed through my mind.

She laughed again. "The only thing a woman ever really needs—information."

Surprised by her answer, I asked, "Information? I don't understand. Information about dressmaking?"

"Don't tell me you're dull, Delilah. You can't be dull with that face. No, not dressmaking. You'd be surprised how much you can learn during a dress fitting. There are not many social situations in which the classes mingle so easily. I have been a dressmaker all my life, as my mother was before me and hers before her. None of us Weaver women got into the business because we loved dresses." She cackled at some joke that only she knew. "With just a glance I can take your measurements and see the perfect dress for you or any woman—tall, thin, short, fat. I can make any woman look and feel good. With that ability comes a lot of trust. Women trust me. And when they trust you, they tell you things."

"And what kind of things do I need to hear?"

"Everyone has a secret, and most people don't want those secrets to see the light of day. That includes the high-and-mighty Claudette Page. In fact, I would venture to say that of all the people in the great city of Mobile, she has the biggest secret of all." She sipped her sarsaparilla and smiled at me through her yellow-tinged teeth.

"What secret might that be?"

"Oh, that's for you to figure out. I don't like Claudette Page, but she is not my mortal enemy—she's yours. Your very existence has threatened everything she holds dear. Her reputation, her wealth, her family's name—these are all things she's willing to die for. But if you find out her secret and confront her with it, she'll slink away like a scolded puppy.

Now," she said, setting her glass down and smoothing her dress as she stood, "I need a dressmaker. Your business is in shambles, and that's not likely to change. Put a sign on the door that says you're closed for remodeling. Have your brother install some new cabinets or something. While he works on that project, you come help me. I'll make sure you get the opportunity to get the information you need."

"Why are you helping me? I'm not ungrateful, but why?"

"I'll keep my reasons to myself for now, if you don't mind. It's not that I don't trust you, but I would like to wait. Work for me for the next six weeks, and I can promise you everything will be different."

I stood up and extended my hand to her. "You have yourself a deal, Maundy."

She shook it and smiled broadly. "Smart girl. I'm Miss Weaver during working hours. I'll see you at Rose Cottage in the morning."

"At your house? I thought I was to work here, in the shop?"

"Oh no, dear. This little shop is for regular folks like you and me. My most exclusive clients have their fittings and consultations at Rose Cottage. It's a private service that I offer them. For example, I have clients who need help with their Mardi Gras ball dresses, but privacy is an issue. Keeping those dresses secret is a must until the big reveal at the ball. It's kind of a local tradition. It's ridiculous how they try to outdo one another, but if it's pearls they want, it's pearls they will get. Or whatever strikes their fancy. That's not going to be a problem for you, is it?"

"Not at all. And where is Rose Cottage located?"

"Turn left on Monterey Street and follow it to Virginia Street. My house is behind the Magnolia Cemetery. You can't miss it. It's the yellow two-story with the green shutters. Do you have a carriage?"

"Yes, I do."

"Bring it. It will rain tomorrow. It always rains after heat like this. And dress nicely, Miss Page. You'll meet your new attorney tomorrow."

"New attorney?"

"My friend, Jackson Keene. He'll help you get all this sorted out."

"I don't know how to thank you for all this."

"One day I'll tell you." She leaned forward and peered into my eyes. "One day I will ask you for a favor. I will expect you to grant it. In the meantime, keep your eyes and ears open and your mouth closed. Don't ask questions. The quieter, the less intrusive you are, the more likely they'll trust you and the sooner you'll hear something. Something useful you can use to put that old woman in her place. I have had enough of her and her moral society."

With a final handshake I slipped out of the house and walked back home. In one conversation I had lost everything and gained it all again. I wondered about my new partner, Maundy Weaver. What did she want from me? It would do no good to ask. I could tell she was not the kind of woman who would be easily persuaded to do anything other than what she wanted. Still, this was better than any plan I currently had. Once again, life had handed me an unexpected fork in the road. I hoped this time I had chosen the right path.

Chapter 3—Henri

I drizzled the bourbon into the hot pan and watched the flames appear. I worked the pan just like a short-order cook, coating the pecans in the decadent glaze. Turning off the flame, I continued to cook the alcohol out, pleased that I hadn't burned the pecans. At least not this batch. Glancing at my wristwatch, I had a moment of panic—Detra Ann would arrive any minute, and I wanted everything to be perfect. I did not want to stop and think about what I was doing, how foolish I was to even dream that Detra Ann and I would ever be anything more than friends. But I did hope and dream. Although I couldn't deny that I cared about her, I didn't know how she felt about me. Not only that, but we were business partners. What was I doing having heart palpitations over a business partner? "Strike one, strike two," as my granddad used to say.

Walking the pan to the dining room table, I spooned the glaze over the plated roasted chicken. I couldn't help but smile and for a moment felt confident that at least she'd like the dish I'd prepared for her. I tossed my dirty apron across the bar in the kitchen and searched for my lighter. No, on second thought, lighting candles would be coming on too strong. With nervous hands, I struggled to open a stubborn bottle of wine when I heard an unusual noise coming from the direction of the bathroom. It sounded like squirrels scratching at the wall— or someone breaking in! I put the wine aside and slipped quietly into my office. Removing my gun from the desk drawer, I went down the hall to investigate the source of the noise. I paused in the hallway waiting to hear the sound again. I was much more agile than I had been a year ago. I'd spent so much time at the gym—I had never been this fit before. My thirty-fifth birthday was last week, and I hadn't told a soul. I didn't need to be reminded how old I was. I couldn't turn back time, but I could get in shape. And I had.

Scratch, scratch…

Nope, the noise wasn't coming from the bathroom. It was coming from the guest room. As I stepped toward the door, I cocked my gun. I stood sweating in my gold-colored polo shirt, silently counting backwards from three. I heard a thud on the other side of the door and swung it open, my gun poised and ready to shoot the invader.

"Get up now!" I shouted in my most authoritative voice. "On your feet! Put your hands where I can see them!"

The intruder didn't respond right away, but when she did I almost fell over. "Calm down, Henri. It's just me," the crumpled figure complained.

"Lenore?"

"Yep, the one and only."

"What the hell are you doing climbing through the window? I could have shot you!"

"If you shoot me, you better hope you kill me. Because if you didn't, you know I would kick your ass!" She dusted herself off and stood up to face me. Her expression let me know that nothing much had changed. She was still as crazy and defiant as ever. From the way her clothing looked, she didn't need to bother trying to tidy herself up. The only time I'd seen my cousin dressed appropriately or nicely was at our grandmother's funeral, and that had been more than twenty years ago. Today's outfit was red leggings and an oversize pink shirt with black combat boots.

"I'm going to ask again, why are you climbing through my window? You plan on robbing me?"

"I don't want nothing you have, Henri Devecheaux—I never have, and I'm sure as hell not a thief!" A little more apologetically she added, "I couldn't come through the front door. You got a damn ghost on the front porch. You know I don't fool with no ghosts."

I laughed, setting my gun down with a sigh of relief. "What do you mean?" Before I could get an answer from her, the doorbell rang. "Um...just wait right here."

"No, Henri! Don't you open that door! I'm telling you the truth, fool! Don't you ever listen? A ghost is out there!"

"Lenore, have you been drinking? That's my dinner guest, Detra Ann. She's a real person, my business partner—not a ghost." I sighed and pointed toward the screwed-up window. "Just fix my screen. Please. I'll be right back." I couldn't believe my luck. My crazy cousin had to show up tonight of all nights. Once again I felt as if the Man Upstairs had it in for me.

Sliding the gun into the back of my pants, I strode to the front door. It wouldn't do to wave a gun around in front of Detra Ann, considering she'd been shot last year. The glass reflected her slender frame. I could tell from the length of her shadow that she was wearing high heels. That was promising. You didn't wear high heels unless you wanted to impress someone. At least that was true for most women I'd met. On the other hand, Detra Ann wore high heels almost every day. I wasn't sure who she was trying to impress. She was a natural beauty, even with bleached blond hair.

I opened the door with a smile, trying to act as naturally as possible. "Hey! Right on time. Come in, please."

"Oh, Henri. It smells wonderful. Nice shirt." She kissed my cheek and handed me a bottle of her favorite red wine. I pretended I didn't notice the smell of whiskey on her breath. "I hope this goes with what you've prepared." She flashed an empty smile.

"This is perfect." Remembering the gun in my waistband, I pointed to the dining room and excused myself. "Make yourself at home. I'll be right back."

"Are you still fussing in the kitchen? Is there something I can help you with?"

"No. Everything is ready. This won't take a minute."

"Okey dokey." She smiled again and walked to the dining room.

As I was returning the gun to the desk drawer, I heard the shower running in the bathroom. What was I going to do with Lenore? She had always been a lost soul, but her behavior had gotten worse after Aleezabeth disappeared. We had been the three amigos—Peas, Carrots and Onions, our grandma had called us. I was pretty sure I'd been Onions.

Aleezabeth…

How long had it been since I'd summoned up her memory? When was the last time I'd called the sheriff of Dumont and demanded an update? Too long ago. I'd let Aleezabeth down, first by leaving her to walk home by herself and now by failing to find her and bring her home.

I leaned against the doorframe with the wine bottle in my hand. So much for a nice, relaxing evening with Detra Ann. I'd have to explain Lenore before she had a chance to crash our dinner.

"Hey, you coming? I'm going to start without you!"

"Yep, on the way." I stopped by the kitchen for the corkscrew and strolled into join her. To my surprise, Detra Ann had lit the candles and was already digging into supper. I poured the wine and sat down with her.

"Hidden talents, Henri. I had no idea you could cook like this. Are you professionally trained? Did you go to culinary school somewhere?"

I took a big swig of the fruity red wine. "No, but I've always loved cooking. I think it's just a part of my heritage. You know, everyone from New Orleans can cook."

She shook her head as she finished a bite of the chicken. "That's not true at all. I had an aunt from New Orleans, and she was the worst cook on the planet. Every Christmas she'd make us these God-awful pralines and then call us the next day to see if we'd eaten them. It was so funny because my dad would lie to her and tell her they hit the spot. She never knew he had a hole dug in the backyard that he lovingly called 'the spot.'"

"That sounds like something my father would have done. He was kind of a jokester."

"I've never heard you talk about your father. Is he still alive?"

I took another swig of wine and eyed the hallway nervously. "I'm not sure."

"What?" she asked incredulously.

"He kind of slipped away. Daddy liked playing music, or he did before he hooked up with my mother. He was a high school science teacher, but he dabbled in music—mostly jazz. One weekend a group of his old band buddies came around, and when they left town, Dad and his sax left too. I assumed he left with them."

"That must have been so hard on you. How old were you?"

"Fourteen. My birthday was the month before he left."

"And you've never seen him in all this time?"

"No, but that's not unusual for my family—we're all a bunch of wanderers. For example, my cousin Lenore showed up tonight. I haven't seen her in years, and suddenly she's here."

Her dark eyelashes fluttered in surprise. "You should have said something. We could have had dinner another night. I hope I didn't inconvenience you, Henri."

"You're never an inconvenience."

She dabbed her mouth with the linen napkin and smirked. I could tell she didn't believe me. After a year, I knew her facial expressions pretty well. At least I thought I did. We chitchatted about work stuff, like the crate of antiques that had come in that morning, a client that refused to pay us, the noise from the construction on Dauphin Street. When our plates were nearly empty and the conversation died down, I felt more relaxed. I was pretty sure that Lenore had passed out on my bed, but at least she wouldn't be crashing our dinner date—I hoped.

"I have to admit I had an ulterior motive for inviting you here."

She set the napkin on the table, leaned back in the chair and appraised me suspiciously. "Not to steal your thunder, but before you tell me, I have something for you. For your birthday."

"How did you know I had a birthday?"

"I took a peek at your driver's license a while back. Since you didn't mention it, I figured you wanted to keep it quiet. You know, thirty-five isn't ancient." Opening her oversize purse she removed a gold box with a royal blue ribbon wrapped around it. "This is for you." She slid it toward me.

I laughed in surprise. "I can't believe you did that. You're full of surprises, Detra Ann."

"Wait until you open it."

I picked up the box and put it back down. "I am sure this is a wonderful gift, but I really want something else."

She froze for a second and said, "Okay, what do you want?"

"I want a dance. I mean, it is my birthday." I walked to the CD player and hit play. I hadn't planned this, but it felt right. Etta James began her sweet serenade.

At last…my love has come along…my lonely days are over…and life is like a song…

With a sad smile, Detra Ann joined me on the makeshift dance floor. Her arms slid around my neck, and I held her close. Her long blond hair rubbed against my hands, and I did my best to breathe slowly so my heart wouldn't beat out of my chest.

"Remember that day, at the ribbon-cutting?"

"Yes, I remember," I said quietly. I knew it was hard for her to talk about TD, even now.

"I don't know what I would have done if I had looked out into that audience and didn't see you."

"You would have been just fine, Detra Ann. You are strong—stronger than you think."

She squeezed me tighter and laid her head on my shoulder. I couldn't help but touch her hair. "I will never forget it." We danced until Etta sang her last notes. When the dance ended, she stepped back and reached for the gift before I could say or do anything else. "Now open it before I change my mind."

Quickly, I opened it, pulling the ribbon first and removing the golden cardboard lid. Inside was a silver key tied to another blue ribbon. I recognized it—this was the key to Cotton City Treasures. Puzzled, I turned it over in my hand.

"I'm giving you my share of the business, Henri. It's time for me to move on. I've taken a job in Atlanta—I'm leaving at the end of the week."

It felt like someone had kicked me in the gut. I put the key back in the box and replaced the lid. "I can't take this. This is too much, Detra Ann. I can't let you do this."

"It's already done, my friend. I signed the papers yesterday, and it is official. You are the sole proprietor of Cotton City Treasures—you own it all. It's just my way of saying thank you. If it weren't for you, I wouldn't be here today. I mean, I know I'm not a hundred percent yet, but you have been a lifesaver. Truly. Thank you for everything."

Stunned, I murmured, "You're welcome."

She sprang from her chair and hugged me, and I breathed in her sweet smell. Detra Ann sometimes wore expensive perfume, the kind you normally only got a whiff of in fashion magazines, but then there were times when she smelled like sun-dried sheets and wildflowers. That's how I always thought of her. And now she was leaving. "I thought this would be easy, but it's not. I will miss you most of all," she whispered in my ear. After a few moments, she reached for her purse and headed out the door. "I have to go. I'll come by and see you before I leave, I promise."

I watched her car lights disappear down Conception Street, and then I closed the door. I felt like my heart had been snatched out. Lenore was standing in the doorway, her hair wild and damp from her shower. Her olive-colored skin practically glowed in the candlelight.

"Please tell me you weren't intending on telling that ghost you loved her. She's not for you, Henri."

"You don't know what you're talking about, Lenore."

She clucked her tongue, "You've always been a fool when it came to women. Remember Peaches?" As she strolled across the wooden floor, I noticed she was wearing a pair of my socks. She peered through the blinds and said, "She was a nightmare, and she left you high and dry just like I told you she would. Then there was that red-haired stripper, Anastasia…"

"She wasn't a stripper—she was a burlesque dancer, and that was over ten years ago."

"Don't correct me. You've got a bad habit of thinking you're the only one that's right, Henri Lamar Devecheaux. You can't love that girl. She's already dead—she's a ghost. At the very least, she's a shade."

"What are you talking about?" I knew I would regret asking, but I did it anyway. "What the hell is a shade, Lenore?"

"Someone who's been touched by Death. A part of her is already gone. Death only got his bony hands on part of her, but all that's left is a shadow—a shade. He'll come for the rest." She stood closer to me now—she touched my hand tentatively as if she thought I was a shade too. "You know what I am saying is true. I can see it in your face. What do you have to do with this, Henri?" I didn't answer her. I wanted her to leave my home, but I was too polite to say so. She touched my arm again. Sure that I was real, her face softened; her voice was unusually soft and kind. "She's someone who should have died but escaped the reaper's hands. But he'll come back for her. And if you're anywhere around her when he does, he might take you too. She's been amongst the dead, seen them, touched them. Death won't let her go—she's his. She can never be yours, cousin."

"I don't believe a word you're saying. You don't either. You just like tormenting me, don't you? This isn't about Detra Ann at all. This is about Aleezabeth. Tell me the truth, Lenore. Why are you here? What do you want? Money?"

As if she didn't hear me, she walked around the room, examining my pictures and my collection of antique silver spoons. "That's probably why she's drinking and taking those pills. She feels cold Death creeping into her bones and thinks she can escape it. It won't work. It never does. She's a ghost already…"

"Shut up, Lenore! If you don't stop talking like that, you will have to go. I don't believe Detra Ann is the only one drinking too much. You're on dope now, aren't you?"

She closed her eyes and held her breath, tilting her head like she was listening to an invisible voice. Then her eyes sprung open and she said, "I'm here to help you, Henri. I didn't come for any other reason. You're about to see the supernatural like you've never seen it before! I want to help you, cousin. You're the last family I got, and I'll be damned if I just let you go." She pursed her lips and scowled at me. "I lost Aleezabeth. We both lost her—I won't lose you too. I am staying right here until that ghost is gone. Have a care for your soul, Henri. Please."

I rubbed my forehead in frustration. "Listen, if you want to stay for a while, fine. But there are some ground rules. Number one, you aren't just lying around the house all day. You've got to get a job. When I leave the house, you leave the house. No climbing in the windows or kicking down doors. Number two, you leave Detra Ann alone. No talking to her about all this crazy stuff—in fact, you don't talk to her at all. She's been through enough. Number three, if you steal from me, you're out of here. All I have to do is call Detective Simmons at the Mobile Police Department and she'll come pick you up *tout de suite*. Those are the rules. You understand?"

Lenore could see I was serious. She didn't argue and nodded her head. "Can I smoke in here?"

"Not in my house, but there's a chair in the backyard if you want to puff on your cancer sticks. You've got the guest room—that's the room you broke into. Do you have clothes?"

"I've got enough, and the guest room suits me fine."

"I'm cleaning the kitchen and going to bed. There's some leftover chicken in there if you're hungry."

"I think I'll go smoke first." Without even a thank you, Lenore slipped out of the house and into the darkened backyard.

With a sigh I went to the kitchen to tidy up. Corking the wine and removing the dishes from the table, I slid on my rubber gloves and let the hot water run in the sink. I had a dishwasher, a nice stainless steel one, but I liked washing dishes by hand. It was therapeutic. After tonight's turn of events, I needed some therapy. The woman I loved—yes, I could admit that now—was leaving me behind. *Isn't that terrific?* I cracked the window a bit to let some cool air in. It was too early in the year to turn on the air conditioning, but the house felt stuffy tonight.

I squirted the blue dishwashing liquid into the sink and watched the suds build. I caught a whiff of Lenore's cigarette. I thought about asking her to move away from the window, but then I heard her whisper into a phone. "Hey! You ain't going to believe this, but I found one." I froze and turned off the water. It was quiet for a moment. "Sure I'm sure." Another pause. "Yeah, probably, but we'll have to move fast."

Chills ran up and down my spine. For a second it was as if the air stopped moving and I stopped breathing. I knew exactly what—no, who—Lenore was talking about.

Detra Ann.

Chapter 4—Carrie Jo

Desmond Taylor insisted that I meet him at Idlewood first thing in the morning, and I was happy to do so. Off the beaten path, the old house stood off Carlen Street about a mile from Seven Sisters. Another forgotten gem crumbling into the Mobile landscape, Idlewood was in nowhere near the condition Ashland's family home had been. It was in far worse shape. And to think I believed restoring Seven Sisters had been challenging. Still, the old house had good bones, as Terrence Dale used to say. And to top it off, it had a fascinating history. One that I couldn't walk away from.

Idlewood was actually a twin home. The original house was the Idlewild Plantation in Derby, Louisiana. The McClellans visited the home and loved it so much they purchased copies of the original plans and reconstructed it here in Mobile. Idlewild was a raised plantation—a unique construction because of its mix of French and English features. Typical for the wild woods of Louisiana, it had been a rarity during its time here in Mobile. The front facade of Idlewood had three dormers, which gave it a graceful look despite the sagging roof. Rusty, ornamental cast-iron balustrades looked promising but in much need of some skilled attention. But the thing I loved the most were the galleries. This type of house normally had molded capitals, but Idlewood's galleries were lined with gorgeous fluted, Doric columns that begged to be restored to their former elegance.

According to Mr. Taylor, Idlewood's current owner, this Greek revival plantation house had undergone at least a dozen changes since the original construction. But fortunately these had been relatively minor and had not taken away from the original owner's vision. Luckily for me, I knew what Idlewood had really looked like, right down to the paisley wallpaper in the hallway—I had seen it in a dream. Once upon a time, about a hundred and fifty years ago, there had been a grand Christmas ball held here at Idlewood. Dr. Hoyt Page and his beloved Christine Cottonwood rekindled their romance in the upstairs nursery. A little boy battled the flu, and rare Christmas snowflakes had fallen, much to the delight of a pair of cocker spaniels and the gathered party. Unfortunately, I could not revisit the nursery or any of the rooms on the top floor, as the stairs were deemed unsafe.

"Tell me, Mr. Taylor, what did you have in mind?"

The older man thought carefully before he spoke. "I'll be honest with you, Mrs. Stuart. I am not sure what to do with this old house. It doesn't seem practical to me to restore it. My wife and the Historical Society seem to think differently, but then again my wife is a sentimental old gal." He chuckled and continued, "I don't have a bottomless pocketbook, but I do have a heart to restore Idlewood, if that's possible. From what I hear about your work at Seven Sisters, you really put that home back on the map. Maybe we can do that here. I don't know. Believe it or not, I've been offered a substantial grant to begin the restoration. But I'm not a foolish man. I've been in business all my life, and I know this kind of project isn't something to take too lightly. We could be looking at a very long project, and I have a construction business to run. I don't have time to manage all this. Not to mention I wouldn't know where to start."

I chewed my lip and looked around the room at the dusty walls and cracked floors. He was right, of course. Restoration was hard work. It took hundreds of hours of research, and then there were acquisitions. Then there was the reconstruction of the property and meeting all the requirements of the local historical society, which could be a major task in itself. I felt sad thinking about working on a new project without Terrence Dale—and probably without Ashland. Still, this was what I did. What I had always wanted to do. Maybe getting the Seven Sisters job *had* been just a fluke—I'm sure Hollis Matthews knew about my dream catching from Mia, and that's why they wanted me in Mobile—but this…this was an opportunity to prove my abilities as a researcher.

"You are right. It is a commitment, Mr. Taylor. Here's how we'll start. Let me ask you a few questions."

After another thirty minutes I got the bottom line. Mr. Taylor didn't want to be involved in the daily decisions, but he did want monthly updates. He would use his construction company to do the work under my team's supervision. Before anything began or any plans were finalized, we would undertake a lengthy appraisal process. He had a dollar figure in mind, and he wouldn't pursue the restoration if the cost exceeded that amount. His ultimate goal was for the home to turn enough profit so all future maintenance would be self-supported. He didn't want to be stuck managing a "money pit," and I couldn't blame him there.

And one more caveat. He had no idea how to collect antiques, but his wife was eager to help. In fact, he wanted her to help. I agreed to his terms, and we ended the meeting with a handshake. Mr. and Mrs. Taylor were going out of town on an extended cruise in a few days, and he wanted to have a detailed project proposal before he left. Which meant I'd have to work day and night for the next forty-eight hours to pull something together. I agreed to do that but reminded him this was just a preliminary proposal. When it came to restoration, there was always that one thing you hadn't considered—like the cost of taking care of any bodies you uncovered.

I left the meeting so excited that my hands were shaking as I dug my cell phone out of my purse. Ashland should have been the first person I called, but after last night, I still couldn't face him. I thought about calling Rachel and then just frowned in the rearview mirror and tossed the phone back in my purse.

You are being a total jerk, Carrie Jo! You can't get mad about some dreams.

Oh, yeah? Well, why is he dreaming about other women? Is he seeing other women?

Sick of my own drama, I flipped on the radio. Bob Marley sang "Three Little Birds," and for the next fifteen minutes I tapped my fingers on the steering wheel as I sang loudly and completely off-key. By the time I made it to my office at Oak Plaza, I felt more like my old self again.

The first thing I saw when I stepped inside was a ridiculously large vase full of pink roses. There had to have been at least a hundred buds crammed into the white ceramic vase. It smelled glorious, but it did seem a bit much. Unless you were at a funeral. As I slid my coat off, I smiled at Rachel. "Gee, who died? Those can't be from Chip."

"Uh, no. Those are for you, actually." She handed me a card and smiled. "Happy anniversary!"

"Oh." I took the card and smiled sheepishly. "Thank you so much."

"You hit the flower jackpot, I think. I'd be lucky if Chip bought me just a half dozen. He's a sweetie but not big on sentimentalism. Me either, I guess. What should I do with these? Put them in your office? I can't leave them here. I don't think the visitors will be able to see my desk."

"I'll take them. I have a table in my office. Let me put my purse and coat away first. Then I'll tell you the awesome news!"

"No bother. I think I can handle this monster." Rachel wrapped her arms around the massive vase. "So what did you get Ashland?"

I felt a bit woozy for a second but caught my balance easily. I wished I could tell Rachel my secret, but I had to tell Ashland first. If I ever got around to speaking to him again. Just a few weeks ago I thought telling Ashland that we were having a baby would be the perfect anniversary present. Now I didn't know when I would tell him. "I'll be honest with you. I've been so busy with our new office that I haven't even thought about it."

"Carrie Jo! Are you kidding me? It's your second anniversary—you have to do *something*." As if she could fix my problem, she asked, "What did you give him last year?"

"Okay, now who's being sentimental?" I helped her position the white ceramic vase on the table and arranged the flowers. Touching the soft petals, I remembered our first kiss. I would never forget that night. It seemed like a lifetime ago.

"Let's see...last year I got him a first-edition copy of *The Jungle Book*, believe it or not. He's a huge Kipling fan."

Shoot! I must be the worst wife on the planet. Spying on his dreams and forgetting our anniversary. Yep, I'm batting a thousand.

Before she could ask me anything else, I told her the good news about Idlewood. Immediately we fired up our computers and began grabbing the research we needed for the proposal. Of course, we had the Seven Sisters model to go by, but each job had its own challenges. Ashland called me sometime around lunch, but I let it go to voicemail. Rachel's eyes widened, but she didn't ask any more questions. We ordered Chinese and kept working. By the time five o'clock came around, I needed a break from numbers and plans and debated on whether or not to head home.

Just then, Chip arrived to pick up Rachel. I'd already asked her to work on a Saturday, and I couldn't very well insist she work past five. She had a life—it wasn't her fault I was trying to avoid mine. "Have fun, you two."

Chip waved goodbye and walked out the door, but Rachel lingered behind. "Carrie Jo, it's your anniversary. Go home, for goodness' sake. Whatever you two are going through, you can work it out. I just know it. We've got a handle on this now. Go home. I'll come and help you tomorrow."

"I appreciate that. I'll go home soon, I promise."

"No need, apparently…your husband is here! Have a nice night! Don't do anything I wouldn't do."

"Which is what?" I asked with a laugh.

Ashland walked in, his expensive cologne filling the room before his arrival. God, that man always smelled so good. And he looked great, of course. I could see he'd bought a new shirt, light blue like his eyes, and he had taken the time to get a haircut. My emotions surged again—on one hand I wanted to feel his hands on my skin, but on the other hand I wanted to slap the smile off his face. This was indeed a dilemma.

Where had even-tempered, reasonable Carrie Jo gone? When would she be back?

"Hey, I tried to call you. Did you get my messages?"

"Were there more than one?" I picked up my cell and saw he'd called three times. "Oh yeah, I've been slammed here. It's been kind of crazy. Sorry about that." I shuffled the papers around on my desk and avoided eye contact.

"You haven't been in business for more than a week. You're slammed already? What do you have going on?" He sounded a little irritated, as if he didn't quite believe me. He picked up the sheaf of papers on my desk and scanned them. A slow smile spread across his handsome face. "You got Idlewood? That's amazing, Carrie Jo."

Snatching the papers away from him I answered hotly, "I haven't got anything yet. I'm working on the proposal, and I have less than forty eight hours to get it to Desmond Taylor. This might be my only chance to work on the Idlewood restoration. I don't want to blow it."

"Oh, I see." He noticed the flowers on the side table and pointed to them. "You like the flowers?"

"Yes, they are very nice. Thank you, and happy anniversary. Your gift isn't here yet. It might be a few days late."

"Carrie Jo, what is going on? You've hardly talked to me all week. I get the feeling you're mad about something, but I don't know what. Please just tell me what's on your mind."

"I don't have time for this right now, Ashland." I added more gently, "When I finish this proposal I swear we'll talk all you want. Okay?"

"Fine, Why not let me help you? I'll cancel the dinner reservations I made, and we'll work on this together. Who else, besides you, knows more about restoration projects than me? What are you in the mood for? Chinese? Italian? I could call Mama's and go pick up something."

The idea of food made my stomach feel queasy. All I wanted was a bottle of water and some oranges. I'd always heard that pregnant women had strange cravings—I didn't want much of anything except oranges. I couldn't get enough citrus fruit lately.

"Are you okay? You look a little pale."

"Yes, I'm fine. I've just been staring at these computer screens all day. You don't have to stay, Ashland. I am sure you're just as tired as I am. Go home—I'll be there in a couple of hours." I sat behind my desk and didn't wait for an answer.

"Damn it, CJ! It's our anniversary! Can't you at least pretend you want to spend it with me?"

Leaping out of the chair I yelled back at him, "Can't you give me some space?"

"Tell me what's going on!" His voice grew louder and I could tell by his body language that he was none too happy with me. I couldn't deny he'd been patient about the proposal, but I still couldn't shake the feeling of betrayal.

"Alright! You want to know so much." I flew to my feet. "You've been dreaming about women—lots and lots of women! You don't even care that I am lying right beside you! Every night it's someone new, Ash. I can't remember the last time I got to sleep without being forced to watch my husband make love to someone else! You tell *me* what the hell is going on!"

"Are you seriously mad about some dream? Like I get to pick what I dream about? Is this really what you're mad about, Carrie Jo?" He laughed bitterly and put his hands on his hips. "All this time I thought I'd done something wrong, and this is why you're pissed? I can't believe what I'm hearing!"

"You better believe it!" Fat, salty tears welled up in my eyes. I felt another wave of nausea. "Why are you all of a sudden dreaming about other women? Are you having an affair? With that brunette you're fantasizing about?"

"Who? What the heck are you talking about—I don't even know how to answer that. You know…" He raised his hands and walked toward the door. "When you're done being crazy, call me."

I stared in shock as he walked out the door, making sure to slam it behind him. I fell back in my seat and cried my eyes out. He was right, I was acting crazy. What the heck was wrong with me? I suddenly missed Bette. I needed someone to talk to, someone who could help me navigate this ball of confusion that I'd wound myself up in. Detra Ann had quietly stepped out of my life, and Rachel and I didn't have the kind of relationship that I felt comfortable sharing my problems with her. Most people had a mother to talk to. Not me.

Ugh, I don't have time to feel sorry for myself. I wiped my face with a tissue and continued to work on my project. Work was probably the best thing for me right now. If I were home, I would just wallow in my misery. At least at work I could focus on something else. I struggled with the spreadsheets for about an hour and then gave up. My mind wasn't here, and neither was my heart. I wasn't going to get anything done tonight except cry all over my paperwork. I grabbed my purse, hoping Ashland had gone home. He was right, we did need to talk, and I would have to start with an apology. I got behind the wheel of my BMW, slid the key in the ignition and turned it.

Click, click.

And that made me cry too. After a few minutes, I rubbed my red face with my now soppy tissue and decided to walk home. At least I'd get some fresh air and have time to rehearse what I would say. It was only four blocks from the office, and I hadn't worn heels. A light winter wind blew, but the temperatures were only in the fifties. It had been a long time since I'd gone for a walk through the streets of downtown Mobile. I thought about Seven Sisters and how hard it would be to get there. *No, you've got enough problems, Carrie Jo.* I kept my eye on the broken sidewalks and tried to enjoy the scenery. This was a particularly nice block, with lovely old homes and cast-iron fences with fleur-de-lis perching atop the occasional posts. I walked past a house with thumping music and excited young people. When was the last time I'd been to a party?

Halfway there now. Just ahead I saw the low-hanging sign that marked one of Mobile's most significant landmarks, the Magnolia Cemetery. Often referred to by locals as the City of the Dead, some of the city's earliest citizens were buried here, along with hundreds of Civil War soldiers. There were even huge mausoleums that housed the bones of entire generations of families. I approached the open gate and slowed my walk. I had always meant to explore this place but had never gotten around to it. I tugged my purse up on my shoulder as if some nefarious purse-snatcher hovered near me in the shadows of the great oak trees.

A flash of light caught my eye. *Must be the night watchman making rounds.* I paused at the open gate. *Hmm…that's odd. I thought they closed this place at dusk.* Well, I was here, and there was a good chance that Ashland would need some time to cool off. Shoving the squeaking gate open the rest of the way, I headed toward the light. I'd let the security guard know I was here, have a quick peek around and then head home. No harm done, right?

The light bounced through the trees, and it was difficult to keep up with it as I navigated the maze of graves. I hoped to avoid tripping over the roots of the massive oak and magnolia trees that littered the cemetery. I couldn't help but squint at the grave markers of some of the cemetery's older residents. Some of the tombstones were so old that the names were hard to read. Since the beginnings of Mobile, bodies had been laid to rest here—neatly at first, and then much more haphazardly as the centuries passed and space became an issue. Everywhere I looked I could see sentimental stonework like weeping angels and broken columns. Besides the children's markers, I found the broken columns the saddest. They represented the last person in a family line. During the Civil War there were a lot of broken columns installed in the Magnolia Cemetery. How many sons had died during that horrendous war?

This was no time to be distracted. Shaking myself out of my reverie, I called out to the security guard. "Hello! Excuse me!" The cemetery was getting darker by the second, and there were no lights besides the bouncing light I had chased from one side of the grounds to the other. Peering through the dim light, I tried to discern a figure. I stepped out from under an old oak covered in Spanish moss into a clearing and watched the light. The air suddenly felt thick and, for lack of a better word, sparkly. It occurred to me that what I was seeing was not normal at all. That wasn't a flashlight! What had appeared to be the beam of a flashlight suddenly changed color to a soft amber glow that bounced ever so softly off the ground about three feet.

"What in the world?" I thought perhaps it could be children or teenagers playing in the cemetery, but that didn't make sense either. I leaned against the oak and called one more time. I had to be imagining things. "Hello?" The light stopped bouncing, expanded and then shrank to half its original size. "Oh my God!"

Yep. This was something supernatural.

Suddenly the light shot across the cemetery toward the gate to the left. Without thinking, I took off after it. It didn't move as I got closer to the gate; it just hung in midair, still bouncing a little. I'd heard of orbs before but had never actually seen one. If that was what this was. Many people thought these were some type of ghost, but I had no idea. Most of the ghosts I saw were in dreams. Well, before Seven Sisters.

It was completely dark now and a chill crept into the air, a chill that had not been there before. Another warning sign. Clutching my purse, I ran ahead, stopping to hide behind a moldy mausoleum wall. I held my breath and silently counted to ten before slowly peering around the corner to take a peek at the light. The reasonable part of my brain told me to call someone, but who would that be? I watched as the light hovered in midair just this side of the gate. Maybe it wanted me to follow? Why else would it hang around?

I looked around the cemetery and saw no one else—no one living, anyway. I was by myself except for whatever entity this was I was chasing. Terrified, I leaned flush against the marble, the cold creeping through my clothing. I heard a noise I couldn't identify—it started as a low moan and quickly became a screech. A small, dark shadow launched itself from the top of the mausoleum and landed on the ground beside me. It was a damn cat! A gray cat with an attitude, upset at the invader who had appeared in his playground. After my heart stopped pounding in my chest, I peeked around the corner again and took a deep breath. It was now or never.

I stepped out quickly, as if I could surprise it. As I did, the light flared and passed through the closed gate, disappearing into the dark Alabama night. I decided to follow it—I'd come this far. The gate was stubborn and didn't give way without a fight. I gripped the cold cast-iron bars with both hands and pushed as hard as I could, and the gate swung open. I felt the chill again, and the hairs on my arms stood up.

Here I was again, completely surrounded by the supernatural with nowhere to run. Still clutching my purse like it was some sort of fashionable life preserver, I took a deep breath and stepped through the gate.

That was the last thing I remembered.

Chapter 5—Ashland

My wife never ceased to amaze me, but lately the surprises weren't anything good. To think she'd been spying on my dreams and accused me of cheating. I couldn't believe this was the Carrie Jo I loved and married. When I first saw her, she took my breath away. The more I got to know her, the more I was amazed at her knowledge, but it wasn't just that. She had a deep compassion for people, even though at times she doubted her own ability to help them.

I will always remember the first time I saw her—a beautiful woman standing at the foot of the stairs of my family home. She wore a red blouse with slightly puffy sleeves and a red and white skirt with a tiny rose pattern all over it. Her legs were tanned and lovely, her face even lovelier with amazing green eyes and wild curly hair. I could tell instantly that she had a sense of humor and that she would not be easily impressed with my southern-boy swagger.

Seeing her there that night was like a sign, or at least I thought it was. But now I didn't know what to think. I stuffed some clothing in my overnight bag and headed out the door. I didn't leave a note for her—why bother? It sounded like she thought I was a disgusting letch. Didn't she know I loved her more than any woman on the planet? Hadn't we been through enough together for her to know that I was hers forever? Apparently not. Locking the door behind me, I looked down the street to see if I could spot her car. I made a deal with God: if I saw it in the next sixty seconds, I would know she wanted to work it out and I would stay. I tossed my bag in the truck and waited. When she didn't come, I sighed, pulled out of the driveway and drove to the marina. I'd stay on the Happy Go Lucky tonight and figure out what my next move was. It would be cold as heck on the water this time of year, but it would have to do. I stopped by the grocery store to grab a few things for supper. I was starving. And to think I had planned on giving Carrie Jo an anniversary gift that she would never forget. I shook my head, did my shopping and headed to the boat.

About an hour later, I was sitting on the deck chewing an overcooked hamburger and watching the moonlight splash on the water. This was not the way I had planned to spend my anniversary. Wiping my hands with a napkin, I checked my phone yet again for a text or voicemail from Carrie Jo. Nothing. Not a peep. I stared off into the distance, sipping my beer and wondering what I could do to fix our current situation. We'd been through too much, seen too much to give up now, but this wouldn't work if only one of us was committed to seeing it through.

To make matters worse, I was seeing ghosts again. Not family ghosts this time, thankfully. Most were strangers, faded people who glared at me from curtained windows and sailed past me at inopportune moments. Even at home. Having other people around seemed to keep them away, though. Thank goodness for Doreen. When Carrie Jo wasn't there, Doreen was. The more living souls in the house, the merrier. People told me my "sight" was a gift, but I wouldn't call it that. I'd hated psychics and mediums when I was growing up, and now I'd become the thing I hated. Yeah, seeing ghosts was never fun. It always surprised me, and unlike on those stupid television shows, they never wanted anything or asked for anything. They didn't speak to me or ask for my help "finding the light." They were always unhappy or fixated on something. And likewise I never spoke to them or tried to communicate with them. Maybe I was going crazy like my mother.

To keep my mind straight, I decided to keep a diary. I wrote down what I saw, where I spotted the ghosts and the dates I saw them and for how long. I noticed that my ability to see ghosts was heightened during the full moon. What was I? Some sort of psychic werewolf? The only place I really found peace was on the water. I never saw anything out here. Once I thought I did, but it turned out to be nothing. And nobody had ever died on my boat—I'd bought it brand new just to be sure. Thank God for that.

Now I really thought I was going crazy. I saw a ghost yesterday, but it wasn't a true ghost—it was Detra Ann, who I knew for a fact was alive and well. What made it stranger was the ghost appeared in my home, on the stairs where she had been shot—probably by another ghost. I had called out to her, but she disappeared, shimmering for a second and then fluttering away like the end of an old movie reel. Her appearance had surprised me so much that I yelled. Doreen had stepped into the hallway to check on me. She swore that there was no one else in the house. I couldn't understand it. Maybe tomorrow I would go by the shop and see Detra Ann and Henri. I missed my friends. I missed my wife. How on earth had my life gone completely nuts?

I checked my phone one more time before I took it below to plug it in. I cleaned up the galley and headed to the shower. Carrie Jo wasn't going to call me. My wife was a stubborn woman but normally not this unreasonable. Why not just call it a night? After my shower, I fell asleep reading a book on mastering extrasensory perception. I woke with a stiff neck to the sound of someone calling my name.

"Ashland! You there?"

"Carrie Jo?" I tossed the book to the side and walked out on the deck. Libby Stevenson, a former schoolmate and my new attorney, stood on the dock with two cups of coffee. Her long dark hair shone in the sunlight. I had never seen her in casual clothing before, but today she wore blue jeans with a purposeful hole in the knee and a comfortable-looking blue t-shirt that read *LA: City of Dreams*. "May I come aboard? I come bearing gifts."

"Sure," I said, running my hands through my wild hair. My eyes felt sticky and my brain was tired—I must have stayed out later than I thought. "How did you know I was here? Did you talk to Carrie Jo?"

"I just happened to be riding by and saw your truck here. I know it's not a workday, but I figured I'd come take a peek at the infamous Happy Go Lucky." She handed me a cup of coffee.

I took it from her with a smile. "Infamous? I wouldn't say that."

"Well, it's the talk of the office. Roger Bosarge says that this is the boat you caught that prize-winning fish in—he thinks either this boat is lucky or you cheated. That was at the Deep Sea Fishing Rodeo a few years ago, right?" I nodded. "Someday you'll have to take me fishing." Pretty white teeth gleamed at me, and I couldn't help but smile back.

"You like to fish?"

"Big time. Growing up that's all we did. My dad believed in teaching us how to fish. I have to admit it's been a while since I've tossed a hook in the water, but I think I remember how to catch one." We sipped our coffees and sat in silence for a few minutes. "How did Mrs. Stuart like her gift?"

"I haven't given it to her yet."

"Oh, I see." Libby's blue eyes widened, and she clamped her lips for a second. "Sorry to hear that."

"It's no big deal."

"For what it's worth, I'd love to get a gift like that. Any woman would. I hope she knows how lucky she is."

"Truth be told, I'm the lucky one." I meant every word. I did love Carrie Jo. Despite this minor glitch, we'd gotten on very well considering the supernatural forces that continually arrayed themselves against us. She had helped me unravel my family's sordid past and set us free from a variety of self-inflicted curses. I was indeed a lucky man.

"That's sweet. You're just too good to be true."

I decided to change the subject. "So how is Jeremy? I heard he started his own veterinary clinic in Clarke County. Has he gotten over Kelly yet?"

Libby pursed her lips and rolled her eyes. "You know how my brother is. He's been in love with Kelly about as long as I've loved—" She stopped short, and I thought I saw a blush rise on her face. Taking another sip of her coffee, she continued, "Well, it's been a long time. At least she didn't leave him standing at the altar. He's got his animals so I think he'll be okay."

"He's got a terrific little sister—I'm sure he'll be fine."

She laughed dryly at the idea. "Relationship advice is truly not my field of expertise. If you need to evict a deadbeat, then I'm your girl. But I'm sure you're right. My brother is kind, handsome and successful—like you. He won't be lonely for long. Frankly, I would like to see him play the field a little more. Get out there and mingle. I think his biggest problem is he doesn't know what he's been missing."

I smiled at the idea of Jeremy mingling. He had been an excellent receiver, the best football player on our team; the guy was fearless on the field, but when it came to women he could hardly put two sentences together, at least before he met Kelly. I was bummed that the two of them had split up, but that kind of stuff happened.

"Which brings me to my next question…what made you get into an all-fired rush to get married? I thought you would be single forever."

"What makes you say that? I have never been a player."

Libby took a seat beside me and carefully removed the plastic lid from her steaming drink. "Oh, come on. It's me you're talking to. The unofficial little sister to the entire Bulldogs football team—I know the truth, Ash. Let's see, there was Shay Dawson, Aimee Wilkinson, Jenna Daughtry…"

"Shay and I are just friends, always have been. Aimee…I did like her, but she moved senior year. And Jenna wasn't the kind of girl to stay with one guy for too long."

"You know, Jenna's changed a lot. Can you believe she married Tony Merritt? Better her than me. I don't think I could ever be a preacher's wife. And then there was Detra Ann. I always thought if I didn't marry you, she'd be the one to put a ring on your finger. Y'all were inseparable."

My phone rang, and I unplugged it from the charger. "This is Ashland."

"Morning, sunshine! Is Carrie Jo coming in today? I told her I'd be here this morning, but she hasn't showed up. If she's going to be late could you ask her to bring some breakfast when she comes in? I'm starving." Rachel Kowalski always talked like that. She threw whole paragraphs at you without taking a breath. Young, ambitious, and completely loyal. I felt guilty that I didn't know what to tell her.

"I'm not at the house right now, so I'm not sure."

"Did she mention coming in? Because that was the plan yesterday. Here I thought I was late. You two must have stayed up too late last night. Oh, the married life."

"Actually, I stayed on the boat last night."

She was silent for a moment. "Sorry, Mr. Stuart. Didn't mean to be nosy. Well, I'll call the house phone again. She's not answering her cell, and her car is here."

"Her car is there? Tell you what—I'll head that way and bring you both some breakfast."

"Sounds yummy. Thanks so much! Bye!"

I dialed Carrie Jo's number, but she still wasn't answering. Her cheery voice asked me to leave a voicemail. I hung up and tried the house phone. Still no dice. Doreen didn't work on Sundays, so I'd have to go check myself. That familiar nagging feeling that something was wrong began to grow in my gut.

"Thanks for the coffee, Libby, but I have to go."

"I overheard the conversation. I hope everything is all right with Carrie Jo. Need me to tag along?"

"No, I'm sure it's nothing. My wife hasn't been feeling well lately."

"I'm just a phone call away if you need me."

"Thanks." I began collecting my things and practically ran down the pier to my car. What a jerk I'd been! I should have stayed home last night instead of pouting on the boat. I haphazardly dialed her phone again as I peeled out of the parking lot slinging rocks and dust. The harbormaster yelled at me, but I didn't have time to explain.

No answer. This isn't good.

Adjusting my rearview mirror as I sped down the causeway, I nearly screamed. For a second it appeared that someone was in my backseat. I saw a face—a man's face. He had pale skin, dark hair that curled around the collar of his crumbling white shirt and empty eyes. I could barely form a thought before he vanished in a less than a second. My car swerved erratically until I got it under control. I swore under my breath as I tried to slow my breathing.

No. This isn't good at all.

Chapter 6—Delilah

I ran as fast as my feet would carry me away from Adam's shop. He shouted my name again, but I didn't stop to answer him. I didn't know where I planned to go—back to Maundy's, I supposed. Where else could I go? Anywhere but with Adam. In my mind I could still see his sweaty back writhing over Blessing Harper, the leatherman's middle daughter. She'd been panting beneath him, repeating his name hungrily, when I walked into the store room of the carpentry shop. I wouldn't have even walked in if he'd bothered to close the door. It was almost as if he wanted to get caught.

Adam came running after me, still shirtless. "Stop, Delilah!" He reached toward me and grabbed my shoulder, spinning me around forcefully.

"Get your damn hands off me!" I shouted at him.

"So now you are swearing? What else has Maundy Weaver taught you?"

"Me? You have no room to criticize me, Adam Iverson! How could you do this?"

Suddenly he stiffened, his chin raised defiantly, and peered down at me with icy blue eyes. "This is your fault," he said viciously as he pointed a finger at me. "You are the one who decided we should no longer be together. Remember the speech you gave me, *sister*? You are the one who wanted to forget about us, and for what? To claim an old name and a fortune you will never have. What would our parents think about you now, Delilah?"

I slapped him as hard as I could right across the face. My hand stung, and his pale skin instantly turned red with the vivid prints from my fingers and palm. He took a step toward me but then froze, his glance riveted to some action over my shoulder. I turned myself, relieved to see Jackson Keene walking toward us, his face dark with concern.

"Here comes your new lover to save you, sister. Now I see why you pushed me out of your bed." I gasped at his insinuation, feeling now as if I had been the one slapped, especially in light of the fact Adam was walking away with bits of straw on his naked back. He didn't wait around to hear my reply, not that I would have given him one. In his mind he would always be right, no matter how wrong he was. He was a fool. His tall, lumbering frame headed back to the carpentry shop.

Some women would have fallen apart; I knew a few who would do just that having worked in Maundy's shop and in her private parlor for the past few months. The stories I'd heard I would never have imagined. Maundy was right—women did talk too much, about too many things and especially about one another. Unfortunately as of yet, I had heard nothing about Claudette Page. But I had heard plenty of tales of adultery, babies born out of wedlock, husbands who asked their wives for strange acts in the bedroom, and it was all proof of what I suspected. Marriage was not so much a thing to be desired as a hardship that crushed the soul—at least the female soul. The more I heard, the less I wanted to be Mrs. Anyone. How could I have ever imagined that I would be Adam's wife?

Instead of weeping like a child, I relished the rebellion that rose up within me. Adam had been the one who wanted to return to Mobile, and I had agreed. He was the one who wanted to come back "home" and make a name for himself, and I had come with him. We had done everything he wanted and nothing else. I refused to live my life according to his whims anymore. I vowed to never be under the control of any man ever again. And I would never surrender my right to my family name and my inheritance. I was going to have everything I wanted in this life—even if that meant living without love! All the passion, all the love I had believed I felt for Adam had been nothing but an illusion.

"Miss Page, may I be of assistance?" Mr. Keene glared toward Adam's shop, obviously ready to defend my honor. If only he knew that I didn't have any honor left. But I did not worry that Adam would tell him. He would rather die than have the world know he had been romantically involved with his "sister." Why? Half the town knew the truth—I was the bastard child of Christine Cottonwood and Hoyt Page. The other half believed everything Claudette Page and her unofficial "morality society" told them. That I was a nobody, an incestuous scam artist bent on destroying the Page family name and with that the City of Mobile. Last week the woman had the nerve to send me a check for five thousand dollars and a one-way train ticket out of town. I ripped up the check and sent it back with a little note of my own.

Keep your money, Aunt Claudette. In the future, please send all correspondence to my attorney, Jackson Keene.

"Yes, Mr. Keene, I believe you can be of help to me. I would like to find a new place to live. I think it's time I moved out of the store. In fact, I would like to sell the whole building." He blinked, his intelligent eyes full of surprise.

"Mr. Iverson may have something to say about that."

"I have full confidence in your negotiation talents. If Adam does cause a fuss, let him know that I am willing to relinquish all the other Iverson properties to him…and remind him that he has as much to lose as I do when it comes to reputation. All I want are the proceeds from this building. I am sure that is what my parents would have wanted."

"I'll make the arrangements, Miss Page, and begin inquiries on a new home. I think we can find something for you…here in town, correct?"

"Yes," I said with a smile, pretending that he didn't look relieved. "I intend to keep working with Maundy Weaver. Maybe something on Florence Street or perhaps Carlen? Is the Winslow home still available? The yellow one with the wisteria out front?" He smiled and nodded. Together we walked back to my shop, side by side on the dusty wooden walkway. I glanced back once to make sure Adam wasn't glaring at us, but I needn't have worried. He didn't show his face again. He wouldn't with Mr. Keene around. Seeing the street now crowded, I decided to take the back way around.

"You know, if you sell the shop, Claudette Page will think she's won."

"Let her think that. What it really means is—what's that poker term? Oh yes, 'I'm all in.'"

He laughed. "I never figured you for a poker player."

"It's a recent hobby I've taken up, and I am told I'm quite good at it."

"I believe that completely," he replied, smiling down at me. "So a small home, like a cottage?"

"Yes, nothing too pricy."

"You know, according to Dr. Page's will, you technically own a few properties near here."

"Yes, and if I step foot near one, his sister will have me tossed out before I unpack the first trunk. No, I don't think I'm ready to go to war. Not yet, Mr. Keene."

"I like your spirit, Miss Page." By his smile, I could tell he meant it. Still, I refused to blush like a teenage virgin. "It is nearly suppertime. Will you do me the honor of having supper with me this evening? We could talk more about what it is you're looking for, in the way of houses. Did I tell you that the judge who will be hearing your case came in on the train today? I have already taken the liberty of introducing myself to him. I think the high-and-mighty Claudette Page may find this new judge less flexible on the law."

"Flexible. That's a nice word for it," I huffed, ignoring his question. "Judge Parker barely even heard our case before he ruled against me." A few people walked down the side street and stared at us, but I had trained myself not to look at their faces. I didn't even mind that some women saw me and crossed to the other side of the street, as if being illegitimate were a disease to be caught. Mr. Keene didn't seem to mind at all.

"You were right to appeal, and you *will* win. Of that I am sure. The morality law that Judge Parker cited is a relic—almost as much of a relic as the judge himself. I feel sure that by this summer you'll be sipping lemonade on the porch of some Page property." He smiled again—it was a nice thing to see.

Jackson Keene was not overtly handsome, not like Adam with his chiseled, Nordic features, impressive height and fit physique. From working in Maundy's shop I could take Mr.

Keene's measure without ever putting a tape to him. Barely 5'10", he had a sturdy medium build with flashing blue eyes and a manicured mustache that hinted at pink lips. I knew for a fact that the ladies enjoyed looking at him because anytime he visited the shop there was a wave of excited chatter after he left and sometimes even while he was there. He was five years my senior but had a young face, and I believed if he ever shaved he'd probably look much younger than he was.

He paused at the back door of my shop as I pulled the key from my purse. I thanked him for walking me home, but he didn't leave right away. He stood with his hat in his hand, waiting for my answer to his invitation.

With a polite smile I answered, "Yes, I will have supper with you. Step inside, Mr. Keene. You can make yourself comfortable in the shop. There are some chairs behind the counter. I would like to tidy up if you don't mind. I won't be a minute."

"Certainly, I will be happy to wait." He followed me into the shop, and I walked up the stairs sure that he was watching me. I changed my clothes quickly. Although Adam no longer lived in the apartment with me—he'd moved into the quarter house attached to the shop—it wasn't beyond him to come stomping up the stairs without warning. Tidying myself as quickly as I could, I scowled at myself in the mirror. Hadn't I just sworn off men? Here I was, going to dinner with my attorney. Tongues would wag, but weren't they already? Again rebellion filled my heart.

What did these people know about me?

I dipped my fingers in the water basin and smoothed my hair in an attempt to tidy up the curls that sprang up around my face. I had a new gray dress with a thin black ribbon that ran across the top of the bodice. It had a modest neckline with three-quarter sleeves, a bit old fashioned perhaps but perfectly respectable for a business dinner.

In a few minutes I was ready, but I lingered at the mirror. I was still young and some called me pretty, although it had been a long time since anyone had complimented me on my appearance.

Like I had so many times since I first read that letter from Dr. Page, I studied my face in the mirror. I wondered whose eyes those were, whose nose? Did my mother have a pretty voice? How did she die? I would never know, but at least I had life. I supposed I should be grateful that I wasn't abandoned at an orphanage or drowned in a river. With a frown I reached for my perfume and sprayed my hair once before I rejoined my guest.

I heard Mr. Keene sliding the wooden chair back; it made a hash sound, and I tried not to stare at the scrape on the floor. He walked toward the back door but I stopped him.

"No, not the back door. Let's go this way, if you don't mind." I waved him to the front. I took the key out of my black satin purse and opened the front door.

"As you wish." He followed me out and waited patiently as I fumbled with the key. My black lace glove caught the metal, but I quickly unsnagged myself and locked the door. "You look lovely," he whispered.

"Thank you, Mr. Keene. Where are we dining tonight?"

"Let's take my carriage. Have you been to Patterson's yet?"

"No, I haven't, but I am quite hungry." I climbed aboard the carriage and arranged my dress neatly. Mr. Keene sat beside me, and together we rode through town with our heads held high. As we traveled, he told me stories about the war, how various businesses and families had fared and what he thought about the prospects for the city. He had been born in Mississippi but had been in Mobile since the end of the war. I did not think it polite to tell him I probably knew more than he did about Mobile society, as I was Maundy's friend and was privy to much information. So I listened and nodded appropriately.

We drove at least twenty minutes, passing the cathedral and the expansive oak groves that lined Dauphin Street. I had not been this far down Dauphin since I was a child, and I could barely remember those times anymore. The carriage turned down an unmarked road, and I suddenly felt a bit panicked. Where were we going? The carriage paused in front of a looming plantation at the end of a wide red dirt lane. As we drew closer, I could see that the house wasn't completely empty; a few lamps shone through the windows, and gas lamps flickered along the carriageway. Despite the light it didn't feel like a happy place, not in the least. I shivered and pulled my wrap closer. "Is this Patterson's? I didn't know we were going to someone's home."

"You've never been here, Miss Page? This is Seven Sisters." I caught my breath. "My mother's home?"

"Yes. She moved here from north Alabama when she married Jeremiah Cottonwood. Truth be told, it was her money that kept this house in the Cottonwood name. It's no secret that her husband could not manage his pocketbook, much less an estate of this size."

In a determined voice I said, "I want to go inside."

"I don't know if that's such a good idea. I had no intention of stopping—I merely wanted you to see the place. I don't think anyone lives there anymore, except for a few of the former slaves and occasionally some obscure relative. And...not to cast aspersions, Miss Page, but the current resident is probably a Cottonwood and thus is less likely to make you welcome. No offense, of course."

"I want to go inside," I said again as I slid clumsily out of the carriage seat. The red clay dirt crumbled into powder beneath my feet, evidence of the long dry spell Mobile had endured recently. Mr. Keene stepped down beside me and offered me his arm.

"Let us go and make our acquaintance." I slid my arm through his and held my breath as the massive front door opened. A tall black man stepped out on the porch. Other faces peered at us from the hallway. My grip on Mr. Keene's arm tightened as we walked up the steps.

The attorney called to the man in a friendly voice, "Good evening. We would like to call on the lady or gentleman of the house. I am Jackson Keene, and this is Miss Delilah...Iverson."

"Delilah Page," I corrected him. I wasn't going to hide my identity like some criminal. He squeezed my hand gently. The tall man showed no emotion one way or another. His dark eyes revealed nothing.

"Please come in, sir, ma'am. My name is Stokes. I will tell Miss Cottonwood you are here. I think she's been expecting you." With a puzzled look, Mr. Keene followed the man into the house and I trailed behind him. Pulling my gray silk wrap even tighter around my shoulders, I nearly fainted at the sight.

The house was easily the biggest home I had ever visited. Maundy Weaver's was nothing in comparison to this place, and I thought her home grand. That was before I set foot in Seven Sisters. Under my feet was a colorful rug with big blue flowers. It looked worn and frayed at the edges, but the floors were neatly kept. A side table held a vase full of dying flowers, the shriveled petals the only flaw in the scene. The place smelled like soap and magnolias. Stokes had walked up the wooden staircase, leaving us to wait in the foyer.

I saw a small fire burning in the room to my left, and like a moth to a flame I walked toward it. Mr. Keene did not follow me, and I did not seek his permission to go. I still couldn't believe I was here—at Seven Sisters. *This may be the closest I'll ever be to my mother!*

So many fine things, and yet an overwhelming sadness pervaded the room. It almost made me cry. A small collection of books lay on a round cherrywood table near the fireplace. I couldn't help but touch them. I thought Miss Cottonwood must like to read, a hobby that I had not taken up faithfully. I read quite well but found that reading for long periods of time made me sleepy. After glancing at the books for a few minutes, I warmed my hands at the fire.

I heard voices in the foyer but didn't turn to look. I stepped back from the fire and saw a large portrait hanging on the wall. I couldn't imagine why I hadn't noticed it when I first came in. The frame was painted gold, and I could see the artist's signature in the corner: *R. Ball.*

It was a portrait of a young woman dressed in a beautiful coral gown. Her shiny brown hair was arranged in a complicated yet flattering hairstyle, and dainty earbobs dangled from her pretty ears. She had a faraway look in her eyes, and on her lips was a hint of a smile. I wondered who she might be. My mother? Some relative I would never know or be able to claim? As if someone were reading my mind, a voice beside me answered my question.

"That is Calpurnia Cottonwood—the daughter of the late Jeremiah and Christine Cottonwood. From what I understand she was the beauty of the county. She disappeared some time ago, before I was born."

I wanted to continue to stare at the portrait, especially now that I knew the woman's identity. To think this was my sister Calpurnia, and not just a half-sister or a stepsister but my true blood sister, if Dr. Page's account was to be believed. She was riveting. Still, I couldn't be rude to my hostess; I had not been invited into this room. The least I could do was be polite.

Pulling my attention from the portrait, I faced the new lady of the house. Younger than me and not as tall, her voice didn't quite match her face. Although she was young, she had a deep voice and intelligent hazel eyes. I could tell she didn't give two figs about her appearance: her clothes were smart but not too stylish, and she wore her dark blond hair in a simple bun. My hostess did not extend her hand or offer a smile. I could sense that she was suspicious, but who could blame her with two strangers showing up at her mansion uninvited? If she did know who I was, then she must think I was crazy or an upstart. Honestly, I didn't know why I had wanted to come inside. Visiting Seven Sisters had not been on my list of things to do. The idea had never crossed my mind before we arrived there this evening.

My attorney cleared his throat and offered an explanation. "Please pardon the intrusion, madam. We were just passing by, and the house is such a lovely Mobile landmark that we could not resist visiting it. Let me introduce myself properly. I am Jackson Keene and this is my friend, Delilah Iverson-Page." I thought I saw her eyes widen a little, but Miss Cottonwood did not comment or ask questions. In fact, she ignored Mr. Keene entirely.

"Yes," she said as she stepped toward me, "you have the look of her. I have seen you before—at Miss Weaver's fitting parlor. Now I remember. But you don't remember me? My name is Karah Cottonwood."

Embarrassed at the slight I stammered, "We see many women on a daily basis. Forgive me if I don't. Did I work on your dress?"

She smiled, and I was reminded of that phrase, 'the cat that ate the canary'. I had a feeling I was the canary. "No, you didn't work on my dress. I came to place an order with Miss Weaver. We have not been introduced, not officially." She turned her attention to the portrait. "Is this why you are here? To assess some claim on Seven Sisters?" She finally spoke to Mr. Keene. "You are an attorney, correct?"

With a courteous wave of his hand, he shook his head. "As Miss Page's attorney, I can assure you that my client has not expressed any desire to make a claim on Seven Sisters. She was merely curious to see the place, and I must confess she had no idea I was bringing her here. Please accept my apology. It was not my intention to inconvenience you." Miss Cottonwood listened, but her gaze didn't leave my face. I felt compelled to speak.

"I have no such desire."

The young lady must have been satisfied with that answer, for she took a deep breath and a sincere smile crossed her face. "Have you had any supper? I was about to take mine, and there is more than enough. Would you two be my guests? I never knew your sister, Miss Page, or the late Mrs. Cottonwood, but I will be happy to answer any of your questions if I can."

Now it was my turn to smile. "Oh, yes. Thank you very much."

"Follow me." Miss Cottonwood walked with her hands in front of her. Wherever she was from, she was certainly trained to behave like a lady. An evil thought crossed my mind. What if

I did claim the house? Shouldn't it be partly mine? Miss Cottonwood was living in grand style in this grand house, enjoying my mother's wealth while I was laboring in the dress shop. Then I instantly felt guilty. My current situation was not Miss Cottonwood's responsibility or anyone else's. She had not wronged me.

We walked down the broad hallway, and I tried not to stare at the oil paintings that filled the walls. We walked to the door and stepped into the most beautiful room I had ever seen. With some pride Miss Cottonwood said, "This is the Blue Room—it is my favorite room in the house. The servants tell me it was once a place for musical concerts and spiritual readings. I think it's a delightful space." For the first time I heard youthful excitement in her voice. "Please make yourself welcome while I go tell Docie to set two more plates." With a polite nod she left us, closing the door behind her.

"Mr. Keene, have you ever seen anything like this place?" I explored the room, curious to examine every nook and cranny. On one wall a built-in shelf displayed a collection of ceramic puppies. I longed to pick them up and hold each one in my hand. I imagined they felt cool and smooth, but I did not dare. My hostess would not appreciate strangers destroying her property.

"I can't say that I have. I have been in some grand old homes, but I have to admit this is the grandest. I hope you hold no grudge toward me because I brought you here without warning. On reflection perhaps this was not a good idea. Perhaps it is wrong to show you all this knowing that you could never claim it."

"I am grateful that you did. I would never have had the courage to come here myself. I suppose I could press the issue if I wanted to, but I am happy with what I have—or will have." Tapping the spines of a collection of books by some obscure author I added, "It's never been about the money, Mr. Keene. I hope you know that. I want my name. My real name. I want to hold my head up high and introduce myself as Delilah Page. It is what my father wanted, or else he would never have written to me."

"Yes, the letter." His voice dropped. "Let us keep that letter to ourselves, if at all possible."

"Why? I'm not ashamed. I am who I am. I'm not less of a person despite my unhappy situation."

"No insult to you, Miss Page, but let me remind you that your father confessed to murder in that letter. In fact, I suspect that he did indeed murder Miss Cottonwood's father."

My face paled at the reminder. "I haven't forgotten that, Mr. Keene."

"Please call me Jackson."

Before I could argue with him, I heard yelling in the hall. Curious to discover the source of the disturbance, I walked to the door and opened it slightly. The young Miss Cottonwood was arguing with an older woman—a woman I had never seen before. "Just stop it! Do what I ask!" The older woman raised her head and stared at me. Miss Cottonwood spun about and saw me standing there. With a swish of her skirts she left the old woman in the hallway and came toward me, her face a mask of determination.

"Come, Miss Page. Let's sit together. Dinner will be here soon." Leading us to a round table in the corner of the room, she sat as if she were a queen at court. She had a natural elegance, an elegance I admired but did not have. As she and Mr. Keene exchanged pleasantries and talked about Mobile, I stared around the room, silently comparing myself to Miss Cottonwood. I was taller by at least a foot, and my dark hair was prone to curl, while hers was smooth and not as dark. Could it be true that we were related somehow? I wondered what Mr. Keene thought about her. I knew nothing about her, but I was dying to know where she was from and who she was related to. As if she read my mind, Miss Cottonwood said, "I suppose you are both wondering about me."

"We do seem to be at a disadvantage. Excuse me for asking, but is that an English accent I detect?"

"Yes, Mr. Keene. I spent quite a bit of time abroad with my mother before coming to Mobile."

I finally asked the question I had been dying to ask, "Who is your mother, Miss Cottonwood?"

With an even, steely gaze she answered me, "My mother is Isla Beaumont, daughter of Olivia Beaumont, sister of Christine Cottonwood."

"Are we related then in some way?" I asked her, my voice shakier than I expected.

"I think we are cousins, Miss Page."

"And your father?" I asked, ignoring Mr. Keene's scowl. It wasn't the proper thing to ask, but people asked me all the time, didn't they?

"Jeremiah Cottonwood. Unfortunately I never knew him." We three sat in silence for a full minute before she spoke again. "It seems there are a great many secrets here in this house. Don't you agree, Miss Page?"

"Yes, I do." A flurry of questions filled my brain. What happened to my mother, to my sister? What did my mother look like? Did she leave me anything? A note or a letter? But it was too soon in our acquaintance to bombard Miss Cottonwood with those queries. I had already broken protocol with my rude question once, but I had to know for sure. The servant, the older angry one with the slick dark hair, came in with platters of food and plunked them down unceremoniously on the linen-covered table.

"Thank you, Docie. Now please bring the wine for our guests."

She glared at Miss Cottonwood, who tried to ignore her. Our hostess placed her linen napkin in her lap, and I did the same. With a shiny gold fork she pierced a piece of ham and placed it on her plate. I helped myself to a piece of warm bread and a pat of butter. It was a simple but delicious meal. As she cut her meat into tiny pieces, she asked, "What are your plans, Miss Page? Do you intend to stay in Mobile?"

"I do indeed. This is my home. Granted, I have legal battles ahead of me, but I don't plan to turn tail and run. Mr. Keene is helping me adjudicate my case with the court. I am sure you have heard all about it."

"Where would I have heard anything like that? Do you think me a gossip?"

Her question surprised me. "I didn't mean to imply that," I said defensively.

Docie returned with a glass pitcher full of burgundy wine. She poured the young woman's drink and set the pitcher on the table. She didn't offer to pour ours or wait to be dismissed but glared at me again before leaving us alone. Aware of her servant's rudeness, Miss Cottonwood's cheeks reddened. She stood and poured our drinks, and then returned to her seat. Mr. Keene kept silent, watching the two of us. I thought I spotted a hint of a smile on his lips.

"I think what Miss Page means is that she is aware her situation is the source of quite a bit of gossip amongst certain quarters of Mobile society. It would not surprise either of us if you had heard something negative about her. However, having enjoyed her acquaintance these past months, I can vouch that she is a kind lady with a good many fine qualities." He sipped his wine and said seriously, "You know, it might be beneficial to you both to form some kind of alliance. Even an unofficial one. After all, you are family and face similar situations."

Ignoring the last part of his statement, she asked, "What sort of alliance?"

"Because of your unique social positions, it might be wise to make a united front against anyone who would deny either of you your heritage. At least you could stand up for one another, if the situation called for it." I watched the candles on the table flicker as I sipped my wine. My lips felt dry, and my heart pounded.

"I agree—if you are so inclined, Miss Page." She set down her fork and knife and watched me.

"Very well, I agree. Do you have an attorney, Miss Cottonwood?"

"Karah, please. If we are to form an alliance, then we should call each other by our given names, I think. And no, not yet."

"Please call me Delilah. And if you don't think it out of place, I would like to recommend Mr. Keene. He's been a great help to me. I am sure he could help you too."

She smiled broadly. "Would you be willing to take me on, Mr. Keene? I have had no luck with finding adequate counsel. At first lawyers were calling on me nearly every day to offer their services, and now I can't seem to find any help. I confess I feel somewhat desperate. If it weren't for my mother's nest egg, I would have nothing at all. While she's away, all I can do is wait—it's most frustrating."

I knew exactly what had happened—Claudette Page. The woman held a lot of influence here. There was no doubt she was using that influence to force us both to leave Mobile.

Mr. Keene nodded. "I would be happy to do some research for you. Let's meet again to talk about the particulars."

His answer pleased her. She raised her glass to me and said, "To new friends."

It must have been the wine, but I smiled and added, "To family."

When we left that evening, I felt happy, happier than I had in a long time. Karah and I had plans to meet the following week. I was to return to Seven Sisters for tea, and my cousin promised me that I would be given full access to my mother's belongings. I could hardly believe it. As the carriage rolled down the long driveway, I looked back just to prove to myself that I wasn't dreaming.

I saw the curtains move in an upstairs room of the house. A dark face peered down at me. It was an old woman, much older than the angry Docie. Even from this distance, I could see her expression clearly: she was afraid. She shook her head and mouthed some words, but I couldn't understand them. I felt troubled and turned to ask Mr. Keene to stop and turn around, but when I looked back the woman was gone. I pulled my wrap closer.

I didn't look back again.

Chapter 7—Carrie Jo

I woke up to a rough tongue licking my face. A friendly cat meowed at me before he stalked off. At least he was friendlier than the furry bag of claws that had assailed me in the cemetery. I sat up, wondering where I was. Cold, stone floor, wooden pews, high vaulted ceilings—I was in a church. I stood and dusted off my clothing. Morning light filtered through the stained glass windows. Under normal circumstances I would've found the imagery beautiful, but these were not normal circumstances. I picked up my purse from the ground and looked around to make sure I hadn't lost anything. Checking my hands and legs, I didn't see any injuries, but the side of my face stung. I touched a ragged scratch on my cheek, probably delivered by the evil cat.

Have I really been here all night? How did I get here? And where is here?

I heard the sound of a key ring jostling; the metal security gate screeched and then the side door of the church swung open. The emerging air felt fresh and warm, and I was thankful for the sunshine. I didn't know whether to call out or to hide. My indecisiveness had me frozen to the spot.

"Well, good morning. Have you been here all night? Get a bit of prayer in?" an older gentleman in a black suit called to me as he shoved the keys in his pocket. His head was semi-bald; white wisps of hair poked out from his temples, and the morning light surrounded him like a halo.

"I'm not sure," I confessed. "I must have fallen asleep. If you'll excuse me." Great. Now I was lying to a priest. In a church, no less.

"No need to rush off. Is this your first time visiting the basilica?" The more he spoke, the more I discerned a heavy French accent. Odd to find a French priest in Mobile, wasn't it?

"Um, basilica?"

"Yes, young lady. You are at the Cathedral Basilica of the Immaculate Conception. I am Father Portier." After a moment he asked, "Are you sure you are all right?"

"Yes, I am. I just…I'd better go. Thank you, Father."

"Very well, thank you for visiting. I must go ring the bells. Can't be late."

"Yes, of course." I strolled toward the open door. The downtown streets were becoming busy now with morning traffic. Then I thought if anyone could answer my questions about the supernatural, surely it would be a priest, right? I glanced at my watch. It was nearly eight o'clock, just two minutes till. "Father if you don't mind, I do have a question."

He smiled pleasantly. "And I will be happy to answer it after I ring the bells. I shall return in a moment."

I sat in a back pew and waited as he began to climb the narrow stairs that led to the belfry. In just a minute the bells began to chime, sure to wake up any nearby residents who were still asleep. It was a beautiful sound. The old man returned to the sanctuary and walked toward me. "Ah, still here. I was hoping you would not change your mind. Not everyone likes the sound of bells, you know."

"I think they're lovely."

"That's nice. Now what is your question, my dear?" He sat in the pew across the aisle from me, resting his gnarled hands on the back of the wooden seat in front of him.

"It's probably going to sound strange, especially coming from someone you don't know, and…I must confess I am not a Catholic."

"We are all children of God. What do you want to know?"

"Thank you for saying that. I am not sure God knows who I am, but it's nice of you to say so."

"I have a feeling He knows all about you, young lady."

"Do you believe in the supernatural, Father? I mean, the world of ghosts and supernatural activity. Is it all evil? Maybe figments of our imagination?"

He considered my question for a moment, then pointed at a nearby statue. It was the Virgin Mary holding the baby Jesus. The statue was painted in bright colors, and on her breast was painted a purple heart. "Do you see that statue?" I nodded. "Do you see the rose she's stepping on?"

"Yes, I do."

"Whenever you see a rose in a painting or statue of the Blessed Virgin, you should look for the secret."

"Secret? I don't understand."

"Look carefully at her hands. Do you see anything unusual?"

I got up from my seat and walked toward the statue. I studied Mary's hands for a moment, then caught my breath. "She's holding something in her hand...it looks like a pearl! What does that mean?"

"That is the question." He rose from the pew, walked toward the statue and studied it with me. He stood looking up at the artwork and then smiled at me. "Not even church scholars can agree on the reason for that pearl. Some say it's a symbol of the purity of the Virgin, while others say it represents the Parable of the Pearl, and there are other more fantastic opinions with which I won't bore you."

"That's interesting, but I'm not sure what that has to do with..."

He chuckled. "Ah, to be young again. So impatient to know all the answers. That is my point. The truth about the pearl's meaning is a mystery. It is there, we can see it, we know it is an unusual thing and this statue is very old. Much older than even me, and that is quite old." He smiled pleasantly. "But we don't know what it means. You see, the world is full of mysteries, not the least of which is the subject of the supernatural. Like this pearl, it is something to be discovered and defined by each man, each woman."

I stared at the pearl and considered his words. He asked kindly, "Does that help you at all, or have I confused you more?"

"Yes, it does help." I did feel more peaceful. He didn't answer my question, not directly, but perhaps he was right. This was a subject that had no answer, no black-and-white definition. "I'd better go now. My husband will be looking for me."

"I am sure he will be. Take care, and mind those steps. I would hate for an expectant mother to trip on the cathedral stairs."

"How did you know?" My hand flew to my stomach protectively.

"When you get to be as old as I am, dear lady, it is easy to spot the glow on a young mother's face."

I smiled and touched my flushed cheek before I turned to walk out of the church. Such a nice old man. Almost made me wish I were Catholic. I walked down the steps and out to the courtyard. I was on Conception Street near the intersection with St. Anthony. Yes, I knew this church; I just never knew the name. I turned around to get a better view of the old building and caught my breath. The place had two huge towers flanking the massive sanctuary. Round domes sat atop the towers, which must have housed the church bells. To my surprise, the gate was locked again. I couldn't believe Father Portier had managed to close it so quickly and so quietly.

Curious now, I walked back to the church, but it was locked up tight. A red-haired gentleman wearing green coveralls walked toward me whistling. "Need to get in there? I was just about to open up. Sorry I'm late. Hey, you're new."

"Yes, I'm new, but I was just in there talking to Father Portier."

He pushed up his thick glasses. "What are you talking about?"

"I was just talking to your priest, Father Portier. Older man, balding, with white hair?"

He looked around as if someone might jump out at him. "Is this some kind of joke, lady?"

"No joke. I swear it's the truth. Just ask him yourself. He's right inside."

With a skeptical look, the man opened the gate and stepped inside. There was no one around.

"He rang the bells a few minutes ago. Are you going to tell me I made that up?"

"Those bells have been on a timer since the early '90s. Listen, I don't know what you're into, drugs, booze or whatever, but you need help, lady."

I backed away and walked out of the church. By the time I made it to the end of the sidewalk, I was already running. I didn't stop until I reached Conception Street. When I got home I wasn't shaking anymore. I was tired and hungry, and I had butterflies. Mostly, I was happy to have something else to think about besides Father Portier and the weird experience I'd just had.

I walked up the sidewalk, happy to see Ashland's truck in the driveway. What was I going to say to him, coming home in yesterday's clothes? *Sorry, babe, I passed out in a church.*

As if he could hear my thoughts, he bounded out of the house. "Thank God! Are you okay? Where have you been, Carrie Jo?" Before I could answer him, he put his arms around me and pulled me to his chest. "You had me so worried."

"I am sorry. I'm a jerk." I clung to him, feeling ashamed that I had not told him the news about our child. Now was as good a time as any. "I will explain everything, I promise, but first I have to tell you something. I can't go another minute without telling you. I should have already told you, but I was so angry. I know it was stupid. I'm so sorry."

"What is it?" His bright blue eyes searched mine, and he held my hands. "Are you sure you're okay?"

"Ashland Stuart, you are going to be a father."

He dropped my hands, and his eyes widened. "Are you serious?"

"Absolutely. But if you don't believe me, you can wait six and a half to seven months and see for yourself."

A big, beautiful smile crept across his face. He picked me up and kissed me passionately. Before I could say "Boo," he carried me into the house. His worries had clearly vanished.

"We'll need a bigger house. And furniture." He put me down and kissed me again.

"Okay, calm down. I've had a rough night. That was the good news. Now I have something else to tell you. It's about

Delilah Iverson, and something else happened. I was at a church. Well, it was a gate and then a church. But Ash, I'm starving. I would love some of your cheese grits."

"I can take a hint. Why don't you call Rachel and tell her you're going to be late? She's been almost as worried about you as I have. Why is your car at the office?"

"It broke down. Brand-new BMW, and it won't start. Food first, Mr. Stuart. I'll go change if you don't mind." I touched his hand. "Are you sure you're happy? We've never actually talked about having kids."

"Of course I'm happy. Aren't you?"

"Yes, I am."

"Good. Then you go change, I'll cook, and we'll meet back here in ten minutes."

"Yes sir," I said playfully as I walked up the stairs.

Chapter 8—Carrie Jo

At 9:45 p.m., I finally pressed the send button on the proposal, shooting it off to Desmond Taylor with a weary smile. I couldn't have done it without Ashland and Rachel. Even Chip helped out by picking up the takeout and pulling up old purchase orders from our Seven Sisters job. It was definitely a team effort, and that felt good. Hopefully we would hear something positive from Mr. Taylor soon. I leaned back in my chair and sighed. What a weird forty-eight hours this had been! I'd been so busy with finalizing the prelim proposal I hardly had time to mull over my supernatural encounter with the cemetery light and the friendly priest. When I retold the story to my husband over breakfast he didn't question my sanity.

Looking as tired as I did, Ashland began picking up our dinner remnants, empty takeout boxes and half-empty water bottles, while I closed up shop on the computer. With bleary eyes I closed the folders, remembering to save our work one last time. I was just about to shut the whole thing down when my inbox dinged. I hoped it was Mr. Taylor emailing me back to confirm that he received the file, but it wasn't my prospective client. The email was from Alice and Myron Reed.

"Uh-oh."

"What is it?"

"I just received an email from the Reeds. I wonder what this is about." I could tell from Ashland's raised eyebrows that he was as suspicious as I was. Nothing good ever came from chatting with the Reeds. Since their daughter's arrest they barely spoke to me, but I suppose I couldn't blame them. A few months after Mia's commitment in the state mental hospital, I got a notification from the Reeds' attorney of a pending civil action, but then they suddenly dropped it. I had no idea what they were thinking—then or now.

"Babe, why don't you wait until tomorrow to read that? I'm sure it's not anything super important."

I tapped my finger nervously on the mouse pad. "You are probably right, but if I don't check it I'm going to spend all night thinking about it. I mean, what if Mia somehow got free? Wouldn't you want to know if she might be lurking in the bushes?" I said with a sad smile.

Ashland sat up straight and tossed the leftovers in the garbage can. "If for some reason that ever happened I'd be on the phone to the governor." With a worried expression he added, "There's no way that woman should be let loose on the public. Here, I can bag this garbage up in a minute. Let's open the message now and see what is happening."

I waited for him to join me, and then I clicked on the email.

Dear Carrie Jo,

We are writing to tell you some sad news. We lost our daughter Mia this morning…

I gasped at what I was reading. This couldn't be true!

Services for Mia will be held Tuesday at Grant Funeral Home in Birmingham, Alabama. We thought it was only right that we invite you to speak on her behalf, as you were her closest friend. If you cannot attend her service we understand, but please know that you always hold a special place in our hearts.

For my part, I cannot claim to understand what my daughter was thinking when she reportedly attacked you…

"Reportedly?" Ashland said with a scowl, but I kept reading.

I will always remember you two as the closest of friends and sisters of the heart. Please know that Myron and I love you and hope for the best for you.

If at any point in the future you find information about Mia's claim, please let us know. I'm sure any light you can shed will go a long way in explaining to us what happened to our daughter.

Please call us when you can.

Love, Alice and Myron Reed

"I can't believe this." Ashland's hands were on my shoulder. I clicked off the computer and leaned back in the chair, looking up at him. "Can this be possible? Is she really gone?"

"What I can't believe is that they would ask you to speak at her funeral. Who are these people?"

"That does seem weird—so it's not just me."

He shook his head and said, "Nope. In fact, I bet my attorney would tell you that it could be a trap. Whatever you said could be used as evidence if they chose to try and sue us again."

"You're right. I'm stunned that Mia is dead. I thought she was dead after she attacked me at the house. I thought they were both dead—there was so much blood and..."

"It's okay. You're safe now, and she's really gone this time."

I knew what he was saying was true, but it still didn't seem real. "I don't mean to sound morbid, but I wonder how she died."

"Let's get out of here. Things might get crazy now, especially if the press hears about this. It's best to prepare for whatever publicity firestorm this might create."

"It could get nuts. If Mia was still in that facility, then only one thing could've happened to her—suicide. I would never have imagined that kind of ending for her. She was always so strong-willed, strong-minded. I swear to you, the girl you met wasn't the one I knew. Something happened to her, and I'm not sure what."

"It's no mystery to me, Carrie Jo."

"What?"

"The house got to her. Anyone who comes in contact with that house has had something happen to them. It's like it's cursed or something."

"You don't believe in curses, Ash."

"Two years ago I would have agreed with you. Now I am not so sure." He shook his head. "Are you ready to go home?"

I grabbed my purse and followed him to the front door. Chip and Rachel were long gone, so I locked up the building and headed to the car.

"Where are you going? Your car is dead, remember? I'll have the mechanic pick it up tomorrow."

"Yeah, I forgot all about that." Determined to give it a try just once more I said, "Let me just try it." I didn't wait for his answer; I hopped in my BMW and to my surprise it cranked right up. Either there was some glitch with my car or unseen forces were indeed at work—perhaps it wasn't a coincidence that I ended up at that cemetery gate after all.

Ashland pulled up beside me with a frown. "See you at home."

***

When Ashland fell asleep I slipped out of bed. It had started to rain. From the sound of it, the drops were heavy and fat, not the typical pitter-patter drops you hear in spring. Low rumbles of thunder warned of an approaching storm, and I felt an urge to watch it roll in. Mobile had no shortage of springtime storms, but we'd been in kind of a drought recently. Tonight, I could smell the rain in the air.

After having made up from our big blowout about his dreaming, I didn't want to risk invading his privacy again. And I couldn't trust myself not to look. In fact, I really couldn't help it. Just like he couldn't control his dreams, I couldn't control my wandering into them. Gathering up my favorite white quilt, I walked down the hall to the guest room. I flipped on the small lamp by the door just so I didn't trip over anything, I didn't need a lot of light to watch the storm. I shuffled across the wood floor in my socks and plopped in the comfy chaise lounge that overlooked the backyard. It wasn't a fabulous view; there were too many trees and tall buildings to see too much below, but I could see the sky perfectly.

I hunkered down in the chair, wrapped my blanket around me, leaned back and watched the lightning light up the sky. At first the blasts of light were subtle, just flashing through black clouds along the distant horizon. It was a beautiful sight. Then the lightning became more defined. It shot through the massive cloud deck, hitting the dark waters of the bay first and then various spots along the edges of the Port City. Thunder rolled and as it boomed and shook the house, sleep seemed impossible. As I enjoyed the scenery, I protectively rubbed my still flat stomach. I was going to be a mother. Was I ready for that? Well, ready or not, I was going to find out soon. I had no doubt that Ashland would be a good father; he was such a good person. "Good night, little one," I whispered to my stomach. Then I thought about Mia, the sane Mia, the one who would have been delighted to be an aunt. Maybe my husband was right—somehow Seven Sisters had gotten to her, had driven her crazy. Strangely enough I couldn't muster up a single tear.

I rubbed my tired eyes and yawned. The gold-toned pendulum clock on the mantelpiece began to chime. I couldn't believe it was midnight already. I was tired, but I also felt unsettled. I glanced at the side table and the worn copy of *THE STARS THAT FELL*. Could I really afford to stay up half the night reading a book? Well, I *was* the boss. I could call in if I wanted to. I had no appointments that I knew of, so I could certainly sleep late. I tossed my wild curls behind my shoulder and out of my face, picked up the book and turned to the worn silk bookmark.

Okay, Delilah. Help me out here. What's going on in your world, and does it have something to do with mine?

Chapter 9—Delilah

My second trip to Seven Sisters was no less impressive than my first. The more I thought of it, the more inconceivable it was that I had lived in Mobile most of my life and had never seen this house. But then again that may have been by design. I would never know if my parents, the Iversons, knew about my true identity; however, it did stand to reason that they would want to protect me. Even though my Iverson family would not have cared about what the upper crust of Mobile thought, I did care. I was left alone to fight for my future. Of course, I had choices. Nothing prevented me from moving away from Mobile and its stuffy social circles. At least I had a small fortune that I could fall back on thanks in part to both my families. Still, as I told Jackson Keene, money had nothing to do with my return to Mobile. I came to claim my name and my family. I was secretly heartbroken to learn they did not want to know me at all.

In a strange sort of way, I felt compelled to pursue my name. Partly because, by all accounts, my mother had no choice but to send me away. She was the unhappy wife of a cruel man, a woman who had found some stolen joy in the arms of my father. I liked to think that whatever her flaws were, she loved me deeply and apparently wasn't afraid to stand up to her tormentor when pressed to. I was hoping to learn more about her, my sister and my cousin this afternoon. I pulled up in the carriage and handed the reins to Stokes, the big man who had met us the other night. He was a man of few words and didn't even walk me in, pointing toward the door with a grunt.

Here in the light of day, I could plainly see that Seven Sisters wasn't quite as grand as she used to be. She'd survived demolition during the war, but she hadn't escaped the effects of time and all those stormy summer afternoons. The rain and humidity had left green mold on the columns, and there were loose boards on the porch and missing side rails. Still, it wasn't anything that couldn't be mended if someone had a mind to invest something in the place. I was curious to hear exactly what plans Karah had. Did she plan to sell the house? Deed it to a cousin? I absently wondered if I could afford to buy the place, and if I could (which was doubtable) would I be allowed to do so? I sighed as I climbed the steps carefully.

I did not invite Jackson, as he now insisted that I call him, to return with me. My cousin and I had much to talk about—some privacy should be expected. Better to leave these things within the family. I walked through the open door and followed the sounds of breaking dishes or something. A woman screamed in anger, and I heard another crash. The idea of someone deliberately breaking the beautiful things in this house starched my collar. I stormed down the hall and walked into the Blue Room like I owned the place.

"Put it down now, Docie. I will not tell you again." Karah said, somewhere between tears and anger. "Do not break another thing! You are mad! Just like her!"

Docie grabbed another ceramic dog from the white painted shelf. I looked at the ground in horror. Several other ceramics had already been destroyed; the evidence of Docie's crimes were scattered all around in piles of broken figurines and ceramic dust.

"You don't tell me what to do! I am not your servant but hers!" She raised her hand and prepared to destroy another pup, but I grabbed her arm.

"You break another thing, and I will have you arrested! Put it down now, madam."

So surprised was she that she did as I told her. The ill-tempered Docie dropped the toy dog on the carpeted floor. Luckily for her it did not break. "Now find a broom and dustpan and clean these things up."

With a sneer she brushed past me, pushing her way out of the room. I doubted she would return, but at least her tantrum had ended. "What happened here, Karah? Is she mad? Are you harmed?"

I walked to her, removing my gloves and tossing them and my hat on a nearby settee. "Let me look at you." She seemed frozen and was staring at a spot on the floor. I followed her eyes. She appeared transfixed by one particular ceramic, a cocker spaniel with a red ball in its mouth. "Karah, are you all right?"

She pulled her eyes away and stared into my face. I don't know what I expected to see, but it wasn't the big black bruise around her eye. "Oh my goodness, Karah! Did Docie do this? You need to see a doctor!"

Finally, realization shone across her face. "Delilah?"

"Yes, it's me. You told me to come, remember. What has happened here, Karah?"

"Cousin?"

"Yes. Here and in the flesh." I tried to sound jovial. I still wasn't sure what I was dealing with here. Suddenly she flung her arms around me.

"Thank God. I prayed that you would come. Don't leave me here again. You must stay with me, cousin. I do not think she wants me here, but I want to stay. I have to wait for my mother. She promised she would come! She always keeps her promises! But she…she…" She pointed to the destruction and then sank to the carpet, crying. Yes, there was more here than met the eye.

"Karah, shhh…all is well. See? She is gone, and I will not let her harm you again. Come sit on the couch." Wiping her face on her brown silk dress sleeve she agreed and let me help her up. Before I could question her further, I saw the face of an old, dark-skinned woman peeping in at the door. When she saw me, her yellow eyes widened, and she did not waste any time getting to me.

"I knew that was you, Miss Calpurnia. I said that you would be home soon, and here you are! I am going to have to tell your mother. She will be surprised to hear that you're home—are you home for good? Would you like some tea? You and your friend? Let ol' Hooney get you some tea, just like you like it." So surprised was I that I did not correct her.

"Yes, Hooney. That would be wonderful. Thank you."

She pinched my cheek with her gnarled finger, and I thought she would hug me, but then her face changed. "You ain't Miss Calpurnia." She stepped back in surprise. "Oh, excuse me, miss. I didn't mean to touch you. I just thought you were my mistress's daughter come to see me. I feel like an ol' fool. I guess I won't need to wake up Miss Christine after all."

"No, I am not Calpurnia. But I am her sister, Delilah. Miss Christine was my mother."

Karah had stopped her crying and watched us.

"Oh Lord, can it be true?" Hooney said. "Hannah told me you was okay. But I thought she dropped you somewhere or maybe laid you in the woods. Was you with the doctor? He was a good man, bless him."

"No, he sent me to the Iversons. I had a new family to take care of me, but now I am back. Karah is my cousin." Then inspiration struck me. "What happened to her eye, Hooney? Did the other lady, Docie, do this?"

"Child, I don't know. I heard the commotion and came to see. It could have been her...she's got a mean streak as wide as the Mobile River. But then again, it could have been someone else."

I sat next to my cousin. "Tell me what happened, please."

"I...I..." She started crying again.

I turned to Hooney. "May we have that tea you offered us, Miss Hooney?"

She chuckled. "Oh, it's not Miss. Just Hooney. Yes, ma'am. I'll make you some tea just like the kind your sister liked. Lots of honey."

As she scurried off, I slid the Blue Room door closed behind her and then returned to the settee.

Without waiting for me to ask again, Karah said, "You will never believe me, Delilah. You do not know what has been happening here. It is like the house does not want me here. Things happen. Strange things, and Docie only makes it worse by doing the things she does. She deliberately instigates them."

"Them? Who?"

"The ghosts. The ghosts of Seven Sisters. They don't want me here, but I have to stay. I promised my mother I would wait for her."

I didn't know what to make of her confession. She had been abused, that much was obvious, but ghosts? I never believed in such things. I suspected that if there were any evil entities in this house, they were all very much alive. I sighed and smiled at my cousin. "I'll be here as long as you need me. We will face these ghosts together."

"You promise?"

Trying to bring a lighthearted moment into a very depressing conversation, I raised my hand and said, "I do so promise and swear."

"Very good. We will have Stokes pick up your things, and you can take your sister's room. Let me show it to you. Nothing has been moved since she disappeared. You may find some clues about her there." To my surprise Docie returned to the room with a broom and a dustpan. She did not speak to us but went about her business tidying up the room. We rose to leave but not before I stopped in front of her.

"Everything you have destroyed here today you will replace. You had no right to do so; these belong to my cousin and to me. If you cannot control yourself and keep your temper, then I am sure my cousin can find someone much more suited to this type of home service." Without a word she continued her work and promptly left us. Karah's eyes were wide as she watched me. Suddenly she smiled, which made her face appear much younger. I had only met her a few times but always thought of her as solemn and serious. Her smile was a good reminder that she was young—that we were both young and had our lives ahead of us. "Now come show me this room. I hope it is close to yours."

"It is very close. I am staying in Uncle Louis' room. I must show you his picture—he was a beautiful man. Quite popular with the ladies in Paris and New Orleans. Maybe one day he will turn up with a new bride. Wouldn't that be wonderful?"

"I have never heard of him. You must tell me everything." For the next few hours, we walked through the house. Our tour began in my sister Calpurnia's room. It was a lovely room, but it looked rather sparse without her personal effects in it. Karah told me not to worry and that all of Calpurnia's things were in the armoire. I could look through any of it and keep whatever I liked. Someone in the household, presumably a servant of Calpurnia's, had neatly wrapped up her pretty hair combs, and we found a velvet bag of her necklaces and small rings. My eyes watered just wearing them. To be this close to my sister and now to be with my cousin—the emotion overwhelmed my heart. Next, we went to Louis' trunks and politely peeked inside them. Karah had been correct; Uncle Louis was unusually beautiful, with white skin that appeared to glow, blond hair and beautiful blue eyes. His oil painting likeness portrayed him in a blue blazer with copious blue ruffles, and he looked quite dandy. We put the picture in a respectable place on the downstairs mantelpiece.

"Now, let's go to your mother's room. I am sure you will want to see it."

Suddenly, a quiet reverence washed over me. I nodded and followed her back up the stairs. We walked past Calpurnia's room to the large room on the right. With a sweet smile, Karah opened the door and moved out of the way so I could take in the sight. Instantly I detected the sweet smell of roses. There were none to be seen, but I could smell them nonetheless. "Oh that smell, it's lovely. Where are the roses? Is that a perfume or something?"

Karah sniffed at the air. "I smell nothing, cousin. Perhaps you washed your hands with rosewater earlier. Anyway, I will leave you alone so you can explore your mother's room in peace." Grateful for her thoughtfulness, I nodded as she closed the door quietly. I closed my eyes and then opened them. Here I was at last, in the room where I last saw my mother. I had been an infant then, but now I was a woman. I was suddenly drawn to the bed, my mother's bed. It was large, with a metal rack that hung above it. It was bare now but I was sure that during my mother's time, it had held mosquito netting so the lady of the house could sleep without the incessant buzzing and biting. There was a white cotton quilt on top of it now, and I rubbed my hands across it.

Like a child, I crawled in the bed and clutched the pillow. Loneliness overwhelmed me. They'd all left me. My mother, my father, the Iversons and even my sister Calpurnia. Death had taken them all, except for my sister. I refused to give up hope for her. She would return one day, surely. I cried hot tears of grief, and the loneliness of my soul felt so deep it was as if it were a drum pounding. When I thought I couldn't cry anymore, the smell of roses became stronger and it so comforted me that I fell asleep. I don't know how long I slept, but it could not have been long because the sun was still high in the sky. I heard the sounds of life downstairs, but at least they were happy sounds. No breaking ceramics, no screaming or beatings. It was a happy day.

Suddenly, the light in the room became bright, so bright I could barely see. I shielded my eyes with my hands and tried to discern its source. The light diminished, and in its place was a woman. I knew, somehow I knew, that this woman was my mother. This was Christine Cottonwood.

I sat up and slung my legs over the side of the bed. "Mother?" She didn't answer me. She held a white dress out in front of her and then looked at her reflection in the long mirror. She spun about and laughed. So happy was she!

"Oh! Callie, darling. You startled me. Don't just sit there— come help me change."

"But I am not Callie, Mother. I am Delilah."

"Now, Callie. We do not have time for those kinds of games today. Dr. Page is on his way to take us on a picnic. Come here and hug Mother." I could not resist her request. I sprang to my feet and ran toward her outstretched arms.

"Mother!" The light returned to the room and flared around her body. She smiled still and seemed not to notice the brightness. I shielded my eyes from fear but kept running toward her. She leaned down with a sweet smile, her arms wide, and I ran into them as she disappeared. I was left clutching the air, feeling the last fleeting bits of her leave me alone in her bedroom. The smell of roses faded in a few seconds and was replaced by the smells of a musty old house and my own sweaty body.

"Mother!" I cried out again. The door opened, and Karah stood in the doorway. She looked at me sadly.

"You saw her." It wasn't a question.

"Yes! My mother. I saw her right here. I was in the bed, and then she came in the room with a bright light around her. She thought I was my sister, but I did not care. She tried to hug me. She disappeared." I didn't cry now. I felt comforted, fortunate that I had seen her. I had seen my mother, not just a painting or a photograph. I saw her with my own two eyes, which should have been impossible. My mother was dead.

"They are all here in this house. I see them too. I never wanted to come here, you know." Karah sat on the bed, her feet barely touching the floor. "My mother made me come. She said she would come soon, that I would see her here. But that was four months ago, and I have not heard a word. Not even a letter or a note. I question Docie all the time because I am sure she knows more than she tells me. She is my mother's servant, not mine."

"Well, we shall have to fix that. You are the lady of the house, at least for now. You will have to have your own maid. We can ask Maundy Weaver. She says there are many hardworking French and Irish girls in Mobile looking for work. And I've heard that if you want a secret kept, you can trust an Irish girl. They are extremely loyal."

"I do not have any secrets. Or beaus or anything requiring a maid. I am just the bastard child of Isla Beaumont and Jeremiah Cottonwood. There—I said it! I am a bastard."

Absently I squeezed her hand. "I am too. Let's not use that name anymore. We are more than a name."

She smiled weakly. "Agreed."

I had to ask her more questions. "Tell me, Karah. You say they are all here in this house. Who are you talking about? Who have you seen?" I no longer doubted that she saw ghosts at Seven Sisters.

"Well, I have seen my father in the room across from the Blue Room, I think it was his study. I have seen a young black woman in the downstairs larder. She pulls my hair and scares me to death. Then I have seen other people, people I do not know. I have looked through all the pictures and cannot identify them. Will you help me? Will you keep me safe?"

"I think we need to call the priest. I hear there is a new priest in Mobile now, a Father Portier. No doubt he would come and pray for us."

"I don't think bastard children are allowed to take communion, cousin."

"We won't ask for it. Surely he would not be opposed to offering a few prayers on our behalf. We are after all very wealthy women."

"Perhaps you are right. But just in case, may I sleep with you tonight? Nothing evil has happened here, has it?"

I was quiet for a moment. I felt nothing but peace and happiness in this room. If something evil had occurred here, my mother's love for her children had washed it all away.

"You can sleep in my bed if you promise not to snore."

"Oh, thank you, cousin."

I hugged her, happy that she felt safe with me.

"I do still intend to work with Maundy, though. I hope you understand that I cannot be here every day all the time. I have to keep my commitments, and I will need to explain to my brother—I mean to Adam."

"I see. I would like to meet your brother sometime, cousin."

I blushed at that idea. I was sure that Adam would be charming—too charming for his own good or for Karah's. I determined quietly to never let that happen. I would tell him nothing. Did he deserve anything more from me? "We shall see, cousin."

She smiled, and we spent the rest of the afternoon walking around the house and waiting for Stokes to return with my things. I also jotted off a note to Jackson asking him to wait on finding my house. I now had a place to stay, at least for a little while. The day ended pleasantly, albeit strangely. This wasn't where I had intended to lay my head at night when I woke this morning, but it felt right.

My favorite part of each day would be when she and I lay in bed together and whispered late into the night. We saw no ghosts, not that first night. It felt as if we were sisters, two cast-off sisters who had finally found one another. I was grateful for that. I was grateful for her. She had no reason to show me such favor, but she did. For the first time in a long time, I fell asleep feeling like I was at home—at last.

Chapter 10—Henri

The Stuarts were on their way—I was looking forward to seeing my friends. I intended to tell them about Detra Ann, if they hadn't already heard that she was leaving, and hopefully enlist their help in getting her to stay. Yes, I had selfish reasons for wanting to keep her in Mobile, but I was also worried about her. She was drinking every day—something she had always hated as long as I'd known her.

Now Lenore referred to her as "the ghost," and that really disturbed me. Detra Ann had cheated death in a very real way…what if Lenore was right? What if the supernatural world wasn't finished with her yet? Moving to another city wouldn't prevent any such encounter. Now how to convey that to her?

I didn't cook this evening, but I had made a few appetizers and mixed a pitcher of hurricanes. Not the syrupy red drink that looked like Kool-Aid, but the authentic New Orleans drink. Lenore, in a rare happy mood, offered to help and even wore a dress for the occasion. I said nothing about her out-of-style baggy denim dress or her mismatched socks. No need to look a gift horse in the mouth, right?

"I think I hear a car."

"Okay, I'll go check." I opened the door and saw Carrie Jo's car in my driveway. The couple stepped out, and CJ waved to me. I waved back and stood on the porch drying my hands on a dish towel.

"Hey, Henri!" Carrie Jo bounded up the steps and hugged me tight. "I am so happy to see you."

"Likewise." I smiled and kissed her cheek and hugged Ashland.

"How's it going, Henri? Things good at the shop?"

"More than good. Come in. I want you to meet my cousin, Lenore."

Lenore flashed a friendly smile, and after everyone exchanged pleasantries I invited them to sit in the living room. "Who wants a drink? I made a batch of hurricanes."

"I'll take one," Ashland piped up. "I guess that means you're driving," he said to Carrie Jo.

Carrie Jo smiled. "I think I can handle that."

"You don't want even a small glass? I use a brown sugar base. It's delicious."

"I have no doubt about that, Henri, but I'm still going to have to pass." The smile on her face told me she wasn't telling me something. She looked at Ashland and said, "Can I tell him?" Her husband nodded, and she smiled even bigger. "Ashland and I are going to be parents."

"Really? That is the best news I've heard in a long time. Congratulations, you two. When is the baby due to arrive?"

"Sometime in May. My doctor says we'll know for sure at the next appointment. I still can't believe it—I'm going to be a mom!" Lenore congratulated them, and we celebrated with a toast. Lemonade for CJ and hurricanes for the rest of us.

"And it's going to be a boy. A boy that looks just like his daddy. A fine healthy young man." Lenore wrapped her hands around her crossed knees and nodded confidently at the couple. Carrie Jo was too polite to say anything except thank you.

"Well, whatever it is, boy or girl, we hope it's just one. I don't think I could handle twins. Especially if they were twin boys."

Lenore shook her head as if she had something to say, but I quickly changed the subject.

"Have either of you spoken to Detra Ann recently?"

"Not me. What about you, Ashland?"

Ashland sipped his drink and shook his head. "She's not returning my calls. I visited her mom recently, and she hasn't seen much of her either. I was hoping you could give us some insight. What's going on with her?"

Lenore let out a little hiss, and I shot her a warning look. "We had dinner the other night. She brought me a little birthday gift—it was the key to the shop. She's moving to Atlanta and leaving me Cotton City Treasures. Everything happened so fast I didn't ask her too many questions because she seemed like she was in a hurry to leave. I'm worried about her."

"You should be. The girl is a shade—she's a ghost already."

Carrie Jo set her lemonade on the table and turned to look at Lenore. "What do you mean, Lenore?"

"I mean the girl has touched Death. She's been in its presence, and it thinks it has a claim on her. It took her friends, and it should have taken her too, but somehow she resisted it. I can promise you that won't last—Death will not be denied. I'm sorry for your friend, but it is the truth."

I tried to keep my voice level. "You don't know what you're talking about. I've asked you to stop talking about Detra Ann like that."

"It's not my fault that you love a ghost, Henri, but I can't lie. She's marked, and she'll pass on soon. And there ain't nothing you can do about it. I am sorry, but it's the honest-to-God truth." She took a big swig of her drink and licked her lips. "I haven't had one of these good drinks in a long time. Pour me another one."

Carrie Jo's eyes were wide with fear. "You can't be right about this. I don't mean to be rude, but what are you basing your statement on? I don't know if you know it or not, but we've been battling the supernatural here in Mobile for over a year and a half. We've seen our share of ghosts and we've beaten them—Detra Ann too. I don't think you realize how strong she is. This can't be true."

Lenore surprised us all by scooting closer to Carrie Jo and taking her hand in hers. She patted it and spoke to her in a soothing voice. "I am sorry that I offended you. I know something about battling the supernatural too. I guess Henri hasn't told you that I've been doing it all my life. People think I'm crazy, and maybe that's true, but there are patterns—laws that the supernatural world follows. Death is hard to escape, especially if it knows what you look like. I'm sure that your Detra Ann is a wonderful person, that she doesn't deserve this, but that doesn't change the fact that she is in danger. Big-time danger."

"If what you say is true, that Death will come for her, then it will come for me too because I was with her. We fought this together. I refuse to abandon her now."

"Maybe you should tell me exactly what happened. If you don't mind. Don't leave anything out. Even small things can help."

For the next hour, Ashland and Carrie Jo caught her up. I shared any relevant bits that they missed but otherwise kept quiet. I was learning a lot too. For example, I never knew about Carrie Jo's dream about Jeremiah Cottonwood and his vicious whip. How unusual that she woke up with the stripe of his whip on her leg. Ashland told us about his first encounter with Isla, and Carrie Jo shared her first dream about Calpurnia Cottonwood. Then we talked about the Moonlight Garden, the treasure, the ghosts of Jeremiah and David Garrett. They told her about the loss of Bette and Terrence Dale, how they saw Hoyt Page and Delilah and Christine. By the end of it, she had more questions, and we answered them as best we could.

"Well, it's obvious that Mobile is a hot spot for the supernatural and that Seven Sisters seems to be ground zero. Everything that's happened to you all has centered around that house. But first, let's deal with the practical things." Lenore took Carrie Jo's hands and stared at them. "Hmm…I never was any good at that. Palm reading, I mean. Let me look into your eyes." She didn't wait to be invited. She grabbed Carrie Jo's wrists and stared deep into her eyes. I almost said something, but Ashland gave me a reassuring look.

Lenore continued, "I know what you say is true about the battle you and Detra Ann did, but she's the shade—not you. No ghost in there. I see only you. As far as your dream catching goes, before you go to sleep at night, you have to put the baby to sleep." Carrie Jo laughed, but Lenore pressed on. "Your little one is who is causing you to wander into your husband's dreams. That little boy will have the same powers his mother does, and maybe some of his father's too. He is already dreaming about you and his daddy. You know more than you think you do, Mrs. Stuart. You didn't have any problems before this, did you? I mean, you could sleep with your husband and drift right off to sleep, right?"

"Yes, that's true."

"It's the baby. He can't control his powers—he doesn't even understand that he has them and that he is special. For a good night's sleep, eat something bland before bed, no sodas or sugar, and sing to him. Sing until he goes to sleep. Then you can sleep without worry."

Carrie Jo nodded uncertainly but then smiled. "It's better than anything I've come up with. I will give it a try."

Then Lenore turned her attention to Ashland. "Start telling your wife the truth about the things you see. Like when you saw that man in the car window…"

"I didn't tell anyone about that." Ashland seemed surprised, and pink rose under his tanned skin.

"It's written on your face. You need to tell her, and you two have to work as a team. I don't know what you have going in your life, but you need to make room for your gift—stop being ashamed of it. It's not going away, and it is only going to get stronger, so be prepared for that. Ask God to help you."

"How do I do that?" He looked confused.

"That's up to you. Go out on your boat and reconnect with Him. He'll help you. He will, I promise."

"So there's no way to make this stop?"

She shook her head emphatically.

"Do I talk to these things or what?"

"You can try, but I doubt they will say anything coherent—just look at what they look at. Pay attention to details. You won't be able to help all of them, but you may be able to help some of them find their rest. I don't have all the answers, but I know pretending it's not happening is not a strategy that works." She touched his cheek, and he didn't back away. "One more thing, Ashland…"

"Yes. What is it?"

"You don't know it all yet. There's something you haven't figured out. You haven't seen the complete truth, the whole truth, the so-help-you-God truth yet. Be prepared for it because the truth won't be denied."

She turned to me with sad eyes. "Now I come to you, Henri Devecheaux. It has been too long since you said her name. She wonders why you do not pray for her, talk to her, look for her. I feel her around this place. Can you see her, Ashland?"

"Not yet, but I sense that someone is very near to Henri." He stared behind me and then shook his head. "No, she's gone."

"That's because you haven't been looking for her." It was more than a statement. It was an accusation. I felt ashamed and angry that she would bring up this subject right now. "You have to find her, Henri. Find her and bring her home so she can rest in peace. When you do, you'll have peace yourself."

I stood up and glared at Lenore. "What if I don't want to know what happened? What good will it do? That was over twenty years ago, Lenore. Am I supposed to spend every day of my life looking for her? I loved her, but she's gone now and I have to let her go—so do you. You have to! I have to! I'll go crazy if I think about it. Is that what you want? Me talking crazy, locked up somewhere?"

"Aleezabeth! Aleezabeth! Can't you even say her name? Quit calling her 'she' and 'her.' She was a living, breathing person—someone you loved!"

"Fine! Aleezabeth! Are you happy?"

Ashland waved his hand. "Um, guys. You said to start sharing. You have a visitor. Tall, olive-skinned girl with long brown hair, a pink skirt, pink knee socks and some kind of white school shirt. She's in the corner of the room. She's barely there." He pointed toward the fireplace as if he were pointing at a clock or a picture, not a ghost. "Can you see her?"

"No, I can't," I said sharply, suddenly afraid.

"Say something to her, Henri." Lenore stood beside me and faced the fireplace.

"I didn't know this would happen. I did not mean for this to happen. I should have stayed with you..." My voice broke, and my heart felt like a rock. "I should have stayed with you. I am sorry, Aleezabeth." I sat on the couch and leaned across the arm, crying. Lenore stared at the corner of the room as if she could see her, and perhaps she could. I could not, but I did feel better.

Ashland gave me a sad smile. "She's gone. I guess that was all she needed to hear—at least for now. I am sorry, Henri. I never knew that you lost someone like that."

I rubbed my eyes with a tissue that Carrie Jo stuffed in my hand. I took a big swig of my hurricane and said, "It isn't something I like to think about too much. I have a life now. I want to keep moving forward, not backward."

He nodded. "I am living proof that sometimes you have to look back to move forward."

Someone knocked on the front door, and I excused myself to answer it. I heard a pretty voice on the front porch and recognized it right away—it was Detra Ann. "Avon calling. Are y'all having a party without me?" I opened it, and she nearly fell inside laughing. It was immediately apparent that she was at least three sheets to the wind. "You know, you really would make a lousy boyfriend. You don't call, you don't come over. That's pretty lousy, Henri." She stumbled into the living room, her red high heels in her hand. "Hey, everyone. I know y'all. Except you. I don't know you—but hey anyway! What are we celebrating? Ooh…are those hurricanes?"

Lenore stepped backward, never taking her eyes off Detra Ann, until she left the room completely.

"Was it something I said?"

"No, that's just Lenore. I don't think you need any hurricanes, Detra Ann. How about some coffee?"

"Whatever you say, doctor." She kissed me on the cheek. I could smell bourbon—it must have been tonight's choice at the bar. "Call me doc-tor love…" she sang off-key and loudly.

"Where have you been tonight, Detra Ann?" I heard Ashland ask as I made a quick pot of coffee.

"Dancing, drinking and saying goodbye to Mobile. I am going to miss this place and all of you. I love y'all, but I have to go." I could hear the stress in her voice now. "I can't stay here, or something bad will happen. I can feel it. You wouldn't understand. I know I should have told you sooner, but my heart couldn't handle it. Yep, my heart…I love you all." Then she began to sing again, "I can feel your heart beat—the heart of love…. Hey! Wasn't that one of your favorite songs, Carrie Jo? That guy William could sing—the band covered all his songs. But don't tell Ashland—I don't think he'd like hearing that too much." I cringed as she rambled on, oblivious to the fact that Ashland was sitting right there. "Hey, where did that girl go? Is that the mysterious cousin—is that your cousin, Henri? I don't think she likes me too much."

"Do you want cream and sugar?" I called to her from the kitchen.

"I want bourbon!"

"You aren't getting any," I replied, shaking my head. At least now I didn't have to explain her drinking problem to Carrie Jo and Ashland. Lenore was right, I sure could pick them. But I couldn't help loving Detra Ann. I poured some of the hot chicory coffee in a stoneware mug, walked into the living room and handed it to her. She thanked me with a pout.

"Ow, that's hot."

Carrie Jo was staring at Ashland. I looked too and saw his face was as white as a sheet. He stared at the front door, and my arms began to feel cold and clammy.

"What is it, Ash?" she whispered.

"I am not sure, but come get behind me. The whole doorway is full of blackness—it's crawling all over the doorframe. Can anyone else see it?"

We all looked, except Detra Ann, who was slow to comprehend the increasing danger. She just stared at us. "What?"

"I can't see it, but I can feel something," I confessed. I sat next to Detra Ann and put my arm around her protectively. Lenore was long gone. *Yeah, battling the supernatural. Right. More like running from it.*

"Carrie Jo, Ashland is right. You need to get behind him—better still, go down the hall." Suddenly frightened, Carrie Jo got to her feet in a flash and would have pulled Detra Ann with her, but I stopped her. "No, leave her with us. We can't risk it following her. We'll stay with her. You go!"

I heard Lenore whisper to her, and Carrie Jo disappeared.

Ashland spoke in a low voice. "That's nothing I have ever seen before, Henri. It's a shape now and he's tall, taller than anyone I have ever known and completely inky black. Oh my God! Do you feel that? It's like all the oxygen just left the room. I think Lenore is right—this is Death we are dealing with."

Detra Ann sobered in an instant. She put down the cup of coffee and clung to me.

"You feel it too? I'm not crazy then?"

"No, you're not. What do we do, Henri? Should I say something?"

"Say nothing," I whispered fiercely. "Be still and pray, both of you. Close your eyes and pray right now!" We did just that. Detra Ann whispered some words, Ashland said the Lord's Prayer aloud, and I poured out my heart to heaven. "God please, protect the woman I love and my friends. She cannot leave yet. Her time is not up. Please, if you have to take someone, take me." My eyes wanted to open, and it was a struggle to keep them closed, but I kept praying, probably louder than I intended. Soon the room felt different. The ominous presence vanished, and the air felt alive again. One by one we opened our eyes. Ashland told us the shape had disappeared. With shaking hands, Detra Ann picked up her coffee. When she realized her hands were too shaky to do her any good, she set it back down on the table.

"It doesn't matter where I go, does it? It is going to follow me. It wants me, I know it. Am I going to die, Henri?"

"We are going to fight, Detra Ann. You won't die—I will be with you the whole time. I swear."

"Can I stay with you?"

"Of course you can." She put her arms around me, and for the first time ever I kissed her. A real kiss, not a friendly, can-I-be-your-pal kiss. She didn't run away or laugh in my face. She kissed me back. I had never been so terrified and so happy in such a short space of time.

That was the moment Lenore chose to step out of the hallway. "Well if she's staying here, I'm leaving. I can't stay with a ghost."

"That's fine with me, Lenore. I didn't ask you to move in."

Detra Ann laughed. "I am not a ghost. I was just drunk, that's all. I am sorry you had to see me like that."

"It ain't the booze, sister—it's the specter following you around. He ain't fixin' to grab me. No way, no how." She crossed her arms stubbornly and stared at me with a perfectly arched eyebrow.

Carrie Jo said sweetly, "Lenore, you can stay with Ashland and me. We have a guest room. I'd like to have you around—maybe you can help us learn what we need to know." I could almost hear her say, "And Henri and Detra Ann could have some time to catch up." She smiled at Ashland, who nodded in agreement.

"Okay, then. Let me get my stuff. Be right back." Lenore left only to return a minute later. "This is it. I don't have much."

"That's great. Well, thank you for the drinks, Henri. I think we'll be going home now. Let's talk in the morning. We have to come up with some sort of plan."

Lenore waited on the porch, still refusing to stay in the room with Detra Ann. I hoped she behaved herself during her stay with the Stuarts. With Lenore, anything was possible. And I hadn't forgotten her mysterious phone call.

I found one…

Chapter 11—Carrie Jo

By the time we made it home I realized how impulsive I had been inviting a complete stranger into our home. But I soothed my nervousness by reminding myself that it was for Henri and Detra Ann. I had privately been rooting for them, and it just made sense to see them get together now. Nobody could ever take Terrence Dale's place, but I couldn't help but believe he would want Detra Ann to be happy. Hopefully Ashland agreed with me; he had to see how good she and Henri could be for one another.

Lenore didn't talk on the drive back to our home. I was dying to ask Ashland about what he saw at Henri's, but I wasn't in the mood to hear Lenore declare Detra Ann a ghost again. When we pulled into the driveway, Lenore didn't move right away. I got out of the car and waited on her. "Are you coming, Lenore?"

She was watching the house, her penetrating eyes examining the exterior for God only knew what. Slowly she opened the car door and stepped outside clutching her two Wal-Mart bags that overflowed with her colorful wardrobe. I sighed and walked up the sidewalk. She'd either come inside or she wouldn't. Ashland opened the door and gave me an amused look. "I know, I know," I whispered.

Eventually she did come in and was the perfect houseguest. I showed her the guest room, guest bathroom and kitchen, telling her to grab something to eat if she got hungry. "What are your plans tomorrow? Are you working somewhere? Do you need a lift?"

"No. I have applications out, but nobody has called me yet. I don't suppose you need a housekeeper or something?"

"No. We have a housekeeper. You will probably meet her tomorrow. Her name is Doreen, and she makes an awesome…well, everything. But if you're interested in that type of work, she might be able to tell you where to go. I bet with the approaching Mardi Gras festivities you could find a job easily."

"That might work," she said, looking hopeful.

"I am going to the office in the morning, but you tell Doreen what you're looking for. If she can't help you, we'll look somewhere else."

Her face softened, and she smiled. "Thank you. That means a lot."

"Good night, Lenore."

"Good night."

I closed the door and went upstairs to pass out. It didn't happen—Ashland was keyed up and ready to talk about what he'd seen. In fact, he wanted to tell me about everything he'd seen. If Lenore helped no one else, she had helped Ash. Sure, she was quirky, but underneath I could tell she had true empathy for people. Plus, she claimed to know a great deal about the supernatural world, and Henri didn't dispute her knowledge. If anyone knew the truth about her, it would have been him.

She seemed like a lost child, wandering through the world depending on the kindness of strangers. She was friendly to everyone...except Detra Ann. I wondered why that was. Perhaps she was jealous of Henri's blooming relationship, or maybe she opposed the idea of her cousin involved with someone ten years younger—or someone white.

Ashland continued talking, and I nodded attentively. He described the ghost man he saw in the car, the many ghosts in the windows of the houses along Conception Street, even the creepy one he used to see regularly when his mother took him to Sunday brunch at the Admiral Semmes Hotel. I listened patiently, pretending that I wasn't creeped out. The poor guy. I couldn't imagine seeing stuff like that all the time and then forcing myself to forget it just to keep my sanity.

I stifled a yawn. I seemed to have no energy today. Boy, missing those pre-natal vitamins even for a day made a difference. I undressed as he talked and finally slid on his old football jersey. I had silk nightgowns aplenty but couldn't resist sleeping in oversize shirts—especially ones that smelled like Ashland's expensive cologne.

"That's not fair."

I folded back the coverlet and slid under the sheets. "What's not fair?"

"You...undressing right now."

I rubbed scented lotion on my hands and feigned innocence. "I have no idea what you're talking about."

He was undressing too and was under the sheets with me in a few seconds. "I love you, Carrie Jo Stuart. I can't imagine spending my life with anyone else."

"That's a good thing, 'cause I feel the same way."

"Say it, then."

I kissed his perfect lips and whispered, "I love you, Ashland Stuart."

For the next hour, we lost ourselves in one another, totally uncaring that someone else was in the house. Afterwards, Ashland dozed off to sleep, but our lovemaking had the opposite effect on me tonight—I couldn't close my eyes. I decided a nice long shower and maybe then a snack would help settle me down. If the butterflies in my stomach were any indication, the baby approved of that idea. After drying off and pulling my hair on top of my head in a messy bun, I padded down the stairs to see what treats Doreen had left me. I was happy to see that she left me a container of mandarin orange fruit salad topped with sweetened pecans. It may not have been comfort food for some folks, but ever since I got pregnant I couldn't get enough of the citrus fruit. Taking the whole container, a spoon and a bottle of water, I slipped into my office and quietly closed the door behind me.

After a few spoonfuls of the tasty treat, I flipped on my laptop in hopes of seeing an email from Desmond Taylor. Nope, nothing yet. I deleted a bunch of junk mail until just the important stuff was left. Digging into the fruit salad, I reread the email from the Reeds. Of course I wasn't going to go to Mia's funeral, but it wouldn't do any good to be mean about it. I felt sorry for Alice and Myron, even though they had considered suing Ashland and me. I wrote them back thanking them for the honor but declining their invitation without giving them a specific reason why. That would have to do. I hit send with a sigh and deleted their original email. That was easier than I'd thought it would be. I hoped that would be the end of the whole sad situation.

Goodbye, Mia.

On a whim, I searched for Father Portier and the Cathedral Basilica of the Immaculate Conception. An image of the friendly white-haired priest appeared. It was the picture of an oil painting—a commemorative portrait from 1829 marking Portier's appointment as the first bishop of Mobile. I could hardly believe it. I had a full-on conversation with a ghost, and I hadn't been asleep. I saved the photo and dug deeper into the history of the cathedral. How was it that I had walked through the gate and ended up in the church three blocks over unless I somehow stumbled into some sort of supernatural portal? Was there such a thing? It had been a common practice in the 1700s and 1800s to build churches atop old religious centers. It was actually a common way to show the natives who the new boss was. I continued to read until my stomach was full and my eyes began to glaze.

That's enough. I need to rest.

I closed the laptop, leaned back in my chair and spun around to enjoy the view of the moonlight bouncing around the backyard. Our little house was quiet except for the occasional sounds of a beam creaking. That sort of thing was to be expected in a home this old. But then I heard another sound, someone talking. It was quiet but distinct. As silently as possible, I went to my door and opened it. Lenore was talking to someone, and from the tone of her voice she was frantic.

"No, I can't do that. You don't understand...I don't know what you mean...."

I knew it was an invasion of her privacy, but I crept into the hallway and stood outside her door. If Lenore was going to do something crazy in my house, I wanted to know about it. I held my breath and took a peek. She had the house phone up to her ear and was sitting on the bed in her pajamas. Her hair looked wild and unbrushed, as if she'd just woken up.

"Why are you asking me to do this? You know I love you..."

Hearing her move around the room, I leaned flush against the wall. *That's enough of that, Carrie Jo. Now go to bed and quit snooping.*

I sprinted down the hall in my sock feet and slid through the open door of my office. I closed the container of fruit salad and put the lid back on my water. I paused to slow my pounding heartbeat.

Lenore's whispering continued, and my hand went protectively to my stomach. I couldn't let it go. I had to know what was going on. Who was she talking to at this time of night, and why was she so upset? My hand rested on the old-fashioned princess phone on my desk. Should I? What if she was in danger? It sounded like someone was trying to convince her to do something she did not want to do. As quietly as I could, I picked up the phone just to make sure Lenore was okay.

"I'm not ready...I can't do it...yes...I understand. I know what this means. This is forever, ain't it?"

There was nobody there—just Lenore speaking into the phone, the dial tone buzzing in the background. With a lump in my throat I put the phone down, left the food on my desk and slinked out of the room. All I wanted to do now was brush my teeth, go to bed and cuddle as closely to Ashland as I could.

This couldn't be good.

Chapter 12—Delilah

As the weeks flew by, the excitement in Mobile grew almost to fever pitch. The city's hotels were filling up as dignitaries and curious visitors from the surrounding counties descended on the downtown area. Lampposts were festooned with purple and gold ribbon, but the city held back a bit on some of the festivities, remembering to honor their war dead with the appropriate decorum. The lost "sons of the south" would be honored during the first parade with an Ash Processional. Relatives of the lost would march in silence dressed in black and doused in ashes, and Maundy and I had spent all morning sewing black ribbons to sell to the supporters. According to Honoree Daughtry, the wife of the commissioner responsible for this year's Mardi Gras activities, this event was expected to help the city begin to "heal from its wounds." I thought the whole thing was morbid, but it kept my hands busy and my mind off my situation.

Parade watchers were already lining the streets and covered the walkways like flies on a watermelon carcass prepared to fully enjoy Mobile's Mardi Gras opening spectacle. We quickly sold our baskets of ribbons, and I took the empty containers back to the shop while Maundy stayed behind to watch.

From what she told me, festivities like the debutante auction and the Night of Masks ball were quite decadent. I wondered what the austere Miss Claudette Page would think about those. I was certain that she would be staging a rally against this sort of revelry, but in fact, Miss Page was a former Boeuf Gras Society queen. Although that mystical organization had dissolved right before the Civil War, Claudette continued to work on behalf of many such organizations. To my disappointment, that had been the most scandalous tidbit I had learned about my estranged aunt thus far. As my court date approached, I began to see my chances of persuading Miss Page to acquiesce to my father's will all but disappear. Perhaps Maundy's idea of gathering information on her had been a waste of my time, just a ruse to hire a decent dressmaker. Thus far, Maundy had gotten much more information from me than I had from her. She pressed me all the time about Adam, leaving me with no doubt that she had was interested in him.

As I pushed my way through the crowd, I reflected on the past few weeks. There had seemed no end to the line of women that flowed through Maundy's parlor and dress shop. We worked as fast as our fingers would allow us, sometimes late into the night. Karah had gotten into the habit of sending the Brougham carriage around to pick me up at five o'clock, which was a blessing. But many was the night when Stokes had to wait for me, sometimes for hours. Regardless of the time of my return, my cousin would be there in the Blue Room with a plate of food and a smile, eager to hear about my day at Mobile's busiest dress shop. I often invited her to visit me at the shop, to come get to know Maundy and the other women I worked with, but she always refused, saying that she did not want to miss her mother's arrival. I pointed out that her mother was not set to arrive for a few days, but she said that she wouldn't put it past her to arrive early.

After all these weeks of being with Karah, I knew very little about her mother other than that she was a popular and gifted actress and quite a beauty. Karah showed me handbills with her image and even shared a tiny portrait of her in a locket that Karah wore about her neck. From what I could see, Karah looked very much like her only thinner and not nearly as flamboyantly dressed. I did not feel anxious about her arrival. I assumed that anyone related to Karah would be kind and friendly.

During one of my late nights at work Adam came by the shop, but Maundy sent him away. She told him we were rushed to finish ball gowns and could not be bothered with a social visit. Listening on the other side of the parlor door, I heard the entire conversation. Maundy was polite but firm in her refusal to let him see me, yet she invited him to visit her for dinner after Mardi Gras ended. I said nothing when she returned but tucked the information away for later use.

The following evening I arrived at Seven Sisters as usual, tired and hungry, but I immediately knew something was wrong. Karah wasn't at her usual place at the round cherrywood table that we often used for our late-night suppers. She was thumbing through one of the many books of poems in the ladies' parlor and barely noticed when I arrived. A stack of books was beside her on the table and I could tell she was looking for something important.

"Good evening, cousin," I said pleasantly and reached for the plate that Hooney left for me. The bread was dry and the soup was cold, but I was so hungry it didn't matter. I dipped the bread into the oniony broth and snacked away.

She turned around, her face in a book, then looked up and gasped. "Oh goodness. What time is it?"

"It's nearly nine o'clock. I didn't mean to startle you. I spoke, but you were immersed in your book. Must be an interesting read."

"I was just…well, you're here now."

"Yes, and I think this is the last late night for me, unless Mrs. Broadus brings her daughter's dress back for some reason or another—which wouldn't surprise me in the least. The way that young lady puts on weight is astonishing. Is there something I can help you find?"

She shook her head and placed the book on top of the others in the nearby stack. Docie walked in, scowled at me and walked back out. Looking even more uncomfortable, Karah said, "Please excuse Docie. She's not used to socializing with other people."

I wiped the crumbs from my hands and said, "Why do you keep her, Karah? She isn't only unpleasant, she also is dangerous and has no regard for our family's things. Not to mention how abominably she treats you. I do not understand. Surely you can find another maid."

She shrugged and absently ran her finger across the spine of the book. Since she was content to stare at her hands, I asked, "What is it? I can see that something is on your mind. Is it your mother? Should I leave?"

"No, I do not want you to go. I think when she meets you she will like you, just as I do. But the truth is my mother is very changeable and I am never too good at predicting her thoughts or her moods. That's not what has me puzzled, though."

"Oh? What is it?" My eyes hurt, and my fingers felt stiff and dry, but I waited to hear her revelation.

"Adam Iverson came by Seven Sisters today."

I sat up straighter and began to apologize. "I will speak with him. I promise he won't come back again. Did he behave inappropriately?"

My lovely cousin pursed her lips in thoughtful expression. The ivory candles on the table sputtered on their shiny candlesticks. I felt an unmistakable draft in the room. The flickering flames cast strange shadows on the wall beside us. "He is in love with you, I think." I could not hide my surprise at her observation. "Mr. Iverson is unashamedly flirtatious, but all he wanted to talk about was you. Do you love him, Delilah? He is rather handsome in a rugged, farmhand sort of way."

"I..." I felt my skin warm, and I toyed with my bread.

Karah quickly added, "Perhaps your affections lie somewhere else now, as Mr. Iverson seems to believe."

How would I navigate this turn in conversation? Until tonight, Karah had never asked me about Adam or our relationship, and I was too tired to play parlor games with her. My rebellious heart won over the intelligent part of my mind that encouraged me to tread lightly.

"I loved him as a brother, until I knew he was not my brother. I thought he felt the same way about me."

"So he mistreated you? Took advantage of you?" She tilted her head and folded her hands in front of her on the table. Seeing my hesitation, she poured me another glass of water.

"No, not intentionally. Adam cannot be anything but who he is. I think we were naïve—I was naïve—but there were no promises made. I had no promise."

"You yielded yourself to him?" Karah leaned forward, the tiny lines on her forehead deepening as she whispered. I sipped my water and did not answer her but merely gave her a glum look. She obviously had never been in love. "What about Jackson? Are you interested in him, Delilah? Not to be crass, cousin, but I do not know any other way to ask."

Surprised by the question I unthinkingly blurted an answer. "Mr. Keene and I have a business relationship. I consider him a friend but only a friend."

"Then you would not mind if he called on me?"

"I have no reason to object."

She reached across the table and squeezed my hand happily. "I am so pleased to hear that. Forgive me for being so forward, cousin. I just had to know. If I thought you had your cap set for him, I would never encourage his attention. I have strong feelings on this matter. I never want to be accused of competing with my dear cousin. There are too many men in the world for that."

I smiled back at her, pretending to be happy. Why hadn't I told her the truth, that I was not sure how I felt about Mr. Keene? Now it was too late say so. Quietly I internalized the meaning of all this. Because of my confession, Karah now knew all about my involvement with Adam and she made it plain she had designs on our attorney. Maundy was right—I was too quick to speak my mind.

"Did you hear me, Delilah?"

"Yes," I lied, then took a sip of my water. I did not drink often, but I suddenly felt the need for a glass of wine or some of Maundy's strong drink.

"Really? What did I say?"

"I apologize, Karah. I guess I am more tired than I thought." I stood up and stretched my sore back.

"It wasn't important. We can talk tomorrow. Can I count on you to help me get the house ready for Mother tomorrow? I want everything to look its best. I am sure Maundy can spare you one day."

"Yes, I will gladly help you. I think I will go to bed now. Do you need help finding your lost bookmark?"

"Bookmark?"

"Yes, or whatever it is you are looking for." I pointed to the messy stack of dusty books piled on the table.

"Oh, bookmark. No, I think I will retire too in just a few minutes. It *is* getting late. Good night, cousin."

"Good night, Karah." Feeling unhappy, I left her in the ladies' parlor and walked down the hall toward the staircase. No candles had been lit in the hallway, and the entire top floor was like a yawning black cavern. The hem of my blue dress had torn as I stepped out of the carriage earlier. I would need to repair it, but now I just wanted to prevent myself from tripping over it and tumbling up or down the stairs. I picked up my skirts to climb up to Calpurnia's room when an odd amber-colored light shining in from the glass door to the Moonlight Garden caught my eye. I paused to decide if I should call out to Karah, but the events of the evening still stung. I decided to have a look myself. It was not unusual to see lights on the property at night, but the color of the light attracted my attention. I had never seen anything like it. As I walked toward the door, the light moved away from the garden entrance, but I could plainly see it shining through the trees.

I opened the door and hoped to avoid waking Stokes, who slept in the small room under the stairs. He was an odd man—an empty man who did not enjoy idle chitchat, especially with women. From what Karah whispered to me on the few occasions we had the opportunity to speak without enduring Docie's disapproving stares, Stokes had been Mr. Cottonwood's right-hand man, never too far from his master. I wondered what the former slave thought about me—if he even knew or cared who I was. The door clicked behind me, and I stepped out on the brick walkway.

Karah and I had walked through the garden during my initial tour of the home, but there had been plenty of daylight to see by. In the day it was a marvelous place, full of hidden spots for reading a book or, as Karah put it, stealing a kiss. But it seemed a forlorn place at night. It was completely dark, with the exception of the half-moon above me and the odd amber light hovering on the other side of the trees.

I walked the half circle to the opening of the maze path, pausing to see if I could determine the source of the light. Tendrils from my usually neat bun slapped my face as a blast of wind blew through the garden, almost pulling me down the path. My hand flew up to shield my face from an unexpected shower of damp magnolia leaves. Then I heard my name whispered on the breeze, "Delilah, Delilah."

"Who's there?" I asked in a near whisper. My heart was pounding in my chest as if I had run through the whole garden. My skin tingled, and my lips felt dry. I stopped on the path, my mind torn between the choices—run back to the house or continue my search to determine the source of the unusual light. "Who's there?" I said in a stronger voice. The wind blew steadily, but at least the trees were not pelting me with foliage. Shielding my eyes with my hand, I watched the light bounce further into the maze. Curiosity won the battle with fear, and I pressed on. In the half light of the moon I could at least see the path ahead of me, and the strange bouncing light seemed to have stopped on the path to wait for my arrival. Walking more quickly now, I called out again, "Who are you? Is that you, Stokes?"

I walked deeper into the twisting garden, to the left and then to the right again until I felt disoriented.

What was I doing? This was none of my business, was it? This was not my house or my property. I was only a visitor here. Who did I think I was, policing the grounds as if I were a true Cottonwood? I had no weapon or any other way to defend myself, but I wasn't thinking clearly as I pushed toward the light that now began to pulsate. The amber color darkened, and suddenly the light disappeared. I scrambled down the hedge, scratching myself on a thorny branch. I swore under my breath—it was a word I had never used before, but I had heard Maundy use it plenty of times. Yet I did not stop. I could not explain this compulsion, but I had to find and identify the source of the light. I stepped out of the maze into a clearing and nearly fell over dead.

Standing in the center circle of the maze was a man, a tall man wearing a fine suit with white collars and no hat. Unmoving, he watched me as I approached just as if he were a statue. I had passed many statues in this garden on my journey here, but none were as frightening as the man who stood before me. I paused about twenty feet from him, waiting for some indication that he was a living being. Another breeze blew through the Moonlight Garden, and on the breeze I smelled magnolias, burning leaves and something else...

My hands flew into fists, and I looked around to see if anyone else had joined us. If there were two men I should certainly run, but I saw no one else. What should I do? Should I turn to flee the garden? I stared in disbelief as a whirlwind of leaves blew between us, blasting my gown and hair. In seconds, it had lashed my hair completely free from its pins. As the wind blew past me I could plainly see that the intruder's hair did not move! He was certainly a statue—or something. A feeling of dread filled my soul with horror, and finally I gained control of my legs. As quickly as I had run into the garden, I began to run out.

I took a right turn down the long hedgerow and ran left, traveling under the blooming dogwoods. I took another left and ran the length of the magnolia-lined trail. My eyes were wide, and my breath came fast and hard. I knew I was heading the right way—there were pods and leaves covering the ground, and the white petals shone bright in the moonlight. My forgotten torn hem caught my foot, and I tripped and went sliding across a pile of damp, musky leaves. I skinned my elbow, but I could not really feel the pain.

I heard footsteps behind me on the leaves and knew I was not alone. I was too afraid to move.

Maybe if I remain very still, he will not see me!

Slowly I pushed my hair out of my face and could see a pair of shoes a few feet from me. With complete horror, I looked up...and there he was, glaring down at me. The stranger reached his hand toward me, and his long nails were dirty and gray. I scrambled away from him, scooting back on my hands and climbing awkwardly to my feet. I stood breathing hard as the thing surveyed me. Since I stood frozen, afraid for my life, I stared back. His unearthly pale skin appeared as if it had never seen the sun. He had a thin, narrow nose, sculpted lips and dark eyes—eyes that had no life in them. On closer inspection I could see that his jacket and trousers were dusty as if he slept in the dirt. My soul was offended on such a deep level, but I could barely understand it. Then it occurred to me. This man was not alive—I was looking into the face of a ghost.

As the awareness of my situation dawned upon me, I could see the amusement in his eyes. I knew who he was—or at least *what* he was, and he knew that too. Since he was not leaving or moving I asked him, "What are you doing here?"

He took a step toward me, and instinctively I moved backwards. In an elegant dead voice he said, "I am waiting for someone."

"Who are you waiting for?" I whispered in the darkness. He moved toward me without moving his feet. It was a sort of glide. He was only a few feet from me now, and as I watched his face began to change…the skin became pinker, the dark eyes took on a dark blue color, and he appeared to breathe. The breeze blew again, lifting the hair off of his collar. Despite the amazing effect, I knew it was all an illusion. He wanted me to think he was alive, but I knew he was not. A smile curled on his lips, and I could see his perfect white teeth.

"It does not matter now, Delilah. She is not here, but you will do. Would you like to take a walk with me?" He offered his hand to me as innocently as a child, but I had no intention of reaching for it.

"No, I don't think I will." There we stood facing one another, he unmoving and my feet locked in place. Then I heard a voice, a familiar voice, a living voice calling to me from the house.

"Delilah? Come inside! There is a storm brewing." The garden intruder glanced at the doorway and then at me. He smiled and rudely licked his lips before he disappeared, melting away until his image vanished. Finally free to move, I bolted toward the door, remembering to lift my tattered hem as I ran. I climbed the steps and scurried through the open door and into the arms of my cousin.

"Delilah! Look at you! What happened? You are as cold as ice. Come inside now and I'll make you a hot cup of tea." I wept on her shoulder and clung to her as if she were the only thing that could save me from death. "Docie! Come quickly!"

Kara's servant walked serenely into the hallway, her hands clasped before her. "Yes? What is it?" The older woman was wearing a long flannel nightgown, and her gray hair hung in a long braid over her shoulder.

"My cousin has seen something that frightened her. Have Stokes search the garden, and please bring us a cup of tea. Quickly now!" Karah led me away, her arm about my waist. I glanced over my shoulder at Docie. The woman had not moved. In fact, she stood in the hallway watching us with a smile on her face.

She knew exactly what I had seen in the garden, and she wasn't surprised by it.

Chapter 13—Carrie Jo

Before I left the house, I checked my email and was delighted to see that Desmond Taylor had replied with his answer: the Idlewood project was a go! I had done it—no, our team had done it! I felt excited by the prospect of beginning a new project. It would take a lot of time, probably a few years, but it would be worth it if we could stop the house from rotting into the Mobile landscape and return Idlewood to its proper place in society.

Ashland had left early for a meeting with his attorney about some mysterious project. I wasn't too sure about this new attorney. She seemed very hands-on, but she was a friend of his from high school; working with him would kind of be her big break. I trusted Ashland. He had been unfaithful to me only subconsciously. I had no reason to believe that there was anything funny going on, but my gut still told me to keep an eye on her.

Rachel greeted me and pointed to the coffeepot. "Made some fresh. Get it while it's hot."

Just the idea of drinking coffee made me queasy, and she must've seen the expression on my face. "What? I thought you loved my coffee."

My hand flew to my stomach, and I nodded glumly. "I do love your coffee, but my child? Not so much."

"Oh my God! Are you serious?" Rachel ran around her desk and put her arms around me. "I'm so happy! I'm going to be Aunt Rachel! When is he due? Or she due? Do we know what we're having?"

I laughed at her excitement. It felt good to tell my secret. "Not yet, but I'm sure we will find out soon enough. I have another appointment in a couple of weeks. Maybe by then they can do the ultrasound and we can see something."

She hugged me again, and before I could get to my office the front door opened. A very happy-looking Henri and Detra Ann walked in. "Hey, guys." I greeted them with a smile.

"Is this how you always start your workday, with a group hug?" Detra Ann laughed and hugged me too.

Before I could say anything, Rachel blurted out, "It's so wonderful! Carrie Jo is going to have a baby."

"I heard! I'm so happy for y'all!" Detra Ann hugged me again.

Henri put his arm around me. "I had to tell her. You and Ashland will make wonderful parents. Congratulations again, CJ."

"Thank you. It is pretty wonderful. So what brings you two by? Not that I'm not glad to see you for any reason."

"Actually I came to talk to you about Lenore."

Thinking that Henri would want privacy I said, "Let's go to my office. Rachel made some wonderful coffee if you'd like some."

"I think we're good."

I sat behind my desk and invited them to take the two seats in front of me. I tossed my purse in the bottom drawer and turned my attention to my friends. "You should know she's gone. I mean, she left this morning before Ashland or I got up. She mentioned something yesterday about getting a job as a housekeeper. I didn't ask Doreen this morning, but I think she plans on talking to her."

Detra Ann leaned back in her chair and glanced at Henri. He said, "Lenore has always walked to the beat of a different drummer, even before Aleezabeth disappeared, but her behavior has gotten worse since. I am grateful that you allowed her to spend the night with you, but that is not a solution. I cannot put you guys in the middle of her mess, especially with a baby coming. I am not sure what she's capable of."

"I agree that Lenore is...quirky. But I'm not sure she's dangerous. Then again, you know her better than I do."

"I think I have a way to help her. What if, somehow, we could find out what happened to Aleezabeth? I mean, I would never ask for myself, but...she needs to know or she is never going to move past it. That's why I am here, Carrie Jo. I know you and Ashland both have skills in this area. What if we could solve the mystery, find my cousin and bring her home? I think that would..." Just then, my phone rang. Despite my attempts to ignore it, Rachel poked her head in the doorway.

"I hate to interrupt, but that's Desmond Taylor on the phone. He's on a cruise. I'm not sure when you could call him back. Do you want to speak with him?"

I didn't know what to say to Henri. Was he asking me to dream about Aleezabeth? "Forgive me, y'all, but I have to take this. Just give me a second."

"We can talk later." Henri stood, and Detra Ann just stared at him.

"It's not that you guys aren't important to me. It's just that—"

Henri raised his hand and gave me a dismissive wave. "I should never have asked." He walked out of the office; I could hear the front door chimes, and I sat staring open-mouthed at Detra Ann.

"What did I do?"

"Don't worry about him. He's just worried about Lenore. And no matter what he tells you, he's not over what happened to Aleezabeth. Tell you what—why don't we meet you for dinner and then we can talk."

"That sounds great. Why don't you guys come over about six? I'm really sorry, Detra Ann."

"Nothing to worry about. You leave him to me. We will be there." She walked out of my office in her shiny taupe heels.

"Okay!" I called after her, still puzzled by what just happened. I picked up the phone.

Desmond Taylor might have been on a cruise, but he was certainly in work mode. He had a slew of questions, and I did my best to answer them. After the thirty-minute call ended, I couldn't help but worry about Henri. It was not like him to be short-tempered with me—I knew something was seriously wrong.

The day dragged by, but finally five o'clock came around and I waved goodbye to Rachel as I headed home. Doreen had graciously agreed to cook for our dinner guests, and my stomach was grumbling. I found Ashland in my office using my computer. I dumped my purse and briefcase on the side table, slid my arms around his neck and kissed the top of his head.

"Whatcha doing?"

"Just checking on a few things. You know, I never did give you *my* anniversary present." He turned the wooden chair around and patted his leg playfully.

"You're right." I slid into his lap and wrapped my arms around his neck. "But unfortunately your gift is going to have to wait. We have dinner guests coming, remember? I texted you earlier."

He smiled wickedly and said, "This will only take a minute."

I blushed and scolded him, "Ashland."

"It's not that, and I'm pretty sure that those kinds of *gifts* take a little more than a minute." I smiled back at him and punched him playfully on the arm. "Open the browser," he said.

"What?"

"Open the browser on the computer. I want you to see this."

I reached over and pulled up the browser window he had minimized. It was a website featuring historic Mobile landmarks. I had to admit that I was puzzled. "Okay, so this is Widow's Row. I have seen this before. What am I looking for?"

"Tell me about it."

"This house was originally part of Widow's Row. It was housing for Civil War widows—there were quite a few of them. But there was something of a scandal there around the turn of the century. At the end of this street would have been the Southern Market. Right here." I pointed to a map that showed the layout of the old city. "One row of houses ran east, and the second ran west, that way. Of course, the county courthouse was across the street back then. It's a shame that most of those houses are gone."

"Not all of them are."

"Really?"

"A few have been wonderfully restored, like the Murray House, but there is one that's kind of been left behind. It's on Eslava Street."

"Eslava...it runs parallel to Virginia Street, right?"

"Yes."

"So what am I looking for?"

He reached around me and clicked on another screen. A tiny house, sometimes called a "shotgun" house, popped up on the screen. "It's yours. I thought it would make the perfect office for your new business. You could restore it and really show off your talents. And of course, you'd be restoring a patch of Mobile. What do you think?"

Tears welled up in my eyes. "I think it's wonderful." I put my arms around his neck again and hugged him. "I love you."

"I love you too."

"And I didn't get you anything."

"Nonsense. You gave me the best gift of all." He nervously touched my stomach. I nodded and put my hand over his. I kissed him, feeling so grateful not only for the wonderful gift but for the fact that I had someone as wonderful as Ashland in my life. What a fool I had been to make such a big deal out of his stupid dreams! I felt blessed beyond belief.

I heard voices in the hall. "Oops. To be continued. Our guests have arrived a few minutes early."

With one last kiss I scooted out of his lap, and together we walked out of the office holding hands like two teenagers.

"Hey, guys!" I called to them. "Glad you could make it. I'll check with Doreen on dinner. Be right back." Ashland squeezed my hand, and I went to see if I could help in the kitchen. As expected Doreen was a whirlwind of activity; a sauce pot on the stove filled the kitchen with delicious flavor. She slid the pork roast out of the oven and set the pan on the stove top before she spun around and gasped.

"Mrs. Stuart! You almost gave me a heart attack." She pushed her eyeglasses back to the bridge of her nose and gave me a goodhearted yet disapproving scowl.

"Sorry," I said sincerely. "Thank you for going the extra mile tonight, Doreen. Smells delicious." I stuck a spoon in the sauce before she could object. "Can I do anything?" The sauce was delicious. Not like Bette would have made, but I couldn't wait to dig in.

"No, ma'am. I have this under control. Dinner should be ready in about twenty minutes. I think your guests are a bit early."

"Yes they are, and we aren't in a big rush," I said as I stole a warm yeast roll from the covered basket on the bar.

"You never said if you wanted me to serve. Did you want this buffet style?"

"Buffet style is perfect. We can wait on ourselves." I resisted the urge to hug her. Doreen didn't enjoy being touched—or surprised. I seemed to always do both. Leaving dinner in good hands, I went to join my friends, but Detra Ann caught me in the hallway and waved me into the bathroom. I giggled as she closed the door behind us.

"What's going on? Are you dying to tell me the details?" I asked teasingly. Her distressed look made me change my tone immediately. "Detra Ann?"

"I thought about calling you after we left this morning, but I didn't know what to say."

"You should have. I'm sorry about that phone call."

"You must think I'm a horrible person. I mean, I never meant for this to happen with Henri. It just sort of happened."

I grinned at her. "What? You must be the only person who didn't see this coming. And of course I don't think you're horrible—this is the way it should be. Nobody expects you to mourn forever, Detra Ann. This isn't the 1800s."

Sitting on the side of the tub with her head in her hands, she whispered, "I just don't know. I don't know if this is right. I don't know if this is what I want. That's horrible to say, isn't it?"

I sat on the floor next to her and waited for her to look at me. Sitting this close, I could see the dark circles under her eyes that she tried to hide with expensive concealer. She hadn't been sleeping and was much thinner than she had been last year. She didn't have any extra weight to begin with. "I think it's time for you to think about yourself. Not your mom. Not Henri. Yourself. It's okay to take care of you. And if you're not sure how you feel about him, then slow down. No one will fault you for that."

"I'm leaving, Carrie Jo. I took a job in Atlanta."

"Oh wow."

"He thinks last night changed everything, but it didn't. He doesn't understand what I've been through. I mean, I know he knows—I've talked about it plenty of times—but he doesn't know how I feel. It's just too soon. It's too much. I just can't. And there's this other thing."

"What?"

"Lenore is right. I am a shade, a ghost. I think I am marked. I think—no, I know—that something bad is going to happen to me."

Instinctively I grabbed her hands and said, "No! Don't listen to her. She doesn't know what she's talking about. We beat those ghosts, and it's over. End of subject. Lenore is crazy—I caught her talking on the phone to nobody last night. There was no one on the other end." No way was I telling Detra Ann what Lenore said or what Ashland saw.

Her beautiful eyes widened, but she continued, "You and I both know that with that house it's never truly over. I can't pretend that I understand why all of this happened. I still don't know why Bette had to go and why Terrence is gone. What was the connection—what made me so special that I escaped? It's not fair, and I think I just got lucky. But my luck is wearing out. If I don't leave, if I don't make a run for it, well, then I'm going to join them. I hear things. I see things. Dark things. If I sit still for too long shadows creep in. I can't even close my eyes for very long. Something is coming for me, CJ."

I heard Ashland call me from the hallway, and I scrambled to my feet and opened the door. "Right here. Be there in just a second." I didn't offer any explanation other than that. He'd have to wait. I closed the door and sat next to Detra Ann.

"Listen to me. If you decide to leave, that's fine if that's what you need to do. But if you're leaving just to run away from some phantom, then you should stay. We can fight this, Detra Ann, and we *can* do it if we stick together. That was the mistake I made the last time. I took off half-cocked into that hospital room, and look where it got us. Bette is gone." A sob escaped my throat. "And that's on me. TD's gone. And that's on me. They had no idea what I was doing, and I put them in a horrible situation. You are not alone, and I'm not going to let you fight this by yourself. Let's go in there right now, tell them what's going on and get everyone on board so we can come up with some sort of plan. Enough with working behind the scenes—we need to be honest and put everything out in the open."

"I can't do that to Henri. He is so broken up about Aleezabeth and Lenore. I don't think he can handle one more thing right now. And let me remind you that you have a baby to think about. I can't have you fighting Death on my behalf. I won't do it. I just wanted you to know that I value your friendship. I am glad I got to know you."

"Me too, but don't talk like I'll never see you again."

"I want you to promise me something." I didn't like the sound of this, but I nodded. "Promise me that you will look after Ashland. If anything were to ever happen to me and you ditch him, I will come back and haunt you."

"Of course I will. But don't talk like this. We're sticking together, remember?" Before she could protest, there was a knock on the door.

"What's going on in there? Carrie Jo are you okay?" When did Ashland get to be so nosy?

"Yes. I was just feeling a little sick. I'm okay now. Coming right out." Detra Ann and I hugged, and I emerged from the bathroom with my hand over my stomach. "Must be evening sickness."

Soon the four of us were chatting, but it was impossible to really have a conversation with Doreen coming in and out. She insisted on waiting on us even though we'd agreed on a more informal buffet style. Thirty minutes later, she waved goodbye, and I gathered the supper plates and quickly carried them to the kitchen. I'd tidy those up later, but I had something to do. No way was I going to lose another friend. I decided it was time to take charge. I meant what I'd said about no more secrets. Wiping my hands on the kitchen towel, I marched back into the living room and stood with my hands on my hips. I didn't give a hoot about what they were talking about. I spilled my guts.

"Detra Ann needs our help, y'all. I know that you have something to say, Henri, and I am sorry about this morning's interruption. But this is a situation that can't wait."

Detra Ann scowled at me. "Carrie Jo...stop."

"Nope. You might be mad at me forever, but at least you'll be alive. We have to tell them. So tell them already!" Ashland and Henri stared at me like I had two heads. "I'm not kidding. You tell them or I will."

Detra Ann shot to her feet and glared at me. "I didn't want you to say anything, CJ!"

"Well, I did, and I refuse to lose another friend! You can hate me later, but tell them what's going on."

She slid her hands into the pockets of her fitted sweatshirt and paced the carpet in front of the big window on the side of the house. The streetlight was on out front, but the side of the house looked dark and gloomy. After a few moments, she leaned against the windowsill and stared out into the darkness with her back to us. "Lenore is right. Something is following me. I knew it the day I left the hospital. At first I thought it was the pain medicine. God, that stuff is awful. That's why I prefer drinking. Booze doesn't make my skin crawl or cause me to hallucinate. Pain medication makes me loopy big time, but that wasn't it. At first it only happened once, maybe twice, a day. I was walking down the sidewalk in front of my mother's house on Palladium Drive, and I passed that big oak that stretches almost into the street. You know the one, Ashland, the one we used to climb. As soon as I stepped into the shadow, I heard it groan, like it wanted to devour me." She shivered, turned around and leaned with her back against the window, her hands still in her pockets. "By the time I got into Mom's house I was shaking so bad I thought I would pass out." She began pacing again.

"Then the shadows in my house began to groan whenever I came close to them. You can't know what it's like having to leave the lights on 24/7 like you're a four-year old! I don't dare turn a light off because the shadows don't just groan now— they call my name!" Detra Ann's voice rose in fear. Henri reached for her, but she raised her hand and shook her head. "No. Let me finish." She took a deep breath and continued, "A month after the hospital event, I was in the shower when the light went out in my bathroom. The bulb blew—that's what I told myself anyway. There I was in the shower, naked and soaking wet, just waiting to die. The groans grew louder and louder—I could feel the darkness gathering. I tripped out of the shower and crawled to the bathroom door. A slimy hand grabbed my foot and pulled me back, but I kept struggling to get away. Finally I remembered the Lord's Prayer. I said it, like you did the other night, Ashland. I said it, and it let me go. I reached the door handle and turned it, and I was free. Then I called Henri to change the light bulb for me." She reached out and squeezed his hand. "You have been so good to me. I don't deserve you."

Henri's dark eyes sparkled with tears. "Don't say that. I am the lucky one. I love you, Detra Ann."

"I know," she said sadly. She turned back to the big window. Nobody said a word; I sure didn't know what to say. "Even now, if I stepped into the yard and stood under that tree where the shadows are the darkest, it would take me and I would never escape." She peered out the blinds, and my skin began to crawl.

"Detra Ann, get away from the window," Ashland warned her sternly. He stood in front of me and waved his hand behind him, and I got off the couch and moved to the doorway. I couldn't see anything, but apparently my husband did.

It didn't seem to faze her. "See? I can see the darkness gathering now. It's just waiting for me. I don't know what's in those shadows, but I know if it touches me, I'll die. Tell me I'm wrong! Any of you! Tell me I'm wrong!"

"Detra Ann, get away from the window!"

Tearing her eyes away from the darkness, she looked at Ashland. As she did, the window behind her shattered with a loud boom, and pieces of glass flew across the living room. Ashland fell on top of me to protect me, and Henri snatched Detra Ann's hand and pulled her to the ground. As we lay there trying to figure out who was hurt and what happened, the chandelier flickered.

"Everyone get up now!" Ashland yelled. "Upstairs, everyone!"

We did as we were told and climbed the stairs like four maniacs. I flipped on light switches as we ran so none of the shadows could touch Detra Ann. She wasn't crying or saying anything at all, just running with fear in her eyes. I couldn't blame her. If Death were chasing me and using shadows to reach me, I would be fearful too. When we made it to the end of the hallway, I grabbed her hands. "Don't run away from us, Detra Ann. Stay close, okay?" She bobbled her blond head. Her makeup was running under her eyes, and her hands shook.

Standing on tiptoe, I tried to see the ground floor, but it was completely dark. I imagined that I too could almost hear an inaudible whisper.

"Oh God, it's calling my name. Lenore was right! It is Death. He wants me! I cheated him, and now he wants me. He's come to claim me!"

"Well, he's going to have to fight us if he wants you because he isn't going to take you, Detra Ann! We're safe here. There is light up here, see?" I heard the light bulb pop above us, and the light faded.

"Oh my God!" she shouted and ran into the guest room.

"Stop, Detra Ann! Wait for me!" I ran to her, flipping on every light I could as I went. "Follow me. I have a flashlight somewhere in my bedroom." Grabbing her hand I called,

"Ashland! Where is the flashlight?" Coming to himself now, he ran to us and opened the closet. Hidden in the back was a huge Maglite that could light up the neighborhood when fully charged. He turned it on. The light was so bright it was nearly blinding. Henri was holding Detra Ann now, and she was weeping.

"I love you. I love you. I love you," she repeated over and over again.

"Shh…it's okay. Shh, now. It's okay. We are all here together."

Then the guest room lights went out and the lamps popped. We were in total darkness except for the Maglite, which lit up the entire room with harsh white light. So far it wasn't flickering, but who knew how long it would last? We heard a sound, a slapping, crashing sound. The tree limbs from the oaks that surrounded our house were slapping the windows—slapping them so hard they were all breaking! Between the crashing and the groaning, it was a horrible cacophony. Surely the neighbors would hear this! Somebody would come help us! But what if they didn't?

"I love you, Henri. I'm sorry. I am sorry…" Detra Ann was crying quietly now. The whispers became louder and more threatening. Henri held her as if it might be his last chance. Tears ran down his cheeks.

"Ashland," I said fearfully as he wrapped his arms around me.

Suddenly the smashing and crashing of the branches ceased, and the door to the bedroom flew open—a tall figure stood in the doorway. We gasped and waited. A tall figure stepped out of the darkness and into the brightness of the Maglite.

I couldn't believe it—it was Lenore!

Chapter 14—Detra Ann

"You believe me now, don't you? I said you were a shade." She spat the words out like she hated me. Like I wanted to be in this battle with Death itself.

"How did you get up here? Is there a way out?" I demanded, suddenly feeling hopeful.

"The only way out is the way you came in, and it's pitch black outside." She leaned against the doorframe staring at me.

Carrie Jo stood by me protectively. "How did you get up here? Did you see it?"

"I saw nothing but the wind blowing and the house dark. I can feel it, though. It's still very close."

"She's right. We're not out of the woods yet," Ashland added.

"I don't understand why this is happening! Why won't it leave me alone? How do I make it stop? Do you know, or are you going to continue to hate me? Why don't you try to help me since you seem to know so much?" Anger and frustration rose up inside me. She could help me, I knew it, but for some reason she wouldn't. "Why? What have I ever done to you? I don't even know you, Lenore!"

She didn't answer but glared at me with her almond-shaped eyes. Her mouth was a pair of hard lines.

"I know who can help us," Carrie Jo said in a rush.

"Who?"

"Father Portier! He'll know how we can defeat Death."

"What makes you so sure, Carrie Jo?" Henri asked.

"Because he's already dead."

"What?"

"There's no time to talk about this." She waved the flashlight and walked out the door. "Let's go before this thing comes back." She grabbed my hand, and we scrambled down the stairs with lightning speed, the guys following behind us. CJ grabbed her purse off the entryway table, and we headed out the door. We climbed into her BMW, and I was surprised to see Lenore climb in the backseat beside me. CJ slid the key into the ignition and we rolled down the driveway onto the crowded street. Ashland passed me the flashlight, and I held it like my life depended on it. Maybe it did.

"Oh no, it's a parade night," Carrie Jo said as we drove down Dauphin and nearly ran into a barricade. "We'll have to go around to Conte Street. Maybe that's not blocked off." She turned right and eased down the street slowly. There were people everywhere.

"Where exactly are we headed?" Ashland asked her in a worried voice. "Not to Seven Sisters, I hope."

"No, I don't think this has to do with the house. Not directly, anyway. We're going to the cemetery. That's where the gate is, and that is where I met the priest. This must be why. I didn't put it together until tonight."

"Hold on now. Nobody said anything about a cemetery. We're trying to escape Death, not knock on his door," Lenore said fearfully.

"As you said, he's not looking for you, right? Then you have nothing to fear." Henri snarled at her impatiently. "And nobody asked you to come."

"Someone has to look out for you, Henri Devecheaux." He snorted and looked out the window.

"What are you thinking? How are these things connected?" Ashland asked, his blue eyes full of questions.

"Detra Ann is a spiritual person. She said that she was able to escape it when it came for her in the bathroom by praying the Lord's Prayer."

"Okay…"

"There must be some prayer we can use to make it leave her alone for good. The priest told me to look for the secret."

Ashland's face was filled with doubt, but I piped in, "Listen, it might be a long shot, but I'm willing to go on a little faith here. Even if it means walking through a cemetery."

"What if the gate won't open? What if we can't get to the priest? You said yourself you don't know how you got there."

"It will open. It has to."

Ashland looked at me in the rearview mirror. "You sure you want to do this?"

I nodded, and Henri squeezed my hand. "I'll be right with you the whole time," he murmured.

Ashland nodded and said, "We'll have to park and walk. This is about as close as you're going to get." Carrie Jo pulled the car to the side of the road, claiming the last parking spot on the street. The sidewalks were jammed with revelers streaming toward the parade route. "Let's see. If we cut through that vacant lot, we should come out on Virginia Street, but the cemetery will still be a few blocks away. Keep the flashlight close and stay close to the group, Detra Ann."

"Got it," I replied. Ashland had nothing to worry about. I was never letting go of Henri's hand. "Let's go!" We emptied the car and walked down the sidewalk away from the gathering partiers. I suddenly wished I'd grabbed my jacket before we left. My sweatshirt provided little protection from the frigid night air. My heart hammered in my chest as I scanned the sidewalks for shadows. There were plenty.

"Go ahead and turn on your flashlight. Just point it down at the ground. We don't want to attract attention," Henri whispered to me. With cold, stiff fingers, I slid the button into the on position and breathed a sigh of relief as the shadows around me vanished. Lenore slipped her arm through mine—I didn't pull away, but I clutched Henri's hand tighter. In the distance a marching band blasted "On Broadway" to the appreciation of the happy parade watchers—the sound echoed through the narrow streets of downtown Mobile. I could hear the occasional blast of police sirens. In a strange way it comforted me knowing that the police were so close. As if they could actually help me.

Ashland paused on the sidewalk. "We're getting closer. How are you doing?"

"So far, so good," I stammered. The cold made my teeth chatter. Lenore's fingers were about to freeze me to death. Of all of us, she was the least prepared for the cold weather. She wore thin tights and an oversize, long-sleeved t-shirt. Henri was the only one who'd had the good sense to dress warmly, but then again none of us expected to be visiting a graveyard at night. I waved the flashlight on the grass in front of me and carefully stepped only in the light. For some reason, I thought about TD. I hadn't thought about him as much lately, but the love I had for him had not diminished at all. Some girls had high school sweethearts, and others had college sweethearts. I had neither of those. TD had been it for me, or at least I thought so until he disappeared. In the months following his death, I had a difficult time sorting through my feelings. TD had left me for a ghost. I had been pushed unwillingly into a battle and fought for my life, and all for what? I felt abandoned. Life was completely unfair. I was reminded of one of my favorite quotes from an English literature class. "Life makes fools of us all."

So why was I thinking of TD now?

"This way, here's the street," a Mardi Gras vendor shouted at us. An inflatable fleur-de-lis hat perched upon his head, and his cart was full of parade swag. Before he could begin his spiel, Ashland raised his hand politely and said, "Sorry. Not today." We left the man staring after us as we shuffled down the street. The parade was a few streets over, so there was nobody else on Virginia Street.

I looked over my shoulder and said to no one in particular, "I wonder why he's over here." To my surprise, the man and his cart had disappeared.

"Don't pay any attention to that. He's just having fun with you. Keep that light on and keep walking." Lenore's furious whisper made my heart pound. I knew exactly who she was talking about. I did as she instructed and kept my eyes on the ground, always stepping only in the light.

"There it is!" The Magnolia Cemetery sign swung gently in the breeze. The gate stood open—it was a foreboding sign, as if someone had expected us to visit.

Carrie Jo paused before we walked inside the graveyard. "There are no lights in here, so you'll have to lead the way. Just walk straight toward the back; that's the gate were looking for. Are you going to be okay?"

I swallowed hard. "Oh God, I hope so." Our little group shuffled together down the narrow walkway. I had been here once before in middle school, but that was a long time ago. I certainly wasn't an expert on navigating this massive maze of graves. Immediately to the right I noticed a row of mausoleums. Even though there was very little moonlight, they seemed to have an eerie glow about them.

Lenore shook her head. "I ain't going in there. Too many ghosts. I'll meet y'all on the other side." Before we could argue with her, she was already halfway down the sidewalk.

I chewed my lip as I watched her disappear down the street. I wanted a shot of whiskey, but it was too late for liquid courage. "Carrie Jo, I've been thinking. What if the gate doesn't work? What if only you can go through it? What if it takes us somewhere else?"

"We connected the last time, remember? I think we can do it again. What choice do we have?" She looked so hopeful, but I felt anything but confident. The last time we went "ghost busting," I ended up the prisoner of a murderous spirit who was convinced that I was his dead wife. The wife he hung from a chandelier until she died. Now CJ wanted to go see another ghost. But she was right...what choice did I have?

"Alright. Then let's do this. Wait." I reached for Henri and kissed him on the lips. "Just to remind myself that I'm alive." I smiled up into his worried brown eyes. "It's okay, right?"

He said, "I plan on keeping you alive. I want a second date." Despite the situation, I couldn't help but love him for saying that. I waved the light around nervously, took a deep breath and entered the cemetery. Some of the newest tombstones were located near the entrance. I remembered seeing these on that middle school trip when we came to take rubbings of the tombstones. I didn't like cemeteries even as a child. I'd found the first suitable grave there was, made my rubbing and waited impatiently for everyone to finish theirs. A few feet into the graveyard, a shell pathway began. It glowed in the dim light. I waved the flashlight around again and gasped. Something ran from the light—it looked like a cat. At least I hoped it was a cat. My eyes couldn't stop flitting about searching for anything that moved.

"How far is it, CJ?"

"All the way in the back." The four of us hurried down the pathway together, Henri and I in front, Carrie Jo and Ash right behind us.

Ashland cleared his throat. "Guys, I don't know whether to tell you this or not, but…"

I spun around, waving my flashlight furiously.

"You're going to blind us, Detra Ann," he complained.

"Sorry. What is it?"

"Lenore was right—this place is teeming with ghosts. And they don't look too happy to see us here."

Carrie Jo asked, "Anyone we know?"

He paused and looked into the darkness. "Not that I can tell, but the shadows are moving now. Just like before…when whatever it was appeared at the house."

"Death. It's Death, Ashland. Just say it."

"We don't have time for this, and we can't stop…go now! Run!" He didn't have to tell me twice. I took off running toward the distant gate. Carrie Jo was beside me. I paused for a second when a looming figure appeared on the right of the path. It was a massive angel statue with his arms stretched to the heavens. "Oh Lord!" I whispered and kept running. The light from my Maglite bounced as I ran, and I could hear the whispers collecting around me. Ashland was right. The shadows were gathering, and now there were many ghosts to contend with. In my mind I could see them reaching for me, demanding that I return to their realm to take my proper place among those who had surrendered life.

No! It's not my time!

My chest burned—it had been a long time since I had gone for a run. I was so out of shape, but adrenaline-fueled fear kicked in and propelled me forward ahead of my friends. I turned the corner of the path, and a gruesome-looking cherub sat perched on top of a moldy gravestone. Long ago, some grieving family member had thought the fat-faced figure would be a fitting tribute to their lost loved one. I couldn't disagree more. Ahead of me, I could see a looming shadow that covered the walkway. I waved the Maglite at it, but it didn't disappear. I came to a screeching halt, and my friends piled behind me. All of us were panting for breath.

"Oh my God!"

"Go around it!" Carrie Jo screamed at me.

Clumsily, I tripped up a small round hill, and the flashlight flew from my hand. Carrie Jo grabbed it and reached for my hand, pulling me to my feet. I heard a swishing sound and felt a disturbance in the air around me. Someone or something was there—I just couldn't see them.

"You can't stop! Believe me," Ashland yelled at me. My friends nearly picked me up off the ground and carried me to the back gate. I was almost in tears and not thinking at all.

"Come on, baby. Almost there," Henri said, looking over his shoulder as he cleared a small row of graves running behind me. It was the first time he'd ever called me baby. I liked it. I suddenly realized that I did love Henri. It was different from my love for TD, but it was love nonetheless.

CJ waved the flashlight at the back gate—only fifty feet away. "Almost there!" she shouted over the growing whispers. Suddenly a flash of light appeared in front of the gate. Then the light disappeared, leaving the figure behind. "Lenore?" she asked.

It wasn't Lenore. I knew that figure just like I knew my own. That was Terrence Dale. I snatched the light from Carrie Jo and shined it at the gate again. He didn't disappear. He stood staring at us, his face not unfriendly or reproachful. It was him! I heard Henri gasp beside me. "Is that..."

"TD..." I whispered, tears filling my eyes. He wasn't dead at all but completely alive. There was even a halo of light around him. Had we gotten it wrong somehow—was he alive but stuck in the past? Maybe he needed our help to break free from wherever he was stuck. I couldn't think straight, and I was freezing. I could see my breath now in the light. He looked directly at me and gave me a heartbreaking smile. Then he vanished.

"No!" I yelled and ran toward the gate. "Terrence!"

Chapter 15—Carrie Jo

Before I could stop her, Detra Ann flew through the gate and disappeared, taking the flashlight with her. The three of us stood in the dark cemetery and stared at the gaping entrance. "She's gone," Henri said. "I was supposed to protect her, and now she's gone." He banged on the gate and walked in circles, his hands on his head. He let out an anguished cry. "Do something! Where is she?"

"She passed through the gate, Henri. She didn't wait for us. She was supposed to wait." I didn't know what else to say. I needed a moment to think.

"What are we supposed to do now?"

"Henri!" A voice called out from the darkness of the adjoining street. Lenore appeared on the other side of the gate. "Where is she?"

"She's gone."

"I was afraid of this." Lenore tapped her lip with her finger. "Well, time for plan B. Do we have one?" Everyone stared at me.

I paced in front of the gate. No, we didn't. My half-cocked plan A was all I had, and now Detra Ann was gone.

"Ashland, what do you see? Are the ghosts still here?"

He peered into the inky blackness and said, "No. They are all gone. There were dozens of them here just a minute ago."

"Shoot! When she ran through the gate, it must have closed the connection."

"How do you know that?" Lenore asked me suspiciously. "You done this before?"

"Kind of. We went through the wall together at the hospital. And when I walked through the gate the other night, I ended up in the basilica. Look, we all saw her. The gate was open, and now it's not and all the activity stopped. That's got to mean something, doesn't it?"

"She's gone." Henri sat on the ground and stared into the darkness.

"We're not giving up. We have to go to the church. Maybe the gate works both ways."

"Sounds like plan B to me. Let's go. I'm freezing."

I walked through the open gate, closed my eyes and half hoped it would work, but nothing happened. Ashland looked glum, Henri wasn't talking at all, and Lenore acted like this was all a joke. As we walked toward the church, the music got louder. We would have to cross the parade route to get to St. Joseph Street. The Order of Polka Dots sailed down the street on vibrant floats, while the crowds roared, pleading for beads, moon pies and candy.

"Carrie Jo? You okay?" Lenore stood inches from my face. "Hey!"

"Yeah, I'm okay." I suddenly realized how lovely Lenore could be if she actually cared about what she looked like. She grabbed my hand and dragged me behind her as we dashed across the street.

"Lenore! Wait! You're hurting me." I snatched my hand away.

She walked toward me and got in my face again. "You don't have time. Death has her, and he ain't gonna wait," she shouted at me over the music. I waved to Ashland and Henri, who were stuck on the other side of the street. A police officer on horseback stepped into my line of sight so I couldn't see them anymore. "Carrie Jo, listen to me. Don't get them involved, please. Trust me when I tell you that it can only be bad. We can do this together. Let's go. They know where we are going, and they'll catch up." A drunken reveler pushed me as he chased after a float. Another one brushed up against me and leered at me. One thing was for sure—we couldn't stand here on the street. Maybe Lenore was right. Could I really put Ashland and Henri in danger? I'd already managed to lose Detra Ann. I looked one more time toward the street, but the crowd was growing and people were pushing and shoving.

"Let's go," I shouted back at her and began following her through the crowd toward St. Joseph and Clairborne Streets. People with painted faces and novelty lighted headbands circled me and shouted, "Happy Mardi Gras!" A man in the parade spun me about playfully as I struggled against him, feeling a surge of panic. Finally I broke free from the crowd and pushed to the edge where I could see the red and white building of the cathedral in the distance. Lenore took my hand, and together we ran as fast as we could. I glanced behind me, half hoping I would see Ashland and Henri close, but they were nowhere to be found. We ran to the cast-iron gates, and I held on to the cold metal as I tried to catch my breath. I could plainly see that the gates and the church doors had been locked. I swore under my breath. Grabbing my hand again, Lenore led me down the sidewalk.

"Give me just a second. I have to catch my breath."

"We're running out of time. This way." Lenore pulled me toward the back of the building. This was the side that faced St. Joseph Street. I'd never explored this area before.

"Maybe we should call someone and ask them to let us in." I knew that was a stupid suggestion, but I was out of ideas. I wasn't sure what I was going to do even if I could get inside.

"Look! We can get in that way!" There were some narrow concrete stairs that led down to the basement of the church. That was unusual in itself, as most buildings in Mobile didn't have cellars. Especially here in the downtown area, as close as it was to Mobile Bay. Yet here it was right in front of me. She tugged on the gate twice, but it would not budge.

I looked over my shoulder again, half expecting to see the red-haired caretaker come running toward me, but the streets were empty. "Let's do it together." Lenore nodded, and we shoved hard on the gate. To my surprise, it worked: the gate rattled open, and we walked down the stairs, closing the gate behind us. The rusty old latch cut my finger, but I managed to wriggle it back into place without locking it. Better to make it look closed so no one suspected anything.

What were the chances that the door would be unlocked? Lenore blew on her cold fingers and then turned the round knob. It opened with a click, and she smiled at me as if to say, "See, I told you this would work." We walked inside the church basement, and I was immediately assaulted by the musty smell. When was the last time anyone had aired this room out? Lenore was fiddling with a lighter she retrieved from somewhere. She flicked the flame and moved it around slowly so we could get our bearings. "Looks like a mission closet or something. Hey! There are some coats!" She walked a few feet away and began digging through a pile.

"We can't take those. They belong to the church, Lenore."

"Okay, you freeze to death, but I'm borrowing a coat."

Standing there shivering while she slid on a warm brown coat was more than I could bear. "Alright, if we're just borrowing them." I grabbed a long black trench with an insulated lining and slid it on. I immediately felt warmer. Seeing a pile of woolen hats, I grabbed one of those too. "Where is that lighter? We have to get upstairs."

Lenore flicked the lighter again, and together we searched for the door. We found it, but it was locked, and no amount of banging would open it.

"Shoot! There has to be another door." I felt along the dusty walls, and Lenore walked in the opposite direction doing the same.

"Hey!" she yelled. "I think I found something over here. Come help me." I ran to her, practically tripping over a box of books that someone had left on the floor. "It's in the floor. Look!" Next to the back wall was a small hatch in the floor with a metal chain attached to it. "Help me." Together we tugged on the chain, and the hatch opened. The smell of moldy earth rose up to greet us. Lenore cast the light around the entrance quickly, but there wasn't much to see beyond a set of dodgy-looking wooden stairs.

"I don't know. Should we be going down those things?"

"It's the only option we have, isn't it?" Without another word, she was climbing down the ladder. I heard the wood creak and complain under her weight, and she was smaller than me.

I heard a thud coming from the entrance of the cellar. It sounded like someone was coming toward us. I hurried down the ladder and reached into the darkness. "Lenore!"

She clicked the lighter, but it wouldn't work. "I'm here. Take my hand." I did, and she clicked again until the lighter released a small flame. "This way."

The historian in me couldn't help but pay attention to the wooden beam that ran along the top of the passageway, the dirty gas lamps that hung from the walls and the random items that I occasionally tripped over like a shovel and a small metal cart.

"What on earth is this place?" she asked as she waved furiously at a cobweb.

"I'd say an underground railroad." I squinted around us in the dim light.

"Are we going the right way?"

"Stop a minute, Lenore. Listen!"

She scowled at me but kept quiet for a few seconds. "What's that?"

I tugged at my coat, pulling it about me tighter. Straining to listen, I heard a voice. It had to be Detra Ann! "That's her! Move faster, Lenore!" We blindly ran until we reached a fork in the tunnel.

"Where now?" she shouted. We stood waiting to hear something.

"Help me! Someone!"

"This way! She's this way!" I took off to the right and stumbled over an unseen obstacle as I ran toward Detra Ann's voice. Shafts of light filtered through the grate above us. I stood under it, looking up into the church, when I heard another noise, a scratching, fluttering sound. "There! Grab that and we'll climb. Maybe push the grate."

"Better idea. Let's go up those stairs."

How had I missed those? We hurried up the curved stairwell and into the church. The only light was dim candlelight. I didn't know when it happened, but somehow we had passed through the "gate" because we were in the old church. The walls were as they had been during my supernatural trip, painted burgundy and gold. According to my online research, the renovations had completely changed the look of the cathedral. In modern times, the basilica had white walls with gold accents.

"Let her go! You have no place here! Leave now!" It was Father Portier, standing in front of the altar. Detra Ann's blond hair swirled around her, moving in an unearthly black cloud that seemed to want to swallow her. "Go, now!" The priest stood rigidly in defiance, but a blast of the black cloud sent him flying backwards into the wooden pews. Horror and dread filled me as I watched the old man collapse into a heap.

"Father Portier!" I yelled, running toward him with Lenore beside me.

At that moment, Detra Ann saw me and screamed, "Run, CJ!" The black cloud expanded, shrank and expanded again. Suddenly it broke into a hundred smaller clouds, and I heard the scratching, fluttering sound again. In the blink of an eye, the clouds became crows that flew straight toward us with deadly focus.

"Get down! Under the pews!" I screamed, dragging the priest to the floor and crawling under the benches. The crows flew above us, diving occasionally to peck and scratch at us. Lenore screamed in pain, and I looked back under the pew toward Detra Ann, who lay on the floor about twenty feet away. "Father Portier! Please! Help us!" I shook him again and again until he began to stir.

The old man turned his head toward me and pleaded, "You have to go. Before it's too late."

"I am not leaving without my friend."

"You have no choice, I am afraid. He will not release her." I peeked out from under the bench at the spinning vortex of birds that threatened us.

"I am not leaving Detra Ann!" My heart pounded in my chest as I crawled under the benches toward the front of the church, crying and praying as I went. When I finally made it to the front of the church, I reached my hand out from under the pew. Just then an angry bird with a sharp beak dipped down and scratched my skin savagely. Crying out in pain, Detra Ann spotted me and shook her head. The black cloud gathered around her thin frame, and a hundred screeches echoed angrily through the church.

Defiantly I slid out from under the wooden bench and stood in the aisle. Lenore and the priest were standing there beside me. The cloud of birds fell to the ground and broke into a thousand pieces of black paper. Suddenly a tall man—taller than any I had ever seen—stood between us and Detra Ann. I could not see his face; a gauzy black fog covered his entire body, and only his pale white hands were clearly visible. He did not speak, but his head rose as he observed us.

"Help us." I said to the priest.

Father Portier said in a sad voice, "There is nothing I can do. He is here to collect a life. If I had one to give, I would gladly give it for your friend. But alas I do not. I am sorry, my dear."

"But it wasn't her fault. She never asked for this! We didn't do anything wrong! For pity's sake, Father. Please do something."

He nodded sadly and said again, "I am sorry, my dear."

I heard Detra Ann crying behind the tall figure, and I walked ahead a few more steps. "You can't have her! It's not her time!" Death did not respond, but neither did he move. Then his answer came. He beckoned me toward him, and I knew what he wanted. He wanted me. He would take me in exchange for Detra Ann. *A life for a life....* I heard the words ringing in my head.

Death waited for my answer. *What about the baby?* Fear washed over me, and tears rolled down my cheeks. Then there was Lenore. "I've got this," she whispered. She stood, hopping up and down in her hand-me-down Reeboks as if she were gearing up for a prize fight. It didn't take a rocket scientist to see she was about to do something stupid.

"Wait! What are you doing?"

"Thinking about someone else for a change!" She grabbed my hands and hugged me. "I knew this was how it was supposed to be. I knew it when I met Detra Ann. She's not the only shade here. I'm one too—I've been one ever since Aleezabeth died. It should have been me that day."

"I don't understand," I confessed. The figure in front of us growled, but Lenore didn't appear moved by it.

"I cheated Death once too. I've been running all these years, but it's time to stop. This is what's right. This is what Aleezabeth wants." She hugged me again and suddenly released me. Then she ran toward the growling figure, screaming, "Aleezabeth!"

I yelled at the top of my lungs, "Lenore! No! Come back!" I watched in horror as she sprang into the air and fearlessly hurled herself toward Death. Then the massive shape vanished, taking Lenore with it. Everything changed. All the coldness, the fear and the dread vanished—even the interior of the church was different. I could smell the freshly painted white walls; the sooty sconces had been replaced with modern-day pin lights that shone from the ceiling. I stood rocking on my heels in shock at the transformation.

I tried to process what had just happened. Lenore had given her life for Detra Ann. My friend lay crumpled on the floor, and I ran to her side.

"Detra Ann! Wake up. Please wake up!" I patted her face desperately. I had to know she was okay.

Her eyes fluttered open, and she looked up at me. "Is it gone?"

"Yes. It's over." We held one another, both of us crying, and then she asked me. "Where is Lenore? I saw her—you came for me. Is Henri okay? Ashland?"

"The guys are fine. Lenore is…she's gone."

"Oh no…" she cried and held onto me as I helped her up from the marble floor. The priest had disappeared too. Detra Ann and I alone stood in the church together, holding one another until Ashland and Henri came up from the basement and ran down the aisle toward us.

"Carrie Jo? Are you okay, baby? Why are you bleeding?"

I glanced down at my hands. He was right—they were bleeding. "It's okay. I'm okay." He put his arms around me and kissed the top of my head.

Henri held Detra Ann tight, tears streaming down his face. "Lenore, where is she?"

"She's gone, Henri," I said softly. "She wanted to be with Aleezabeth. She said it was right."

Detra Ann held him closer and whispered in his ear. I couldn't hear what she said, but I didn't need to know. They had each other now. He nodded and wiped his eyes. This would be hard for him. Lenore was all the family he had. Except us. We were a family. A strange, wonderful family.

Chapter 16—Carrie Jo

The next few days were strange to say the least. I felt like I was walking in a fog. I closed the office while we worked out the details of Lenore's memorial service, then the four of us took the Happy Go Lucky out into Mobile Bay. The only one who seemed truly happy was Detra Ann, and who could blame her? Our first evening out was quiet. The water was like smooth glass, and the air felt warm and welcoming. We were sailing to Point Clear, where we would stay for a few days. With just a quick phone call, Ashland had managed to book two suites at the Grand Hotel. It was a beautiful place with a breathtaking view of the bay. Naturally, I was fascinated with the history of the place and promised myself that sometime during my stay I would explore the older wings and the grounds.

After dinner on the boat, Ashland and I spent an hour looking out over the bay, enjoying the lights and the stars that glittered above it all. We held hands and quietly enjoyed the peaceful view.

"How are you?" he asked softly, his eyes still focused in front of us.

"I'm fine. The baby is too. Everything is okay."

"That's good to hear."

"What about you? How are you doing with all this?"

"I haven't seen anything in forty-eight hours. Any ghosts, I mean. It's like everything went quiet again. It's times like this when I question if I ever saw any of what I thought I saw. But I know I did."

"Don't question it. You did see those things. Just enjoy the quiet for as long as it lasts." I smiled at him and squeezed his hand. Then I asked, "Are you sure you want to stay in Mobile, Ashland? I think the Port City has more than its share of ghosts, don't you?"

"I love Mobile, but I want you to be happy. Do you want to leave?"

I squinted at him in the dim light. "Nope. You're stuck with me, babe. Wherever you are—that's where I want to be. We made a promise, remember?" I slid out of the white leather chair and climbed into his lap.

He kissed me like he meant it. I kissed him back, and I definitely meant it. With a wicked smile, I led him to the shower, stripping off my clothes as I went. I loved this ridiculously large shower stall. It had four shower heads, a smooth stone floor and sultry blue lighting. Just perfect for what I had in mind. I kicked on the wall stereo and turned on the water as Ashland raced to join me. It was a nice way to end the day.

Afterwards, I pulled on a giant t-shirt and climbed into the feather bed and fell asleep almost immediately. For once, I didn't have a worry in the world.

***

I woke up with Hooney's face so close to mine that I could feel her breath on my cheek. She whispered to me, but I was half asleep and had difficulty understanding what she said.

"Your mother wants you to go. Leave this place, Miss Calpurnia. Leave now."

I had given up trying to convince the old woman that I was not my sister. In a perverse sort of way, the misidentification made me feel closer to Calpurnia.

"Why? Why should I go?" I pressed her, but Hooney's tight grimace let me know that I would get nothing else out of her. She had passed on the message and believed it should be enough. "Where is my mother? Why does she not tell me this herself, Hooney?"

"You know good and well why." I heard a noise from the hallway...someone was here! Karah was not in the room with me, and I could see that her rose pink dress was no longer hanging in the armoire. She must have dressed in one of the other rooms because she never dressed quietly. That meant Isla would be here any moment—if she had not yet arrived.

"Tell me, is Karah's mother here? I have to get dressed."

"She is, Miss. But if I were you, I would run the other way. She's the devil, that one." With that, the old woman left me without another word or

glance. I flopped on the bed wondering what to do. If Hooney was truly relaying messages from my mother, was I wise to ignore them? I snorted at myself. When did I begin believing in ghosts? Gooseflesh ran up and down my arms. Then I remembered. Probably when I saw the man in the Moonlight Garden…the one whose hair did not move in the breeze!

I dressed quickly and managed to arrange my hair in a decent fashion with the few pins that I found remaining in the bowl on the vanity table. Sliding on my purple heels, I dabbed perfume on my neck and headed toward the stairs when I heard Karah's voice. The sound was coming from the guest room, so I politely tapped on the door and waited. Nobody came, but I could still hear muffled voices. With a frown, I opened the door slowly and hoped it wouldn't give me away. Of course, it groaned as I pushed it open, and I cringed. "Karah, I am sorry to interrupt, but I could not wait to meet your…"

I left off speaking, surprised to see that no one was in the room. There were trunks and packages everywhere; obviously Cousin Isla intended to stay in this room. I heard the voices again and followed the source. I discovered that the sounds were coming from the floor grate. Not wanting to intrude, I turned to walk away, but something in Karah's voice compelled me to listen.

"Please, Mother. You could not be more wrong. She is not your enemy or mine. I like her!"

"You always…take my side for a change…weak, just like your father!" Isla's voice wasn't as clear. It sounded like she was moving about. Where were they? The Blue Room? "Maybe you have already found it. Are you keeping it from me, Karah?"

"Never! I would never do that, Mother. I have searched high and low, and I cannot find it. I swear to you, I do not have it!"

"If that is true, you had better get her out of here before she finds it. Oh, if only you had been a boy. None of this would matter."

I heard Karah's voice, soft and sad, "I am sorry, Mother. I will find it if it takes me…"

"What are you doing there, Miss Page?"

I rose from the floor to find Docie in the doorway, her arms crossed. She wore her usual black dress and severe bun. I stammered, "Well, I thought I heard Karah, but I was mistaken. Nobody is here." I walked towards the doorway, intending to slip out, but Docie would not let me pass.

"You should not be in here without an invitation. This is Miss Beaumont's room, and she is very particular about her things." She suddenly frowned and walked to an open trunk, examining the sumptuous gowns inside. "You have not touched these, have you?"

"No, of course not."

"Good. You will stain her fine gowns. Such lovely fabrics, don't you agree? It would be a crime to damage such an elegant wardrobe."

The voices from the grate had faded; the women had obviously left the room below us. "Very fine. Excuse me."

"Wait, Miss Page."

I froze in the hallway, and Docie purred, "Remember my warning. I hope I make myself clear." I knew that was a threat, and I would be a fool not to heed it. Docie was dangerous, and it sounded as if her mistress had a secret of her own.

Instead of running downstairs to greet Karah's mother, I went back to my room to catch my breath. I knew that Karah had been looking for something, but what? A book, a love letter, a will? The only way I would find out would be to ask her, but I did not want to put my cousin in such a position. Her mother sounded like a hard woman to please. After seeing Isla's gowns, I changed mine, choosing instead a bright yellow dress with plenty of lace and a respectable neckline. I loathed the idea of presenting myself as the "poor cousin" who had nowhere to go. I was a dressmaker, for goodness' sake! I changed shoes and earrings too and then headed towards the stairs for a second time.

There was no one in the ladies' parlor, but I could hear the musical sound of tinkling laughter. The beautiful Isla Beaumont was now holding court on the patio near the Rose Garden. From the half-open door I could see Jackson Keene, Karah and a man I did not recognize listening to a riveting story told as only an actress could. Isla was the most beautiful woman I had ever seen, with dainty facial features and hair like an angel's, blond and perfectly curled. Even though she was Karah's mother, she barely looked old enough to have had a child. Isla paused her monologue and tilted her head toward me.

"Come now. Don't be shy." I immediately felt embarrassed to have been spotted dawdling behind the door like an awkward child. She rose to

her feet and neatly arranged her ethereal blue dress before making a beeline for me. *"You must be Delilah. I am Isla Beaumont."* I felt ill at ease, perhaps because all her attention seemed to rest upon me now. It was as intense as her storytelling had been.

I blushed and said, *"I am Delilah Page. And you are Karah's mother. It is very nice to meet you at last."* The older woman flinched at my words even though I could not fathom why. Had I offended her already?

"You do have the look of your sister. I am sure you hear that all the time."

"Only since I have been here, but I never tire of hearing it. You knew her?"

"We spoke a few times."

"A few times? Surely you jest, dear Miss Beaumont. You were Miss Cottonwood's constant companion for some time. I've often wondered how she managed to escape Seven Sisters without your knowing anything about it." The man who spoke to her had a round belly, a balding head and an obvious love for sweets. Even now his fingers could not resist plucking sugared grapes from the silver platter on a nearby table.

"Why yes, Mr. Ball, we did spend some time together. But Calpurnia was very shy and not one for social gatherings, and as you know, I spent much of my time out and about getting to know our neighbors. Ah, but that was before the dreadful old war. Tell me, Delilah, do you suffer the same maladies as your sister?"

I blinked at her, unsure how I should respond. *"What do you mean? What maladies?"*

She giggled and smiled at the audience watching us. *"Am I speaking out of turn? Please forgive me, Karah. You know what I speak of, Mr. Ball. But I promised Karah I would not embarrass you, dear girl. Come join us, Delilah. What a lovely name! Have you ever considered becoming an actress? You have the name for it, you know. I wonder why your mother bestowed such a name on you. Not a very proper name, is it, and Christine Cottonwood was nothing but proper. Or so we all thought."* She giggled again as if she knew some great joke and I was the butt of it. Sadness welled up in me. This woman did not like me, and I had so wanted her to. The gathering appeared shocked and embarrassed by her description of my mother, but nobody said a thing against her. My first instinct was usually wrong, as Maundy often reminded me. So I kept my mouth shut and sat *quietly listening to Isla's news about the London stage and how wonderfully she had played Claudia DuMont in some play called "The Delight of New York." Everyone nodded and asked the appropriate questions, but I could not help but notice she did not look in my direction again or shower her smiles upon me. Those she reserved for the men and occasionally for her faithful servant, Docie, who was never more than a few feet away from her mistress. Karah appeared to be as miserable as I was, but there was something else there too. I could not understand it. I watched the silent interactions carefully, just as I had been trained to in the dress shop. It was obvious that Docie worshipped Isla and waited on her as if she were the Queen of England. Karah seemed a mere afterthought to her mother. Isla had a way of selfishly stealing all the air out of a room.*

Jackson Keene received more than his share of Isla's attentions, and I wasn't the only one who noticed. Karah's pretty face was awash with red color, obviously flushed with embarrassment at her mother's forwardness. Once Isla even touched Jackson's leg as she spoke. Although she acted like it was an accident, I believed no such thing. As quickly as I could politely arrange it, I excused myself; I was eager to remove myself from her presence. But where would I go?

As I walked through the patio door into the ladies' parlor and then down the downstairs hallway, Docie followed me, watching every step I took.

"May I help you, Docie?"

"No, miss." She did not move but stood in the hallway like a sentinel, her hands clasped in front of her. I wanted to go upstairs and hide, but then thankfully Jackson stepped into the hallway.

"Miss Page, may I speak to you for a moment?"

"Yes, of course. Why don't you take a walk with me, Mr. Keene? It's a lovely night, and it's much too stuffy in here."

"Indeed it is."

As soon as our feet hit the path of the Moonlight Garden, I felt the burden lift. "What do you think of Isla Beaumont, Jackson?"

He mulled over his answer and then said, "How can the daughter be so different from the mother? Karah is the picture of virtuousness, but her mother has no such restraint." That wasn't exactly the answer I had expected. I had no idea that Jackson thought so highly of Miss Cottonwood. He looked about him; when he was finally convinced that no one was listening he said, *"I have had a difficult time of proving your cousin's parentage."* We strolled down the brick path together, circled the fountain and walked into the garden maze. *"Everyone in the county says that her mother was never a respectable young woman. Isla herself was born out of wedlock, and now her daughter shares her status."* He glanced over and added quickly, *"I mean no insult. I am merely repeating what others have said."*

"That is gossip, Jackson, and I am surprised to hear you repeat it."

"No, it is fact. As Miss Cottonwood's attorney, I have a professional duty to investigate these matters. Supposedly, Miss Beaumont took up with a riverboat captain, a David Garrett, but he was murdered a few years ago. By all accounts he was a man of few restraints. I should not like to shock you, but I have it on good authority that this Captain Garrett once had designs on your sister, until he met Miss Beaumont. After that, he cared for no other woman. I am almost convinced that he is Karah's true father, but what can I do?"

"I can hardly believe what I am hearing. No wonder Isla does not like me—I take it she was no friend of my sister's, then?"

"Not in the truest sense of the word, no. And to make matters more complicated, she had an affair with Jeremiah Cottonwood, while he was married to your mother."

"I see," I said as I pondered what he had told me.

"However, I have good news to share. I have had an offer from Claudette Page. Would you like to hear it? Perhaps I should wait until tomorrow to tell you the details?"

"No, please I want to hear her offer now. I need something else to think about." I sat on a nearby bench and waited.

"Very well. Your aunt came to my office yesterday and says she will agree to acknowledge you in name and will not contest any deed you possess if you agree to leave Mobile. She says she will give you everything that her brother wanted you to have but insists that you must leave and remain away from the city until her death."

I shot up from the bench. *"How dare she ask me to leave? How can I leave Karah and Seven Sisters?"*

"My dear, Karah could always come visit you wherever you reside. Think about what this would mean. You would never have to work again—no more late nights at Miss Weaver's shop. You could travel and

see the world. With this act, Miss Page has sealed your future. You are a very wealthy woman now, Delilah. The world is your oyster!"

Exasperated, I stormed off, walking deeper into the garden.

"Delilah! Wait!"

"You don't understand, Jackson! It was never about the money."

"Please, just think about this."

"No! And don't follow me!" I turned to the left, then to the right and then to the left again, slapping branches out of my way as I went. After all this time, Jackson still didn't understand. Yes, I would have money and possessions, but I would still be denied the thing I wanted most—a family! I wanted to belong somewhere...to someone. Claudette Page was willing to sacrifice her fortune to see that I never had that.

I was so angry that I barely noticed the dark-haired man watching me from the other side of the clearing. Yes! There he was—near the Atlas fountain. It was the same man who had followed me the other night. I froze on the spot. He smiled, and my stomach twisted. I turned to walk away and nearly walked into Isla Beaumont.

Her eyes were fierce—she reminded me of a wild animal. One that was trapped inside the body of an innocent sheep and desperately wanted to be released. "Oh, sorry. I didn't hear you," I said. "I think we should go, Miss Beaumont. There is an intruder in our garden."

She stared at me and then turned her attention to the man standing at the Atlas fountain. She could see him too! The wind picked up, sending her ethereal blue dress fluttering. I just watched as she took down her hair and let her blond tresses blow freely behind her. I looked from her to him and felt my unease growing.

She took my hand and tugged on it, dragging me after her. She was walking toward the man and taking me with her! He hadn't moved, but he had an evil smile plastered on his pale face. "Let go of me!" I yelled at her, wrenching my hand free from her deathly grip. She did not seem to notice. She continued toward him as the wind continued to blow.

I ran! I ran as fast as I could all the way back to the entrance of the maze. I ran so fast that I collided with Jackson Keene. "There you are," he said, steadying me. "Have you changed your mind? Delilah, what is it?"

"Didn't you see Isla? She was just here with that man. The evil-looking one with the dark hair. He...she...they are just in there."

"Nobody came out here. Just you and me. I wish you would reconsider Claudette's offer. I do believe she is being sincere."

"Very well. Make the arrangements. I am ready to leave Mobile." With one more glance over my shoulder, I practically ran back into the house. I could hardly believe it...when I passed the ladies' parlor, Isla was still there, regaling her guests, except for Jackson and me, about her experiences on the stage. How could I have seen her just now in the garden with that evil man? With that ghost? As if she knew what I was thinking, she stopped talking and smiled at me innocently.

Yes, I was ready to go. I would go to my room and pack, and then leave first thing in the morning. I heard Jackson's carriage leave almost immediately, but I went upstairs and asked Hooney to help me pack. I went to my mother's room and plundered her hope chest and treasures. If I was going to leave, I would take something of hers with me. Karah had told me repeatedly to take whatever I liked. She had no need of it. In fact, she hinted that when her mother left Seven Sisters, she wished to go with her. Then no one would live here, except a few forgotten former slaves.

I found a few books, ribbons and sewing pieces that I decided to take with me. Walking back to my room, Hooney surprised me by bringing supper to me. I ate it, hungry now that I did not have to entertain Isla any longer. "Please ask Stokes to come get my things, Hooney. I am going to stay in town tonight."

"It's too late, Miss Calpurnia. Stokes isn't here now. He had to go somewhere for that lady. I suspect he won't be home until late."

I tried to keep the tremor out of my voice as I replied, "Well, I can send for these things tomorrow. I'll just take one bag with me." My hands shook as I sorted through everything. Just as I was ready to leave, Isla walked into my room. Hooney scurried out, making the sign of the cross as she went.

"What's this, cousin? Are you leaving when I just got here? I was hoping we would have some fun, get to know one another. I have so much to tell you."

"I saw you in the garden, Isla. I saw you with that man." I said, nervously clutching my bag. "I think I will stay in town tonight. Stokes can bring my things tomorrow."

"Hmm...you act like you are the lady of the house here, Delilah. You don't command my servants. In regards to what you think you saw, I must *confess I am at a loss as to what you mean." Then in a sad, sweet voice she added, "You know, those are just the maladies I was referring to when I spoke about your sister. She had...such an imagination. It must be a trait the two of you inherited from your father. A Beaumont would never go about saying such things."*

"How dare you..."

"How dare I what? Tell you the truth?" She sat on the bed and ran her hands across the leather suitcase. As quick as lightning she opened it and began rummaging through my things. She plucked out the things that belonged to my mother. "This is thievery," she said indignantly as she rose from the bed. "Are you stealing from me, cousin?"

"These are my mother's things. You can't stop me from taking them."

"Everything in this house belongs to me." Her voice sounded sharp and angry. "You put those things back, or I will call the sheriff and he can settle this."

"You would call the sheriff to report a sewing kit and a few keepsakes? I can't believe it!"

"You should believe it."

Just then Karah poked her head in the room. "Are you leaving, Delilah?"

"Yes, I am afraid I must. Thank you for your hospitality, Karah."

She went to hug me, but Isla prevented it. "You are not leaving with these things. You empty those cases now! I do not make empty threats— just ask my daughter."

"Mother, I told her she could have a few of her mother's treasures. Surely that is permissible."

Isla slapped her across the face. "Get out!" Karah scurried out of the room sobbing.

I grabbed Isla's arms and shook her. "How dare you hit her? You evil woman! Don't ever touch her again!"

To my utter surprise, she smiled and then kissed me. In revulsion I pushed her away and ran out the door after Karah. "Karah! Where are you?" She was not in her room, and Hooney was nowhere to be found. The balcony door overlooking the Moonlight Garden was open, and I walked toward it. "Karah!" I did not see her and turned to walk back inside when Isla stepped in my path.

"Move out of my way!" I said angrily, but she only laughed. Then her beautiful face hardened. She shoved me toward the balcony, and I fell to the floor. "What do you think you're doing, Isla?"

"I am doing what I should have done a long time ago. I should have done it when you were too stupid to know who you were, but it is no matter. You are worm food now, I suppose." She giggled as she brandished an evil-looking knife.

"Oh God, what are you doing?" I lay sprawled on the floor, my mind racing. I looked about me, hoping to find something to defend myself with. But there was nothing, only a chair and a table. "Why are you doing this, Isla? I am your blood."

"Now, now, don't be difficult. Be still, cousin. I don't want to get your blood all over my new dress." The knife arced toward me as I rolled and scrambled to my feet. I was standing now, but she still blocked the only exit. "Very well. If you prefer to jump, I won't stop you. Go ahead." She pointed her knife to the balcony's edge.

"No!" I shouted. "Karah!"

"Leave my daughter out of this unless you want to get her killed too. Now be a good girl and do as I tell you. Keep moving—this will all be over soon." I heard a noise below and saw Karah looking up at me. Isla sliced my arm with the blade, and I screamed.

"No! Go away!" I kicked the chair at her as I cried and moved out of her reach. Blood poured down my arm as she herded me to the edge of the balcony just as she'd promised. "What do you want? Why are you doing this?"

"Since the first day I arrived here, I knew this was mine. My adulteress sister didn't deserve this place—neither did her fool of a daughter. Calpurnia was so stupid—it was mind-numbingly easy to make her believe that David loved her, but he never did. He only ever loved me!" She shouted and waved her knife. "Now there is just one untidy loose end left. You. The forgotten bastard. I told Claudette that you wouldn't be so easily dissuaded, but she was too proper to agree to my solution. But here we are, just the two of us. I sent Stokes away, and Hooney is so old and blind, she'd never hear you even if you cried day and night."

My back was against the railing now. There was nowhere else for me to go. Only down, down, down to my death. I looked down again but only for a second in case she sliced me again. "Help me! Somebody!" I screamed *into the fading light. Nobody answered. I turned to see Isla waving her blade again, and this time she tore through my dress and cut my abdomen. I cried out in pain.*

"Mother! Stop it!" Karah reached for an old wooden cane that stood in a bucket near the doorway. She raised it high and swung at her mother.

Isla crumpled to the ground and squealed angrily. "Stupid girl!" She clutched her arm and reached for her knife.

"Stop, Mother! You are out of your mind!"

"Such a coward! How could I have raised such a coward? I never wanted you, did you know that? All I ever wanted was my captain—and my home. That's all I ever wanted. Now you want to throw it all away like it meant nothing. Like what I did meant nothing. You stupid coward!" She ran toward us with her knife raised, but Karah struck her again. She fell again, but I knew it wouldn't stop her—she was truly mad.

"Run, Delilah!" My arm was slick with my own blood and I felt cold, but I tried to keep up with her. Then Docie appeared at the top of the stairs, her hands in her pockets and a murderous look on her face.

"Stop them, Docie!" Isla yelled as she tried to stand after Karah's latest attack.

"You heard the mistress. Where do you think you're going?" Karah's face turned white, and I could see fear arresting her reasoning. It was my turn to do something. I snatched the cane and swung it toward Docie, hitting her square in the stomach. Without a sound she fell backwards down the stairs and landed at the bottom, her head turned at an awkward angle. Karah pulled me out of the way as Isla ran toward her, leaving her knife behind.

"No! Docie!"

"Run, Karah! Come with me!" We scrambled down the stairs and out the back of the house. A half hour later, my cousin and I appeared at Jackson's door, and the last thing I remembered was Jackson lifting me out of the carriage in his strong arms. How I wanted to stay in his arms forever...

***

The first thing I did when I woke up was examine my arms. I had felt every painful slice Delilah had endured, and I was happy to see that those wounds had not followed me into my own life. I tried to still my breathing, and the baby fluttered about as if he too had seen and experienced the drama. I hoped I was wrong about that. I hoped Lenore was wrong.

Shh…sweet little one. It's all right now. We're safe.

As always, I reviewed what I dreamed, remembering details I thought would be important later. That surely hadn't been the end of Delilah—I knew she had become a celebrated actress. But what about her and Jackson? Did they have a happily ever after? It would be nice to know that someone in Ashland's family did. Ashland stirred beside me and put his arm around me. I lay back down and snuggled up next to him.

"Still dreaming, Carrie Jo?"

"Yes, still dreaming."

"How about this once you just dream about us?"

"I like that idea. Now how do I do it?" I sighed, feeling tired but suddenly very peaceful.

With a devilish smile and a twinkle in his blue eyes, he whispered, "Let me help you with that."

With a smile of my own I agreed.

The Sun Rises Over Seven Sisters
By M.L. Bullock

Dedication

To the ghosts of the South, we remember you.

MIDNIGHT has come, and the great Christ Church Bell
And may a lesser bell sound through the room;
And it is All Souls' Night,
And two long glasses brimmed with muscatel
Bubble upon the table.
A ghost may come;
For it is a ghost's right,
His element is so fine
Being sharpened by his death,
To drink from the wine-breath
While our gross palates drink from the whole wine.
—William Butler Yeats
"All Souls' Night"
Autumn 1920

Prologue—Isla

This morning's chilly air had long since evaporated, replaced by the pungent fragrance of the nearby docks. No cool breeze blew off the water. Not one strong enough to wind through the stale rooms of the Holy Angels Sanitarium. I supposed building the hospital near the Mobile Bay was meant to soothe the facility's patients, but it did not bring that kind of relief for me. The eternal slapping of the water on the shore and the constant churning of the steamboats passing by made me think of my Sweet Captain.

Oh, mon amour! How I miss you! Rescue me, my darling! Take me in your arms once again!

Never had I met a man so beautiful and amiable. So far above all others. Until he failed, and then all of heaven wept at his fall. I was sure some lovely angel with long limbs and golden skin was loving him even now, and the thought of it filled me with anger all over again. Yes, in the end he had been like all the others. Unfaithful to the bone was he, and the fact I missed him so only reflected on my poor character.

Yet, I did miss him. Especially during the quiet moments of the day. Wouldn't any wife miss her husband? Even an unfaithful one?

I could not think of him now. Not with so much to plan.

I would never give up my claim on Seven Sisters. It was mine now, that and the Beaumont fortune. They would both be mine! I clamped my lips together in determination.

One of the dull girls who shared a room with me—Angela, I believe her name was—muffled a cry at the sight of my grimaced face, but she did not speak to me. She knew better. Yes, she had learned that quickly, in spite of her madness. We shuffled down the hall to eat our morning meal, looking like a string of prostitutes, our hair unbound, gowns hanging loosely. The guards made the women here surrender their ribbons and corset ties for fear we might hang ourselves. Who ever heard of doing yourself in with a corset ribbon? I could not imagine ever doing such a thing, but then I was not the kind of woman to take her own life. I might be compelled to take the lives of others. Whenever necessary.

I had a clever mind, but I would remove anyone who stood in my way. It was as simple as that. I tried to explain all this to the physician. When I saw I shocked him, I used my prettiest pout and even twisted my hair playfully, but he was not moved. After a few hours of constant interviewing, I told him what I thought about him and demanded that he release me.

"My dear lady, I did not put you here. You are a ward of the city now and due to stand trial. Only the judge can issue a release, so I suggest you make yourself comfortable. Take time to reflect upon your deeds, and perhaps the judge will have mercy on you." I knocked over his ink well and slapped his papers around before he yelled for the guard. Upon later reflection I realized that I had been foolish to act so rashly, but I felt sure I could persuade Dr. Hannah to petition the court on my behalf. I was still pretty. I had charms and skills that many women did not. From that day forward I did not stir up the staff or the other patients. Not openly, at any rate.

After stuffing a piece of dry biscuit into my mouth and swallowing a few gulps of water, I walked into the open yard looking for a quiet place where I could sit alone. How I longed to have a meal that required a knife and fork. Never would I enjoy that here. I could not abide the company of such madwomen! Even now they were behaving like idiot children. One of them, a tall, thin wisp of a woman, slapped her own face constantly. She had near permanent red marks on her cheeks. Most days, a guard would eventually tire of her self-destruction and tie her hands together. Then she would sit and moan and whine until bedtime. If anyone cared to listen, they would hear her repeat the same phrase, "My boy, Dimitri. My boy, Dimitri." She had a heavy Russian accent; I had heard it before during my travels with my captain!

Oh, David! How I miss you! What will become of me now, my love?

Another patient always pulled at the hem of her sleeve or dress. She pulled away inches of fabric every day and seemed absolutely riveted by the destruction. In the short time I had been at Holy Angels Sanitarium, she had been issued two garments, both essentially sacks made to look like dresses. I did not think she minded much because she quickly unwound them and then sat naked, crying that she had nothing to do. Mrs. Ambrosia, she was called, and she appeared as if she would come sit by me this morning with her missing sleeve and hem to the knees. I hissed at her under my breath to discourage her without making an open fuss. She took the hint and wandered off in the other direction, tugging at the string on her sleeve.

Now, where was I? I said to no one in particular. I stared at the nearby waters of the Mobile Bay from behind the cast-iron bars. I made plans for after this unnecessary excursion. A girl had to have plans, didn't she? I was always a girl with a plan. I would demand, pleasantly, to see the physician tomorrow. I would apologize most humbly and explain to him the great distress I had been in since the death of my husband. He would understand. Men always understood pretty faces.

I frowned into the sun and closed my eyes. Where had Docie been? She had visited me only once, and even then she acted as if she did not want to linger too long. I suspected my former maid had vanished—probably with my remaining fortune. That would be a mistake for her. I treasured loyalty above all things.

The sound of mewing pulled me back to my present circumstance. I had seen the kitten before, but it had not amused me to help it in any way. Fortunately for the lost feline, my situation had changed. I knelt on the ground near the fence and pulled a few biscuit crumbs from my pocket. I knew the guard was watching me, for he always watched me, but thus far he had been careful to keep his distance and had not spoken to me directly. He was a portly man with a bushy brown mustache and thinning hair. Just from observing him I could tell he was secretive and quiet. Those men were the most dangerous kind because they were hard to predict and sometimes hard to please, but he did not frighten me. I pushed the biscuit pieces through the metal bars and spoke sweetly to the animal.

Hunger drove it to trust me at least long enough to accept my offerings. It was a sad-looking tabby cat, underweight with missing patches of hair. I did not imagine it would live very long, but anything was possible.

After it got a taste of the biscuit, it naturally wanted more. I pretended I had not noticed the guard step closer to observe me. I held another piece of biscuit out for the kitten to see but put it in my lap. I let the loose gown fall from my shoulder, exposing my skin. Since I was pretending that I did not see the guard, I did not bother to tug it back into place. I kept my eyes on the kitten, who was not cooperating too well. If it wanted something to eat, it would have to take a chance. "It's okay, Mr. Buttons," I purred loudly enough for the guard to hear, "you can trust me."

"What do you plan on doing with that animal? You cannot bring it in here, miss."

Artfully placing my dainty hand over my eyes, I peered into his face with my most innocent expression. "Oh no, sir. I have no intention of keeping him. I only meant to help him along a bit. Look how small and helpless he is."

"Keep that cat out of the yard, miss."

"Oh, have I broken a rule, sir?" I turned my upper body, arching my back slightly, and my hand flew to my mouth as if I were surprised. "Forgive me. May I toss the last of my crumbs to the poor thing?"

He shuffled his feet and hesitated but finally said, "Yes, you may."

"Thank you, sir. Here, Mr. Buttons."

I tossed the crumbs through the gate and stood clumsily, pretending I might trip and fall on my loose gown. His hands quickly went out to steady me, and I did not push them away. "Again, I thank you," I whispered as a small smile spread across my face. I did not meet his eyes but looked at his hand as he removed it nervously. This was too easy. I did not know yet what my plan was, but I felt sure that if I needed to, I would be able to call upon the very helpful guard. Who knows? Maybe Dr. Hannah would not see reason and release me. In that case,

I would need help from someone else. I left the guard to watch me walk away, looking back once over my shoulder to give him a demure smile. I picked up the skirts of my untied dress just as I would if I were climbing the steps at Seven Sisters.

He did not follow me. The lady warden, a stern woman named Miss Calypso, came toward me, her shiny black kid boots clicking on the grimy floor. "Miss Beaumont, you have a visitor."

"I have a visitor?" I could not hide my surprise.

"Your mother has come to see you. Straighten your dress and make yourself presentable. As presentable as you get, anyway. The physician has given you permission to sit in the private yard to speak with her. This way, miss."

I thanked Miss Calypso politely and followed her. How clever of Docie to claim to be my mother! Surely she could manage that disguise! She had seen me on the stage for years pretending to be Ophelia, Lady Macbeth and a dozen other characters. I smiled more, thinking of what her choice of disguise might be. Would she have colored her hair? Surely she would not have borrowed a gown, for she did not fit into my clothes at all.

I stepped through the physician's office, and he greeted me briefly. I could tell by his suspicious look and tone that he had not yet forgiven me for my outburst the week before. The lady warden opened the door that led to the doctor's private garden. It was a meager garden at best, but it did have a pleasant shade tree, a young magnolia, two benches and a few scant patches of Bourbon roses. My eyes were on none of these but on the woman who sat on the farthest bench. Her cold blue eyes clamped on my face. This was certainly not Docie, and I could not place her although she was familiar to me in some way. Perhaps she was a fan of my work? I smiled pleasantly, but it was not returned. She studied me as she rose from her peaceful spot in the shade of the tree. She came closer, and the unsettled feeling climbed up my spine.

This woman was my mother.

There we stood appraising one another, not in an overtly threatening manner, just curious. One would have imagined that I would have questions, and perhaps someone other than myself would have been overwhelmed with love or sadness. I experienced none of those things. It did not occur to me to wonder what she might be thinking. Did that matter? I knew one thing—she had been a fool for sending me away. I was beautiful, intelligent and clever at solving puzzles.

Olivia Beaumont had a chiseled, lovely face for an older woman. She must have been at least forty, but she was far lovelier than her sister Christine had been. Olivia had dark blond hair that appeared to have been tinted recently, perhaps to hide silver strands? I smiled at that. She wore it in an upswept, feminine fashion like the women in London. Her hairstyle held plenty of decorative pins, and she wore carefully placed curls at her neck and ears.

I wondered what she would do if I told her about her brother, how he died beaten in the head with a garden curiosity by his brother-in-law's young black lover. *Worm food now, I suppose.* Would she collapse into a pile and whimper as her fragile sister had? I knew she would not. She was not a frail thing but someone with a will and soul of steel, despite her lacy appearance.

Her lips were carefully painted a dark color, but it did not make her look a whore. It made her light blue eyes lovelier and more expressive. At her ears were modest pearls, and her gown was also in the London style with a smaller bustle than the hoopskirts we Southern women were forced to endure. So was she more than a fashion plate? She appeared wealthy and lovely, like a great woman should. I wondered how she came to be here. Who had summoned her to the Holy Angels Sanitarium?

There we were, mother and daughter, standing in a sparse garden and silently staring at one another. I suddenly felt foolish for looking so out of sorts. When had I last bathed? When had I washed my hair? She seemed not to notice those things but instead focused on my face.

"Ah, thank you for waiting, ladies. I did not mean to be so long." It was Dr. Hannah, the tall, fleshy physician with the white hair and the monocle. His pale skin had a touch of pinkness, like a baby's or an albino rat's. I suppressed a giggle at the thought of Dr. Hannah as a rat. Olivia stared at me, her blue eyes like two glass marbles that could see right through me. I quieted and sat with my hands folded in my lap, just as I had learned from Christine and Calpurnia.

"Thank you for coming, Mrs. Torrence. How disappointing that I will not meet your husband. Typhoid, is it? Very nasty illness, that. If I were you, I would keep far away from home until he is completely clear of the disease."

Abruptly she stood and interrupted his speech. "Would you mind if I had a few minutes alone with Isla? As you can imagine, we have many private things to speak of."

With a serious pursing of his lips he answered her, "Certainly, Mrs. Torrence. I will be in the office if you need me. I would like to speak to the two of you together, but there is no need to hurry. Take your time."

"In fact—Dr. Hannah, is it? We will not be speaking with you at all, today or any other day. This is for you." She handed the man a scroll of papers. He could not hide his surprise as he scanned the documents.

"Everything looks to be in order, but I am afraid I haven't yet completed my examination of Miss Beaumont. This is most irregular." His objections availed him nothing, and he knew it after a few more stern looks. "Will you be leaving right away?" Olivia stared at him as if he were the mental patient. He sputtered and stammered, "Yes, of course you will be. Very well, I will ask the warden to collect your daughter's things. Good day to you then, Mrs. Torrence." She did not smile or thank him, just watched him disappear back into the white painted building.

I marveled at the whole thing. I had planned to seduce my way to freedom, but Olivia wielded a power I had never seen before, all without saying please or smiling even once. I wanted to learn how to use this power. I wondered if she would share it with me.

"Now you and I need to talk."

"Yes, Mother," I said sweetly.

"Drop the act. Do not call me Mother. I am not your mother. I am your aunt. You may call me Mrs. Torrence."

Now I felt like Dr. Hannah, completely unprepared to withstand Olivia's stare and authoritative manner.

"Your mother was a common street woman from New Orleans, a woman who convinced my brother that he was your father. He was foolish to believe so, but he did."

"What do you mean you are not my mother? I have always been told that you were. How can this be wrong?" I frowned in suspicion.

"I am not. I would think I would know whether or not you were mine." No smile, no expression of sadness or regret. No expression at all. To her, this was a boring conversation forced upon her by the judge who had summoned her to speak on my behalf. Or so I assumed.

"Then why the charade with the judge and the physician?"

"Why not? It is what they believe, so who am I to tell them different? I refuse to share family gossip with them or shame my family further."

I stepped toward her, uncaring that my gown had fallen off my shoulder again. "What about the shame it brought on you? Having a cast-off child, having me believe you did not want me as your daughter."

"It is my brother who should feel the shame. On the other hand, he is dead, so I doubt he feels much of anything." I gasped at her total lack of concern for my feelings on this matter. "Are you going to cry now? If so, do me the courtesy of waiting until we are in the carriage. I cannot abide public outbursts."

Sniffing away the wash of emotions, I answered her confidently, "I will not make a fuss."

She appraised me again. "I *should* leave you here. I am sure you could finagle your way out if you chose to. Probably already have a plan, don't you?"

I should never have admitted it, but I nodded slowly.

"Yes, you are your father's child. Scheming and planning. Let us go now."

"Where are we going, Mrs. Torrence?"

"To Seven Sisters, of course. I want to see what's become of my sister's fortune. You sure have made a mess of things, haven't you?" She walked toward the door, but I had to correct her. I had done everything—everything imaginable—to keep the family fortune. I would not let this slight pass.

"No! Your sister did that by having two children out of wedlock. Cottonwood knew all about it. However..." I smiled proudly here. I was anxious for her to respect me. *No need to wait. Let us establish the facts now,* I told myself. "He has left everything to his rightful heir, my own daughter, Karah Cottonwood."

Olivia's hard stare elicited another sentence from my lips. It was probably not wise to say aloud, but the words came anyway. "That leaves nothing to the Beaumonts, I'm afraid."

"Is that what you truly believe?" she asked, her face a pretty, unemotional mask. It wasn't really a question; it was more of a challenge. "My carriage is outside." She walked into the office, down the hall and out the door without looking back once. Good thing for her she didn't. I stuck out my tongue at her at least a half dozen times during the trek to the entrance. To my surprise the raggedy-looking tabby cat waited for us as if he too wanted to escape. He rubbed against my leg as if I were his only friend. Perhaps I was. More was the pity for him.

Olivia eyed me as I petted him once. "Your pet?"

"Hardly," I answered as I climbed into the carriage behind her. I was ready to go home and take a bath, eat real food and find a new dress. I watched Mrs. Torrence as she instructed the driver which way to go. Frigidity masked as decorum. Did she think I would be intimidated by her folded hands, her elegant kid gloves? I looked down into my own hands. Broken nails with dirty beds and torn skin. I stared at them intently. I did not hide them. Maybe these weren't the hands of a lady, but they were the hands of a fighter, someone accustomed to fighting for everything.

I could feel her cold eyes on me, but still I smiled at my hands.

No, these hands would not let me down.

We would fight, and we would win.

Chapter 1—Carrie Jo

The tap on the front door woke me from my nap. That was aggravating, as I could just feel myself slip away into a pleasant dream. With my recent influx of nightmares and sleep paralysis, dreaming about something nice would be a godsend. Thankfully I was no longer invading my husband's dreams. I shuddered to think about what he would be dreaming now that I was as big as a house. Although our love and commitment to one another remained strong, Ashland and I argued a lot lately. The worst part was, our disagreements, as he called them, were mostly over insignificant things like who misplaced the hammer or how the puppy got out. As I reminded him frequently, the new dog had been his idea and I never used the hammer. Well, hardly ever. I did hang a baby calendar in my office. And I found some cute wooden monograms to hang in my room.

Ashland's dog, a cute white Maltese, demanded constant affection and attention, and quite frankly he was a lousy watchdog. In fact, he was in full-blown nap mode at the foot of the couch when the visitor came to my door. He hadn't even budged at the knock. *Yeah, right. Big-time watchdog. Thanks, fella.*

Ashland and I would have to talk about that later. Well, maybe not. I think we had fulfilled our mandatory couple's argument quota for the year. Especially after last night. That had been the fight of the century, and I couldn't understand it. Why was Ash being so unreasonable? Apparently the subject of baby names was a hill that both of us were willing to die on. He hated the idea of naming our child anything "old-fashioned." I hated the idea of giving our son or daughter this year's trendiest name. Well, it couldn't be as bad as Carrie Jo. What had my mother been thinking?

"Just a second," I called to the unscheduled visitor who tapped again at the door. I tossed the soft throw blanket to the side and slid carefully off the couch. Navigating life with a big old baby belly had proved a challenge, but I liked being pregnant. Whenever he or she arrived (I still held out hope for a girl) I would miss this experience. The closeness with my child, the feeling of life growing inside me. It was like my love with Ashland had created a bit of magic, and now that magic would become an amazing person. "Whatever, Carrie Jo," I muttered to myself. I had become too sentimental lately. Too many sappy movies.

Peeking through the glass door, I could see the mail lady waiting patiently for me. I arranged my sloppy t-shirt and flyaway hair before opening the door with a smile.

"Good morning! These are for you, Mrs. Stuart." I accepted the bundle of letters and the package she handed me. I dropped a few items, but she graciously picked them up for me. No way was I going to bend down, not without some help getting up.

"Thanks. Anything good in there?"

"More baby catalogs. Almost time, isn't it?" Sharone Pugh and I had become quite familiar with one another the past few months. Too many late nights spent shopping online for baby clothes, furniture and whatever else struck my fancy. Sharone showed up day after day with something new. I gave up apologizing after a while. She didn't complain. Not too much, anyway. I joked with her that I would have the best-dressed infant in downtown Mobile, but at this point the only colors in the child's wardrobe were yellow and white. (Lenore had declared we would have a boy, but I wasn't so sure.)

"Can you believe my doctor says three more weeks? I don't think it's humanly possible to get any bigger."

"I was as big as a hippo when I delivered my first child. Gained seventy pounds too. You look wonderful. I'd better go. I have a ton of mail to deliver, and I can't leave my truck on the street. Have a nice day." She walked away as I said goodbye.

Closing the door behind me, I set the package on the foyer table and flipped through the stack of envelopes. The third letter in, I froze. It was from my mother. I stared at her name written in the familiar handwriting.

Deidre Jardine

Dumping the rest of the mail on the table with the package, I took the letter with trembling hands, grabbed the blanket and plopped back on the couch. As if he or she knew my heart was pounding, the baby turned in my tummy and pressed on my bladder. "Hey, cut that out, kiddo." After a few seconds the baby got comfortable again, and I leaned back on the pillow hoping to get some relief from the dull ache in my side. The clock struck half past the hour. It was 9:30 on Saturday morning, just a few hours before the baby shower. Plenty of time to take a nap. Ashland would not be back from his latest deposition for a while, and lately he had been in no mood to just hang out. I tried to be understanding, but I'd had my own crankiness to deal with. I blamed it on the pregnancy, but I knew it was stress. For the past six months Ash had been battered with lawsuits about the most mundane things, from claims on the estate to an unhappy tenant who claimed he was a slumlord.

And now this letter.

It was just one more thing. What could she possibly have to say to me? We had not spoken, emailed or messaged one another in over two years. Sure, I had stared at her contact info in my phone a few times, but I never actually called. Then again, she never called me either. Feeling tired and tearful, I put the letter on the coffee table and lay down again. The house was quiet, and there were no shadows. Maybe it would be safe to sleep. Safe to dream. I needed the rest. I could read the letter later. I touched it once again and then wrapped the blanket around my shoulders and snuggled into the plush couch. I had so many reasons to be happy. So why was I so unhappy? I told my mind to be quiet, and after a few more minutes of unhappy rumination I fell asleep.

***

Olivia Torrence had spoken barely a word on our journey to Seven Sisters. Obviously she had been here before. She did not crane her neck out the carriage window or gawk up at the white-painted edifice that shone brightly in the late morning sunlight. She was not overawed by the sheer size of the plantation or the obvious wealth that commanded it. I reminded myself that Olivia Beaumont Torrence was probably the wealthiest woman I had ever met. If I could have her as my ally, then who could stop me? But for that to happen, I would have to show her I was worthy of her partnership. No flattering words or innocent smiles for her. She would appreciate intelligence. I had to show her I was worthy of her trust.

The carriage shifted, and I slid across the seat. I noticed that she had barely moved a muscle. How was that possible? Was she made of stone or marble? She did remind me of the statues in the Moonlight Garden. Elegant, pale and forever frozen in one position. Despite the uncomfortable nature of our silence, I refused to be the first to speak. Instead, I peeked out the window at the house, uncaring that she thought me a fool. Once the carriage arrived, Stokes came to the door and pushed the latch, freeing me from my latest prison. It was good to be home! This was my home! I had broken every commandment in the Holy Bible to have this place, and I would not be denied. Not now and not ever. Hooney lingered in the doorway, but she did not offer a glass of lemonade or a bite to eat.

I frowned at her, and she made the sign of the cross. I laughed and strolled into the house like I owned it. Over my shoulder I said to Mrs. Torrence, "Forgive me, Aunt. I need to bathe and change. It has been far too long since I had a proper scrub."

She slid off her gloves and ignored me, which aggravated me to no end. She strolled into the ladies' parlor with Stokes on her heels. I heard her speaking to him in low tones, and I stomped up the stairs happy to be out of her company. "Hooney! I need a bath. Send someone up here with some hot water." She also did not answer, but I noticed she shuffled her old feet to fulfill my request. What did I care if she carried the water up herself? I doubted she would, though. Soon I heard wood being tossed in the upstairs stove and the sloshing of water. When the water was heated, I would soak my bones and wash away my cares.

I had claimed Christine's old room. Seemed appropriate—this was where the lady of the house slept, wasn't it? To my utter shock and amazement, all my things had been packed in trunks, stuffed away like yesterday's rubbish. "Hooney!" I yelled in my most aggravated tone. She never came. It was Hannah who came into the room, drying her hands on her yellow checked apron.

"Yes, miss?"

"I am hardly a miss, am I? Why are my things stuffed away? Look at my dresses! Everything is wrinkled. How can I wear these now? They must be pressed immediately."

"Mrs. Torrence told us to pack your things. I tried to pack them proper. I can try again. I am sorry, miss."

"What do you mean pack my things? I am not going anywhere!" I snapped at her. She looked at me, unsure about what I was saying. I shoved her out of the way and stomped out of the room. I suddenly did not care that my hair was a mess or that my dress hung off my thin, dirty shoulders.

In my bare feet I stomped into the ladies' parlor to find Olivia, but she was not there. Angrily I sailed through the Blue Room and yet again found no sign of her. Crossing the hall, I could hear her shuffling around in Jeremiah's study. She sat straight-backed in a cherrywood chair—not the master's chair, but a more petite one. She had shoved Jeremiah's monstrosity to the side as if it were something she could not abide touching. Perched on her nose were a pair of spectacles, and she was sorting through a stack of crumpled papers.

"What do you mean by having the servants pack my things? I have no plans to leave Seven Sisters."

"I am not prepared to speak with a madwoman," she said, barely breaking her gaze from the papers.

Her answer surprised me, and I sputtered for a moment. "How dare you! I am nowhere near mad. I do not know what plans you think you have for me, but I can tell you mine. I am not leaving Seven Sisters. This is my home."

She tossed her glasses on the desk and stood behind it, looking tall and rigid like an oak tree. "Speak to me like that again, and I will put you back where I found you. You are here only by my good graces. The sooner you understand that, the easier things will be."

"Easier? You have no idea what I have endured—the price I have paid."

"No more than any woman has, I am sure," she said flatly. "That is your problem. You think yourself a victim. You are weak, like most women. You are too old to play games like a spoiled schoolgirl."

Feeling the thrill of rage rise again, I smiled at her and stepped closer to the desk. I subtly searched for a weapon. My eyes fell on a letter opener with a black enamel handle.

Her perfect brows rose astutely. "See? Weak. Murder is a common solution for common minds. Imagine that I would waste my time rescuing

*you when I heard you described as clever! I shouldn't have bothered."
Without waiting for my response, she picked up her spectacles and sat back
down in the chair. She pretended to read her many papers.*

"I am not leaving Seven Sisters, Aunt."

*"I don't think you have much choice in the matter, do you? Dead or
alive, you will do as you're told."*

*I stared at my aunt with a ferocious glare. How dare she judge me!
Call me old, would she? She who wore a high collar and long sleeves,
undoubtedly to mask her age? Should I tell her that the neck and hands
were the first to go? There wasn't enough lace in the world to hide those
telltale signs. She was entirely too thin, but I still had a young, firm body
with plenty of soft curves. As I stood with my head held high, I caught a
whiff of myself. I had the stench of the asylum on my skin. It humbled me.
For a moment.*

*I left her without a word and went upstairs to take my bath. I needed
to think and not act. How many times had my Sweet Captain reminded
me of that very thing, "Think first, then act, my love." According to him, I
was too spontaneous, too ready to act without first thinking through a
matter. I should have taken his advice. But in the words of old Ben
Franklin, it was never too late to try. I had not yet made up my mind
about Olivia. Would I kill her? Rob her? Befriend her? I pondered these
options as Hannah washed my hair with lemon-scented soap. The aroma
was intoxicating. Then she scrubbed my feet with the bristle brush and,
when I was dry, rubbed my skin with coconut oil. I felt like a debutante
when her ministrations were completed.*

*"Dinner is almost ready, miss. You want me to help you dress? I
think this pink gown is less wrinkled than the others. I promise to finish
pressing the others tomorrow. I do apologize."*

*"No pink. Bring me the dark blue dress. The one with the blue lace
on the sleeves."*

*A few minutes later I walked down the stairs to dine with my aunt.
As I walked ever so slowly, I thought about her words. She considered me
weak, but she was wrong. Oh so wrong! I had survived when she and the
rest of the Beaumonts had cast me off as unworthy. And all this time I
had lived. I had nothing to hang my head about. A celebrated beauty, I
had traveled the world like a queen with David by my side, sometimes
performing, other times watching him win his precious card games.*

I took a few more steps, remembering the first time I saw David standing near this bottom step. How direct he had been! How I wanted to stare into those eyes of blue velvet forever! When we failed in our mission to lead Calpurnia into finding the Beaumont treasure, I made another plan and achieved it. My own mind had conceived those plans! None other. Still determined to win, I had a Cottonwood baby. Although she was a girl, I had delivered a promised heir. Could anyone imagine how difficult it was to seduce a man who preferred boys? I had taken great pains to capture his attentions, but I had managed it. It was easy to do with Calpurnia neatly locked away in her prison. And I had been the one who convinced Jeremiah to finish Christine. I watched him pull the rope as her body went up and up. If not for Hoyt Page, the adulterer doctor, I would have the deed to this place and plenty of freedom to find the missing jewels.

Later, when my Sweet Captain considered leaving me, I made another hard decision. Never could I forget the feeling of his warm blood seeping out of his body and into my hands. And he had never known it was me who pulled the trigger. But now he would never leave me.

I reached the bottom of the stairs and stood in the foyer of Seven Sisters. This was mine. I had made a deal with a devil named Cottonwood.

I had paid the price.
I would not be denied.

Chapter 2—Carrie Jo

I saw Lenore's face. Her dark eyes wide, she mouthed a word to me, but I could not understand her. No sound came out of her mouth. I woke with a start. The puppy yelped in surprise as my body jerked awake. "Oh, sorry, little guy. I forgot you were there." I swung my legs around and sat on the edge of the couch, my head in my hands. How was I dreaming about Isla again? I took a moment to "feel" my environment. There were no ghosts, as far as I could tell. I heard no giggles and saw no gray spirits with bloodless lips and ashen hair. But I had learned something, hadn't I? Olivia was not Isla's mother after all. Why was I seeing this now?

I did feel Lenore's presence, but only for a fleeting moment. She was here, or she had been. Warning me about something. The fat puppy whined beside me, and I stared at him. "Need to go out? Come on, chunky boy." He hopped off the couch and trotted to the door, waiting impatiently for me to get up. I glanced at the clock again. Darn! I had only 30 minutes to get ready. I told myself I'd have to think about all this later as I tried to shake off the remnants of my dream.

The puppy (I would have to give him a name sooner or later) wandered around the garden for a while, entranced by flowers, butterflies and anything that distracted him from his potty task. With some coaxing he finished his business and ran back in the house to find a snack. A snack sounded good, but I had to get going. I was sure there would be plenty to eat at my shower. Especially if Henri was involved. Man, that guy could cook! I trekked upstairs and found something mommy-ish to wear. It was kind of Detra Ann to host this shower for me, but I honestly didn't need anything. Still, it would be good to see Rachel, Detra Ann and the rest of the folks in my small circle of friends. We were like a family. We celebrated one another's birthdays and anniversaries, and we spent holidays together. In a sense, we were a band of broken people, a tribe of weirdos, each with their own supernatural power. Except perhaps Rachel, but then again I considered her research skills pretty amazing. I hoped she'd have some updates for me on that project we were working on. I was curious to see the end result. Ashland would be so surprised!

Speaking of, I hoped he remembered to show up at Detra Ann's. This was supposed to be a couple's baby shower, not just a party for me. I hoped the attorney didn't invite herself as she tended to do at times. I didn't care for her too much. She reminded me of someone, someone from my past that I couldn't trust. But I did trust my husband. He wasn't the kind of guy to be unfaithful. He hated that his father had been that sort of man. Ashland Stuart's life goals included being the complete opposite of his father. I can't say that I blamed him. His father was a terrible husband, by all accounts. In fact, two of the recent lawsuits came from two different individuals claiming to be the misbegotten sons of the late Mr. Stuart. I wondered what kind of father-in-law or grandfather he would have been. My phone dinged, and I read the text from Detra Ann.

Come on, slowpoke!

I sent a smiley emoticon back and slid my swollen feet into my sandals. I tossed my wallet, keys and makeup bag into a purse that matched my dress, then scanned myself in the mirror. I suddenly regretted my attire choice. This bright yellow dress made me look like Big Bird, but I couldn't change now. It was sleeveless with white flowers at the collar and along the hem. It was still warm out even though fall was approaching, and I wanted to wear this dress at least once more before the baby arrived. As if he heard me thinking about him—*oops, did I say him?*—he moved a foot or an elbow and jammed me in the side.

"Okay, settle down. We'll have lunch soon. You ready, kiddo?"

As I pulled the yellow purse strap over my shoulder, I heard a nearly inaudible whisper. I froze in the doorway trying to discern where it was coming from. I glanced down at my phone, hoping it was an audio text, but there was nothing on the device. "Who's there?" I called, my voice echoing down the hall of my Victorian home. "Doreen?"

Nobody answered. I walked slowly across the hardwood hallway and stood at the top of the stairs. This was a dangerous place to stand. Isla had tried to kill Detra Ann here in this spot. I did not linger but moved quickly and carefully down the stairs. "Hello?" I called again. The only response was from the curious puppy, who believed I must have had a snack hidden in my hand. His fuzzy round face took the fear out of me, and I smiled at him and inelegantly squatted down to pat his head. "I'll be back. No accidents while I'm gone, okay?" He jumped up and licked me affectionately. I doubted he really understood a word I was saying.

I made the short drive to Detra Ann's house. Well, it was really Detra Ann and Henri's house. The two were nearly inseparable now. It was only a matter of time before they took the big step. I wondered when Henri would pop the question. He sure was taking his time. Detra Ann rarely talked about TD anymore.

Henri, on the other hand, was actively searching for Aleezabeth, as he had promised Lenore he would. He was committed to the task, and he spent quite a bit of time traveling to Louisiana. We'd traveled with him a few times and spent some weekends in New Orleans with him. The food, the people, the beautiful architecture—I could see why so many people loved the place.

I pulled into the driveway of Detra Ann's home and took a deep breath. There were at least a dozen cars, most of which I recognized. It looked like Ashland had made it on time. I smiled, hoping he would be in a good mood. I didn't plan on telling him about my dream, not right now. He had enough to worry about, but I wanted to mention that I had seen Lenore. Maybe he was seeing her too? For some reason, Ashland was always reluctant to talk about the things he saw unless forced to. He was a private man, but he had a warm heart and the most beautiful smile I had ever seen. I was completely in love with him. He had changed my life.

I suddenly remembered the letter from my mother. "Oh, shoot!" I muttered. I had left it on the coffee table at home. I couldn't worry about that right now. Maybe Ashland and I could read it together later.

Grabbing my purse and locking my car, I walked up the brick walkway to the lovely Creole home. Detra Ann had finally bought her own place, and it was chock full of antiques from her store, Cotton City Treasures. She had a flair for displays, and it showed. I rang the bell, and she opened it dramatically. "Should I say surprise?"

I laughed and hugged her. "Not unless you want me to pee on myself."

She laughed too. "I'm just teasing. Come on in here. Look at your belly. That's going to be a big boy! I mean girl. Maybe you'll have one of each."

"Please don't say that," I said, ready to cry at the idea.

She hugged me again, "I'm sorry. I forgot how sensitive preggos can be. I'm sure there is just one baby in there. And he—or she—is perfect."

"Hey, baby!" Ashland walked toward me and scooped me into his arms. "What's this? Are you crying?"

Detra Ann frowned a bit. "It's all my fault, Ash. I'm an insensitive friend. The kind who suggests she's carrying two youngins in there. Just for that, I volunteer to babysit anytime you need me." She kissed my cheek, and I smiled back, wiping away the ridiculous tears. "Y'all come out to the patio when you get ready. Henri thought it would be fun to have this shindig by the pool, and it's only a 'little' hot. He's been cooking, and it's going to be delicious."

"Sounds wonderful. Don't worry about me. I've just got the blues today. And my side is killing me. This kid can kick like you wouldn't believe."

She laughed and said, "I'll get you something to drink and meet you on the patio."

Ashland looked down at me with concern. "What kind of pain are you having? Should we call the doctor?"

With a weak smile and faux confidence, I shook my head. "I don't think it's anything to be concerned about. The last time I mentioned it, Dr. Gilmore said it was probably just my ligaments stretching. I have never heard of contractions in your side, but hey, I'm new to all this childbearing stuff. How did it go today?"

"Nothing I can't manage." He gave a small laugh that didn't sound too cheerful. "Did you hear back from the project manager for the Idlewood house?"

"No. I get the feeling that he wasn't expecting all the red tape. I'm going to back off on the project until after the baby. I'll call him tomorrow and tell him. He'll probably be happy to hear it. Might give him some time to get his act together. Are you sure you're okay?"

He held me in his arms and kissed my forehead. "Stop worrying. Today was just another Monday."

"It's Friday, babe."

"Exactly." He hugged me and whispered, "I love you, Carrie Jo."

"I love you too, Ashland. Please don't make me cry again."

"Ha! How is telling you I love you going to make you cry?"

"You've obviously never been pregnant." I kissed him and released him.

"What's going on that I don't know about?"

With a guilty look I answered, "How did you know?"

"I just know."

"Nothing big, just a dream and a letter. Can we talk about it after the party? Junior or Junior-ette is starving."

He didn't like the compromise, but how could he argue with a hungry child? "All right, but no secrets, remember?" I nodded in agreement. "Oh, wait. I got you this."

He walked to the nearby table and handed me a corsage box with a genuine smile. Ashland was definitely one to shower a girl with flowers. I loved that about him. "How beautiful! Are those Bourbon roses?" I knew they were, but I was enjoying the conversation. This was the first time in recent days that he'd smiled. "Put it on me." I held my arm out, and he slid the fluffy corsage arrangement on my wrist. "I love it, Ashland. It's beautiful."

"Not as beautiful as you, Carrie Jo Stuart."

I rubbed my hands over my belly and turned sideways. "Really? Even with this big belly?"

"Yes, and you get more beautiful every day." I kissed him again, and we walked hand in hand to the patio where our group of friends waited patiently. They applauded as we walked through the open French doors. I smiled at all the faces and accepted hugs from everyone. Chip and Rachel were the first to wish us well. They were on-again, off-again, but I was happy to see them together, at least for the moment. Henri wore one of his many aprons; this one said: *Cooking Up Something Good*. By the smell of it, I knew that was true. Nobody cooked like Henri. And as I predicted, Libby Stevenson, Ashland's attorney, made an appearance. I noticed she recently ditched her long dark hair in favor of a sassy bob. It flattered her angular face. I wondered why she bothered to come when we barely spoke to one another, except in passing. I supposed she came as Ashland's guest. Libby had one of those smiles that never quite made it to her eyes, the kind of smile you couldn't trust.

Whatever, lady, I said to myself. I chose to ignore her but shot Ashland a look. He gazed back at me questioningly. I didn't bother explaining; I shouldn't have to. Less than a minute ago, we were practically making out. Now I wanted to choke him.

Detra Ann spoke up, "Let's get this party started! We're here to welcome Baby Stuart. Thank you all for coming—now let's play some games." For the next 45 minutes we played goofy games and ate crab puffs, gumbo and mini cheesecakes. I laughed about a hundred times and opened a seemingly endless pile of gifts. Jazz played quietly in the background, and Henri surprised me with a beautiful cake.

"Oh my gosh! You bake too?" I dipped my finger into the frosting and tasted it. It was my party, right? Cream cheese frosting so light it tasted like heaven. "When are you going to marry this man? He can do it all." Everyone got quiet, and I felt embarrassed. I hadn't meant to meddle in their business!

Detra Ann just smiled at me. "Funny you should mention that." She held up her left hand and waved her fingers at me.

"What? Does that ring mean what I think it does?" It was almost as big as mine, and it shone beautifully against her tanned skin. "Oh my gosh! That is beautiful! When? Where?"

Henri smiled and put his arm around Detra Ann. "Last week at the LSU game. I have a friend who works in the booth, and they let me pop the question over the Jumbotron. You should have seen her face."

She squeezed his hand and smiled at me. "Only Henri would do something like that. I thought he was pranking me at first. Until he whipped out this big ol' ring. How could I say no?"

"Why didn't you tell me? Ashland, did you know about this?" He smiled sheepishly and raised his hands as if to say, *I had nothing to do with this.*

"We didn't want to overshadow the shower. This is y'all's party. We planned to have an engagement party after the baby arrives. We'll tell the whole world then."

I felt the tears again for about the fifteenth time that day. This was getting beyond ridiculous. "You guys. That is so wonderful. I am so happy for you both." I hugged Detra Ann, thankful that she had made it through her dark times and found someone as amazing as Henri. She hadn't drunk a drop since Lenore's death, and her antique business was booming. I was so happy for her. She deserved some happiness. Didn't we all?

It appeared that most at the shower had not heard the news, and everyone offered congratulations. "I'm so happy for you both," Libby said in her deep, sultry voice as she hugged Detra Ann halfheartedly. Detra Ann accepted the hug, but I saw her stiffen a bit. She gave Libby an icy smile and moved on to the next person.

I accepted a slice of the cake and sat by the pool listening to Bob Marley and the Wailers and watching my friends. Soon people began to say their goodbyes. Rachel was one of the first.

"Sorry, CJ, I have to go. Chip's mother is being a pain in the arse."

"Hey, that's my mom you're talking about," he said defensively.

"And she's a pain in the arse." Rachel rolled her eyes at him and hugged me. "You coming in tomorrow? I have that tree mapped but..." Her voice dropped to a whisper. "I think there's something you should see."

"Really? What is it? Are there pirates in the Stuart tree? I would expect nothing less," I joked.

"It's better to show you than tell you. I promise I'll fill you in tomorrow. I'll be there at 9."

"Call me curious! Of course I'll be there. Thanks, Rachel."

She smiled and left with Chip. I started picking up plates when Detra Ann stopped me. "No, ma'am. No cleaning of any sort. This is your party. Henri and I will take care of this. I think you better figure out where you're going to put all these gifts. Did you drive the BMW?"

"Yep, and Ash drove the Jeep, so we should be okay. I hope. You guys are so generous. I'm going to have to get a bigger house just to have enough room for all this," I said with a laugh.

"No doubt you will." She finished off her glass of punch and observed the remnants of the party. "Wonder why she came?"

"Who's that?" I asked, munching on sugared pecans. She glanced toward Libby. "Oh, her. I don't know. Well, I probably don't want to know."

"Remember when she said, 'I wish you both happiness,' or however she put it?"

"Yes."

"She didn't mean it. My bells went off big time. I mean, why say anything? She's such a liar. Like I said, I don't know why she came. I sure as heck didn't invite her. I don't think she likes anyone here, except Ashland. But then she always was a loner, even in school. Her brother was pretty nice, though."

"Really? I didn't know you guys went to school together. I think we both know why she's here, right?" I rolled my eyes. The young attorney wouldn't be the first woman to have a second thought about my husband. He had practically been a household name before the stranger from Savannah nabbed him. I knew for a fact that half the Historical Society still held a grudge because Ashland married a girl from Georgia and not a "belle from Mobile proper."

"Libby is barking up the wrong tree if she's after Ashland. He's not going to do you like that."

I wiped the sugar from my lips with a yellow napkin. Detra Ann had Ashland's and my initials printed on the napkins, cups and plates. It was a nice touch. I had to remember to keep one for my neglected scrapbook.

As if she heard her name, Libby strolled over to us, her mules slapping on the brick. "Can I help you ladies with something? Need help loading your stuff, Carrie Jo?"

"I think we have it. Thanks."

She stared at me a moment and said, "Well, I guess I'll go, then. Nice party."

As she walked away I felt like a jerk. Not every woman on the planet wanted my husband. Right?

"Nice of you to come, Libby," I called after her. She didn't act like she heard me. Instead, she stood on tiptoe and whispered to Ashland. He leaned down to hear her, and she took advantage of the nearness. Her arms went around his neck, and she hugged him. With her whole body. It was kind of embarrassing. Ash seemed surprised, and he patted her back like she was a child. My raging pregnancy hormones wanted me to slap her into the pool, but I kept my head. *Always listen to your instincts, CJ*, I warned myself.

Detra Ann made a disgusted, snorting sound and yelled, "Ash, we need your help over here."

He said something to Libby, and she left the party. I felt my face flush with embarrassment. Henri sensed the tension and said, "Let's see if we can get this bassinet in the Jeep. If not, I know it will fit in the truck."

"Wonderful party, Detra Ann. Thank you." Avoiding Ashland's eyes, I grabbed a couple bags and headed to the door. I was ready for this day to be over. I felt tired, I had eaten too much, and the green-eyed monster threatened to make an appearance. Detra Ann smiled understandingly and helped me carry the baby's gifts to the car. Thirty minutes later I was headed home with Ashland's Jeep behind me. The way I was feeling, most of this stuff was going to stay in the car overnight. I couldn't imagine hauling it all inside. My puffy feet would never allow that. What made me eat all those crab legs? I felt the sharp pain in my side again, and this time it was so severe I caught my breath.

"Oh God, oh God, oh God," I said as a kind of chant against the pain. Soon it subsided, and I pulled into the driveway. Putting the car in park, I leaned over the steering wheel and waited, hoping it didn't happen again. Ashland seemed oblivious as he juggled pastel-colored gift bags and house keys. When I was sure I was okay, I got out of the car with my purse and a few bags.

Walking up the drive I could feel an oppressive cloud, an unhappy fog unseen by human eye but felt by the spirit. It wasn't a presence, per se, more like bad mojo—or something. I looked up and down the street; the sun was going down now, and the afternoon traffic had dissipated. Compared to my neighbors' front yard, my flowerbeds looked forlorn and forgotten. Even my newly planted mums had croaked. Why did everything in my yard look dead? I walked up the driveway and almost tripped over a cat. It was the largest black cat I had ever seen outside of the zoo.

"What in the world? Where did you come from?" Like a bolt of lightning, Chunky Boy (that's what I'd decided to call him) ran out of the house after it. "Hey! Come back!"

Ashland was out the door and running past me. "Damn! I'll get him."

I wanted to say something smart like, "Serves you right for leaving the front door wide open," but I kept my mouth shut. I shook my head and headed for the front door when I heard a car slam on its brakes. Chunky Boy yelped, and I dropped my bags. As I ran down to the end of the driveway, I could see Ashland bent over in the street. He picked up Chunky Boy as the driver got out to apologize.

"Oh, I am so sorry. He came out of nowhere. Is he okay?"

Even from this distance, I could see he wasn't. His white fur was covered in blood, and he was clearly lifeless.

For the umpteenth time today I let the tears flow. This time I actually had a reason.

Chapter 3—Rachel

"I've been an unofficial member of the Seven Sisters ghostbusting team from the beginning, but nobody talks much about what happened over there," I complained again. Chip nodded as I continued, "I do believe that Carrie Jo is a dream catcher, though. She's not a huckster. In fact, she's one of the most honest people I know."

His eye roll revealed he had a different opinion. *Gee. That's pretty close-minded of you, Chip.* I decided to change the subject a bit. "What have you heard about the house?"

"I know I'm glad to be out of there, and I can't wait until you've finished up with it completely. Then I won't worry so much. Too many rumors about that place. Did you know it's on the Ghost Hunters website? I think those guys are trying to get in there. You know, to investigate."

"Oh really, nonbeliever? If there's no such thing as ghosts, what would they possibly investigate?"

"I never said there wasn't, but dream catching? I thought that was some Indian myth."

"I think the term you are looking for is Native American," I scolded him. Chip always said the most inappropriate things. He was so unsophisticated. I couldn't believe I'd even agreed to go out with him, much less do anything else with him. I quickly added, "But for your information, I'm not afraid of the house. I like helping out the Historical Society, and it's a big deal for Mobile. Besides, if I didn't manage the tours at Seven Sisters, who knows what they'd tell the visitors? I wonder about what they teach kids in school these days. Everyone should know the history of the city they live in."

"You sound like an old lady, Rachel Kowalski."

"Me? Because I believe in the unseen, the supernatural? I think you've got that the other way around."

He squinted at me through his glasses as if he didn't quite believe me. The truth was, he was right in a way. I was kind of an old lady. I did worry about everyone and everything. "You didn't answer my question, Chip. Did you see something in the house?"

He said, "I never saw anything, but more than once I felt like someone was watching me. Especially in the Blue Room. Got worse after Hollis Matthews died. It was more of a feeling, that's all. What about you?"

I didn't know if I was ready to tell Chip about my experience. He might think I was losing my mind, as he clearly thought Carrie Jo was a bit loony. He wasn't a deep thinker at all and certainly not spiritual. Once again I wondered how on earth I could be serious about a guy like him. I was totally a spiritual person. I didn't go to church as much as I used to, but I believed in God and the supernatural world. Why did people separate the two? God was a Spirit, right?

I decided to change the subject to a less controversial one. Chip had a short attention span, and he probably wouldn't notice anyway. "Do you believe in curses? Like family curses?"

"Come on, Rachel. You've met my mother," he joked, sipping the remnants of his Starbucks coffee.

"I'm serious. Do you believe in curses, like the Kennedy curse or the Rockefeller curse?"

"Are the Rockefellers cursed?"

I shrugged, aggravated that he was missing the point again. "Just something I heard. So you admit that you believe the Kennedy family is cursed?"

He snorted at the idea. "I didn't say that. I mean, they've had an unusual amount of bad luck. They might be cursed, if that's what you want to call it. I think it's just luck, though. Some families are luckier than others."

"What makes them lucky?"

"I don't know. It's too early in the morning for philosophical discussions, Rachel. You up for dinner tonight? I'm thinking deep-dish pizza from Mushrooms."

"I'm thinking of washing my hair." I opened the car door and grabbed my purse.

"Hey! Don't leave mad. What do you want me to say?" He got out of the car and leaned over the roof of his Volkswagen.

Chip had money. Not Ashland Stuart money, but he came from a wealthy family. He wasn't the handsomest guy on the block, but he wasn't bad-looking either. My biggest complaint was that he lacked imagination. I knew I shouldn't have hooked up with him the first time, let alone again. We were just too different.

"I'm not mad. I just can't make it tonight. I have some major studying to do, but I'll call you. Okay?"

He believed me. I could tell because he beamed from ear to ear. Boy, did he have large ears. *Come on, Rachel! Stop being so damn picky!* He tapped the top of his car happily and watched me unlock the office door before he drove away, completely oblivious to the fact that we were headed for another—permanent—breakup. I would have to deal with that later.

I flicked on the lights, tapped the security code on the alarm pad and made some coffee. CJ never drank coffee anymore, not since her pregnancy, so I made a half a pot. I was firmly committed to drinking every bit of it. I felt tired this morning. Not so much from Chip's snoring but from my constant work on this family tree project for Carrie Jo. I dropped my purse on my desk and went to the conference room, where I arranged the sheets of paper to show CJ my ridiculously detailed research. I looked at it again. Yep, I wasn't imagining things. An entire page of male ancestors dead between the ages of 30 and 40, and most on the lower end of that time frame. I felt a wave of clamminess hit me. *This can't be right*, I'd thought in the beginning. *This has to be some kind of weird coincidence.*

Then I began digging deeper, and that's when things got real hairy. The Stuarts were plagued by freak accidents. For example, one guy got hit by lightning while fishing; another was working on a car, and the dang thing fell on him. Too weird. Things were okay on his mother's side of the tree, but his father's was an entirely different story.

I knew Southern family trees often had tangled roots, but this was crazy. I had traced the Stuarts back to the Cottonwoods—but not Jeremiah Cottonwood. Ashland was related to Isaiah Cottonwood, Jeremiah's brother. In the words of my father, "That puts a whole 'nother spin on that, Sparky." Sparky. Who nicknamed their daughter Sparky? My brother Andy used to tease me and call me "Sparkly" just because he knew it ticked me off. I'd rain down curses on him for all the good it did. Nothing bad ever happened to him. I was lousy at cursing, and I sure as heck knew something about curses. My mother firmly believed in them, as did her sisters, and as a child I tossed salt over my shoulder, avoided crossing streams while wearing a skirt and never, ever stood on a stump—all activities that could have brought down the curses upon myself and my family. Publicly I scoffed at the idea of curses. I often agreed with my childhood friends—curses were superstitious nonsense for scaredy-cats—but after they went home, I crossed my fingers, said the prayers and did whatever it took to keep the curses away.

I knew that what I was looking at was nothing short of a curse. A straight-up curse. I had to tell Carrie Jo. And if she thought I was crazy, well, she wouldn't be the first friend of mine to think so.

"Good morning, Rachel!" she called from the front door. "Coffee smells great! Have a cup for me."

"I will! You need anything?" I called back, delaying a face-to-face meeting for a few more seconds.

"Nope. I'm peachy keen," she said as she poked her head in the doorway. "Oh, cool. Let me go drop this stuff on my desk, and I'll be right back." As she turned to walk away, she groaned and froze, reaching for the doorframe.

"What is it? You okay?" I sprang to my feet, nearly sloshing hot coffee on my starched white blouse.

Her face was pale, which wasn't like CJ at all. All throughout her pregnancy she had amazing skin. Before that she had a nice warm-looking tan. At the moment she appeared near death. "You don't look so hot, girl. Can you walk? I think you should sit down."

"I think you're right," she gasped, holding on to the door like a wavering drunk. Finally, whatever pain had hit her subsided. "Okay, I think I can move now. Darn! My side is killing me."

"You have to go to the doctor, Carrie Jo. You could be in labor."

"Can't be. This pain is in my side. I thought labor pains were in the back or the front."

"I'm not a baby expert, but if I had pain anywhere and I was pregnant, I'd be on my way to the OB-GYN. Can I at least call Ashland?"

"No. Please don't do that. Let's just keep an eye on it. See? It's easing up now." I gave her a disapproving look, and she added, "I'll call my doctor in a few minutes. Promise."

I watched her as she sat at the desk and the color finally returned to her face. "Wow, that was a sharp one. I wonder if I pulled something."

"What have you been doing?"

"Trying to tie my shoes," she said with a laugh. "I'm fine. Stop worrying about me. The pain is gone now. What did you want to show me? I'd be lying if I said I wasn't super-curious."

"I've got everything spread out in the conference room, but I can bring it in here if you like," I offered.

"No. I'm good." She cracked open a water bottle and smiled up at me. Carrie Jo had a beautiful face, a cleft chin, startling green eyes and naturally curly hair. She was a natural beauty, and I often wanted to ask her the brand of coral-colored lipstick she wore. It really played up her light olive skin. You could easily describe her as the girl next door, but she was also usually the funniest girl in the room. I both admired her and felt a bit envious. She'd had some amazing luck in life, including landing the chief historian job at Seven Sisters. Of course, her bestie had almost killed her, and quite a few of her friends had died. I suddenly felt ashamed for the envy.

"Great. Whenever you're ready, just come to the conference room."

"Okay, be there in a second."

After a few minutes she joined me and sat next to me, looking over the sheaves of paper. "Beautiful work, Rachel. How's it going in school? Ready to graduate?"

"Dear Lord, yes. Did you get the graduation invitation?"

"Yes! And if I'm not having a baby, I'll be there." She laughed and made a face that let me know she was ready to get on with the whole childbirth experience. I didn't blame her. She was all baby now. Her arms and legs were much thinner than before, and it seemed like the baby was stealing all her nutrients. But then again, what did I know?

With a smile I handed her the first piece of paper. I used the Alari software to create the family tree. I thought it would be easy enough, but filling in the slots on the electronic tree had been anything but. Alari verified each entry, and when it couldn't find source records it forced the user to provide verification via GEDCOM, Rootsweb or one of the dozens of other genealogical sites. I sat beside her and allowed her to look through the papers before I spoke up.

"So this is the completed version. It took me about forty hours of research to find all the connections."

"Oh no. I had no idea I was asking you to work that many hours. I expect to compensate you, Rachel. This is wonderful work."

I shook my head. "No way. This is my baby gift. Remember? As you can see, Ashland comes from a long line of tangled relations." I smiled tentatively at her. Maybe I shouldn't tell her anything. She had enough going on now. What with the pain and the baby.

"Hey, what's the deal? Is this right?"

I peeked at the paper she was holding. It was the information about Isaiah Cottonwood and his connection to Ashland. "Yep, it's right."

"So Ashland is not a direct descendant of Jeremiah Cottonwood? I can't say I'm disappointed. I've never heard of Isaiah. Or maybe I have, but I just don't remember him."

"He never came up in our previous research, Carrie Jo. Funny thing is, Ashland is both a direct descendant of the

Cottonwoods and a cousin to the Beaumonts. See here? In 1870, Dara Beaumont married this guy, and that's the cousin. Not unusual when families stick close to home. Apparently in this family group, people kind of hung around and didn't move away when they got older. Except Calpurnia, but she didn't have much choice. See?" I pointed to another section of the genealogy.

"I wonder what this will mean for his estate."

"I'm not sure, CJ."

"Here's something even more surprising. There is a codicil to Jeremiah's will."

"Yes, I heard about that."

"You knew?" I asked, surprised.

Her cheeks went pink. "Not until recently."

"Here is a copy of it that I made from the archives downtown. It clearly transfers all property rights to Isaiah. Jeremiah must have been quite a jerk. This codicil was created just a month before he died, and with it he basically took the family fortune away from his daughters and his in-laws and gave it to his brother. Which sucks since most of the money probably belonged to the Beaumonts originally."

"That does suck," Carrie Jo added, still staring at the pages. I promised myself I wouldn't say a word unless she did. The idea of talking about a curse seemed ridiculous to me now. Except for the evidence. I handed her a copy of the spreadsheet that displayed the birth dates, death dates and ages of the deceased. Maybe she would notice it herself. She said, "Good work, Rachel." She scanned the printed sheet down to the bottom.

Carrie Jo stared at Ashland's name for a second and then scanned back up. She saw it too! With wide eyes she looked at me. "And you are sure about these ages?"

"I doubled-checked everything, CJ. It's all accurate. I even had Chip look at it with me. You know he's got a photographic memory."

Carrie Jo didn't say much but kept staring at the page. "Why so young? I mean, I know people back then didn't live as long as we do, but 35 seems very young to die. And it's men only? How many generations does this phenomenon go back?"

"Near as I can tell, right around the time of the codicil. Isaiah's sons, Jacob and Christian, died at age 31 and 34, respectively, but his two daughters both lived into their sixties. Next generation, these three men, all dead before 35. And it goes on until today."

"And Ashland is about to have a birthday." I could hear the fear in her voice.

"I'm sure it's nothing, Carrie Jo. I mean, I noticed it too, but what could it mean? The Cottonwood line has had some bad luck, but a lot of families experience tragedy. Try not to worry about this." I regretted pointing this out; the look on her face said it all. "Don't obsess over this stuff. It's nothing to worry about." *Or nothing you can do anything about, anyway.*

She didn't look at me but kept staring at the papers. She pulled her phone out of her purse. "Maybe not, but I know someone who can tell me what I'm looking at—I hope." I watched her dial the number, and my heart beat faster. "Hey, Henri? You got a minute? I'd like to come see you. I need your opinion on something. Sure, I can be there in a few minutes. Yes, breakfast sounds great. No, Ashland isn't with me. Just Rachel. Great. We'll be there in 15."

She put the phone down and stared at the papers again. I was dying to ask so I did, "How can Henri help?"

"He's a bit of a spiritualist. He knows a thing or two about supernatural subjects. You up for some pancakes? He's got extra."

Happy to finally be included in something beyond answering phones and creating reports, I nodded with a smile.

"Grab your purse and let's go. We need to bring these papers too."

"I've got these. You get your purse. I'll drive, CJ."

"I'll let you." As I slid the papers into the envelope, a shadow crossed the window outside. The sky suddenly seemed darker. Was there a storm brewing? This changeable weather was one of the things I disliked the most about Mobile. You could be lying out in the sun in the backyard one minute and getting drenched the next. A flash of lightning popped across the distant sky. It came from the direction of the harbor.

Yep. There was definitely a storm brewing.

But what kind?

Chapter 4—Carrie Jo

The two of us didn't talk much as we drove to Henri's. I could tell Rachel wanted to say something to comfort me, but what could she say? Suddenly everything I'd been through the past few days made sense. The arguments, the bad luck, the feeling of oppression. Sounded like a curse to me, but I was no expert.

Henri now lived in the apartment over Detra Ann's antique store, but honestly that wasn't much of a move. Cotton City Treasures was only two streets over from his old digs. And it wasn't a permanent move, now that they were getting married. I loved his apartment, though. It was in an old building with fabulous gargoyles perched at the corners of the roof. A rarity in Mobile. There weren't many such objects in the downtown area. There was an interesting pyramid building with two sphinxes at the door. Some kind of Masonic lodge, probably. I'd never asked about it, but it was on my to-do list. If I ever had the time.

And if I could ever get the supernatural stuff cleared away. Between the ghosts, the dreams and the specter of Death, I'd been a little busy. Now I suspected that something else hung over us, over Ashland and our child. Maybe that was why I had been so resistant to the idea of having a son. Did I somehow psychically know that the Cottonwood boys were cursed? I needed to show the evidence to Henri and let him tell me what he thought. He came from a family who understood curses and hexes, as he had related to us many times.

I did the math while Rachel drove. Two men in that generation, then three, then two, then four more. I couldn't remember the second page, but I would never forget seeing Ashland's name at the bottom. No way could I tell him about this.

"Oh my God!" I said as a flock of crows hovered in front of our car. They hung in the air for a moment, then flapped their wings and flew away. "Holy smokes! What was that about?"

"I...have...no...idea," Rachel said slowly. She was gripping the steering wheel so tightly her knuckles were white.

We pulled in front of the antique store, and I waved at Detra Ann as I got out of the car. I looked over my shoulder to make sure the evil birds weren't stalking me. She waved back but didn't stop to chat. An excited customer was purchasing a blue and white tray and asking the pretty ponytailed blonde a bunch of questions about other items in the shop. I pointed to the stairs, and she nodded at me as the breathless patron kept up with her queries.

I didn't know how Detra Ann worked with the public, but she loved it. It took someone special to take a public relations degree and use that to run an antiques shop. One of the things I loved about her new business was that every item came with a story. Not just word of mouth, either. No, Detra Ann had hidden talents. She wrote what she knew about each item and made sure the new owner got a copy of her story. The community and its visitors loved her place. *It's like she was born for this.*

We walked up the narrow stairs to the apartment and opened the glass door that led to Henri's loft. After Lenore died, he had sold his house and moved in here instead. I didn't blame him. It was a gorgeous open space with warm painted walls and to-die-for fixtures and extras.

"So what's up, ladies?" Henri tossed off his apron, which read: *Boo-yah.* "Who wants some pancakes? I made enough for a small army—I had a feeling I'd have guests this morning." He rubbed his hands together as he served us with gusto. He was obviously proud of both his premonition and his pancakes. I took a bite. He had reason to be.

"I'll take a few of these. As always, it smells like heaven in here."

"You want the syrup warmed?"

"Whatever is easiest, Henri. Thanks for this." Rachel blushed as he handed her a plate of hot pancakes. I smiled a bit. I never knew Rachel had a crush on Henri, but then again I had been kind of self-involved for the past few months. I knew she liked Detra Ann, though, so I didn't worry about any shenanigans there.

After he poured the juice and set everything on the table, I handed him the stack of papers. "Take a look at this and let me know what you think."

With a curious look he accepted the envelope and put on a pair of gold-rimmed glasses.

"Glasses, huh?"

"No jokes, CJ. My eyes may be old, but I'm not."

I chuckled and covered my mouth with my hand as I chewed a delicious bite of pancake. I was hungrier than I thought. And to think, I'd walked away from Doreen's omelet this morning. But then again, our housekeeper's cooking didn't stack up against Henri's. I'd often told him he needed to open a restaurant. So far, I hadn't convinced him.

"Okay, what am I looking at?" He stared at the papers and looked up at the light. "Did it just get dark outside? The news didn't say anything about bad weather this morning. That storm is way off the coast." He hopped up and flipped the light switch, and the beautiful fleur-de-lis embellished chandelier filled the dining room with warm light.

"What storm?" Rachel asked.

"Looks like we have a late tropical storm brewing off the coast, but it's pretty far away." He went to the window and looked outside. It had gotten dark quickly, first at the office and now here. As the old folks used to say, it "looked like the bottom would fall out of the sky" any minute.

I loved Henri's place. It had so much New Orleans flair; cool photos from his time there covered the living room walls. A collection of fleur-de-lis candle holders rested on a side table. One of the walls in the living room was painted a dark red, and an elegant gold-rimmed mirror hung in the center of it.

He slid the papers out of the envelope and shuffled through them quickly before he began intently studying them. He didn't ask me what to look for, and I could tell when he spotted it. "So he has a birthday in about a month?"

I nodded, wiping my mouth with the linen napkin and pushing the plate to the side. It was wonderful, but I'd lost my appetite again. "Do you think it's possible that we—that we're..."

"Cursed?" Rachel answered for me.

"Yeah, what she said." If I didn't say the word, then we wouldn't be, right?

"Let's look at the facts, and then we'll look at the rest. According to this, every man in Ashland's family tree—in this particular line of ancestors, anyway—has died at an early age. From these notations about the causes of death, it looks like a string of accidents."

"Some. I can't be sure about a few of the others, so I left question marks beside their names. Even if you assumed that those men died of natural causes, that's still a lot of early deaths." Rachel added in a serious voice, "Men usually died around age 55 to 60 during the early to mid-1800s. There's definitely a trend of men dying young in that particular family."

"No doubt there is. How old is Ashland now?"

"He'll be thirty. We've joked about the baby coming on his birthday. And that's another thing—what about the baby? What if I have a boy? What will that mean?"

"Hold up, let's not jump to any conclusions." Just then a bolt of lightning cracked through the sky and illuminated our faces in blue light. I winced at the closeness of it. The lights flickered, but the power didn't go out. I heard the shop door ring downstairs; we'd left Henri's door ajar on accident. I heard footsteps coming up the stairs. Feeling creeped out about curses, I turned to look and was relieved to see it was Detra Ann.

You are being ridiculous, CJ. All the ghosts have settled down. You're just looking for trouble. If you're not careful, you'll find it.

Detra Ann slid her arms around my neck and hugged me. I needed all the hugs I could get right now. I squeezed her back, and she grabbed a plate. "I'm stealing some breakfast, but help me keep an ear out for customers. I've got the buzzer set. It sure got dark outside, didn't it? I might have to bring my antiques table inside, Henri. I think it's going to flood any minute. What are y'all up to?"

It was just like Detra Ann to talk in a constant stream of consciousness. She plopped down in the empty chair with her plate and dug into the pancakes.

"We've found something weird. It has to do with Ashland. Have you ever heard about a, well, I guess the thing you could call it is a…" Why was this so difficult to say?

"A curse, she's talking about a curse." Henri filled in the blank this time.

"What kind of curse? Like a hex or something?"

"No. More like a family curse," Rachel said. "All of Ashland's male relatives from the Cottonwood line died early deaths. We're just concerned about him since his birthday is around the corner."

"So you think Ashland is cursed? What would make you say that?" She put her fork down and stared at the three of us.

Henri handed her the family tree, and as she flipped through it he questioned me, "What's been going on? He mentioned he's had some legal troubles recently. What else is happening?"

"I don't know. What am I supposed to be looking for?"

Rachel raised her hand. "Um, I can answer that. The women in my family are experts on curses."

"Oh, so like they're witches?" Detra Ann asked innocently between drinking orange juice and nibbling on her pancakes.

"Lord, don't tell them that. No, they aren't witches at all. They're just very superstitious. My mother and her four sisters break curses all the time. They can spot them a mile away too." She snapped her fingers. "I am sure they would be able to tell if you or Mr. Stuart had one!"

"Whoa, let's not get ahead of ourselves here. We don't know if he's—if we're…"

"Cursed?" Detra Ann finished for me.

"Well if you believe in curses—and I've always been taught that you have to believe in them for them to work—a number of things can cause them," Henri began to explain.

"Not to contradict my elders," Rachel said with a smile, "but that's not entirely true."

Henri leaned back in his chair and drank his coffee as another pop of lightning came close to the shop. "What can you tell us about curses, Rachel?"

"Well, they manifest differently, and they can fall on individuals and families gradually. The way I understand it, curses work the opposite of a blessing. You know, when you say a blessing over food or you bless someone for some special reason?"

"Or say, 'Bless her heart'?" Detra Ann joked, obviously trying to lighten the mood.

"Not quite like that, no. Bad stuff happens to people all the time, but when it hits you nonstop it might just be a curse. A curse is basically negative energy that gets bound to a person for some supernatural reason. For example, in our family, we believe that if you steal, you've put yourself under a curse. Negative acts bring curses. Sometimes someone can send a curse to you, but you would have to do them wrong in a major way for them to be able to curse an entire family for generations. I'm talking about a serious curse here."

"What other evidence do you have to support the idea that Ashland might be cursed?" I could tell by her tone that Detra Ann wasn't convinced, and I was glad for that. I still couldn't even say the word.

"You know what? We have had some issues lately. He's had lawsuit after lawsuit, things keep breaking around the house, we argue all the time. It's like we're in this funk and can't get out of it."

Nobody spoke for a minute, and then Henri asked, "What about animals? Any weird encounters?"

"On the way here, a flock of crows nearly caused us to have an accident." Rachel's voice sounded even quieter now, and I shivered when I saw her spill salt in her hand and toss it over her shoulder.

I cleared my throat and made a confession. "That's not all. Some stray cat on our street lured our puppy into the road, and he got hit by a car. He died." I chewed on my lip for a second while my friends stared at me wide-eyed. "Also, things keep coming up missing, like we've got a thieving gremlin in the house. I just chalked it up to me being absentminded because of the pregnancy, but I'm thinking it's something else now. Can this be possible? I mean, everyone here knows that the supernatural world exists, but this kind of thing…a…"

"Curse, Carrie Jo. It's a curse. Saying it won't make you more cursed, I promise." Rachel patted my hand.

"Yeah, well, curses. That's a whole other ballgame. This can't be right."

"But that's the thing about a curse. It's not in your face. It's sneaky. Most people don't even seem to notice they are under one."

"I agree with Rachel. If we can do something to prevent it, break it, we should. If his birthday goes by and nothing happens, then we know we're good."

"Until next year," Rachel mumbled.

"So I'll just stress out for the next ten years every time he has a birthday? No. If Ashland is cursed, I want to break it, right now—today! It's not just Ashland. It's the baby too, if we're having a boy. And there's another thing." I turned to Henri, who watched me intently with his warm dark eyes. "I saw Lenore, Henri. She was speaking, trying so hard to tell me something, but I couldn't understand her. It was a word."

"If Lenore is involved, then the chances that something is wrong have increased dramatically. She would want to help, no matter where she was. No clue at all what she was trying to say?"

I took a sip of milk and shook my head. "I had a dream and was about to wake up. That's when she came, at that in-between place. I can't explain it any better than that. I could see her pretty clearly, but it sounded like she was trying to talk underwater. Then she was gone and I was awake. It was so fast I couldn't work out what she said."

Detra Ann reached across the table and grabbed my hand. "Hey. We're with you. We all love you and Ashland. If there's a curse, we'll figure out how to break it. But…I have to say this. I think it's a good idea to keep this to ourselves for now. No need to freak him out. We all know how much he hates this kind of stuff. You said yourself, he's been under quite a bit of stress recently."

Rachel's forehead wrinkled with concern. "What? If I was cursed, I would want to know it. I know I'm not as close to Ashland as you guys are, but I wish you'd reconsider that."

I looked from one face to the other, not sure what to say. "I think Detra Ann is right. For now—just for now, Rachel— we don't say anything to Ash. But didn't you say that for a generational curse to work it had to be sent by someone who was done wrong in a big way?"

"Yes, that's what I understand. Let me check with my mom, though. Like I said, she and my aunts are the expert on curses."

Henri put the papers back in the envelope and handed them to me. "While she does that, I'll check with a friend in New Orleans. He's a pastor there. Whenever I need prayer, he's the guy I call on. Let's get him praying over this situation. Maybe he can get some spiritual insight into what we're dealing with. I think the big question is who put this curse on Ashland's ancestors, and how do we break it? It's going to be difficult to make things right if the curser has been dead for over a hundred years."

For some reason I just had to laugh. Like the old-timers said, "You either laugh or cry." Everyone looked at me like I was sure-enough, put-her-in-the-loony-bin crazy. "I don't mean to laugh. I swear. It's just what you said." I stifled more laughter. "About the curser being dead. I mean, these Cottonwoods and Beaumonts don't die. I don't know why you're worried about that." Then the tears came, and Detra Ann put her arms around me. I cried on her shoulder, feeling more tired than I had ever felt in my life.

She whispered kindly to me, "It's going to be fine, CJ. I promise you, I'll stick close to Ashland. He'll think we're joined at the hip. Maybe I'll start by meeting him for lunch today.

Keep an eye on him. I can call Cathy in to work the shop for me."

I gave a sigh of relief. Not because I had all the answers. Quite the opposite. I had a bunch of questions. But at least I had my friends. We had friends.

"That leaves me. I'll do the one thing I know I can do." My friends knew what I meant. I'd be dreaming, but with a purpose this time. It had been a while since I pursued the past through the dream world. I'd had plenty of dreams, but those came naturally and were less taxing than dreaming with a purpose. I didn't mention what I had seen about Olivia and Isla. That might not be relevant…oh, who was I kidding? I was pretty sure the evil blonde cherub would be involved somehow. But why bring up Isla to Detra Ann? The dead girl had tried to kill her!

It was always risky going back to Seven Sisters, but now that the spirits had settled down, I was sure it wouldn't be so dangerous.

I hoped.

Chapter 5—Karah

Sitting on the worn blue quilt, I shook my blue silk purse and listened to the sound of the last of my coins. Hoping it was more than it sounded, I loosened the cord and dumped the coins on the bed. This wasn't enough to make it through the week, much less another month in Mobile. Out of sheer embarrassment I had refused to stay with Delilah, but my pride had cost me. I was no charity case, and I refused to allow Jackson to cover the expense of my continued stay here at the boarding house. I had to make plans for my future, but the truth was I had nowhere to go. Mother had sold our home in Virginia, and God only knew what she did with the money. Docie probably knew, but she would never tell me. She was always Mother's creature, although I suspected she had abandoned her and taken Mother's meager supply with her.

This trip had cost me all my savings, but it cost me even more than that. I had been spent emotionally in ways I had not expected. Why had I come to Mobile? Why had I trusted Mother? The small stipend she gave me had long since disappeared, and I had no other means of support. When Mother sent me to Seven Sisters, she assured me that all would be well. Ah, she excelled at lying, and I excelled at believing her. But no more.

She had made claiming my inheritance sound like a mere formality. She had assured me that my father had made provision for me and that local society would not question my parentage. "They will see your beauty and know right away that you are a Cottonwood. No, *the* Cottonwood." But society had not accepted me at all, and neither had my father's family; none had accepted my invitations to visit me at Seven Sisters. I had received a few letters from an uncle I did not know, but I had not been allowed to read them. Docie snatched them up and kept them secreted away until Mother arrived.

"You let your mother deal with this man," she warned me as tersely as possible.

All I had to do was wait for her, care for the house and most importantly of all—find the Beaumont treasure.

But she had been wrong, and no treasure had yet been found. Jackson informed me that the will was very specific and that I needed proof that I was who I claimed to be. I had no proof, only the word of my mother. I wrote her and informed her of the many challenges I faced in Mobile. She wrote me back, but it was only one line:

I will succeed. I am on the way.

I received no more letters, but a short time later Docie returned. She had hard eyes and a cruel grip, which she did not mind applying to my young wrists. Easy enough to hide the bruises. "Wear gloves, Karah," my mother would tell me. She did not care one whit what Docie did to me.

It wasn't until I was almost ten that I understood that Mother went mad sometimes. During those dark times I would be sent away to a nearby girls' home until she recovered. I had a few happy times, though. Especially when Captain Garrett came to us. He insisted that I call him Uncle David, which I liked. I much preferred pretending he was my father, but from my earliest age Mother made sure I knew he was not.

"You are a Cottonwood, my dove. That is much better than being a Garrett." I hated seeing the hurt on the captain's face, but I did not dare argue with her. How I missed the captain! He brought joy into my dim life for a time, and when he left us for good, darkness descended.

I had heard it said that Mother had been a great actress in her prime, but she did not speak of it much anymore. How I loved seeing her standing in the spotlight, although I had to witness her performances in secret. "Theaters are for mature minds," she would say before she stepped into the carriage and disappeared into the night with a wave or a scowl. Thankfully Docie would leave with her and I would be alone.

Occasionally, I would steal into Mother's rooms for a while and read her plays. If the trunks were left open, and they rarely were, I would grab a gown and hold it up to my small body pretending that I was my beautiful mother. Of course I had to be careful to put the dresses back the way I found them.

Once, while we traveled through Virginia, I did sneak into a theater to see her. It wasn't hard to do. We traveled with a company of actors through a string of Virginia cities, and the hotels were often very near the theaters. I crept out at quite a few of them; often I pretended that I had to deliver something to Isla Garrett, as she sometimes called herself. The usher let me pass, but I never made it to the dressing room. I hung back in the shadows of the stage and chewed on my fingernail or a stolen apple as I waited for the play to begin. It was like watching someone I did not know. She wholly transformed herself each night and became whomever she pretended to be. I could not believe this breathtaking, living doll was my own mother. She was a magical creature full of light and laughter. It was almost as if she could change her features, her voice, her body shape. She could have played Hamlet himself if she had taken a mind to.

That seemed a hundred years ago; now she sat in a mental asylum awaiting trial for attempted murder. I could hardly believe it!

The weeks went by and shamefully I had not seen her once. How could I, after what she tried to do? That did not stop Docie from coming to see me. She demanded that I attend my mother, defend her, help her in some way. I refused. I did not know the devil she had become.

But I had found a friend in Adam Iverson. One early evening, when I ventured out long enough to find needed toiletries, I ran into him on the sidewalk outside the boarding house. He was kind to me and offered to help me with my packages. I refused, of course, but he begged to take me to dinner. Overwhelmed with loneliness I accompanied him to a small dining room on the outskirts of town. He was flirtatious, as he had always been, but not too inappropriate. The following day he left a bouquet of flowers for me at the front desk, and I had spent much time with him since that first dinner. I had other visitors too. Jackson came a few times. He carefully let me know that it was Delilah who sent him. It was clear to me that she was the object of his true affection. I cared not, for I had my eye on Adam. He was strong, clever with his ideas and amiable enough. At least for a little while.

But I did miss Delilah, and I was happy to hear that she got stronger every day. The slice on her leg had become infected, but she had recovered and was apparently anxious to see me. I couldn't face her either. I made my apologies to the attorney and promised I would visit my cousin soon. I did not bother to inquire about my own legal status. How could I make a claim now when my only true witness to my parentage had gone mad?

Imagine my surprise when Stokes showed up at my door. My mother had been released and was residing again at Seven Sisters, he told me in his loud, deep voice. Not only that, but a relative of mine, a Mrs. Torrence, requested my presence at the house. I considered calling Mr. Keene, as he had been gone only a few minutes, but I felt better about making this trip by myself. I left a message for Adam with Mrs. Shields, my landlady. I asked him to wait for my return at his shop. I would come see him soon. How could I involve any more innocent people in what could only be considered my family's madness?

Curious now, I collected my purse and followed Stokes to the carriage that would take me to the grand old house. Of course I knew the name, Olivia Torrence. She was Isla's mother and my grandmother, but I had no knowledge of her involvement in our lives at any point up until now, and so naturally I was suspicious of her. If I learned anything from my mother, it was to be suspicious and to question the motives of everyone around me. Especially my mother's.

As the carriage pulled into the long driveway of Seven Sisters, I did not experience the wonder and happiness that I had the first time I made this journey. The white columns used to rise up like a welcoming temple in the promised land. Now the massive home seemed more like a mausoleum, for there was no one about. A massive mausoleum full of secrets and lies. There were only a few lights burning in the windows this evening. The dim light added to the solemnity I already felt. Whatever could Mrs. Torrence want with me? She had cast off my mother as a child; I could not hope for better, could I? Then the likely truth occurred to me: she wanted what all Beaumonts wanted—the return of their fortune. Like my mother, Mrs. Torrence pinned all her hopes on me to be the one who brought her the reward. I would disappoint her too because I knew nothing at all and had found nothing at all. Whatever treasure had been there, it was long gone now. Or hidden so carefully in the house or grounds that it would take ten lifetimes to recover it.

To continue to seek it would be madness.

I made my way into the house cautiously, as if someone or something would jump out at me any moment. I fully understood the phrase "on pins and needles" as I made my way from the open foyer to the ladies' parlor. The first thing I saw was the pale face of my mother as she sailed toward me with a smile.

"Mother? Why are you here?"

Ignoring my question, she said gaily, "Here is my lovely daughter, Aunt."

I raised my eyebrows at both her greeting and her address of "Aunt." I had always thought Olivia to be my grandmother, not my great-aunt. While my mother was animated and showering me with forced affection, the older woman hardly moved. She sat like a thin, tall statue in the largest chair in the ladies' parlor.

"Karah, this is your aunt and mine, Olivia Torrence."

"How did you get out, Mother? I thought you were to stand trial for what you did to us?" I didn't bother with the formalities. We were not a formal family.

"Yes, and little you did to help me! Imagine not helping your mother when she needed you the most! I sat in that jail with all those other women! No family. No friends. Barely any food at all. Do you know what I went through? The guards mistreated me—of course, men only want one thing. That's all they think about. Like your father! You ungrateful—"

Mrs. Torrence exclaimed, "Isla! That is enough! Sit down before I have Stokes tie you to a chair and gag you. You will contain yourself, or you can return to Holy Angels Sanitarium. Now, Miss Cottonwood, please have a seat here at the table."

I cast an angry look at my mother but took the seat across from her. How different the two women were in spirit, though they were very much alike in physical appearance. Olivia stood a near head taller than Mother. That I could tell even though she had not yet stood. They had similar etched features, like two lovely porcelain dolls, but they were made of ice, not porcelain. Olivia dressed more demurely than Isla, but she was older. Old enough to be Isla's mother. I wondered again how this family tree ran.

"You must have many questions for me, and I certainly have some for you."

I nodded but kept my mouth shut. It seemed better to collect information than share it, and I could do that only if I kept quiet. "Are you the daughter of Jeremiah Cottonwood?" Olivia asked.

"I have been told all my life that I am." I held my head high and stared daggers at my mother.

"You have the look of the Cottonwoods. The wide mouth, the colorful cheeks. I would say that you could be."

"She most certainly is! Even Jeremiah acknowledged her."

"Yes, but the courts haven't, have they? And your recent performance makes it less likely that they will. However, all is not lost yet."

"Truly? Tell us, Aunt. What do you have planned?" Isla smiled broadly as if she had been given a long-awaited gift.

"I do not need your help in establishing Karah. You leave that to me."

"She is my daughter!"

"Unfortunately for her. But she is not yours to worry over anymore, Isla. She is my ward and in my care until she is established. The only thing you can bring her is shame and notoriety. Imagine working as an actress! What were you thinking?"

Isla stood up and slung the chair back. It made a scraping sound as it slid across the floor. "I did what I had to do! You cannot keep me from my only child."

Without standing or arguing, Aunt Olivia rang the bell beside her. Stokes came immediately. "Please escort my niece to her room and make sure she stays there until I summon her," Aunt Olivia said coolly.

"You cannot imprison me, Olivia! I will not have it."

"You have nothing to say about it. Now go peaceably, or Stokes can pick you up and carry you. Whichever you prefer." With an angry scowl, Isla did as she was told. It was likely the first time in her life she had obeyed anyone. It was certainly the first time I had ever witnessed such a thing. Even Uncle David had not been able to command such obedience. I immediately feared and liked my great-aunt.

"Will you imprison me as well?"

Olivia poured me a cup of tea and slid it to me. "Come. Let us put the knives away. As the daughter of a madwoman, you will appreciate the honest truth."

I sipped my tea nervously and said, "If you knew she was mad, why did you leave me with her? Why have I never met you, Aunt Olivia?"

She toyed with a sugar cube as if she weren't sure what to say to me. With slender fingers she tossed the cube into the lukewarm tea and stirred it with a golden spoon. "She was Louis' daughter. Who was I to interfere? If he wanted to leave her in a girls' home or send her overseas, I had nothing to do with it. If it pleased him to tell everyone that she was my bastard daughter, then that was fine too. Nobody who knew me believed his stories. Louis was one to tell tales. He and Christine were both such dreamers. I was the practical one. I married a practical man and have lived a very respectable life, all told. It wasn't until I learned what Louis had done with our fortunes that I decided I must do something."

"I see. You gave no thought for me at all until your fortune became involved…"

"This will be the last time I remind you, put the knives away, girl. You are no match for me, and I will not be swayed by your insults. Do nothing foolish; I am the only one who can help you."

"Really? You want to help me now?" I swallowed the anger and resentment that began to brew within me. "How do you propose to do that?"

She leaned back in her chair and closed her eyes for a moment. I watched and waited to see what would happen next.

"When I met my husband, Louis practically disowned me. If it weren't for our mother, God rest her soul, I am sure he would have. You see, he was the son, the heir to all our fortunes, but he was not a wise man. He arranged for Christine to marry Jeremiah, knowing full well that she loved another."

"The doctor?"

"I see you know your family history. Yes, the doctor." She opened her eyes and smiled, but not at me. She was thinking about something. "Louis loved Christine and me, but he was easily influenced. He wouldn't think twice if he needed to use you for something. And as we all loved him so much, we tolerated him."

"Why are you telling me this?" I asked her.

She seemed not to hear me. She stood, walked to the French door and stared out of it. "He cared for Jeremiah, in his way, but he did not love him the way Jeremiah wanted him to. So he gave Jeremiah the next best thing. He gave him Christine. I told our mother all about it. I begged her to stop the marriage, to save Christine, but she believed Louis. Louis thought it would be a good match. The two most powerful houses together, joining their bloodlines and their wealth to establish a dynasty. He had such dreams and hopes."

"But Jeremiah didn't love Christine. He loved Louis. He treated her badly and swore at her in my presence. My own husband tried to stop the marriage, but to no avail. I knew nothing but disaster would come of it." She sat down again. Sitting up straight, her arms on the armrests, she looked like a beautiful queen, a tired old queen reflecting on her life on the last day of it. "Then the gossipers came. Jeremiah was burning through the money. He made poor investments, spent money on new slaves, the kind he liked, and God knows what else. He was a devil of a man.

"At that time, I went to Isaiah, Jeremiah's brother, and pleaded with him to intercede. I told him about the love his brother had for Louis. I told him Jeremiah would ruin us both, but he laughed in my face. He told me to stop interfering in my sister's marriage. If she wasn't complaining, who was I to do so? I almost believed him, but I went to Christine. She confessed to me her love for Hoyt Page. What could I do? Mother died, and there was no one left who could influence Louis to do what was right. Soon he began traveling to New Orleans, and for a time, I thought he fell in love. Unfortunately, she was a whore. Imagine how I greeted her when he brought her to our family home. I turned her out before she could put her feet up. How he hated me for that!"

She sighed sadly and straightened her dress. "After that, he had nothing for me. No more brotherly love. We were estranged. I stayed out of his business and tried my best to salvage whatever was left of the family fortune. Then your mother came here. She made things worse. She got pregnant with you and complicated things even more. Somewhere, she says, there is a codicil that names you as sole heir to Seven Sisters and the other Cottonwood properties. Without it, everything will go to Isaiah, Jeremiah's hateful brother. Now my sister is dead, my brother is dead, and I am left to clean this mess up! How cruel fate can be!"

She slammed her fists down on the table, causing the candles to flicker in their heavy brass holders. It was the most emotional thing I had seen her do.

"Fortunately, niece, my husband has a great amount of influence in the government of Alabama. One stroke of his pen, and he can make you legitimate. You will inherit Seven Sisters, as the late Mr. Cottonwood wished. You will have your own money, so you can live comfortably. And best of all, your mother will not be around to steal it from you. I plan on taking her back to north Alabama when I leave, provided you agree to my terms."

My mind swam at what she offered me. I would be legitimate—at least legally. I could be free from my mother's shadow and her ever-reaching hands. I knew there must be a catch.

"Why would you do this for me? I know there is a reason. Please do me the courtesy of telling me what that reason is, madam. I deserve to know the truth."

"You will allow my investigators to locate my missing property. If they are unable to do so, you will sell whatever lands and assets you possess to provide me with the return of the Beaumont money. Minus this house, of course. I would not dream of claiming your family home. And one last thing. You will testify against Miss Page and refuse to recognize her as your relative. Neither she nor her sister, if she should reappear later, will have any claim on this place or the Beaumont fortune."

I shot to my feet, boiling with anger. How dare she demand anything at all! Of all my so-called family, only Delilah had been kind to me. In fact, she loved me. That much I knew, even though I had not been as kind to her recently. I felt even more ashamed that I had not seen her or spoken to her in weeks. "You cannot demand such a thing. Why would I renounce the only family I have for your gain? You ask too much. I am nothing without loyalty."

Olivia rose to her feet, but her voice stayed calm and cool. "If you want my assistance, those are the terms. I have everything I need with me. We can visit the courthouse to see the judge whenever you like. Think what this could mean for you, girl. Think about yourself for a change. I will give you a day to think about it. If you refuse, then you will never see me again. And you will have no one to support you."

How was it that I could be denied love so frequently? Was I not worthy of love? I had not chosen to be born, and I had not chosen my parents. Yet, everyone rejected me again and again. Except Delilah. She alone had accepted me. Without her, I would have no family at all. I had not wanted this fortune, and I was not willing to pay the price that my mother and aunt apparently were. Such beauty. Such cold hearts.

"I am glad to hear that you are taking my mother with you. I have long since known that she needed the care of someone skilled at managing her. I do hope you know what you are undertaking. As far as this house goes, I have no attachment to it. I do not care if you burn it to the ground. And as for my cousin, I will not deny her, either privately or publicly. She is the only family I have, and I will not disown her, even if it means I will be penniless. I would like to say it was pleasant to meet you, but it hasn't been. Good day to you, Aunt Olivia. You promised me I would not see you again—it is a promise I hope you keep." I swung my skirts out from under the table and walked toward the door.

"Where are you going? Do you intend to walk back to the boarding house? How long do you think you will live on the change you have in that purse? I suppose you could earn a living on your back. Maybe that is a talent your mother can teach you."

I did not take her baiting. I walked into the foyer and out of the house. I could hear my mother screaming upstairs and feel my great-aunt's cold eyes burning at my back. I kept walking. If I had to walk all night, I would.

I would never go back. Not now. Not ever.

Chapter 6—Carrie Jo

I woke myself with a scream of pain. The contraction was so powerful that it took my breath away. I had no doubt I was in labor. I had no time to dwell on what I had dreamed. No time to consider Olivia's threats or Karah's emotions. I reached out and suddenly remembered that Ashland wasn't there. He had left early this morning to secure the Happy Go Lucky. Against all odds, Tropical Storm Jasmine was growing and heading our way. Catching my breath, I reached for my cell phone as I tried to sit up. Sweat beaded on my forehead, and I gasped for air. Thankfully the pain eased and the muscles relaxed. I looked at my alarm clock, remembering somehow that I needed to time these contractions.

"You can't come now, baby. You have a few more weeks before you make your appearance. Stay inside where it's safe." My child did not respond as he usually did. He lay quiet and still. And that bothered me. "Hey! I know you hear me. Let Momma know you're okay." Still nothing. Not a kick. Not a punch. He—or she—was as still as…

No, I'm not going there. The baby is fine. I am fine. Everything is going to be okay. Tears of panic welled up in my eyes. Everything *would* be okay, wouldn't it? Only one way to find out. I was going to the hospital. I dressed as quickly as I could in a voluminous summer dress. As I slid it over my head, the next contraction hit me.

"Agh!" I doubled over and managed to ease myself back on the bed. I looked at the clock. Five minutes. These were really far apart. I was in the early stages of labor. I gasped and focused on breathing. I swore at myself for not taking those Lamaze classes when I had the chance. Ashland wanted to go, but I thought it was dopey. I just wanted to get through it with as much dignity as I could and have a healthy baby. Breathing as calmly as I could—*that's what you're supposed to do, right?*—I waited for the pain to ease. When it finally let up, I slid my feet into my sandals and grabbed my overnight bag and purse. By the time I made it to the bottom of the stairs, nearly five minutes had passed. I sat in the foyer chair and waited for the next contraction. I grasped the corner of the table as the pain hit me again. It seemed stronger this time. Oh God! Should I call an ambulance? It would take me at least ten minutes to get to the hospital. There was no way I could drive. Knowing that Ashland probably wouldn't have a signal out on the water, I called Detra Ann.

"Hey, girl!"

Breathing heavily, I said, "Girl, I need you to take me to the hospital."

"Oh my God! Where are you? Is it the baby?"

"Baby, yes. Home. Please come now." My breathing came quick, and I forgot again how I was supposed to breathe.

"I'm on the way now! Henri! Bring me the keys, babe! It's CJ..." She hung up the phone, and I didn't call her back. I scribbled a note for Doreen and left it on the foyer table where I hoped she would find it. I panted through the pain and waited patiently for Detra Ann to show up. When I heard the car screech into the driveway, I opened the door and stood leaning against the doorframe.

"Oh my God! Help me, Henri." She said slowly and loudly, "It's go-ing to be all right, Carrie Jo!"

The pain eased up a bit, and I growled at her. "I'm not deaf, Detra Ann. I'm having a baby."

She didn't seem to mind my snappiness. "I'm calling Ashland now."

"He's going to tie up the boat. He doesn't have a signal out there."

"I'm try-ing any-way, o-kay?"

"Fine!" I said as I rolled into the front seat. "I told you I'm not deaf!"

"Your seat belt!" She reached for me, and I swatted her hand away.

"Oh my God, Detra Ann. If you put that seat belt on me, I'll kill you." She danced around me and climbed in the back, ignoring my crabbiness like the true friend she was.

Henri put on his flashers and drove us to the hospital in record time. "You're right. No answer."

I didn't respond. I stared at my watch and waited for the contraction. I could feel it building, and I knew it would be a strong one. I suddenly prayed I didn't pee on myself. I had to go, and I didn't want to pee in Henri's car.

"This sucks so bad!" I yelled as I clutched the dashboard. We pulled into the ER driveway of Springhill Memorial, and Detra Ann bounced out of the car and inside to get a wheelchair.

A nurse chased her, and together the two women managed to get me into the chair. Henri yelled at us, "I'm going to the marina to get Ashland. I'll be back soon."

"Okay, thanks!" I yelled at him like I was crazy.

"Breathe, Carrie Jo, breathe. It's all right. You are going to be all right. Oh my gosh, I'm going to be an aunt."

"This your sister?" the nurse asked as she pushed me through the double doors.

"Yep," I lied. I knew they wouldn't have let her stay with me if I'd said no. She was like a sister to me. That had to count for something.

For the next fifteen minutes a swarm of nurses worked around me, hooking me up to intimidating machines that supposedly monitored the contractions and my heart rate. The on-call doctor was coming to check my dilation. When she arrived, I cried, "It's too soon. The baby isn't supposed to be here yet. And he's not moving. What's wrong?"

"It's okay. Babies sometimes get still before they are born. If he's in the birth canal, there isn't much room for him to move around. Let's just check." The doctor moved her stethoscope over my stomach and listened intently. As she moved the cold round piece over my stomach, my panic grew. Shouldn't she have found him by now?

"Ah, there he is. He's fine. You want to hear him?" I nodded and accepted the stethoscope. Yes, I could hear his heart beating strong and evenly. I knew he was a boy. I had known it all along. I didn't know why I'd tried to deny it. I tried not to think about what that might mean.

"Let's take a look now. See how far you have to go."

Detra Ann stood at the head of the bed holding my purse and my hand. I looked at her, and she smiled down at me like a cheerleader-angel.

"Hmm…not that far along after all. Only dilated two centimeters."

"That's bad, isn't it? Is the baby going to be okay?"

The doctor smiled patiently. "Yes, he is fine. Early labor happens to many women. Your doctor is on the way. We'll consult, but if the due date is three weeks away, then he'll probably want to stop those contractions for a while." She looked at her watch and said, "If your doctor isn't here within the next half hour, I'll write the order myself. Either way, you'll have to stay overnight so we can keep an eye on you and the baby. We don't need the baby to come today. He needs to wait a bit longer, if possible. Would you like something to help with the pain?"

"No, I think I'm okay for now. I'll wait."

"Okay. I'll be back soon. Hopefully with the orders for that drip. It will stop the contractions. Let the nurse know if you need anything."

She smiled at me and rearranged my blanket before leaving us alone.

Detra Ann put our bags on the nearby table and sat beside me. "Don't worry, CJ. It's going to be fine. You heard the doctor. This happens sometimes. I have seen it in my own family. My cousin Lanie came to the hospital four times before she actually had the baby. She just about wore us out."

"I don't mean to be an inconvenience to anyone."

"That's not what I meant. I hope you know that."

"I'm sorry to be such a jerk. I want the baby to stay where he is because I know he'll be safe in there. What happens when he comes out? What about this curse? I can't stop thinking about it."

"Well, you need to. That baby needs you to think happy thoughts. All right? I mean, think about this in the light of day. Are curses even real? What if it's all just a big coincidence and you're worried over nothing? Lots of people die young. It's not a reason to believe in curses. I think you should tell Ashland and let him worry about it."

"But you were the one who said we shouldn't tell him," I said, frowning at her as I prepared for the next contraction.

"Well, I know, but I changed my mind. If it's going to make you go into labor and make you sick, then you need to tell him."

"Carrie Jo?" I heard a voice call from the doorway.

"Yes?" I answered and froze. It was my mother. "Momma?"

"Yes, it's me. Your housekeeper told me where to find you. I hope it's okay that I came."

It wasn't, but I didn't want to argue with her. I was so shocked at seeing her that I didn't bother to introduce her. She wore a neat dress that came past her knees. To my surprise, it didn't have long sleeves and it wasn't black. It was cobalt blue and completely out of style; she probably bought it at one of her favorite secondhand stores. The dress had a conservative neckline and three-quarter sleeves. She wore cheap shoes and carried an even cheaper black purse. Deidre Jardine had once been a pretty woman; today she wore light pink lipstick and a bit of mascara, which made her look prettier than usual. How long had it been since I had seen her wear makeup? I thought it was against her religion. She had gotten ultra-religious about seven years ago and given up worldly things like makeup and jewelry. I was surprised to see she wore gold stud earrings, like the kind girls wore when they first got their ears pierced.

Before I could say anything else, a wave of pain hit me. I closed my eyes and focused on making it through the agonizing half minute. The machine beside me sputtered out paper and beeped. A nurse appeared and studied the paper. "That's a good one. If you decide you need pain medicine, just yell."

"Breathe, baby," my mother coached me patiently.

"Mom is here too? That's great. Between your sister and your mother, you will do just fine." Thankfully Deidre didn't make a fuss, but when I opened my eyes I could see her looking at Detra Ann questioningly. My friend shrugged and didn't say anything.

"What are you doing here, Momma?"

"Didn't you get my letter, Carrie Jo?"

"Yes, but I haven't had a chance to read it yet. I've been a bit busy."

"I see," she said sadly. "It's not important. What can I do for you?"

"You can tell me why you're here, Deidre." I said curtly. Detra Ann's eyes widened, but she kept her mouth shut.

"I wanted...I didn't know you were having a baby. Your housekeeper told me you were going to the hospital. I didn't mean to interfere. I'll go now." She sounded on the verge of tears. She picked up her purse and headed out the door.

As she disappeared, Detra Ann scowled at me. "I had no idea you could be so mean, CJ. I know y'all are estranged, but she is that baby's grandmother."

"You don't understand," I said woodenly, offering no further explanation.

"You're right, I don't. I'll be right back." She stomped out of the room after my mother and left me alone. I instantly felt guilty. Of course she was right, but she didn't know what I'd been through with Deidre. The humiliating childhood. The horrible teenage years when I couldn't keep friends. Coming home from school to find a circle of strangers praying over your bedroom, touching your things, rebuking the devil. She had done that. Not me. If Detra Ann wanted to be mad at me, so be it.

I lay in the bed, tears sliding down my face, when another contraction came. My phone rang in my purse, but I couldn't reach it. Feeling desperation rise within me, I said a prayer. "It's me, God. I know we don't talk as much as we should, and that's totally my fault, but I need your help. Please protect

Ashland and our baby. Help me know what to do because I haven't got a clue."

Just then, Detra Ann came back in. My phone rang again, and she dug it out for me. Without waiting for permission she answered. "Hey, Ash. Sure, she's right here. Everything is fine."

She handed me the phone, and I took it with shaking hands. The contraction was passing, and I felt like myself again. "Hey, babe."

"You okay? I'll be on the way soon. Henri found me."

"Sorry to mess up your day."

"Stop that. You just hold on, okay. I promise you it's going to be all right. You just do what the doctor says and listen to Detra Ann. We'll be together soon, the three of us."

"All right." The tears sprang up again, against my wishes.

"Hey, hey," he said in a low and comforting voice, "don't cry. You can do this. I promise you I'll be there soon."

"I can do this," I repeated obediently. "Be careful."

"Will do. Talk to you soon. Let me speak to Detra Ann."

"All right." I handed the phone back to her. A nurse hustled in the room and reviewed the paper. She let me know my doctor was coming down the hall now. Detra Ann smoothed my hair and kissed my forehead after she hung up the phone.

"That's from Ashland. And me. You know I love you, CJ."

"I love you too." I leaned forward and fell into her arms. We hugged until the next contraction came.

"Is she still here?" We both knew who I meant.

"Yep. She's in the waiting room, crocheting and praying."

"That's good. For once in my life, I'm glad to hear that. I can use all the prayers I can get."

Chapter 7—Ashland

Everything went wrong that morning. I fell off the boat for the first time ever. The engine didn't want to start, and when I finally thought I would be able to get her going, Henri came running down the pier. I knew right away it was about CJ, and that made the weight of the day feel even heavier.

"Baby is coming, Ashland. She's at the hospital."

"He's not supposed to be here yet." I couldn't help but worry. This wasn't normal, was it?

"Somebody better tell that to the baby because he's absolutely determined to arrive. You want to ride with me?"

"No, I better take mine."

"You sure?" he asked, studying my face.

"No, I'm not sure."

"Get in. I'm driving. You look like you need a minute to think."

"Yeah, probably so." I left the boat where she was, climbed into his Dodge Charger and put on my seat belt. We didn't say much as we drove out of the marina parking lot, but I was glad for his company. I sensed he wanted to say something, but he didn't. I wasn't one to push someone to talk. It was a trait that drove my wife batty.

The dark clouds gathered above us and seemed to increase as we drove. "I can't remember when I saw the sun last. Weather seems weird lately."

"Yeah. You can't ever tell about the weather down here."

"What's going on, Henri? Is it the baby? I can tell there's something you aren't telling me. Don't hold back now. I want to know what's happening. Is Carrie Jo sick or something?"

"As far as I know, the baby is fine. Carrie Jo is fine too. I swear." He was trying to play it cool, but I knew he was holding back. I started to ask him again, but something caught my eye. It was a lone figure standing at the edge of the road. For a millisecond I thought he was alive, but as we approached him I saw that I was wrong. He was a ghost, and if he didn't move, we would drive right through him. His black suit was covered with dust, and it looked like something from the early 1900s. His hair had a dingy white tinge, but his skin was even whiter. Then he jumped into the road as we drove through him, and instinctively I gasped and tried to move out of the way like a wild man. His face lingered in front of mine for a long, agonizing moment, and he grinned at me. His dry, dead lips pulled back from his yellowed teeth. I screamed as he passed through my body, and Henri screamed too. The soul-sucking phantom pulled all the warmth out of me.

Henri slammed on the brakes. "What the hell was that about?" he demanded. "You seeing things?"

"Hell yes!" I said, trying to calm my breathing. I wiped my face furiously with my hands as if I could wipe away the ghostly residue from my soul. "I guess you didn't?"

"No, but I felt something. Coldness. Gone now. It is gone, right?" He glanced over his shoulder into the backseat, and I followed his lead. Nothing there. Thank God.

"Yes, it's gone."

"Anyone we know?"

"Nobody I have ever seen. And I hope I never see him again." I kept my eyes glued to the road ahead and tried not to look around me. So that's why I had been out of sorts this morning. The spirits were back. "I don't think I'll ever get used to this. I thought by talking about it and, you know, embracing it and all that jazz, it would get better. But it hasn't."

"What do you mean?"

I didn't have time for this right now. I had to get to my wife. Why did I even bring it up?

Henri glanced at me and said, "What's up?"

"It's been months since it happened last, so I thought it went away. I've seen things at a distance, but that just now was right in my face. It's like he was taunting me. Laughing at me. Something isn't right."

Henri's jaw clenched, and I could see him struggling with something. We were just ten minutes from the hospital now. "For the love of God, tell me what you know, Henri."

"The girls didn't want to tell you, but there is a rumor…no, that's not it. There is some concern that you might be cursed."

"What?" I said, laughing.

"Carrie Jo wanted to surprise you with a family tree print. You know the swanky kind you hang in a picture frame? During the research, Rachel noticed something strange about the date of expiration for some of your relatives."

"Date of expiration? Rachel is involved with this?"

"I don't know what else you would call it."

"Sorry, go on. You were saying?"

"The bottom line is the men in your family never live past forty. CJ wants to make sure that doesn't happen to you or your son."

"My son," I said, enjoying hearing that. Carrie Jo had been so insistent that we would have a girl. I always knew that was wrong. Even Lenore knew. I wished she were here now to tell me if I was going crazy or not. "Cursed? How can a whole family be cursed? Is that even a legit concern, or is my wife finding things to worry about?"

"I saw the genealogy, and she's not exaggerating. It is a real phenomenon. Your family never talked about this?"

"Not to me. My dad died when I was a kid, and my Uncle Robert…damn. He died too. Both before they were forty. Great. Does that mean at age forty I'm going to keel over?"

Henri said nothing but kept his eyes on the road. Finally, he said, "Stop holding out. Tell me the truth."

"Most of them died right after they turned thirty. Very few made it to forty."

The car hit a pothole and made a crunching noise. It seemed appropriate. Here we were talking about curses, and Henri's car was tearing up.

"So what's the cure?" I asked. "I mean, how do I get rid of this bad mojo or whatever it is? I can't deny I've been in a kind of funk lately, but I chalked it up to being a new dad. Sometimes crap just happens, and up until now it seemed I had no problem with luck. Now I guess that's all changed?"

"It has to have something to do with your gift. Curses are supernatural, and you have a supernatural ability. Where did you get your gift from? Do you know where it started? Did your mother see ghosts? Your father? Anyone give you clues about where this supernatural stuff came from? Maybe if we knew the answers we could trace the curse."

"Not really. My mother talked to the air all the time, but I didn't chalk it up to ghosts. I thought she was just pretending, playacting. I was a kid, so that kind of stuff didn't bother me. Later, though, she really pursued the supernatural, always dragging me to séances and whatnot. I couldn't tell you about my father. He didn't really share things with me."

"Too bad we can't ask your mother."

"Yeah, I know she'd love being a grandmother. She loved children."

There was an awkward silence as we zipped through a yellow light on Government Street. "We could ask her. If you'd be willing."

I bit my fingernail. I had my elbow on the window ledge. It made me feel ready to act if I needed to. Why did I think I could run from a ghost? Hopefully we wouldn't drive through any more of those.

"What are you talking about?"

"A séance would do the trick. I'm sure we could contact her."

I ran my hands through my hair. "I can't even begin to tell you how opposed I am to that idea."

"I figured you would be. CJ mentioned it, but considering what you're up against.... I'm only trying to help."

"I know it, but there has to be another way."

"You're probably right." Henri banked the vehicle to the right. We were close now, just a mile away. I was so anxious to get there I unbuckled my seat belt in anticipation.

"You'll be a great father."

I couldn't help but smile. "You think so?"

"I know so. Here we are. I'll drop you and then follow you up. Don't wait for me."

"Don't worry, I won't," I said with a smile as I practically jumped out of the car. As soon as the smoky glass door slid open, I knew I was in trouble. There in the lobby were two ghosts, and both of them knew I could see them. "Oh great," I muttered to myself.

"Can I help you?" an older lady with a nametag that read 'Dot' asked me. She must have thought I was talking to her.

"No, ma'am. I know where I'm going." I didn't tell her that an old man and a young boy were standing behind her. Why creep her out like that? The two ghosts weren't frightening like the roadside apparition had been. They whispered to one another, and the younger one pointed to me. The boy's hand passed by Dot's ear as he nudged the man. Dot patted her hair-sprayed hair as if she could feel it. Without much more notice to me or her hair, she answered the phone in a bright, cheerful voice, "Springhill Memorial Hospital. How may I direct your call?"

I sailed past her and caught the elevator. The baby floor, as it was affectionately known around here, was the fifth floor. I stood in the elevator with four other people and a ghost. He had a slack jaw, and the remnants of yellow hair circled his large head. Suddenly as if a magnet drew him, he moved closer to me. He stared at me with his empty gray eyes. "You know, don't you? You know where she is. Tell me," he pleaded with me. I tried not to fly across the elevator and scare the other passengers. As soon as the door opened I jumped ahead of the ladies who stood closest to it. "Tell me!" the ghoul screamed after me. I had gotten off on the wrong floor. Two more levels to go now. I flew past a crowd of people; I wasn't sure if they were dead or alive, and thankfully none of them followed me into the stairwell. By the time I made it to the fifth floor, I was so panicked I had to stop and catch my breath. I heard a sound behind me. Peering down the railing above me was another specter, a ghostly janitor with bloodless skin. His phantom mop plunked to the ground, and he eased down the steps toward me.

"Oh God, oh Jesus!" I prayed loudly. To my relief the words seemed to repel him enough to give me time to slip out the door. I pushed open the door from the stairwell and stepped onto the fifth floor. The atmosphere was very different here. Instead of lingering spirits and angry black clouds, there was an abundance of light and a thick, peaceful feeling. I breathed a sigh of relief as I walked to the nurses' station.

A young nurse with a dazzling white smile greeted me. I said, "I'm here to see my wife, Carrie Jo Stuart."

"Yes, Mr. Stuart. Follow me." She stood to show me the way. She wore yellow scrubs with tiny rainbows all over them. Very cheerful.

"No need to bother yourself. Just point me in the right direction."

She smiled and waved to the left. "She's that way. Room 542."

I glanced down the hall, making sure I had the right direction, and then turned back to her to say thanks. "Thank you..." The nurse was gone. She'd vanished in just a second.

Another woman walked up. "May I help you?"

"No, I know the way."

All I could think of was getting to my wife and son. I needed this day to be over soon. I couldn't take much more. The window at the end of the hallway suddenly clouded. The sunshine departed. Storm clouds were rolling in.

Somehow, it seemed appropriate.

Chapter 8—Ashland

Detra Ann hugged me and, as she typically did, fussed over me and brought me endless cups of coffee. Carrie Jo looked beautiful, but I didn't bother telling her so. She wouldn't believe me, and it didn't seem like the most sensitive thing to say during this painful and stressful process. Thankfully her doctor finally ordered the medicine that would stop the contractions. Carrie Jo had been in pain for several hours. She didn't complain, but I hated seeing the woman I loved suffer. The drip took effect quickly, and her contractions weakened. I breathed a sigh of relief knowing that Baby Boy would be indoors a little longer.

Baby Boy. Funny name, but I liked it. If my wife and I couldn't settle on a mutually approved baby name, I'd be forced to call him that. Now that his arrival was closer, I wondered how important names were anyway. I kissed CJ's hand and didn't say too much. I let the nurses do their work and tried to keep out of the way. I kept my eyes trained on my wife and not the creatures that occasionally sailed past the door or popped in to stare at me.

Seeing ghosts wasn't like the movies. Not at all. The spirits weren't trying to communicate with me or convince me to help them. Not in any kind of coherent way. Most of the ghosts I saw were a little eccentric—a bit mad, really. It was more like they sensed I was different, and that difference drove them even crazier. I got the sense that when you died, if you didn't pass on to wherever you were supposed to, you were left to amble about the spirit world trapped in your own nightmare. It wasn't a fate I wished on anyone. Especially someone I loved.

I used to believe that like Carrie Jo, I would get better at my "gift" or whatever you wanted to call it. But it hadn't happened for me, no matter how many books I read or how much I practiced. The appearance of a ghost scared the hell out of me every single time. Regardless of how much I prepared to see one, they always caught me by surprise. I prayed constantly, more so than I ever had before, but so far my prayers appeared to be unanswered. At least I had my friends, and until this latest session of ghost-seeing passed, I would keep them close. The more living beings around me the better.

Here we were all crowded in the room together now. The living collective appeared to repel the majority of the ghosts. Of the six of us, CJ and me plus Rachel, Chip, Detra Ann and Henri, only Henri and I knew what was happening. He looked at me encouragingly but like a true friend kept his mouth shut. One nurse complained about the number of people visiting, but I assured her it was okay. I was pretty sure I hadn't heard the end of her unhappiness, but let her try and run them out.

Suddenly everyone got quiet again. The machine bleeped to life as Carrie Jo squeezed my hand and sweated through another contraction. "I'm good, babe. Promise. I'm good," she whispered as she turned in the bed trying to find a comfortable spot. Miss Henrietta, the name I gave the unhappy nurse, came back in a deeper frown on her face.

"Okay, everyone. I have to insist you step out. The doctor is coming to check Mrs. Stuart again. If she hasn't dilated any more, he'll probably send her home. Clear the room," she said with a wave of her hand.

CJ frowned at her. "It's not like I haven't been trying," she sassed back at her. "Go ahead, babe. I'll be fine."

I kissed her forehead and walked out with a growing feeling of dread. Henri stayed close. "I've got your six, Ashland," he whispered as we stepped outside.

"Detra Ann, is she going to be okay? What's going on?" A petite brunette stood between us and the waiting room. Her dress hung off her small shoulders, and her lips quivered nervously.

"Oh yes, she's fine, Mrs. Jardine. I don't believe you have met Carrie Jo's husband yet. This is Ashland Stuart."

If she'd told me the woman was the pope, I wouldn't have been more surprised. I extended my hand to her and studied her face. Now that I knew she was CJ's mother, I could see the resemblance. "I didn't know you were here. I'm sorry. I would have come to speak to you sooner had I known."

"I'm sure it's not something my daughter would want everyone to know. We haven't been on the best terms, but I do care about her," she offered as a kind of apology. Her bright hazel eyes glossed with tears, but I was suspicious. I knew what Carrie Jo had been through with this woman. The nervous lady before me hardly appeared threatening, but looks were almost always deceiving.

"Her doctor is with her right now. Maybe when he completes his exam you can see her. If she's up to it," I said carefully.

"I saw her earlier, but only for a few minutes. I'll see her when she's ready. As long as she's okay. I had no idea she was having a baby."

As she spoke, a young spirit sailed past, holding a bundle of blankets in her arms. I tried not to stare at the ghost, but she stared at me, her pale face too close to mine. Mrs. Jardine turned around to investigate. I couldn't be sure, but as she faced me again I thought I saw her eyes widen a bit. Could she see the girl too? The spirit paused to listen to our conversation, but when no one acknowledged her she began to fade away. That was something else I had learned about the spirit world. The more attention you gave the creatures, the stronger they became. In some cases simply ignoring them was enough to send them back to wherever they came from.

I shivered involuntarily, and Henri touched my shoulder. "You need anything?" he asked.

"Coffee?" Detra Ann offered me.

"Please, no more coffee. I'll be up for the next two days if I drink another cup," I said as she frowned at me.

"Mr. Stuart, the doctor would like to talk to you." The crotchety nurse waved me back to CJ's room, and I excused myself from the gathering. Chip and Rachel crowded around Mrs. Jardine and asked her about her stay in Mobile. I was glad to see it. I didn't have a bad feeling about her, regardless of her history with Carrie Jo.

"Mr. Stuart, nice to see you."

"Dr. Gary. Good to see you too. Are we having a baby tonight?"

"I was just telling your wife that she's made some progress. She's dilated to four centimeters now, but I'd like to wait if the baby will allow it. She isn't due for a few more weeks, and that time is crucial for good lung development. I know you're miserable, dear," the older man said to Carrie Jo as he squeezed her hand, "but if you two can hold out a little longer, it will be better for both of you." He turned to me and continued, "Mrs. Stuart appears to be responding well to the medications; the contractions have diminished, and that's a good sign. I'd like to keep her overnight, just to watch her. If all goes well, I'll send her home in the morning, and then we'll see what Junior decides to do." Relieved, I hugged the doctor. He good-naturedly patted my back. "I know it's a nerve-racking process for both of you, but I assure you that you will get through it and everyone will be fine. The baby's heartbeat is strong and steady. Mother's health is good too. I see nothing to worry about."

"Thanks, doc. That is good news."

"I'll see you two in the morning."

"Thank you, Dr. Gary," CJ called as he walked out the door. "Sorry, babe. Didn't mean to make you worry about me," she said with a small smile.

I kissed her forehead again and sat in the chair beside her. "You had nothing to do with it. You heard the doctor. It's up to Baby Boy, not you."

She wrinkled her nose at me. "That's the name you want?"

"Well, no. It's just a nickname I came up with."

"You're convinced he'll be a he, aren't you?"

I couldn't help but grin. This moment was the happiest I had been all day. I nodded and confessed, "From day one."

"All right, so what names do you have in mind?"

"Really?"

"Yep, whatcha got?"

I squeezed her hand and said, "I was thinking Richard or James."

"Aren't those Bible names?"

I laughed aloud. "I don't think there were any Richards in the Bible."

She laughed too and wiped tears from her eyes. "We're going to be okay, right? No matter what?"

"No matter what. Yes, we will be fine."

I held her until we heard a knock on the door. It was Carrie Jo's mother. "Hi. I just wanted to say goodbye before I go back to the hotel. It's getting dark, and I don't really know my way around here. I'll be praying for you, Carrie Jo."

CJ looked at me, and I smiled at her as if to say, *It's okay. I'm right here.*

"Stay for a minute, Momma." That delighted the older woman to no end, and she dropped her purse in the chair and walked to the bedside. As she and CJ talked, Henri and Detra Ann stepped in the room to watch us. Detra Ann waved me over, and we walked outside for a minute.

"Listen, I know they have a rough history, but her mother is telling the truth. She didn't know CJ was pregnant, and she really does care about what happens to her. Let Carrie Jo know, okay?"

"Yeah, I will."

"Henri told you, didn't he?"

"I knew anyway. I just didn't know what to call it."

"So you think you're cursed?"

"Who's cursed?" Mrs. Jardine asked, standing a few feet away.

Detra Ann piped up, "It's just a figure of speech. Ashland's had some bad luck lately is all."

Without waiting for an invitation, Carrie Jo's mother grabbed my hand and began to pray, "Dear God, break this curse on this young man's life. No weapon formed against him will prosper, just as your Word says. Keep him safe as he fights the good fight. Amen."

Surprised by the impromptu prayer, I murmured "Amen" and thanked her.

"No need to thank me. I can't have my only son-in-law cursed. I'll keep praying. That's something I know how to do." She smiled brightly, and I had to admit, I did feel better. My space wasn't ghost-free, but the spirits had diminished a bit and none were in my face. Always a plus. "Your friend said he'd take me home. I'll come back in the morning, if that's okay."

"Sure. Carrie Jo is supposed to go home in the morning, but I'm not sure what time. Are you sure you're comfortable at the hotel? Which one are you staying at?"

"Don't worry about me. I am very comfortable in my room. You be with your wife."

"Hey!" Detra Ann said. "I'll ride too. Here comes Henri now. See you in the morning, Ash." She kissed my cheek, and I could feel her glossy lipstick on my skin. I waved goodbye and hurried back to CJ's room.

She'd snuggled up in the blankets and had her eyes closed. She stirred and made sure I was there, then went back to sleep. A few hours later I hunkered down in the chair and thought about the simple prayer that Deidre had said over me. It comforted me, and soon I fell asleep.

Chapter 9—Carrie Jo

Before nine o'clock, Ashland and I were headed home. I'd made it through the night with no other contractions, and we both breathed a sigh of relief. I think everyone thought I would be disappointed that the baby's arrival had been delayed, but I wasn't. Not at all. As long as Baby Boy stayed close to me, I knew I could protect him. *Oh no! Did I just call him Baby Boy?* I smiled at Ashland and shook my head.

"What?" he asked innocently.

"You. You've got me calling our son Baby Boy."

"You're okay with a son, then?"

I leaned back against the seat and smiled even bigger. "Yep, I'm okay with it. I don't know why I was so dead set against having a boy." We pulled into the driveway and weren't a bit surprised to see cars already there. Doreen's old truck was on the street, and of course Rachel's and Detra Ann's vehicles were in the driveway.

"I know why. And I know what you think."

Suddenly all the brightness of the day seemed to vanish. One of my well-meaning friends must have told Ashland what we discovered, and now he was going to say it—the word I didn't dare say.

"I know about the curse, Carrie Jo."

There. He said it. Now it was real.

For all three of us.

I couldn't meet his eyes, so I stared at the yard. It was so sad-looking, with dead flowers and moldy sidewalks. How did they get moldy? We had the place power-washed just two months ago. It sure as heck didn't look like it.

"Now what, babe? How do we break it?"

"*We* can't break it, Carrie Jo, but you can help *me* figure it out. This is my deal. And I want you to promise me something."

"What's that?" I asked suspiciously.

"I don't want you to do anything that will put you or our son in danger. Our son...yeah, I like that." He squeezed my hand. "I couldn't stand it if I knew you two were in danger. I mean it, CJ. Nothing. No visiting the house. No stirring up spirits. You let me do this. Okay?"

I bit my lip and searched his face for any kind of softness. There was none to be found. He was dead serious about this. "If you won't promise for me, do it for Baby Boy."

My hands rubbed my stomach as our son adjusted his foot, shoving it deeper into my ribs as if to say, "Yeah, I agree with Dad."

"Okay, I promise not to do any of those things."

It was his turn to be suspicious. "And don't do anything else I haven't thought of yet, okay?"

"Scout's honor." I held up two fingers. "Now let's go in the house before the bottom falls out. It looks pitch black out here. The weather is so unpredictable."

"This has got to be from Hurricane Jasmine—the storm is on the way, but it's only a Cat 1. We'll be okay." He chuckled at Rachel waving from the front door. "Looks like we're home base this time around. I guess that's fair since we camped out with Henri for the last tropical storm. Do I need to send everyone home?"

"No, I like having our friends around. This storm will be like the last one, I'm sure. It will fizzle out before it gets here."

"Looks like we have an extra guest."

I could see my mother's petite figure through the big bay window. How did I miss her? I sighed and nodded. Ash didn't need me losing it right now, and so far Momma had behaved. I promised myself I would get to the bottom of her appearance here right away, though. I couldn't have my baby around someone so judgmental, so unpredictable.

Stop being so negative, Carrie Jo. What if she's changed?

I had given her chances before. I loved her, no doubt about it, but it was easier not dealing with her. Not talking to her. Not hoping things would change. Yeah, that was way easier than seeing her, daydreaming about a "normal" relationship. Here we were, dealing with a curse, and she showed up out of the blue. What was up with that? She did seem different, but maybe that was also a ploy. The old Deidre Jardine would have recited at least five Bible verses at me by now. I wondered what she was up to. I hoped and prayed this wasn't about money.

Doreen came barreling out the door. "Here she is! Mrs. Stuart! I am so glad to see you. You had me worried! No baby yet, huh? No worries. He will come in his own good time. I stocked your pantry for the storm, but I didn't know all these people would be here. Do I need to make another trip to the store?"

I smiled at her and followed her into the kitchen. "Hey, everyone!" I waved to the rest of the group camped around the widescreen television in the living room. "No, Doreen. This is fine. You didn't even need to do that. If we need something else, I'm sure one of these guys will go. I hope you made me some fruit salad. I'm starving."

"Of course. Right on the top shelf. Just for you."

"You go home and be with Stephan. Are you staying in Mobile?"

"Oh no. I never stay for these storms, and I wish you would go too. We go to Stephan's mother's house in Evergreen. No storms there." I smiled at her and insisted that she go home. The skies were darkening, and according to the local weather reports that blared from the next room, Hurricane Jasmine would be bearing down on us in the next few hours. I didn't know what it was about hurricanes that made my friends want to gather around a television. But I imagined that was the way it would be for the next few days. I was glad. I wanted them close to me right now. And close to Ashland.

"I am sorry about your puppy, Mrs. Stuart. He was a sweet dog."

"Thanks, Doreen. Me too. You go to Stephan now. I'm fine. We'll see you when this is over."

With a nervous wave, she grabbed her purse and left out the kitchen door.

Doreen's powder blue Ford backed out of the driveway, and I waved at her as she pulled into the frantic street. Pretty busy out there. Hm…maybe I did need to pay attention. It was dark enough for the streetlights to come on already. Yep, this was going to be a doozy of a storm.

"Hey, babe. I have to go to the boat. I never did get her secured, and I'd hate to lose her. We've had some happy memories there."

"Ashland…shh…" I said, giggling and kissing him. We had long speculated that we'd conceived during an overnight trip on the Happy Go Lucky.

"Relax. No one can hear me." He kissed me back. "Henri's going with me. Won't be gone but about an hour."

"Sure, but hurry back. No hanging out on the boat."

"In this weather? No way, crazy lady." He laughed and shook his head. "Be back in a bit."

"Better be," I said, kissing him square on the lips before smacking his behind playfully.

"Be kind to your mother," he said to me before he walked out the door. For a second I thought I heard Chunky Boy whine after him as he always did. Chunky Boy and Baby Boy. What a pair they would have made! I sniffled and felt someone beside me.

"You want a cup of tea?" That someone was my mother.

"Yes, but could you make sure it's herbal? Caffeinated drinks make the baby very active."

"Good idea. I was hoping we could talk. Your friends went upstairs to put your shower gifts away. Looks like you were really blessed with all those gifts."

I followed behind her. My back felt sore, but I reasoned it was from the hospital bed. That had been one long night and one stiff mattress. "I have to ask, Momma. Please don't take this the wrong way, but why are you here? I haven't heard from you in over two years. Now you're here?"

She put the lid on the teapot and set it on the stove. "Cut to the chase, hmm? Sometimes you remind me of your Aunt Maggie so much."

"I don't want to talk about Aunt Maggie, Momma. I want to talk about you. And me. It can't be like it used to be. I won't let it be. That's not what I want for my child."

She nodded and looked me square in the eye. She didn't argue or get defensive. "Okay, cards on the table." She sat across from me at the small, round breakfast table. "About a year ago, I had what they called a cardiac event." I waited to hear what else she would tell me. I would hold my sympathy until after I heard the rest of the story. Not that she would lie about such a thing. Deidre Jardine was many things but not a liar. "I am fine now. They put two stents in me, but I can do everything I used to do."

"Sorry to hear that. Does heart disease run in our family?" I wasn't asking for me. What about the baby?

"Not that I am aware of. I know it's a bit of a shock seeing me after so long, but I've come to realize something." Just then the teapot screamed and Deidre got up to pour our cups. I didn't hurry her, but I was dying to hear what she had to say.

Setting the cup in front of me, she stirred in a cube of sugar and put her spoon down. "I don't blame you for not trusting me. For wanting to keep me away. I needed help, Carrie Jo, and I didn't know how to ask for it."

"What kind of help, Momma?"

She laughed nervously. "I'm still not sure. But I have made peace with the Big Man Upstairs. That happened when I thought I was going to die. You know how you hear that your life plays before your eyes when you are dying?" I nodded, unable to sip my tea or even move. I couldn't distract her now, just when she was about to tell me something significant. I could feel it rising, like the crest of a wave. "Well, that's not what happened to me. I didn't see my life—I saw yours."

"Really?"

"Yes. And I had no idea. It was like I could feel what you felt, see what you saw. I realized that while I thought I was protecting you, loving you, saving you, Carrie Jo, I was terrorizing you instead. Every incident. The time I came to the classroom to get you after Ginny's stepfather...I walked through that whole thing as you." When she met my eyes, the hazel color appeared a bit green now. I had forgotten they changed color like that. "You needed someone to protect you from me. I hurt you. In my desire to shield you, I did the thing I dreaded. Please believe me, protecting you was really all I wanted to do."

"Protecting me from what?"

"From who I was. And who I was afraid you'd become."

"I don't know what you mean." The baby moved around, and I rubbed my stomach to still him. "Tell me what you mean."

"Where do you think you got your dream walking from?"

"Dream walking?"

"Yes, that's what my mother used to call it."

"Used to call what?" I asked incredulously.

"Going back in time and sometimes forward, through dreams."

I heard a puppy whine somewhere. Must have been the neighbor's dog. A vehicle with a screaming siren whizzed past my home and down the bumpy street. I held my breath as she whispered the truth at last.

"You, my daughter, come from a long line of dream walkers."

Chapter 10—Ashland

"Ash, you have to call me back. Like ASAP!" Libby's voicemail sounded urgent, as if someone's life hung in the balance. As Henri navigated the traffic, I dialed her office number. I had enough stress in my life right now without Libby losing her mind on me. She wasn't the one being sued. By multiple people.

Without saying "Hello" or "How's your wife?" she immediately began throwing a tantrum. "It's like I said! Someone opened the floodgates. It's open season on Ashland Stuart. What the hell did you do? Post your net worth on a forum? We have another lineage claim! Myron and Alice Reed, whoever the hell they are! And just to make it worse, plaintiffs Rhodes and Hines have teamed up and are asking for nothing less than half—of everything!"

"Hello to you too, Libby. In case you haven't noticed, we are in the middle of a hurricane right now. Can't this wait? I can't imagine the wheels of justice moving so quickly that I need to head to the courthouse right this minute. That has never been the case."

"Screw the hurricane! Aren't you listening? You are in major trouble, Ashland." She was talking too loud in my ear; I held the phone away from my head and seriously considered throwing it out the window into the gray, choppy waters of the Mobile Bay. I should never have hired Libby. Once again I let my loyalties to friends and family get me into trouble. And my track record with lawyers wasn't the greatest. Henri shook his head in surprise at Libby's tone but kept his eyes on the dangerous roads.

I put the phone back to my ear. "Okay, reality check, Libby. You work for me, remember? Bring your voice down and breathe between sentences. I don't need this right now, so say what you need to say and be done with it. Now what happened?"

"I got a phone call about a half hour ago from a clerk in Judge Carmichael's office."

My phone beeped, and I glanced at it quickly. It was Rachel. Probably wanting me to pick up something for Carrie Jo, like those chicken-flavored crackers she snacked on constantly. I'd have to call her back after I handled this situation. "And?"

"It's true. All of it. Those jerks down at Rodney and Waite came up with this idea—no doubt about it. It's bad, Ash. Whoever drew up your mother's will left a lot of loopholes for crazies to jump through. Unbelievable! The only thing you can do now is settle with these people, and quickly. Then we can make the changes to the original document official and stop the bleeding. I think you need to start thinking of a number you can live with, and let's get them to the table. It's the only way you'll be able to walk away with at least the shirt on your back."

My blood boiled as I listened to the not-so-surprising news. Who in the world sues someone just because they share some DNA? Now the Reeds too? This was unreal. "What? Listen, I'm not prepared to talk about this today."

There was suddenly a deafening silence. "This isn't like you, Ashland. How can you be so blasé about being sued? Don't you understand what I'm saying? Come see me now, and we can get the prelim stuff squared away. I'm sure Carrie Jo would understand. How can I help you if you won't let me?"

"I'll come to your office Monday, after this storm blows through. My wife comes first, Libby. In case you weren't paying attention, we are about to have a baby."

"Well, I *know*," she said with an extra edge of snark to her voice. "I was at your shower, remember? But I would think you'd want to protect your child from all these lawsuits. And I doubt this storm is anything to worry about. It's down to Category 1 status now. Just come by. I've got lunch."

"Goodbye, Libby."

I hung up the phone, shaking my head, turned on the radio and stared at the rising water. We had time to make our trip to the Fairhope Pier and back, but beyond that would be sketchy.

High winds are expected. Hurricane Jasmine has produced gusts up to eighty miles per hour, and she's just getting started. Let's go to Meg, who has an update on this surprisingly powerful storm…

"When it rains, it pours, huh?" Right on cue, fat raindrops slapped the windshield and soon covered the car in sheets of water.

"Literally. If there was any doubt about it before, there isn't now. I've definitely stepped in a streak of bad luck. Are you sure you want to be riding in a car with me?" It was a joke, albeit a bad one, but Henri didn't laugh.

"Stop making that your confession, Ashland. You'll only make a curse stronger by agreeing with it."

"Yeah, whatever." I paid no attention to the spirit that stood in the waters off the causeway. We were driving too fast for him to reach us. At least, I hoped.

"Curses aren't bad luck. Bad luck happens to everyone. That's not the same thing as a curse."

"I'm listening."

"Curses that affect generations of people have to have some weight behind them. You can't just speak a few negative words about someone and hope it hurts them. For a true curse to work and affect a family for generations, there had to have been some major wrong done to someone. Its source must be a great injustice. A wrong that needs to be made right."

"I get that, and I believe it, but how am I supposed to know what that is?"

"Do you believe in God, Ashland?"

We sloshed along the causeway and turned off the bridge onto Highway 98. The watery streets were nearly empty, except for a few people making last-minute provisions. I thought about his question; it was important to answer truthfully. "I've always believed there was, and I still do, but I have a lot of questions for him. If I ever get to see him."

"Do you talk to him at all?"

"Are you asking me if I pray? Sure, I pray." My mood went from bad to worse. This wasn't the time to be having a heart-to-heart about my spiritual life. "What's your point, Henri? Cut to the chase."

"Well, I'm trying to say that I don't have the answers, and even if Lenore was here with us, she wouldn't either. Carrie Jo can't find out, because she's in no shape to perform her 'dream' detective work. Rachel knows about curses but nothing specific about your case. Yet you say you're seeing ghosts again, right?"

"Yep, unfortunately."

"I think God is trying to talk to you, Ashland. I think you have to trust him to show you the truth. If you haven't already, ask him to reveal the source of the curse to you. Tell him you are willing to make right whatever wrong has been done. That's what I would do, if I were in your shoes. Because when you boil it all down, it's about you. This is your battle, and it always has been. From the finding of the Beaumont treasure to the battle in the ballroom. You've been the focus of all this spiritual activity, although it's not always been in an obvious way. God sent you Carrie Jo, and us, if I may say so, but this battle has been for Ashland Stuart."

The car came to a stop at the marina, and we sat in the parking lot. The windshield wipers sloshed back and forth, slinging the water onto the already soaked pavement.

I knew every word he said was true. It had been about me. I'd spent all my time trying to protect Carrie Jo, but Seven Sisters had been *my* house. The Beaumont treasure was also mine. The ghosts had been from *my* past. Now this curse threatened my son and someday my grandsons. Unless I stopped it.

"Pray with me, Henri. I don't know what to say."

He nodded and grabbed my hand. "Lord, nothing is hidden from you, for you see all things—everything in the past, present and future. I know you can see this man's heart and his desire to break this curse over his life and his family. Please, Lord, speak to Ashland. Speak in a language he will understand. Show him what he needs to know. Show him what to do. Give him what he needs to set himself and his family free. We put this in

your hands and trust that you will give the answer. In Jesus'
name, amen."

"Amen," I whispered. I wiped my eyes and stared at my
boat rocking in the marina. I hoped he was right. "Well, no
time like the present."

"Need some help?"

"Sure, come on. Let's move her away from the floating
dock—that's the worst place to leave a boat during a hurricane.
Hey, actually, you should move the car to the other side of the
marina. That's where I'm taking the boat. I'll meet you over
there."

"All right."

I got out of the car and was soaked to the bone before I'd
taken two steps. I walked quickly to the Happy Go Lucky and
dug for the keys in my wet pants pocket. I untied the boat and
turned the key.

Click, click.

"Come on, are you kidding me?"

I adjusted the throttle and turned the key again.

Click, click.

Smacking the dashboard in frustration, I tapped the gas
tank gauge. How the heck was I out of gas? I went below deck
and grabbed a half-empty can. It wasn't much, but it would be
enough to get me the few yards I needed to travel. The boat
rocked and rolled in the rough water of the Mobile Bay. My
phone rang in my pocket again, and I suddenly remembered I
needed to call Rachel back. I climbed the steps, shielding my
eyes from a spray of water with my hand.

I couldn't answer the phone now. Suddenly the wind
became so savage I could barely stand up. I waited until the
blast of wind passed, then raced to the tank. With clumsy hands
I poured the gas into the tank and replaced the gas cap. Closing
the outer cap, I stowed the empty can under the railing,
latching it secure with a bungee cord. Just as I stood up, the
boat lurched, sending me hurtling across the deck.

As I struggled to get up, I thought I saw someone standing
near me. It wasn't Henri. It was a woman—it had to be. She

wore a moldy dress with a torn hem. I tried to look up to see her face when I felt and heard the sound of wood hitting the side of my head. *Wait!* I thought as the blow came. The boat tilted again, and this time I rolled into the water.

The shattering pain overwhelmed me. I slipped down, down, down...

Chapter 11—Olivia

As I waited for my host to join me in the garden, I watched a line of black ants steal sugar crumbs off the top of a forgotten cake. I felt no need to interrupt their work, nor did I feel a great deal of sympathy for the person who would leave such a treat unprotected in a den of ants. I did not accept the mint tea offered me or eat any of the sweet delicacies before me. Isaiah took his time. I knew it was his way of toying with me, reminding me who had the upper hand.

Of all the confrontations I could have hoped to avoid in this life, and I was not one to fear anyone, this would be the one I dreaded the most. I was about to face the man I rejected to marry another. Why did men believe that a woman who possessed a modicum of attractiveness could not possibly be sensible? That a woman must always be guided by the heart or its inclinations?

I was and had always been a sensible woman. I had not come in tears, as I was sure my sister would have done if she had been in my shoes. And I had not come as a servant—I had come as a Beaumont, the last Beaumont, unless God saw fit to give me another child, which seemed unlikely considering my age. In my world, women who were twenty and five and had not had a child were considered old maids, barren, cast-off spinsters. They were whispered about and never invited to social events. Useless dried husks without value.

I had a child, a girl-child, whom I had summarily given up to have the marriage alliance I preferred. I lied to her and told her that she belonged to my brother; it was better for her to believe that. Better for everyone. But Isaiah would not likely be willing to ignore the truth. Our daughter, Isla, had seduced her own uncle Jeremiah, and from that unholy union had come Karah. No, I doubted that Isaiah would be pleased at all.

And I knew he would never let me forget my change of heart, especially now. Not when he heard the whole truth. But still I was here, despite my better judgment, and I had a purpose.

Isaiah must make this right.

The fool girl, our own daughter, convinced her uncle to sign a codicil that named only her children as his heirs. If she'd just left things alone! Claudette and I had arranged a settlement for Christine's youngest daughter, Delilah, and God knew where poor Calpurnia was, probably at the bottom of the Mobile River. My personal investigation into the matter had revealed nothing. It was as if the girl had disappeared from the face of the Earth. Everything had been perfectly arranged until Isla and her schemes interfered. Since there was no male heir between her and Jeremiah, and Karah's parentage was being questioned by the courts—also thanks to Isla—the Cottonwood property, including the missing Beaumont fortune, would go to Jeremiah's brother, Isaiah.

All of it. The irony of the situation did not escape me. He would have what he had lost. But he would never have me.

I had not seen my former lover in ages. For the first five years, he would send me the occasional vague letter asking again why I had rejected him. I never responded.

In the first pleading correspondences, he shared the depth of his despair and pledged his undying love. "I shall never feel again what I felt with you, my darling. Oh, have mercy on me and let me hear you call me that once more. I could have any wife I choose, but my only desire is for you, my own Olivia."

I would admit this to no one, but I kept those letters. On the many nights when I was alone, I would unfold them and read them again and again, pretending that I would write him back. How could I explain to him why I did what I did? I could not, so I never picked up a pen.

Lost in my silent reverie, I did not hear the dogs barking at first, but then I saw Isaiah approaching. He leaned on a silver-headed cane and wore a finely woven black suit that had obviously been made for his trim body. He wore no hat, and I could see that time had been kind to him. He had all his beautiful dark hair, now flecked with white. I did not ask why he used the cane. I still had my manners when I wanted them.

Without a word, he sat down across the small table from me. Spotting the ants, he snapped his fingers and the dogs came running. He put the china dish on the ground, and the nearest hound devoured the food. Isaiah did not seem to care that his dog's pawing and excited eating broke the fine dish.

I raised an eyebrow but said nothing. With some swagger he leaned back in his chair and stared at me. I could see he was taking in every line, every change, every less than firm inch of my skin. He did not hide his amusement at my appearance or my situation. He had the advantage, and he enjoyed it.

This was not going to be easy, I feared. It was he who spoke first.

"This business with the codicil. Did you plan this, Olivia? Was that your plan all along? To use our daughter to seduce her uncle?"

"What kind of woman do you think I am, Isaiah?"

He spun his walking stick and said, "The kind of woman who leaves her intended at the altar while she runs off to marry another. The kind of woman who refuses to tell me where my child is or what's become of her. That's the kind of woman you are, dear Olivia."

"You can't think that I…"

"Can't I?" He smiled at me, rubbing the silver horse head atop his cane.

"To what end? I am not clever enough to dream up such a scenario. I can only assume it was Fate that caused these things to happen."

"Ah." His eyes looked playful. "As do I. It was Fate that left me the inheritance, all the inheritance, Olivia. See, you should have married me, for it was always mine anyway. And I would have loved you without it. That is the truth. Now I will have the fortune without your love. Things change, my dear, and so have I. I found peace with my wife, Virginia, and she has given me many sons and even a daughter. So you see, it was the Hand of Providence that led you away from me to marry Calloway James Torrence, that well-known adulterer. How is life with the old man now? Is he even still alive? My wife tells me you have no children. Well, besides our child."

"You have no right to speak so personally to me! I am not a child anymore, Isaiah." I stood, ready to leave immediately. "You have not changed at all. You are a small man, ruled by your pride and ambition, and obviously I cannot reason with you. Do the right thing, Isaiah. You must set this codicil aside and leave Christine and Jeremiah's original will to stand."

"Too hasty, my dear. You always end things too hastily. I am sure you want to hear me out on this. I have something to say to you, Olivia. Or rather, I have someone you should see."

He rang a little silver bell on the table, and to my utter surprise our daughter walked down the leaf-covered path to our outdoor dining space. She mocked me with a curtsy and sat next to Isaiah in an outfit that was obviously intended for the stage. She showed far too much cleavage, and I kept my face a mask as she leaned forward and kissed her father on the mouth like a wanton.

"Isla, I told you to stay home! What are you doing here?"

"Imagine my surprise, Aunt Olivia, to learn that this man, Isaiah Cottonwood, is my own father. Imagine my great surprise! For I am *truly* surprised! And an even greater surprise, *Aunt* Olivia, is that you are my *mother*! Can you imagine how surprised I was to learn this? You tricked me, Mother! What can that mean for my daughter, Karah? That her father was also her great-uncle? We are one big happy family now, aren't we?" Isla walked toward me with a rare, serious look on her face. "And I want what belongs to me. I will not let this go. You should know that by now."

She got in my face and smiled. "You left me with the general, and he took his liberties with me, Mother. His hands were all over my body. When he got bored with violating and hurting me himself, he invited his friends to do the same. I learned many tricks from the general. Cruel to the last was he, but in the end, I took care of him. One last time. And there were others too, all except my sweet Captain. And even he failed me like all the rest. But now I have my own father!" She walked over to stand beside him, her hand on his shoulder. "He will make sure I get what I deserve. Won't you, Father?"

She slapped the table and yelled at me, "I told you that you would never take Seven Sisters away from me! That it was mine. That it belonged to me. Now we know why, don't we? I will live there until the day I die. Then my daughter…"

"No, you are coming home with me. I have left you too long in this world." I masked my shock, regret and revulsion. I would deal with those later.

"You cannot command me, Mother," she said in a mocking voice.

"Maybe not, but I have legal custody of you until your next court appearance. You *will* go where I command you."

"She can't, can she, Father?" Her sickeningly sweet voice was too much to bear. I left the two of them at the table, her giggles in my ears. Isaiah did not call after me, nor did I wish him to. I left his estate at Park Hill and headed back to Seven Sisters. This was too heartbreaking. I decided I would retrieve my ill-begotten daughter tomorrow and go home. That would be that. I would tell my husband the truth about our fortune and let him do what he could to solve the problem. He might even abandon me, as would be his right. I had failed to deliver a fortune or a child. I was doubly cursed.

As I finished dinner alone, Stokes came in. I could tell by the way the old man shuffled his feet that he wanted to announce someone. "Who is it, Stokes?"

"It's Isaiah Cottonwood."

"I see. Well, let him in, please."

Twice in one day. Apparently, Isaiah had thought of something else to hurt me with. What would he do now, bring Karah before me?

"I am sorry to call on you so late. I realize this is most inopportune of me."

I did not rise. I wiped my hands on a thick linen napkin and waited for him to get to the matter at hand. "Why have you come, Isaiah?"

"I come because—I wanted to tell you—she's not…"

"Ah, Isla," I said, smiling at him sadly.

"I do not know how it happened, but it did happen. I was asleep, and the next thing I remember was her naked body on top of mine. I hardly know how to say this to a lady, but when I woke up, we were... she was...." He shuddered, and I could see he was overcome with disgust and shame. "Once I knew it was not some sort of bizarre dream, I threw her off of me. She laughed at me, her own father! Our daughter is mad, Olivia! Mad and dangerous! I threw her out of the house, and I do not know where she has gone. Perhaps to this captain she speaks of."

"He is dead, Isaiah. She shot him. In Roanoke. He has been dead for three years now."

"That's impossible, for I saw him earlier at my home. He stood outside the door waiting for her. She went to him when she left me. I locked the door behind her."

I took a sip of the dark claret. "Then you saw a ghost."

His eyes were even wider. "That's not all. She said—she cursed me, Olivia. Already I feel it taking effect. I am sick now, and I fear I shall die."

"You are being dramatic, Mr. Cottonwood. An angry woman—a madwoman—assaulted you. That is all. Do you really believe in curses? What woman has the power to do such things?"

"Don't talk to me about women, Mrs. Torrence."

"You expect me to help you after you confess to me that you have had carnal knowledge of our daughter? You expect me to assist you at all?" I smiled at him and watched the low light of the candelabra flicker. The candles burned low, and their red wax dripping made the moment that much more somber.

"You don't understand. I feel—my heart—the doctor says I am not supposed to have— Ahh...help me, Olivia."

I stood up as Isaiah slumped over the table, panting for breath and pounding at his chest. "I do understand you—and I curse you too! How dare you molest our daughter. How dare you refuse to help me! You thought you'd take advantage of my situation, but it has turned on you, hasn't it? Fate is a cruel mistress, Isaiah. This is why I did not want to marry you. You have always been unsteady. How does the saying go? 'A double-minded man is unstable in all his ways...'"

I rubbed his shoulder with my pale hand and whispered in his ear, "You are that man, and you are unstable in all your ways." All the emotions I had locked away, had carefully forbidden myself from feeling, rose to the surface. And despite my sudden tears, the emotion I felt most strongly was anger. All of it fell on Isaiah. My reasoning renounced its position as my chief counsel. Raw anger took control, and for the first time in my life, I welcomed it and allowed it to flow through me like dammed-up water through a pipe.

I sobbed, "I curse you, Isaiah—and your sons too. May you die, may they die in the prime of their life! May they feel happiness but have it stolen from them before they can fully possess it! I curse you for stealing my soul! You never cease to disappoint me, and now you would do this to me. You will not have what you seek. No peace for you or any of the Cottonwoods! Just as you did this to my blood, I curse your blood!

"I leave you now, Isaiah. I will never see you again. Except when they bury you. And they will bury you soon. Probably tomorrow."

Just then another guest joined us. It was Isla. "Mother, I can explain."

"What is there to say? I have cursed the man who hurt my daughter and stole my fortune. Now he is doubly cursed. See, he is dying. Leave him be, Isla. Why don't you go be with your captain in the Moonlight Garden before we have to leave this place?"

"You know about my sweet Captain?" Her voice sounded frail, quiet, pretty.

"The Moonlight Garden has always been a special place. Go now and leave your father to me."

***

I sputtered the sea water out of my lungs. How long had I been lying on this piece of foam, floating around the harbor? I'd woken up long enough to throw up, and now I was dying of thirst. Thankfully the storm had been during a warm season, or I was sure I would have died.

"Hey! Somebody! Help me!" I shouted about a hundred times. I heard nothing but the winds roaring and the waves crashing in response. Yelling into a storm was futile, so I waited for the waves to diminish and then tried again. The sun was rising now. How long had I been out here?

Long enough to know that Henri's prayer had been heard. God showed me what I needed to know, how the curse began and how I could break it. I had no doubt I would be found, because this had been his plan all along.

When the Coast Guard ship sailed in my direction, I cried. Not just because I had been found but because I knew how to break Olivia and Isla's curse. I would live to break it.

Carrie Jo! I love you! I know what to do now! I'm coming to you, baby!

Chapter 12—Carrie Jo

"I spent my whole life trying to prevent this dream walking, to prevent it from developing in you, but I failed—and I caused you great pain in the process," my mother said earnestly. "Please believe me when I tell you that I begged God a hundred times to take it from us. To take it from you. If you had seen the things my mother went through…she got so obsessed. All she wanted to do was sleep, and then one day she didn't wake up. I think the dreaming killed her, and I didn't want that for you. I thought if I followed the rules, you know, went to church, lived a holy life, if I became pure in the eyes of God, I could save you. I can't explain my reasoning. It all seems so crazy now."

"I can't believe this." The pain in my back worsened, but I didn't move. I stared at her. "You mean you knew what was happening to me and you didn't tell me? You knew all this time? I thought I was crazy. I thought you hated me!"

"I'm sorry, Carrie Jo. I am very sorry that I let you grow up not knowing what I knew, even if that wasn't very much."

A blast of wind moaned around the eave of the house. I heard the television bleeping a weather alert in the other room, but I was frozen to the spot. Rachel and Detra Ann were upstairs, laughing about something. The surreal moment lingered and I said, "How could you do that?"

She wrung her hands and covered her mouth. Finally she said, "All I can say is I am sorry."

"And I'm supposed to do what now?" I stood up. "Act like a 'sorry' makes it all better. That it erases it all? You're wrong, Momma. I'm not going to forget and…" I felt the need to get away, but I wasn't done giving her a piece of my mind. Kind Carrie Jo warned me to watch my mouth—that I would regret it if I said something stupid—but as sure as I was pregnant, I didn't listen to the voice of reason.

"I'm not asking you to do anything, Carrie Jo. Nothing at all. It's up to you if you want to accept my apology or not."

My hands were clenched into fists. My ponytail felt limp and my back pain kicked into high gear, but the tears were coming. There would be no stopping them now. "With Ginny, you knew I wasn't crazy? And that time when I kept seeing that old man in my dreams—the one who hurt himself? You knew those dreams were real and you let me sleep in that house anyway?"

"We had nowhere else to go! It was that or the street. Your dad left us high and dry. I had to take whatever we could get." Her eyes narrowed in frustration. "I'm not proud of what I did, the decisions I made. Not proud at all. I know it's too late to ask you to trust me now, but I could not let one more day go by without telling you that I am sorry. I am sorry about it all."

"What about my father? How come you never wanted to tell me about him? You know what that's like when you're a kid? What it's like now? He hates me, doesn't he?" The pain in my back grew more intense, and I could see flashes of light around the corners of my eyes. I put my hand on the table to steady myself.

"No! No, Carrie Jo. He doesn't hate you. He was afraid of us. Afraid of me. He's not a bad man, just a fearful one."

Angry words were poised at the tip of my tongue, but they didn't spring forth like I wanted them to. To my surprise, a splash of water landed on the floor between my legs. It felt warm and sticky. It didn't stop. My sandaled feet were all wet now. All I could think to say was, "Momma?"

She jumped out of the chair. "It's okay, Carrie Jo. This is normal. Your water broke. The baby is coming soon. We've got to get you back to the hospital." She put her arm around me and led me to the side door. "Oh, shoot! My car isn't here. Detra Ann? Rachel?" The girls bounded down the stairs, still smiling until they saw me.

"Does this mean what I think it means?" Detra Ann asked.

"Yes, her water broke. We've got to get her back to the hospital right now."

"Why did they send her home? I knew that was a mistake. Let's take my car." She ran to the living room, grabbed her purse and came back. "Let's do this, CJ. You've got this! Rachel? Would you mind cleaning this up?"

"Sure, I'll clean up and turn everything off. I'll meet y'all up there. Should I call Ashland and Henri?"

"Yep, that would be great." I hated the way everyone was talking so calmly. Like one of us had a baby every day. "See you there. Oh, and grab her suitcase by the front door!" Detra Ann said as she hurried me down the steps.

"Can't I change my clothes first? I look like I peed on myself."

"Um, no, girl. You don't have time for that. Once your water breaks, labor could start any—"

Just then I screamed. If I thought yesterday's contractions were anything to brag about, I was sorely mistaken. "Shoot! Shoot!" I said as I tried to remember how to breathe. I kicked myself again for not taking those Lamaze classes. "What do I do? What do I do, Momma?"

"Take slow, deep breaths when you can. I ain't gonna lie. It's gonna hurt like hell, but you'll survive."

"That's one hell of a pep talk, Deidre," Detra Ann scolded her.

"Well…. Oh, and don't push yet. For the love of God. It's not time to push. Let's get to the hospital first. We'll start timing the next one."

"Okay, okay," I said, breathing as slowly as I could. It was hard as heck to do with my heart pounding and my pulse racing. Detra Ann practically shoved me in the backseat and began backing the car down the driveway like a wild woman. *Should I tell her my purse is hanging out the door? Breathe, breathe, breathe!*

"Too bad it's not a girl. We could call her Jasmine, in honor of the storm," Detra Ann said, smiling at me in the rearview mirror.

"Never," I promised her. "But Ashland would love that. I hope Rachel got a hold of him."

"Don't you worry about it, CJ. He'll be there." Detra Ann shouted at me as she ran a red light.

Deidre gasped and grabbed my hand. "Sweet Lord!"

"Get your watch ready. I feel another one coming. I'm sorry about your backseat, Detra Ann."

"Son of a b! Did you see that guy? I don't care about the backseat, but don't have the baby in my car! Jasmine deserves better."

Between pants and twists of pain I panted, "I'm—not-calling-her—Jasmine. Oh God, oh God!"

Detra Ann hit a curb trying to avoid a car. It was like being on a painful bumper car ride. My mother prayed beside me the whole time. Detra Ann grinned like a maniac when she wasn't honking at someone or threatening to cut their body parts off.

"Here we are! Pulling in the driveway now!" she yelled, forgetting once again that I was pregnant and not hard of hearing.

"Great! Perfect timing! Here comes another one!"

"Three minutes apart! That baby will be here soon!" My mother opened her door, rescued my purse and practically dragged me out of the backseat. "Hey! My daughter is having a baby! Like right now!"

"Momma! That's an ambulance guy. Not a nurse!"

It didn't matter. She was going to make sure someone helped me, and all I could do was hold my breath and hope the pain quit. A dark-haired young man squatted down in front of me. "What's your name?"

"Carrie Jo. It's Carrie Jo."

"Okay, Carrie Jo. I've got a chair here. Think you can stand so we can get you in it?"

"In just a second." I held my breath and waited for the contraction to let up.

"Don't hold your breath. Try to breathe through them. It will help with the pain. That's better. Take your time. I'll wait." Over his shoulder he told the approaching nurse what was happening.

"I think I can stand up now."

"They are three minutes apart," Deidre told the nurse as she pushed me through the hospital doors. "And her water broke."

"Sounds like we have a baby on the way. If it's a girl you could name her Jasmine."

I rolled my eyes at Detra Ann, who ran along beside me. "Never," I mouthed to her.

My clothes were drenched, my forehead was covered in sweat, and I was exhausted already. "Detra Ann, call Ashland, please. I need him here."

"I will. Deidre you stay with her while I find out what's going on."

Before I knew it, the nurse had me in the elevator and we were headed to the fifth floor. No long registration process for me. "Got no time to waste. The doctor says to bring you up now. Baby's coming! It's going to be okay. We're going to get you an IV started, he'll check to see how far you've dilated and then we'll go from there. How does that sound?"

"Like a dream. I'd like to wait for my husband."

The nurse, a young woman with pretty, soft-looking brown hair, smiled sympathetically. "Hopefully he will make it in time. But either way, I think you will meet your baby soon." Sure enough, another nurse came in quickly and had me rigged up to the IV in no time.

Dr. Gary arrived, apologizing that he had sent me home. A quick examination confirmed it. "Eight centimeters dilated. It's almost time."

"I know!" I practically screamed at him as another contraction, the strongest so far, took my breath away.

"How about an epidural to help with the pain?"

"Please? I would love one." All my pledges to "go natural" went out the window. I wondered if breast-feeding would hit the chopping block too.

"Be right back," Dr. Gary said as he pulled the blanket back down.

"Momma, please find out where Ashland is—he needs to get here."

Detra Ann walked back in, her phone in her hand. I could tell by the look on her face that something was wrong.

Something was dead wrong.

"Ashland is missing. Henri saw him fall in the water. He's with the authorities. They are looking for him now." She flew to my side and rubbed my hand. "You listen to me, Carrie Jo Stuart. We are not going to entertain anything negative about Ashland, you hear me? He is going to be fine. Right now, you have his baby to think about! I know you want to cry and fall apart, but you can't! You don't have that luxury! Let's have this baby so we can find out what's happening."

"Detra Ann, no! I can't—you have to go be with Henri! Help him find Ash! Please!"

Dr. Gary heard the shouting and came in; a nurse was tying on his face mask. "What is this? What's going on in here? Trying to have a baby, people."

"You don't understand, Dr. Gary. Carrie Jo's husband, Ashland, has disappeared off his boat. He's in the water and they haven't found him. But they will!"

"You had to tell her that now?" He sat on the rolling chair and rolled to my side. "I know you wish you could be doing something else right now, but this child needs you. Your son needs you. Let's welcome him into the world and make sure he's healthy. That's the number one thing right now, got it?"

Still in shock from the news about Ashland, I said, "Yes, that's the number one thing. Ashland's baby. Oh God, please protect him. Momma!"

"Yes, darling."

"I know you wanted to be in here, but I need you praying for Ashland. Let Detra Ann stay with me, and you go pray. When Rachel gets here, get her praying too. Please, Momma. Pray your very hardest!" I cried as the sweat poured off my forehead.

"What's the air on?" Detra Ann asked the nurse. Without waiting she checked the room thermostat and immediately dropped it. It didn't do any good because just then the lights went out. In the momentary silence I could hear the winds rattling the windows of the hospital like moaning ghosts demanding to be let in.

"I've had enough of ghosts! You hear me? Enough!"

Dr. Gary stared at me. "Carrie Jo, are you with me? Nurse, check her IV bag. I did not order anything that would make her hallucinate."

Detra Ann assured him I was fine, that I was just worried about Ashland, and then the labor began in earnest. "Okay, let's check. Yes, fully dilated. That was fast once you got started. That's a good thing. Some people have the worst time opening up. Let's see…oh yes, I see a little head already. Now it's important that you push when I tell you to push, okay. Are you in pain?"

"No pain, just a lot of pressure. Can I push yet?"

"Let me get in position. Okay, let's push."

I sat up and held my knees, pushing with all my might. *This isn't right. This shouldn't be happening. Not without my husband. Ashland, I love you. Where are you!*

I need you right now!

Chapter 13—Carrie Jo

"Of course you know this will open you up to a ton of lawsuits now, right?" Libby said, frowning at Ashland. "And that you've just signed away seventy-five percent of your net worth? That's a big deal, Ashland. I'm not sure you understand how far this decision reaches. This could haunt you for the rest of your life."

Libby couldn't know how apropos her choice of words was. "We hope so," he answered cryptically.

"I just can't believe this. You're normally so level-headed. Is this because of your son? Or something else?" She glanced at me as if I were the culprit. I kept my face completely expressionless.

"Yes and no," he said. "That's all I can tell you. I appreciate your help with all this."

"I still don't get it. I don't get this whole thing. I need a vacation." She tapped her head with her pen in frustration. "It might be the last one any of us take."

"Don't tell us you're breaking up with us, Libby," I said with a smirk. Ashland laughed, and boy, did that sound good. Money was all Libby really cared about. Well, money and stealing my husband. Now she would lose on both counts.

"Two of these claimants can't even prove they are related to your family. You do know that, right?" He nodded, and I could tell he was starting to feel a bit aggravated about this whole conversation. "This sets a bad standard, Ashland. Not just for you but for many of the older families here in Mobile. You haven't heard the last of this, I'm afraid. Not by a long shot."

"This is the right thing to do, Libby," he replied. "Not just for us but for everyone involved. I know you don't understand my decision, our decision, but this is it. This is how it should have always been."

Libby shook her head, her stylish bob swinging as she did. With perfectly manicured hands she stamped the documents and folded them up neatly. She placed them in the thick manila envelopes and looked at us like we were both out of our heads.

"As long as you know what you're doing. Who am I to say?"

Ashland and I walked out of the building and stepped into the warm sunshine. It was hard to believe that a major storm had blown through here just two weeks ago. Most of the fallen oaks had been removed, but there were plenty of houses missing shingles, windows—you name it. I closed my eyes for a moment as we stood outside the car. I felt lighter, like an unseen weight had been lifted off my shoulders, and I was sure Ashland felt the same way. After a minute, I poked him in the side. "One more stop before the event, babe. Can't daydream now."

"I'll leave all the dreaming to you."

"As well you should. Speaking of which, Deidre says she'll meet us at Seven Sisters with Baby Boy. Did Mr. Chapman from the city call you? He said the sign arrived and they'll be installing it in front of the house today. I can't believe Seven Sisters won't be called Seven Sisters anymore, but I like the sound of the Beaumont-Cottonwood Manor. It sounds...right. Oh, I almost forgot. Doreen and Rachel are coming too. I can't believe this is going down without Henri and Detra Ann. Are you sure we can't wait?"

"We'll throw them a huge party when they get back. And yes, I'm sure this can't wait. You know, I've heard people talk about getting married in Vegas, but I've never actually met someone who did. Can't believe they went without us," he said with a smile.

I laughed. "I can. Those two don't need us there. They'll have Elvis and Marilyn Monroe as their witnesses. I promise you this, though, Detra Ann's mother is going to have a nervous breakdown when she finds out they got hitched. She's the only girl in that family, and I'm sure Cynthia's always dreamed of throwing her a big wedding."

"Probably so."

He turned the car down the forgotten road. His Jeep found every bump and pothole, but it didn't matter. We were on a mission. It was hard to believe fall was here, with the way the sun beamed down on us. The balmy weather made me want to slip off my shoes and prop my feet up on the dash, but now wasn't the time for that. The Jeep came to a stop, and in the distance I could hear the river lapping against the sandy riverbank.

"This is about it," I said. "I remember seeing this place in a dream. There was once an old oak tree that stood there. Isla used to climb it and watch the boys swim. The Delta Queen used to roll along here, and just a way down was where she embarked the night Calpurnia landed in the water."

"When we ceded the house to the city, I thought that would be the end of all this. I hope this truly is the end. Do you think it will be?" he asked me, grabbing the roses out of the backseat.

I slid my sunglasses up to the top of my head. "No matter what happens, this is the right thing to do. I am proud of you, babe, for wanting to make it right. I think the ghosts of the past will know that you've tried, that we've tried, and they'll accept that."

He squeezed my hand, and we walked down the steep hillside to the riverbank. "I don't know how we managed to talk the city into changing the name of the house. Usually this kind of thing takes years. The Beaumont-Cottonwood Plantation. That has a nice ring to it, doesn't it?"

"Yep, it does." He handed me some roses. Thankfully, the florist had been nice enough to clip the thorns from the stems. I took the flowers, and we stood by the water with our heads bowed. "You ready?" I asked him quietly.

"Yes, I am. Finally." With his eyes closed, he tilted his head up toward the blue sky.

"Dear Lord, my wife and I ask you to lift the curse that was placed upon my family all those years ago. I know that wrongs were done, many wrongs. I know that many people were hurt as a result of those wrongs. Although I did not personally do these things, I take responsibility for them as the current representative of our family. I repent, Lord. We stole from others, we made our brothers slaves, we hid our secrets and refused to repent of them. Many of us did murder and many other sinful things in your sight. But I, Ashland James Stuart, do repent, Lord, on behalf of my sinful ancestors. I am sorry." I squeezed his hand as a tear rolled down his cheek.

As he wiped his face with his hands, his eyes looked even bluer through the tears. Still speaking to God, he said, "I have given the moment to the people who deserved it. I have a clean conscience, God. I have given the house the name it deserves. I hope this is enough. But if it's not, please tell me what to do and I will do it. If not for me, Lord, for my son and my wife. She is innocent."

"No, I am not so innocent either," I said to Ashland. Then I spoke to God as Ash had, toward the blue sky. "I have been bitter and unforgiving toward the people I love. I had no idea that you were trying to help me, that my mother was doing what she thought she should. I was wrong to hate her. For that I am sorry. I do not know how I am related to Muncie yet, if at all. But if I am, I will not be ashamed to call him my cousin. Or uncle. Or whatever he may be. I accept him. Thank you for keeping Ashland safe. Thank you for our family."

It was my turn to cry now. I put my face in Ashland's chest and cried my heart out. When my tears had flowed, I prepared to throw the flowers in the water as a kind of tribute to the many Cottonwoods, Beaumonts and others caught up in the centuries-long curse, but I froze. Standing on the water, just as she would have described Reginald Ball as walking out like "Holy Jesu," was Calpurnia. She was not the sickly, defeated girl I remembered from my dreams but happy and smiling. She walked toward us, the hem of her coral gown skimming the water.

"Ashland, do you see her?"

"Yes," he whispered without looking at me. She floated closer, and the bright sunlight sparkled in her intricate hairstyle. With shaking fingers, Ashland handed her a red rose. Her fingers never touched his, but she accepted the flower from him. "Be at peace," she whispered to him. She smiled at me too, and the coral earrings bobbed at her ears. Suddenly, Muncie stood beside her. He was no longer Muncie the boy but Janjak the man, the teacher in a three-piece suit. He took her hand, and I held out a flower to him with shaking fingers.

"Be at peace," he said to me in a soothing, rich voice. Together they stepped back on the water and soon faded away with smiles on their faces. We breathed a sigh of relief, but then there were others, walking to us across the river.

Isla came next. She wore her powder blue gown with the full lacy sleeves. I could feel Ashland tense beside me, but he offered her the rose. "Forgive me, cousin," he said in a sincere voice.

"Be at peace," she said. She accepted the rose and vanished immediately. Others came too, Christine, Delilah and finally Olivia.

I had seen Olivia only once in a dream, but I knew Ashland had seen much of her, either in dreams or as a ghost. He handed her a rose as she drew close, her hair still upswept with not a hair out of place. She looked at the flower for a moment and leaned closer to his face. "So you are the curse-breaker? Be at peace, cousin." She too vanished as Isla had done.

We tossed the rest of the roses on the water and watched them float away down the Mobile River.

"The curse is broken, Ashland. It is over, at last!"

"Yes, I believe it is. Thank God!"

"I was so nervous. I hardly expected to see Janjak or anyone!"

"Me too!" We were all smiles.

"We better get going. Little AJ will be missing you," I said with a smile.

"I can't believe you named our son Ashland James."

"Well, if it was good enough for you, it's good enough for him. At least it's not Jasmine."

"What do you have against Jasmine?"

"Nothing, really. Maybe we'll consider it for our daughter."

"Daughter? Whoa! We just gave away all our money. Maybe we should slow down on growing the family for a while."

"No way. We've got to restock the family tree, babe." I put my arms around his neck and kissed him.

"And what good stock it is too," he purred playfully. As I kissed him I pretended I didn't hear a giggle or two coming from the direction of that old oak tree.

"You hear anything?" I asked cautiously.

"Nope. Let's go."

We drove out of the woods and down the bumpy, beaten path, back to the road that would lead us to the future. Our good future. It *was* going to be a good one. A curse-free one.

I felt overwhelmed with gratitude. "Thank you," I whispered to no one in particular. I knew everyone who was supposed to hear it would.

Author's Note

Thank you for taking this journey with me. When I wrote book one of the Ultimate Seven Sisters Collection, I had no idea I would end the series with six books! What is even more surprising to me is how much you all love Carrie Jo, Ashland and all the folks at Seven Sisters. Seven Sisters was my first book, and it will always hold a special place in my heart. From the Blue Room to the Moonlight Garden, I know every inch and visit it myself often in the books.

I am often asked if Seven Sisters is a real place. I am sorry to say that no it isn't. But then again, who really knows? So many of the old houses have been lost, and I am sure somewhere down the line there was a house like it, complete with a creaking staircase and plenty of ghosts. We have an abundance of haunted houses in the South. I based the house on a combination of houses you can find in Mobile, Alabama including the Historic Oakleigh House and the Bragg-Mitchell Mansion. Mobile is a lovely city with plenty to see and do. If you haven't been, come on by!

I get other questions as well, like, "How is Mia still alive when Carrie Jo said she was dead?" The answer to that is Carrie Jo was wrong. She has been wrong before—but in the end, it all works out.

Because we all love this series so much, I've begun a spin-off series. Carrie Jo and the gang need a new house to explore, so we are headed off to Idlewood. The Ghosts of Idlewood is Book One of the new Idlewood series. It will be available sometime in 2016.

If you love historical fiction, check out my Desert Queen series. It's about Queen Nefertiti and her ill-fated love with Akhenaten.

I've also begun a series set in Dauphin Island, the Sirens Gate series. My heroine, Thessalonike (called

Nik by her friends), gets into plenty of trouble. It's an urban fantasy with a touch of humor and snark.

I have other series planned too, many featuring ghosts and great Southern families. I would be honored to have you follow me on Facebook. Just look up Author ML Bullock or sign up for my mailing list at www.mlbullock.com and get updates on new releases right in your mailbox. I don't send spam, and I only email about new releases.

Thank you again for every kind email, Facebook post and message. I appreciate you.

All my best,

M.L. Bullock

Read more from M.L. Bullock

The Seven Sisters Series
Seven Sisters
Moonlight Falls on Seven Sisters
Shadows Stir at Seven Sisters
The Stars that Fell
The Stars We Walked Upon
The Sun Rises Over Seven Sisters

The Desert Queen Series
The Tale of Nefret
The Falcon Rises
The Kingdom of Nefertiti
The Song of the Bee-Eater (forthcoming)

The Sugar Hill Series (forthcoming)
Wife of the Left Hand
Fire on the Ramparts
Blood by Candlelight

The Sirens Gate Series
The Mermaid's Gift
The Blood Feud (forthcoming)
The Wrath of Minerva (forthcoming)
The Lorelei Curse (forthcoming)
The Fortunate Star (forthcoming)

The Southern Gothic Series
Being with Beau

Connect with M.L Bullock on Facebook. To receive updates on her latest releases, visit her website at MLBullock.com and subscribe to her mailing list.

About the Author

Author of the best-selling *Seven Sisters* series and the *Desert Queen* series, M.L. Bullock has been storytelling since she was a child. A student of archaeology, she loves weaving stories that feature her favorite historical characters—including Nefertiti. She currently lives on the Gulf Coast with her family but travels frequently to exotic locations around the globe.

CPSIA information can be obtained
at www.ICGtesting.com
Printed in the USA
BVHW042126030320
574035BV00009B/85